The Moves That Matter in Academic Writing

全美最強教授的
17堂論文寫作必修課

150句學術英文寫作句型

從表達、討論、寫作到論述

建立批判思考力與邏輯力

杰拉德‧葛拉夫 Gerald Graff

凱西‧柏肯斯坦 Cathy Birkenstein ——著

周中天 教授 ——審訂推薦

丁宥榆 ——譯

「我很高興發現自己批改研究生論文的原則，在許多地方剛好符合這本名作的精神。我也期待研究生在他們的論文中營造一個『眾生喧嘩』的言論空間，讓研究生得以站在國內外資深學者的肩膀上發言，並且跟同儕交叉辯論。這本書特別適合傾向自說自話、閉門造車、不敢發表『個人意見』的論文寫作者。就連寫論文、教寫作的大學老師也會覺得這本書有用。」

—— **紀大偉**／政治大學台灣文學研究所副教授
「研究生青紅燈」、「研究生三溫暖」專欄作者

「國內研究生的論文常淪為資料堆砌，而非建立堅實論證。句與句也常缺少銜接，無法做延伸推論。本書提供明確易懂的邏輯思考模式、學術語彙、轉接語和論述範本，是實用、有效的研究生入門書籍。」

—— **陳錦芬**／台北教育大學兒童英語教育系教授

「本書闡明學術觀點的敘事架構，並提供模板格式（template format）方便初學者隨學即用，立馬開展學術寫作和口說的有效論述。」

—— **廖柏森**／台灣師範大學翻譯所教授

「綜觀其他同類型論文寫作書籍，作者以實用取向編寫本書，從四個步驟由淺而深，將精緻深奧的學術寫作觀念精簡而出，使之通俗簡單化，並以淺顯的範例練習協助論文寫作者逐步驗證、補充，並改進自己的寫作。」

—— **蔡素薰**／台北市立大學英語教學系助理教授

目錄 *Contents*

PART IV In Specific Academic Contexts
應用在其他學術領域

PART V Readings 範文集

Demystifying Academic Conversation

作者序 學術對談一點都不難

杰拉德・葛拉夫（Gerald Graff）
凱西・柏肯斯坦（Cathy Birkenstein）

經驗豐富的寫作老師很早就明白，所謂文章寫得好，就是能與他人展開對談。學術寫作中尤其不能只是表達自己的觀點，更要回應別人的論述。在我們任教的大學，大一寫作課的教學目標就要求「學生參與重要學術與公共議題的持續對談」。另一門課也提出相似的教學目標：「有內涵的論文，幾乎都要為回應他人的文本。」這些說法呼應了幾位修辭理論大師的見解，如肯尼斯・柏克（Kenneth Burke）、麥可海爾・貝克汀（Mikhail Bakhtin）、韋恩・布思（Wayne Booth），以及幾位近期的寫作學者，如大衛・巴梭洛梅（David Bartholomae）、約翰・賓恩（John Bean）、派翠西亞・畢札爾（Patricia Bizzell）、愛琳・克拉克（Irene Clark）、葛瑞格・哥倫布（Greg Colomb）、莉莎・埃德（Lisa Ede）、彼德・艾爾博（Peter Elbow）、約瑟夫・哈里斯（Joseph Harris）、安德莉雅・郎斯福德（Andrea Lunsford）、伊蓮・麥蒙（Elaine Maimon）、蓋瑞・歐森（Gary Olson）、麥可・羅斯（Mike Rose）、約翰・史威爾斯（John Swales）、克莉斯汀・斐克（Christine Feak）、緹麗・沃納克（Tilly Warnock）。還有其他人也主張，優秀的寫作必須納入別人的聲音，並讓他們的寫作也納入我們的聲音。

然而，即便這樣的共識不斷增強，公認寫作是一種對談、一種互動行為，但要協助學生實際參與對談仍是項艱鉅的挑戰。本書的目標就是要克服這個挑戰，**透過淺白的方式說明學術寫作**。本書採取的方式，是將學術寫作分解成數個基本步驟，並加以說明，並透過**套句範本**的方式呈現。希望這樣的方式，能協助學生在學術界以及更廣闊的公共領域裡，積極參與重要的對談。

本書緣起

　　本書最初的構想來自於我們兩人的共同興趣，也就是將學術文化大眾化。首先，是杰拉德・葛拉夫教學研究多年的心得：大專院校都需要鼓勵學生參與周遭的對談和論辯。具體來說，這是其新作《Clueless in Academe: How Schooling Obscures the Life of the Mind》（茫茫學海：學校教育如何蒙蔽了心智生活）的中心理論，本書正好與之印證。杰拉德先採用認為學術對談晦澀難懂的人的觀點，來看待學術討論，接著提出破除這種困境的方法。

　　其次，凱西・柏肯斯坦在 1990 年代擔任寫作和文學課上，發展了許多套句範本，正好用在本書內。許多學生在課堂討論中，都知道引用證據支持論點、考慮相反論述、辨識文本矛盾，也會質疑某些論點並加以回應，但卻不知道如何將這些概念實際運用到寫作上。然而，只要提供了具體可用的詞語和句型，學生的寫作以及思考品質都大幅進步。

　　於是，我們綜合彼此的想法，發現這些套句範本能啟動並釐清學術對談，便著手撰寫本書。本書的出發點是，所有寫作者都要用既定的寫作公式，這些公式不是他們自己發明，而早被廣泛使用，因此可以整理成範本，供學生套用、架構，並從中發展出自己的論點。

▶ In discussions of _____, a controversial issue is whether

_____. While some argue that _____, others contend

that _____.

討論_____的時候，一個爭議點在於是否_____。

有些人爭論說_____，有些人則聲稱_____。

▶ This is not to say that _____.

這並不是說_____。

　　上述套句範本讓寫作者的注意力不僅放在所要陳述的論點，也聚焦在要用**什麼「句型」來架構論點**。換言之，套句範本讓學生更加意識到論述技巧，這是學術寫作成功的關鍵，卻常被忽略。

套句範本的實用性

　　閱讀和寫作緊密相連，學生若是學會本書所提出的學術寫作技巧，也更能辨識出文中相同的論述。我們認為，有效論證需建立在與他人的對談上，如果這樣的思維是對的，那麼為了理解在大學中所指派的艱深文章，學生就需要能辨識文中所回應的是哪些觀點。

　　這套寫作技巧也有助於創作發想，找到要說的內容。從我們的經驗來看，要找出想談的東西，最好的方式不是閉門造車苦思，而是閱讀文本、仔細聆聽其他作者的說法，並且找尋加入對談的時機。

　　對那些有想法不會表達、甚至連想法都沒有的學生來說，本書的套句範本特別有幫助。這些學生往往認為自己的論點已不證自明，不需多做說明。然而，我們給他們一個簡單範本，要他們試著寫出一個反論（見本書第六堂〈將反面論點納入文中〉，他們反而能說出更多的想法：

▶ **Of course some might object that** _____ . **Although I concede that**
_____ , **I still maintain that** _____ .
當然有些人可能會反對_____。雖然我承認_____，我仍然主張
_____。

　　這個套句範本幫助學生使用一個違背直覺的寫作技巧，也就是質疑自己的
想法，從反對者的觀點來檢視自己觀點。這麼一來，範本可以啟發學生未曾察
覺的思維，就像有些學生會說，他們根本不知道自己有這些想法。

　　書中的其他套句範本，同樣能幫助學生練習細緻的寫作技巧，如總結他人
言論、用自己的話作一段引述、找出要回應的他人觀點、在他人問點與本人論
點之間轉移立場、為本人論點提出證據、思考並回答相反論點、點出重點。向
學生示範這些範本的使用方式，不僅能協助學生組織想法，更能幫助他們**產生
想法**。

| 本書結構

　　本書核心是「人們說／我說」（they say / I say）這個套句範本，因此我們
用它作為全書的架構。

　　Part 1 先說明聆聽的藝術（they say），由〈先聽聽別人怎麼說〉揭幕，解
釋一般文章開場為何多先引用他人論點，而非直接表達自己的論點。接下來，
繼續探討如何概述並引用他人的論述。

Part 2 接著說明如何提出自己的論點（I say），先說明三種不同的回應方式，接著建議如何在「他人論點」和「本身論點」之間轉換，如何引用反論並加以回應，並且協助寫作者回答以下重要的問題：「那又怎樣？」（So what?）、「誰會關心這件事？」（Who cares?）。

Part 3 提出〈使文章前後連貫〉的方式，首先介紹銜接句子與通篇一致性的技巧，接下來介紹正式與非正式用語，說明學術論文和日常使用的非正式語言並非截然不同。接著鼓勵寫作者在論文中使用後設評論（metacommentary）技巧，引領讀者理解文本。最後以〈運用範本修改文稿〉一章作結，並提供一篇小論文作為應用示範，並加上註解說明該文所運用到的套句範本。

Part 4 陳述各種學術領域的對談方法，分別說明口頭討論、網路寫作、閱讀文本，以及文學、科學、社會科學領域之論文寫作。

最後提供五篇範文，並將本書所提到的所有學術寫作句型作成索引，作為本書的收尾。

▎哪些不是本書的目標

本書並不探討邏輯推論原理，如三段論證（syllogism）、立論理由（warrant）、邏輯謬誤（logical fallacy），或者歸納法（inductive reasoning）和演繹法（deductive reasoning）的區別。這些概念相當實用，但是我們相信，多數人在學習議論文寫作時，不該是研究抽象的邏輯原理，而是要實際參與討論與論辯、嘗試不同的回應方式，並且用這種方式去說服各種讀者。在我們看來，比起去研究歸納法和演繹法的差異，以下套句範本 **You miss my point. What I'm saying is not _____, but _____.**（你沒聽懂我的意思，我所說的不是_____，而是_____。）或 **I agree with you that _____, and would even add that _____.**（我同意你說的_____，我還要補充_____。）更能幫助學生學會如何論述。這樣的寫作範本能讓學生彷彿參與了公眾討論，而這是研究抽象立論原理或邏輯謬誤所做不到的。

與他人論點交流

本書的核心目標是讓學術寫作回歸到互動與對談，進而使學術寫作平易近人。雖然寫作需要某種程度的安靜和獨處，但是這套寫作技巧能讓學生知道，若要將自己的論證發揮到極致，不僅要關注自己的想法，還要像平常與好友高談闊論一樣，傾聽別人的話，關心他們的想法。

這種寫作技巧，不只是讓寫作者證明並重申他們相信的論點，還能與那些不同、甚至完全相反的論點互相對照，並以此延伸出自己的論點，因此，這本書還有一項道德訴求：在一個日益多元、全球化的社會當中，能夠與別人的論點交流，對於民主公民素養（democratic citizenship）可謂至關重要。

透過文字，與讀者暢快對談

周中天／台師大翻譯所教授

語文是溝通的重要工具；書面文字交流，更是文明社會資訊記載傳遞、知識發展建構的基本條件。因此，寫作一向是各國教育重要的基礎。

可惜，許多學生並不了解寫作的意義，只當作是老師交代的苦差事。從小學起，我們都上過多次的作文課。包括我自己在內，常常都是對著黑板上的作文命題，腦中一片空白，不知如何下筆。

現在，由於視聽媒體的發達，影音訊息五光十色，網路資訊彈指傳遞，更讓年輕人忽視文字精練的必要，少有耐心閱讀、寫作。

其實，寫作的最大價值，不在於書寫的行為，甚至不在於完成的作品。更重要的是，寫作過程中，我們要發揮縝密思考與判斷，收集各種資訊，經過篩選整理，再確立自己的見解，好脈絡清晰地表達，使讀者理解並進而接受我們的論點訴求。我們對許多事情都隱約有各自看法，但是未必認真加以分析整理過，有時不加思索便隨口高談闊論、言不及義，事後回想才發覺漏洞百出，連自己都不知所云，如何說服他人。因此，透過寫作的過程，冷靜地慎思明辨，才能真正認清自己立場、了解他人態度，並互相作理性交流溝通，這才是最好的邏輯思考訓練，也是現代民主社會中人人應有的公民素養。

一般學生視寫作為畏途，看到「學術寫作」更會不知所措，以為那必是象牙塔內老學究壟斷的禁區，閒人免進。這本書打破了這樣的迷思。兩位作者用最淺顯易懂的比喻，點出了寫作的基本意義，也就是「對談」。一般寫作如此，學術寫作也是一樣。每個人隨時都在與自己、與他人對談，我們只要冷靜地聽他人說什麼（they say），認真理解辨明真正的意思，再整理自己思緒，清楚有條理地表達回應（I say），就是成功的對談。再高深專業的學術論辯，其本質也不過如此。

　　本書由英文迻譯為中文，原文輕快活潑，沒有學術文字艱澀難懂的困擾；譯者也忠實反映原文風格，以流利順暢的文筆，陪伴讀者體會學術寫作的歷程。許多讀者都看過一些「譯本比原文更難懂」的書，不明究理，只能慚愧自己程度太差。相信閱讀本書，不僅不會有苦讀經典的壓力，還能藉著譯者巧思翻譯，心領神會，輕鬆愉悅地與作者對談。也祝福大家，將來都能以作者身分，跟你的讀者暢快對談。

Entering the Conversation

導言　**進入對談之前**

試想一個你擅長的活動：烹飪、彈鋼琴、打籃球，或是開車這類基本的事也行。你會發現，一旦精通了這些事，就不需刻意回想做這些事情的各種步驟。換言之，你需要先學會一連串複雜的步驟，才能進行這些活動 —— 對於還不會這些事情的人，這些步驟就顯得很神祕很困難。

寫作亦是如此。成功的寫作者習慣仰賴許多既有的寫作技巧，他們只是沒有意識到，而這些方法對於傳達複雜思想是非常重要的。文章要寫得好，寫作者不僅要有能力表達吸引人的思想，也要嫻熟一系列基本寫作技巧，他們可透過廣泛閱讀其他成功的寫作作品而學會這些寫法。反之，經驗不足的寫作者，往往對這些基本寫作技巧感到生疏，不知道怎麼運用在寫作中。我們希望本書是一個簡潔好用的學術寫作指南，讓大家認識學術論文的基本寫作技巧。

本書的重要前提之一，是這些寫作技巧相當常見，因此可以用寫作範本的方式呈現，讓學生立即套用、架構，進而寫出自己的論文。本書最獨樹一格之處，就是提出許多寫作句型，幫助學生踏入學術討論與寫作的殿堂，並且能參與更廣闊的公民談話與事務。

本書不鑽研抽象的寫作理論，而是提供學術寫作範本，協助學生化學術理論為實務。當你應用這些句型時，就能進行大學程度、未來職場和公共領域所要求的批判性思考。

有些寫作範本相當簡單卻關鍵，像是概述一般看法：

▶ **Many Americans assume that** _____.

許多美國人假設_____。

有些範本則較為複雜：

▶ **On the one hand,** _____. **On the other hand,** _____.

一方面，_____；另一方面，_____。

▶ **Author X contradicts herself. At the same time that she argues**
_____, **she also implies** _____.

作者 X 的論述自我矛盾。她既主張_____，卻又暗示_____。

▶ **I agree that** _____.

我同意_____。

▶ **This is not to say that** _____.

這並不是要說_____。

　　當然，批判性思考與寫作比任何句型範本都要來得深入，它要求你質疑假設、建立有力的主張、提出支持的理由和證據、考慮反論等；但是，唯有擁有可以釐清想法、讓思想有條理的一套語言，才能實踐這種更深層的思考習慣。

▍陳述自身想法以回應他人

　　書中最重要的寫作範本就是 **They say** _____; **I say** _____.，也是本書的英文書名。我們最希望各位讀者從本書中學到的，就是表達自我想法，並回應某人或某個族群的想法。有力的學術論文——以及負責任的公眾談話——其基礎不僅在於陳述自己想法，也在於傾聽周圍其他人的聲音、以他們認可的方式概述其觀點，並且以同樣的方法回應出我們的想法。整體而言，學術論文屬於議論文，我們相信，若要論說得宜，就不能只是堅持自己立場，而是要進入對話，用別人的說法作為個人論點的跳板或傳聲筒。因此，本書最重要的建議，就是把別人的聲音寫進你的論文。

於是，好的學術論文需具備一個基本特色：**以某種方式深入關照別人的觀點**。然而，學術寫作卻經常被教導成與世隔絕、只把「真的」或「聰明的」事情說出來即可，彷彿不需要與別人對話就能完成學術寫作。如果你曾經受過傳統五段式論文（five-paragraph essay）的寫作教學，就知道如何開展一個主題，並且舉證支持。這是個不錯的寫作建議，但是卻忽略了一個重要事實：在真實世界裡，我們不會無端展開辯論。相反地，我們之所以會展開辯論，是因為有人說了什麼話或做了什麼事（或者沒說什麼話、沒做什麼事），而我們需要做出回應，像是「我不明白你為什麼這麼喜歡湖人隊。」「我同意，這部電影真的很好看。」「那個論點很矛盾。」若沒有別人致使我們去質疑、同意或回應，根本毫無爭論的理由。

身為一個寫作者，若要產生影響力，就不能只是寫出合乎邏輯、舉證充分、前後一致的陳述。你還必須想辦法與他人的論點——they say——展開對話。如果你的論點沒有說明是在回應何種「他人觀點」，就很容易出現矛盾。聽眾或許知道你在說什麼，卻未必清楚你說這些的理由。正是因為他人的言論和思想，激發了我們的寫作，使之有了存在的理由。於是，**你自己的論點**——**I say**——務必都要是對他人論點的回應。

許多寫作者在他們的文章中運用了「有人說／我說」寫法。一個著名的例子是小馬丁・路德・金恩（Martin Luther King Jr.）所寫的〈來自伯明罕監獄的一封信〉（Letter from Birmingham Jail）。八位神職人員發表了一份公開聲明，強烈譴責金恩所領導的民權抗議活動，而金恩便以此信作為強力回應。這封信寫於 1963 年，當時金恩在英國伯明罕領導抗議種族不公的遊行而入獄。整封信的內容幾乎都是概述和回應他人看法，金恩先是概述對方的批評，然後逐一回答。其中一個段落寫道：

You deplore the demonstrations taking place in Birmingham. But your statement, I am sorry to say, fails to express a similar concern for the conditions that brought about the demonstrations.

你們對於現在發生於伯明罕的示威遊行感到惋惜。然而我很遺憾地要說，你們的聲明並沒有對示威活動之起因表現出同樣的關心。

—— 小馬丁·路德·金恩，〈來自伯明罕監獄的一封信〉

接著，金恩對批評者表示認同，他說「伯明罕正在發生示威遊行，此事固然遺憾，」（It is unfortunate that demonstrations are taking place in Birmingham,）緊接著說「然而這座城市的白人權威結構，令黑人社區別無選擇，這才是更加遺憾的事。」（it is even more unfortunate that the city's white power structure left the Negro community with no alternative.）事實上，這一整封信已經可以改寫成對話或劇本的形式：

批評者：_____
　金恩：_____
批評者：_____
　金恩：_____

顯然，正因為批評者，金恩才會寫下這封舉世聞名的信。他不將批評者的觀點視為反對自己的異議，而是將之視作自己論點的源頭，是自身論點得以存在的理由。他不只引述批評者的言論，如「有人問：『你們為什麼不給新的市政府做事的時間？』」（Some have asked: 'Why didn't you give the new city administration time to act?'），同時也點出對方可能的說法，如「有人或許會問：『你們怎麼可以提倡違反某些法律，然後又遵守其他法律？』」（One may well ask: 'How can you advocate breaking some laws and obeying others?'）──這些都是金恩為自己想說的話布局。

社會評論家卡莎‧波利特（Katha Pollitt）也用了類似的架構，展開一篇美國愛國主義的論文。她用自己女兒的意見來代表 911 事件後席捲全美的愛國狂潮。

> My daughter, who goes to Stuyvesant High School only blocks from the former World Trade Center, thinks we should fly the American flag out our window. Definitely not, I say: The flag stands for jingoism and vengeance and war. She tells me I'm wrong—the flag means standing together and honoring the dead and saying no to terrorism. In a way we're both right...

> 我女兒就讀的史岱文森高中距離前世貿中心僅幾條街之隔，她覺得我們應該在自家窗外懸掛美國國旗。我說，絕對不行。國旗象徵沙文主義、復仇心態和戰爭。她說，我錯了──國旗代表著萬眾一心、紀念亡者，以及向恐怖主義說不。某種程度我們都是對的……

> ──卡莎‧波利特，〈別掛國旗〉（Put Out No Flags）

從波利特的範例可以看到，鋪陳自己論證時所回應的「他人論點」，不見得要是知名作家或某位讀者，也可以是像她女兒的家人，或是與你見解不同朋友或同學。又或是某人或某團體說的話──或是你自己的一個立場，一個你曾經相信但如今推翻的想法，或是你半信半疑的事。重點在於，「他人觀點」（或「你的其中一個觀點」、「她的觀點」等）代表的是讀者所認同的廣大族群。以波利特的例子來說，「他人觀點」就是那些主張懸掛國旗的愛國主義者。從這個例子也可以看出，回應他人的觀點不一定要無條件反對，波利特藉由贊同與不贊同女兒的說法，做出了我們所謂的「對，也不對」（yes and no）回應，使明顯互不相容的觀點可以和平共存。

金恩和波利特的例子，皆明確點出他們所回應的論點為何，但是有些寫作者不會明確陳述他人的觀點，而是留給讀者自行推斷。舉個例子，你能看出下列主張所未言明的「他人論點」嗎？

I like to think I have a certain advantage as a teacher of literature because when I was growing up I disliked and feared books.

我倒認為我具備當文學老師的某種優勢，因為我小時候很討厭並且懼怕看書。

──杰拉德・葛拉夫，〈小時候不愛看書〉（Disliking Books at an Early Age）

上述例子所暗藏的「他人論點」，就是一般人所認為的，要成為好的文學老師，一定是在書香中長大、喜愛看書的人。

如同以上範例所示，寫作者所運用的「人們說／我說」寫作技巧，都是先質疑他人意見或某種既定的思考模式，並以此展開辯論。如果你向來以為，在學術寫作上成功，就得步步為營、避免爭議，並做出無可反駁的陳述，那麼這樣的觀念可能會讓你震驚。雖然這個觀念看似合理，實際上卻會讓你寫出平淡無奇、枯燥乏味的文章。此外，這種寫作觀念也沒有回答「那又如何」（So

請見第 **4** 堂更多在同意中表達歧見的說明。

what?）和「誰在乎這個論點？」（Who cares?）的問題。「莎士比亞寫過許多知名戲劇和十四行詩。」這句話也許千真萬確，但正是因為沒有人會反對，就是如此理所當然，因此說了也沒有意義。

回應的方式

即使大部分的議論文是出於反對他人論點而寫，但不代表你不能同意他人論點。雖說論證往往與衝突和反對有關，但是本書所強調的「人們說／我說」對話式論證法，無論用來表達反對或贊同，都一樣好用。

▶ **She argues ＿＿＿＿＿, and I agree because ＿＿＿＿＿.**
她認為＿＿＿＿＿，我同意，因為＿＿＿＿＿。

▶ **Her argument that is supported by new research showing that ＿＿＿＿＿.**
新的研究顯示＿＿＿＿＿，支持了她的立論。

不一定只能在同意或不同意之間擇一，如同前面波利特的示範，你也可以兩者兼顧。

▶ **He claims that ＿＿＿＿＿, and I have mixed feelings about it. On the one hand, I agree that ＿＿＿＿＿. On the other hand, I still insist that ＿＿＿＿＿.**
他主張＿＿＿＿＿，我覺得各有道理。一方面，我同意＿＿＿＿＿。另一方面，我還是堅持＿＿＿＿＿。

我們特別推薦同時表達贊同與反對的寫法，這讓你的回答不落於簡單的是或不是，也讓你得以提出更複雜的論點，你可以使用上面範本中條理分明的「一方面；另一方面」（on the one hand / on the other hand）句型。

你可以透過本書的範本架構句子，也可以視需要增減句子，如下面這個「人們說／我說」範本就相當複雜：

▶ In recent discussions of _____ , a controversial issue has been whether _____ . On the one hand, some argue that _____ . From this perspective, _____ . On the other hand, however, others argue that _____ . In the words of _____ , one of this view's main proponents, "_____ ." According to this view, _____ . In sum, then, the issue is whether _____ or _____ . My own view is that _____ . Though I concede that _____ , I still maintain that _____ . For example, _____ . Although some might object that _____ , I would reply that _____ . The issue is important because _____ .

在最近_____的討論聲浪中，有個爭議的問題就是_____。一方面，有人認為_____。從這個觀點來看，_____。然而另一方面，其他人又爭論說_____。用這個論點的主要提倡者之一_____的話來講就是：「_____。」據此觀點，_____。那麼簡而言之，這個議題即是_____還是_____。

我個人的看法是_____。即便我承認_____，我還是堅持_____。舉例來說，_____。雖然有人可能駁斥說_____，我會回答_____。這個議題至關重要，因為_____。

再看一次這則範本。裡頭運用了許多高難度的寫作範本（後續章節會逐一討論）。首先，它點出某個正在討論中的議題，作為文章開場（In recent discussions of ＿＿＿＿＿, a controversial issue has been whether ＿＿＿＿＿.）。接著描繪此爭議下的一些聲音（on the one hand / on the other hand）。這個範本也帶出引述的技巧（In the words of），並且用自己的話闡釋之（According to this view）。接著另起一段陳述自身的觀點（My own view is that）、進一步補充說明觀點（Though I concede that），然後舉證支持（For example）。

此外，這個範本也運用議論文中最關鍵的寫作技巧「將反面論點納入文中」，利用這個寫法，先概述一個可能的反對論點，再加以回應（Although some might object that ＿＿＿＿＿, I would reply that ＿＿＿＿＿.）。最後，這個範本教你怎麼在普遍而宏觀的主張（In sum, then, the issue is whether ＿＿＿＿＿ or ＿＿＿＿＿.）和略而微觀的支持性主張（For example）之間轉移。

沒有人生來就懂這些寫作方法，尤其是學術論文寫作技巧，因此才會需要這本書。

套句範本會扼殺創造力嗎？

你或許和我們的學生一樣，對範本抱持懷疑的態度。許多學生在一開始抱怨，套用範本會剝奪他們的創造力，讓他們的文章看起來如出一轍。其中一個學生堅稱：「它們會把我們變成寫作機器人。」另一個學生附和說：「欸！我是爵士樂手，我們不照固定形式演奏的，都是自己創作。」還有學生說：「我都已經上大學了欸，這是國小三年級的玩意兒吧。」

不過在我們看來，本書的寫作範本可不是什麼「國小三年級的玩意兒」，它們是精細思考下的產物，是寫作必須的技巧，需要花上大量練習和指導才能運用自如。至於認為套用句型會扼殺創造力的看法，是過於侷限視野，未能窺得創造力的全貌。寫作範本能讓寫作產生更多創意；就算是最有創意的表達形式，終歸是建立在既有的模式和結構上。舉例來說，多數作曲者，都是依循行之已久的主歌—副歌—主歌模式；莎士比亞的十四行詩，還有被他發揮得如此精采的戲劇形式，並不是他發明的，但是很少有人會說他沒創意；就連走在時代尖端的前衛藝術家（像是即興派的爵士音樂家），也需要先嫻熟基礎音樂形式，再以這些基礎去創作、脫離、進而超越，否則只會像是小孩子的成果表演。那麼歸根究柢，創造力與獨創性靠的不是揚棄既有形式，而是發揮想像力，好好運用它們。

再者，這些寫作範本並不會限制住你要陳述的內容。你要怎麼獨創內容都可以，範本幫助你梳理陳述的內容。一旦你對這些寫作範本得心應手，就可以根據自身狀況和目的，修改範本，也可以在閱讀時發現其他範本。換言之，本書提供的寫作範本更像是一套入門的學習工具，而非僵化的限制。等你上手之後，甚至可以完全棄之不用，因為它們所示範的修辭技巧已在你指尖，憑直覺就能信手拈來。

如果你仍然需要我們證明寫作範本不會扼殺創造力，可以看看下面這段探討速食產業的論文開頭，本文也收錄在本書最後一個部分（第 268-271 頁）。

If ever there were a newspaper headline custom-made for Jay Leno's monologue, this was it. Kids taking on McDonald's this week, suing the company for making them fat. Isn't that like middle-aged men suing Porsche for making them get speeding tickets? Whatever happened to personal responsibility?

I tend to sympathize with these portly fast-food patrons, though. Maybe that's because I used to be one of them.

假如真有個話題是為了傑·雷諾脫口秀的開場獨白而特意製作的，那就非此莫屬了：本週兒童迎戰麥當勞，控告該企業害他們發胖。這豈不就像是中年男子控告保時捷害他們被開超速罰單？個人責任感到哪裡去了？

不過呢，我倒是相當同情這些肥胖的速食常客，或許是因為我也曾是其中一員吧。

——大衛·辛善寇（David Zinczenko），
〈別怪吃的人〉（Don't Blame the Eater）

儘管辛善寇採用的是「人們說／我說」句型的變體，他的論文卻一點也不枯燥、僵硬或沒有創意。他沒有使用 they say 和 I say 這類字眼，但這個段落實際上仍然是基於這個架構：

They say that kids suing fast-food companies for making them fat is a joke, **but I say** such lawsuits are justified.

人們說，兒童控告速食業者害他們發胖是個笑話；但是我說，這種控訴是合情合理。

▍這是抄襲嗎？

「難道這不算抄襲嗎？」每年至少有一個學生會這樣問，我們會回問：「這算嗎？」我們把這個問題變得有建設性一些，好讓全班能從中受益。我們對學生說：「畢竟我們是在要求大家在自己的寫作中，運用別人的語言 —— 是你『借』來的，或者講難聽一點，是從別人那裡偷來的。」

接踵而來的便是一場熱烈的討論，像是作者的所有權、剽竊、合法使用他人言論以及敘述方式等問題會被提出並討論，這樣的討論有助於釐清抄襲與合理使用兩者之間屢被混淆的界線。學生們很快就會知道，像 on the one hand...on the other hand... 這樣的慣用句型，並不專屬於某個人，a controversial issue 這樣的片語也已司空見慣，而且被一再使用，是可以自由使用的共有財產。但是，如果在這樣的句型空格中所填入的文字，是未獲許可就取用的他人內容，那就是抄襲。簡單來說，使用慣用句型並非抄襲，但取用他人文本中的實質內容，卻未舉出出處或原作者，就是嚴重違反學術道德（academic offense）。

▌插入自己的想法

雖然本書現階段目的是協助讀者成為一位更優秀的學術寫作者，不過就更長遠來看，是希望讀者能成為具批判性、具智慧的思考者，進而能夠積極主動、自信地參與辯論和對話，而不是當個被動的旁觀者。簡而言之，本書的終極目標就是：讓你成為具批判性的思想家，能參與如哲學家肯尼斯·柏克在下列廣被援引的段落中的場合。他把智力交流的世界比做聚會裡毫無止盡的對話：

> You come late. When you arrive, others have long preceded you, and they are engaged in a heated discussion, a discussion too heated for them to pause and tell you exactly what it is about...You listen for a while, until

you decide that you have caught the tenor of the argument; then you put in your oar. Someone answers; you answer him; another comes to your defense; another aligns himself against you...The hour grows late, you must depart. And you do depart, with the discussion still vigorously in progress.

你遲到了，當你抵達的時候，大家早就先你一步開始討論了，他們討論得如火如荼，沒人有閒工夫告訴你究竟在討論什麼……你聽了好一會兒，終於聽出個端倪，然後插了話。有人回答你；你回答他；有人幫你辯解；有人反駁你的看法……時候不早了，你得告辭，而你也就走了，討論依然熱烈進行下去。

—— 肯尼斯·柏克，《文學體裁之哲理》
（*The Philosophy of Literary Form*）

我們喜歡這段敘述，是因為它暗示著：唯有與他人對話，才能陳述一個論點，進而「插入自己的想法」。我們都不是以孤立之姿踏進活躍的思想世界，而是以社會人的身分，和其他重視我們言論的人緊密連結。

在現今 911 後的多元世界裡，我們急切需要能參與複雜、多面向對話的能力，我們在未來需仰賴這種能力，讓我們能換位思考。本書的核心建議 —— 傾聽他人的聲音，即使是反對的聲音，然後以慎重尊重的態度做出正面回應 —— 能讓我們不侷限於自己偏愛的理念，因為那未必是所有人的共通理念。光是寫出以 Of course, someone might object that _____.（當然，有人或許會反對_____。）開頭的句子，或許不能改變世界，但是卻能帶我們離開舒適圈，用批判的角度省思自己的理念，甚至改變我們的想法。

1. 閱讀下列節自傅爾曼大學（Furman University）的學生愛蜜麗·波（Emily Poe）的論文段落，先不管她說的內容，把重點放在她用來架構言論的用語上面（以粗體標示）。接著以波的段落為模範，將她的素食主義主題換成其他主題，寫出一個新的段落。

The term "vegetarian" tends to be synonymous with "tree-hugger" in many people's minds. **They see** vegetarianism as a cult that brainwashes its followers into eliminating an essential part of their daily diets for an abstract goal of "animal welfare." **However**, few vegetarians choose their lifestyle just to follow the crowd. **On the contrary**, many of these supposedly brainwashed people are actually independent thinkers, concerned citizens, and compassionate human beings. **For the truth** is that there are many very good reasons for giving up meat. Perhaps the best reasons are to improve the environment, to encourage humane treatment of livestock, or to enhance one's own health. **In this essay**, then, closely examining a vegetarian diet as compared to a meat-eater's diet will show that vegetarianism is clearly the better option for sustaining the Earth and all its inhabitants.

2. 寫一篇短文，概述我們支持本書範本的理由，接著清楚表達你的立場作為回應。你也可以用下面的範本來組織段落，必要時可加以延伸和修改，讓它符合你想要表達的內容。

In the Introduction to *"They Say / I Say": The Moves That Matter in Academic Writing*, Gerald Graff and Cathy Birkenstein provide templates designed to _____. Specifically, Graff and Birkenstein argue that the types of writing templates they offer _____. As the authors themselves put it, "_____." Although some people believe _____, Graff and Birkenstein insist that _____. In sum, then, their view is that _____.

I [agree / disagree / have mixed feelings]. In my view, the types of templates that the authors recommend _____. For instance, _____. In addition, _____. Some might object, of course, on the grounds that _____. Yet I would argue that _____. Overall, then, I believe _____—an important point to make given _____.

PART I

They Say
有人說

學術寫作不僅只是表達自身觀點，
而要把它當作是回應他人的論述。
第一部分便從〈先聽聽別人怎麼說〉揭開序幕，
解釋論文為何多從引用他人論述作為開場，
而非直接切入自己的論點。
接下去的章節則繼續探討如何概述，
並引用他人言論。

第 1 堂　先聽聽別人怎麼說

"They say..."
「有人說……」

　　不久前，我們在一場學術研討會上聽到一場演講，講者說某位社會學家——姑且稱之為 X 博士——在該領域許多方面貢獻卓越。講者接著將 X 博士的所有著作詳細引述介紹。這位講者顯然很有學問，也充滿熱情，但是我們卻聽得一頭霧水；X 博士的研究很重要，這個論點很清楚，但是第一個最大的問題是：「**講者為什麼一開始就提出這一點？**」有人質疑過這一點嗎？有該領域的評論者反對 X 博士的研究或提出質疑嗎？講者沒有針對上述問題提供任何提示或答案。我們只能納悶，為什麼他要滔滔不絕講述 X 博士的事蹟。直到演講結束、聽眾開始提問時，我們才理出頭緒。他在回答一個提問時，才提到 X 博士的論點確曾遭受質疑，且若干社會學家認為 X 博士的研究並不嚴謹。

　　這個故事給我們一個重要教訓：如果要讓文章言之有物，寫作者不僅要**明確提出自己的論點（thesis）**，還必須**將該論點與他人做更大的對話**。當天講者沒有提到其他人對 X 博士研究的看法，因此聽眾不明白他為何有那樣的立場。在場的其他社會學家或許比我們更了解有關 X 博士研究的爭議，或許更聽得懂講者的論點。但是，如果講者能提出其論點背後的對話背景，提醒聽眾「其他人說」（they say）了什麼，並以此為背景說明自己的論點，那麼，其他社會學家，也會更了解 X 博士的論點。

這個故事還告訴我們另一個重要教訓：**敘事順序很重要**。如果要吸引讀者持續關注你的主題，就要先說明你的論點要回應的對象是什麼，越早越好。倘若你在小論文或部落格文章的一、兩個段落之後，或長篇論文的三、四頁之後，或一本書的十多頁之後，才點出你要回應什麼，這就違反了讀者理解的自然順序，也與寫作者構思的順序相違背。畢竟，會議上那位講者既然是專家，他必是先聽到批評 X 教授的言論，然後才會想到去做辯駁維護。

因此，建構一個論證時（不管是以口說或寫作的方式），請記住，你是在進行一場對話，因此，要如同本課標題的建議，從「別人怎麼說」開始，接著才說明自己的意見作為回應。我們尤其建議，在文章中要儘早概述別人的看法，並隨著文章鋪陳到關鍵處再次提醒讀者。雖說並非所有文章都要遵循這種做法，但我們認為，應該先熟悉這個寫作方式之後，再發展其他技巧。

這並不是要你一開始就洋洋灑灑列出所有談論過相同主題的人，接著才提出自己的看法。當天那位講者，要是大部分時間都概述對 X 博士的批評，卻不提出自己可能立場，聽眾還是會不明白：「他到底為什麼要這樣？」因此我們建議，盡早表明你的立場與你所回應的立場，而且要將兩者一起呈現。一般而言，最好在文章的開頭簡短帶出你所要回應的論點，稍後再詳細解釋。這裡的關鍵在於，讓讀者快速預覽你的論證動機，而不是一下子就把細節說盡。

一開頭就概述別人的論點，看似與一般的寫作建議 —— 要先寫出自己的論點 —— 相悖。但我們也相信，你應該在他人論點當中找出想支持、反對或修正，或是要進一步改善之處，換言之，你必須將自己的論點與其他論點形成一個對談。盡早概述他人論點還有一個好處：以他人論點協助你構思並釐清你所撰寫的議題。

想想喬治・歐威爾（George Orwell）在其知名論文〈政治與英語〉（Politics and the English Language）中，是如何以別人的話起頭：

Most people who bother with the matter at all would admit that the English language is in a bad way, but it is generally assumed that we cannot by conscious action do anything about it. Our civilization is decadent and our language—so the argument runs—must inevitably share in the general collapse...

[But] the process is reversible. Modern English... is full of bad habits... which can be avoided if one is willing to take the necessary trouble.

對這個問題略為關切的人大都認為，英語使用水準低落，即使有意振作也無法改善。我們的文明日益衰落，而我們的語言 —— 有此一說 —— 也勢必無法倖免於難……

〔但是〕這個趨勢是可以逆轉的。現代英語……充滿的那些不良用法……只要肯下功夫，仍可以避免。

—— 喬治·歐威爾，〈政治與英語〉

基本上，歐威爾要說的是：

Most people assume that we cannot do anything about the bad state of the English language. But **I say** we can.

許多人認定我們對英語的現況不佳無能為力，但我說我們可以做到。

讓文章開場強而有力的方式有很多，如果不直接用另一人的論點起頭，也可以用一段生動的引述、一件具體事實或統計數字，或是如本課開頭的做法，先以一則軼事揭開序幕。重點是，不論你選擇的是上述何種方式，一定要盡量在最少的步驟內導出你想表達的論點。

以本文開場白為例，我們先以一則軼事開場，下一段，就以此講者的表現為借鏡，指出寫作時容易發生的錯誤。以下這段是取自《紐約時報書評》（*New York Times Book Review*）的一篇文章開場白，作者克莉絲緹娜・聶琳（Christina Nehring）同樣以一則軼事開始描述她不喜歡的事，接著迅速進入自己的主張——愛書人士太自以為是。

"I'm a reader!" announced the yellow button. "How about you?" I looked at its bearer, a strapping young guy stalking my town's Festival of Books. "I'll bet you're a reader," he volunteered, as though we were two geniuses well met. "No," I replied. "Absolutely not," I wanted to yell, and fling my Barnes & Noble bag at his feet. Instead, I mumbled something apologetic and melted into the crowd.

There's a new piety in the air: the self congratulation of book lovers.

黃色胸章寫著：「我是愛書人！你呢？」我打量了配戴黃色胸章的主人。他是個高大魁梧的年輕小伙子，正在鎮上舉辦的書展會場走動。「你一定也很愛書吧？」他自動幫我回答，彷彿我們是兩個天才相見歡。「不會耶，」我回答：「完全不會。」我真的好想大叫一聲，然後把我的巴諾書店紙袋朝他的腳砸下去。不過我忍住了，我咕噥了幾句不好意思，就沒入人群之中。

有種新的虔誠心態正在滋長：愛書人士的自命不凡。

——克莉絲緹娜・聶琳，
〈書讓你變成無聊的人〉（Books Make You a Boring Person）

發生在聶琳身上的趣聞，可以用來呈現以下的「他人論點」：愛書人士總是自命不凡。

範本 1：提出「他人論點」

用來引導出他人論點的方式很多，對於研討會上那位講者，我們會建議這麼說：

▶ A number of _____ have recently suggested that _____ .
最近有些_____提出，_____。

▶ It has become common today to dismiss _____ .
今日，我們普遍不去考慮_____。

▶ In their recent work, Y and Z have offered harsh critiques of _____
for _____ .
Y 和 Z 在最近的研究中，對_____提出了嚴厲的批評，說他_____。

範本 2：提出「一般論點」

下列句型可以幫你引導出一般論點（standard view），所謂一般論點，就是該論點已廣為大眾接受，如今想到某個主題就會習慣性以該論點思考。我們可以用以下範本來帶出這樣的論點。這些範本可以幫助寫作者快速有效進行最重要的工作，就是：對廣為接受的信念提出質疑，用放大鏡檢視其優劣。

▶ Americans have always believed that _____ .
美國人向來相信_____。

▶ **Conventional wisdom has it that** _____.

一般看法是_____。

▶ **Common sense seems to dictate that** _____.

基本常識似乎認定_____。

▶ **The standard way of thinking about topic X has it that** _____.

關於 X 這個主題，標準的思維模式是_____。

▶ **It is often said that** _____.

大家常說_____。

▶ **My whole life I have heard it said that** _____.

我一生中總不斷聽到別人說_____。

▶ **You would think that** _____.

或許你會認為_____。

▶ **Many people assume that** _____.

許多人假設_____。

範本 3：將他人論點轉換成自己的論點

第三種回應他人論點的方法，是以自己的觀點來討論。你要回應的論點未必全然是他人的看法，也可能是你自己曾經贊同或者仍然不太確定的想法。

▶ **I've always believed that** _____.

我一直認為_____。

▶ When I was a child, I used to think that _____.

小時候，我常覺得_____。

▶ Although I should know better by now, I cannot help thinking that

_____.

雖然我現在想法更周延了，但不禁還是認為_____。

▶ At the same time that I believe _____, I also believe _____.

我既認為_____，又認為_____。

範本 4：提出暗示或假設的想法

另一種較精緻的寫作法，就是指出別人隱含預設的論點，但不直接引述他的說法。這些句型有助於你對某個主題進行分析思考——不僅要看了別人到底說了什麼，還要考慮其言下之意，聽出其弦外之音。

▶ Although none of them have ever said so directly, my teachers have often given me the impression that _____.

儘管我的老師們未曾直言，他們卻常給我這個印象，_____。

▶ One implication of X's treatment of _____ is that _____.

X 對_____的論述蘊含了_____之意。

▶ Although X does not say so directly, she apparently assumes that

_____.

雖然 X 沒有明講，但她顯然假設_____。

▶ While they rarely admit as much, ＿＿＿＿＿ often take for granted that ＿＿＿＿＿.

雖然他們不會承認，＿＿＿＿＿經常把＿＿＿＿＿視為理所當然。

範本 5：提出一個尚未定論的爭議點

　　有時候，你也可以提出兩三種互斥的論點作為開頭。這種開場方式顯示你能從多角度思考問題，展現你對該主題的熟悉，讓讀者感受你的說法可靠而值得信賴。再者，以一則爭論做開場，能幫助你在提出自己的論點之前，先對該議題進行探究。這個方式能讓你利用寫作過程，發覺自我立場，而不是在還不確定時就採取某個立場。

　　以下是以爭議作為開場的範本：

▶ In discussions of X, one controversial issue has been ＿＿＿＿＿.
On the one hand, ＿＿＿＿＿ argues ＿＿＿＿＿. On the other hand, ＿＿＿＿＿ contends ＿＿＿＿＿. Others even maintain ＿＿＿＿＿.
My own view is ＿＿＿＿＿.

在對於 X 的討論中，一個爭議點一直是＿＿＿＿＿。一方面，＿＿＿＿＿指稱＿＿＿＿＿。另一方面，＿＿＿＿＿聲稱＿＿＿＿＿。有些人甚至堅持＿＿＿＿＿。我的看法是＿＿＿＿＿。

　　認知科學家馬克・阿洛諾夫（Mark Aronoff）在其探究人腦的一篇論文中，運用了這種寫法：

Theories of how the mind / brain works have been dominated for centuries by two opposing views. One, rationalism, sees the human mind as coming into this world more or less fully formed—preprogrammed, in modern terms. The other, empiricism, sees the mind of the newborn as largely unstructured, a blank slate.

關於心靈／腦部如何運作的理論，幾世紀以來一直有兩個對立的論點。一為理性主義，認為人來到世上時腦部多少已經完全成形，以現代術語來說，就是已預先寫好程式。另一說為經驗主義，認為新生兒的大腦大部分尚未建構完成，等於一張白紙。

——馬克‧阿洛諾夫，〈華盛頓在此長眠〉（Washington Sleeped Here）

另一種以爭議點起頭的方式，就是提出一個許多人起初看法一致，但是他們最終見解互有不同。

▶ **When it comes to the topic of _____, most of us will readily agree that _____. Where this agreement usually ends, however, is on the question of _____. Whereas some are convinced that _____, others maintain that _____.**
談到_____這個主題，我們多半會異口同聲認為_____。然而，到了最後，卻往往在_____的問題上產生歧異。儘管有些人相信_____，有些人仍主張_____。

政治作家湯瑪士‧法蘭克（Thomas Frank）就以這種寫法略加以變化：

That we are a nation divided is an almost universal lament of this bitter election year. **However,** the exact property that divides us—elemental though it is said to be—remains a matter of some controversy.

在這個令人苦悶的選舉年中，舉國上下幾乎都在感嘆我們是個分裂的國家。然而，究竟是什麼原因讓我們分裂 —— 即使有人說是一些基本核心矛盾 —— 仍有待商榷。

—— 湯瑪士·法蘭克，〈美國精神〉（American Psyche）

範本 6：持續關注他人論點

從開始寫論文到尾聲，請務必時時關注「他人論點」。在一開始回應他人論點之後，更重要的是持續關注。惟有不斷提醒讀者你所回應主張為何，他們才能理解你所進行的複雜議題。

換言之，即便你已經在論述自己的主張，也都應該持續回顧他人論點。文章越寫越長，內容更加錯綜複雜，讀者越容易遺忘你的寫作動機 —— 無論你在一開始表達得有多清楚。因此，我們建議你在整篇文章的關鍵處使用「回顧句」（return sentence），像是：

▶ In conclusion, then, as I suggested earlier, defenders of _____ can't have it both ways. Their assertion that _____ is contradicted by their claim that _____.
那麼最後，如同我先前提到，主張_____的論點有無法克服的矛盾。他們說_____，這和他們_____的主張是相悖的。

有人可能說，好的寫作只要針對主題做真實、明確、合乎邏輯的陳述，不太需要提到他人的說法，甚至完全忽略也可。在本書中，我們不厭其煩提醒各位，對這樣的主張，我們非常質疑。

透過回顧句提醒讀者你所回應的論點，可以使你的文章自始至終顯示使命感和迫切性；可以顯示你的論點是對他人論點的認真回應，而不僅是對特定主題的自說自話。這兩者間差異甚鉅。先提到別人怎麼說，並且讓讀者一直記住，這樣才能回應他人論點，形成對談式的論述。

練習

1. 下列的論證少了「他人論點」的部分，不知道誰該聽這些主張，也不知道誰持有相反想法。請你在本練習中，為每一條論證提出一個反論。你可以自由使用本課所提供的範本。

   a. Our experiments suggest that there are dangerous levels of chemical X in the Ohio groundwater.
   我們的實驗顯示，俄亥俄州地下水中一種化學物質 X 含量過高，到了危險程度。

   b. Material forces drive history.
   物質條件決定歷史。

   c. Proponents of Freudian psychology question standard notions of "rationality."
   佛洛依德心理學派的倡導者質疑對『理性』的標準看法。

d. Male students often dominate class discussions.

主導課堂討論的多半是男學生。

e. The film is about the problems of romantic relationships.

該影片在探討情感關係中的問題。

f. I'm afraid that templates like the ones in this book will stifle my creativity.

我覺得這本教科書裡這些範本只會壓抑我的創造力。

2. 下面是採用辛善寇的論文〈別怪吃的人〉（見第 268 頁）的起始段落所作的一個範本。請自選一個主題，運用這個範本組織一個段落。首先，找到一個自己認同，但別人不僅反對，而且根本就視為荒謬的主題（用辛善寇的話來說，就是值得被脫口秀藝人傑·雷諾拿來調侃的）。你可以從先前練習列舉的主題中擇一書寫（環境、性別關係、一本書或電影的意義），或任選一個你有興趣的話題。

▶ **If ever there was an idea custom-made for a Jay Leno monologue, this was it: _____. Isn't that like _____? Whatever happened to _____?**

I happen to sympathize with _____, though, perhaps because _____.

假如真有個話題是為了傑·雷諾脫口秀的開場獨白而特意製作的，那就非此莫屬了：_____。這不是很像_____嗎？到底_____發生了什麼事？

我倒是認同_____，雖然這可能是因為_____。

The Art of Summarizing

第 **2** 堂　概述的技巧

"Her point is..."
「她的說法是……」

　　如果本書的主張是正確的 —— 要使自己論證有說服力，就得形成一段與他人的對談，那麼，如何在寫作時概述他人論點就是必要的核心能力。「概述」（summarize）就是將他人的論點用你自己的話轉述出來。要提出強而有力的主張，就要**釐清自己主張與他人論點的異同**，因此，有效概述別人的說法，至為重要。

　　許多寫作者會避免概述別人的看法，或許是他們懶得閱讀文本、不想思索裡面說了什麼；或許怕花太多時間在別人論點上，會削弱自己的主張。這樣的寫作者要回應他人論文時，可能只會針對對方論文主題提出主觀看法，卻絲毫不提對方真正論述了什麼。另一個極端的情況是，作者全篇只有概述他人的論點。這樣的作者對自己的想法缺乏信心，於是在論文裡大量概述別人的論點，導致自己的聲音都被淹沒。因為寫作者沒有投注興趣，這些概述也就失了生氣，讀起來好像只是條列某甲想了什麼、某乙又說了什麼，而沒有明確的焦點。

　　一般來說，好的概述要在他人論點和本人關注的焦點之間取得平衡。寫概述時，要正確簡述原作者論點，同時強調出其中吸引你的部分。要達到這樣的微妙平衡並不容易，因為你要同時處理兩個面向：你所概述的作者，還有你自己。換言之，你一方面要尊重原作者的論點，另一方面在轉述時，要設想好論述架構，以便配自己即將提出的論點。

▍站在別人的角度思考

要寫出真正精采的概述，就必須先把自己的想法放在一旁，站在別人的角度思考，也就是要玩一場寫作理論家彼德·艾爾博（Peter Elbow）所謂的「**信任遊戲**」（believing game）：試著進入你想對話的人的世界觀裡──即使你不同意他們──從他們的視角看待他們的論證。好的寫作者就如同好演員一樣，要能暫時放下個人定見，「變身」成為現實生活中自己很厭惡的角色。你如能把信任遊戲玩得爐火純青，讀者甚至看不出你對該概述的理念是同意或反對。

若是不能或不願意暫時把自我理念放在一旁，就容易寫出充滿偏見的概述，降低讀者對你的信賴。看一下以下這段概述文字：

> David Zinczenko's article, "Don't Blame the Eater," is nothing more than an angry rant in which he accuses the fast-food companies of an evil conspiracy to make people fat. I disagree because these companies have to make money...

> 大衛·辛善寇的論文〈別怪吃的人〉全篇都是憤怒的謾罵，他在文中控訴速食業者的邪惡陰謀，意圖使人發胖。我不同意，因為這些業者也是得賺錢⋯⋯

如果你再看一次辛善寇的實際說法（請見第 268 頁），就會發現，這段概述偏頗且扭曲事實。辛善寇的確認為速食業者的確是使人發胖的原因之一，但是他的語氣一點也不「憤怒」，也不認為速食業者存心不良，蓄意讓人發胖。

另外，上述文字只用了一句話就結束概述，就急忙跳到自己的回應，這也說明他並沒有合理恰當地轉述辛善寇的論點。他急於表示反對，不僅浮誇了辛善寇的說法，解讀上也流於草率和膚淺。在一般寫作情況下，你的確因為考量篇幅比例分配，可能只做一、兩個句子概述。如同寫作教授凱倫·郎斯福（Karen Lunsford，專攻論證理論）所指出的，在自然科學和社科領域中，只用一個簡潔有力的句子或片語來概述他人論點，是常見作法，請見下例：

Several studies (Crackle, 2012; Pop, 2007; Snap, 2006) suggest that these policies are harmless; moreover, other studies (Dick, 2011; Harry, 2007; Tom, 2005) argue that they even have benefits.

有些研究（克拉克爾，2012；波普，2007；史奈普，2006）主張這些政策並無害處；其他一些研究（迪克，2011；哈瑞，2007；湯姆，2005）甚至認為它們有益。

然而，如果你的寫作是為了回應單一作者，如辛善寇的文章，那你就要讓讀者充分了解該作者的論述，讓讀者自行評估價值，而非受你影響。

概述他人論點時，如果不夠完整，或是有所疏漏，往往就會落入所謂「**近陳腔濫調症**」（the closest cliché syndrome）的陷阱。在這種情況下，寫作者所概述的內容並非對方真正的意思，而是把一個最接近對方意思的陳腔濫調誤認為其觀點（有時是因為寫作者自己這樣認為，就錯誤假設對方也是如此）。舉個例子，小馬丁·路德·金恩在〈來自伯明罕監獄的一封信〉中情緒激昂地維護「公民不服從」（civil disobedience），就可能被描述成不是為政治示威活動發聲，而是呼籲人人「和睦相處」，但其實前者才是其初衷。無獨有偶，辛善寇針對速食業的評論，也可能被描述成是在呼籲肥胖人士為自己的體重負責。

因此，你在寫作中與他人進行對談，務必要回歸到別人真正的論點，務必將他人論點詳細研究，切勿與自己既存的信念混淆。若是無法做到這一點，你其實只是和自己先入為主的觀念對談。

另一方面，要知道「自己」的方向

即使你必須暫時採納他人論點，以便有效地寫出概述，這並不代表你要完全忽視自己的想法。這聽起來很矛盾，不過，在概述別人的論點時，一方面你得公平客觀地陳述，一方面又得同時讓你的回應默默發揮影響力。換言之，一則好的概述會有一個重點或輪廓，讓它既符合你的論述架構，又不曲解你所概述的對象。

因此，如果你要寫篇論文回應辛善寇的論點，就應該要了解，你的論點可能會是針對整體速食業，也可能是針對親子教養、企業規範、或警告標語這三項議題；因為主題不同，其概述方式也大不相同。假如你的論文涵蓋的是後面三個議題，就必須先將這三個議題放在辛善寇的中心論點的架構中，從辛善寇的中心論點，開始鋪陳你的論述。

假設你想要說的是，該為孩子的肥胖負責的是家長而非速食業者，為了建立這個論證，在組織概述的時候，就要強調辛善寇對速食業以及對家長的看法，看看下面這段示例。

In his article "Don't Blame the Eater," David Zinczenko blames the fast-food industry for fueling today's so-called obesity epidemic, not only by failing to provide adequate warning labels on its high-calorie foods but also by filling the nutritional void in children's lives left by their overtaxed working parents. With many parents working long hours and unable to supervise what their children eat, Zinczenko claims, children today are easily victimized by the low-cost, calorie-laden foods that the fast-food chains are all too eager to supply. When he was a young boy, for instance, and his single mother was away at work, he ate at Taco Bell, McDonald's, and other chains on a regular basis, and ended up overweight. Zinczenko's hope is that with the new spate of lawsuits against the food industry, other children with working parents will have healthier choices available to them, and that they will not, like him, become obese.

In my view, however, it is the parents, and not the food chains, who are responsible for their children's obesity. While it is true that many of today's parents work long hours, there are still several things that parents can do to guarantee that their children eat healthy foods...

　　大衛・辛善寇在他的論文〈別怪吃的人〉當中，譴責速食業者是加速當今所謂肥胖症的元兇，不僅因為他們未在高熱量食物上面提供充分的警告標示，也因為父母親為了工作疲於奔命，孩童三餐都靠速食充飢。辛善寇表示，許多父母親因為長時間工作，無法注意孩子的飲食，導致現在的孩子很容易受到速食連鎖店大量供應的低價、高熱量食物所危害。以他自己兒時為例，他的單親媽媽外出上班，他都習慣在塔可鐘、麥當勞等速食連鎖店解決吃的問題，造成他過重。辛善寇希望藉由這些接連爆發的控訴事件，讓其他雙親必須工作的孩子能有更健康的選擇，而不要像自己一樣發胖。

　　然而在我看來，該為孩子的肥胖負責的是家長，而非速食業者。當然，現在許多家長的工時很長，但他們仍有方法可確保孩子吃得健康⋯⋯

第一段的概述是成功的，因為它同時指向兩個方向——一方面引出辛善寇的文本，一方面幫第二段鋪陳，建立自己的論證。第一個句子包含了辛善寇的中心主張（速食連鎖業者該為孩子的肥胖負責）以及其兩個主要論點（警告標示和父母親），但最後以寫作者所關注的重點作結：父母親的責任。如此一來，不僅公平呈現辛善寇的主張，也順勢帶出後續的評論。

概述原作者的論點，以利提出自己的論點架構，這個原則大家應該已明白。但是，在寫作過程中，寫作者往往容易忘記自己的論文重點，而在原作者的某個觀點上面打轉。為了避免這種情況發生，你要確保「他人論點」和「自己論點」在內容上密切配合。事實上，將兩者並列，也是論文編修時，特別要用心的地方。

概述他人看法時，如果沒有適時帶入自己論點，往往會流於所謂的「條列概要」（list summaries），也就是把他人的各種論點列成清單，卻沒有使它們集中，圍繞著一個更大的整體主張。如果你聽到一場演講中，講者只用 and then（然後）、also（而且）、in addition（此外）來連結陳述，你一定會昏昏欲睡了。就像以下的例子：

> The author says many different things about his subject. **First** he says... **Then** he makes the point that... **In addition** he says... **And then** he writes... **Also** he shows that... **And then** he says...

> 作者針對他的主題說過許多不同的看法。首先他說……；接著他說明了……的論點；此外他說……；然後他寫道……；他還表示……；而接著他又說……

這樣的條列概要沒有意義，可能讓人誤解貶抑了概述的價值，甚至會致使一些教師提醒學生不要寫概述。

因此，一段好的概述，不只是忠實轉述原作者的論點，更要讓它符合你自己的論述架構。一方面，要玩艾爾博的「信任遊戲」，合理轉述他人論點。如果概述時忽略他人論點，或是未能詳實敘述，就會讓人看出你的偏見與破綻；另一方面，公正客觀地作概述時，也要採取一種取向，準備開始鋪陳你自己的論點。一旦你在論文中概述他人論點，那就是原作者與你所共有，它要同時反映出他人的和你自己的論點。

諷刺性概述

我們剛剛已經說明，好的概述通常要在別人所說的話與你身為寫作者所關注的重點之間取得平衡。不過，現在我們要舉出一個例外：諷刺性概述（satiric summary）。在諷刺性概述中，寫作者巧妙地把自己的立場置入別人的論點，目的是為了暴露其漏洞。雖然我們在前面說過，好的概述是既留意到他人的論點，也保有自己的觀點，並在兩者間達到平衡，但是採用諷刺手法有時不失為一種力道十足的論述方式，因為它可以讓對方的論點不攻自破。假如你看過《每日秀》（The Daily Show）這個節目，你一定記得，節目中經常只是回顧政治人物說蠢話或做蠢事的畫面，讓他們自己的言行舉止來自曝其短。

再來看看另一個例子，2011 年 9 月，當時美國總統小布希（George W. Bush）在國會發表演說，呼籲全國「持續參與美國經濟，並且要有信心」，以期能從 911 恐攻中振興起來。記者艾倫・史龍（Allan Sloan）對此說法做了概述，實則是批評，他說總統「將愛國主義和購物畫上等號。在購物中心刷爆你的信用卡可不是縱欲，而是報復賓拉登的手段。」史龍所展現的立場相當明確，他認為小布希的提議荒謬至極，或至少是過度簡化問題了。

使用具體貼切的示意動詞

撰寫一段概述時，盡量不要用 she "says"、they "believe" 這類平淡乏味的動詞，雖說這樣的用語有時足以達意，卻往往無法正確反映引述者的立場。在某些情況下，使用 say 這種動詞甚至會讓你所概述的想法毫無情意可言。

在概述的時候，我們可能不太想清楚描述對方的實際行為，所以會養成這種習慣，就是前面提到的，以為寫作要打安全牌，避免爭議；把寫作過程當作只是堆砌事實和知識，而沒有將其視為和別人的互動過程。我們和朋友聊天時，不假思索就會說出：「某某人根本就亂講（misrepresented）／抨擊（attacked）／熱愛（loved）某件事」，到了寫作的時候卻常常選擇「某某人說（said）」這種比較溫和甚至不夠精確的說法。

研究生所閱讀的論述，作者不會只是在「說」（say）什麼或「討論」（discuss）什麼，而是「疾呼」（urge）、「強調」（emphasize）還有「抱怨」（complain about）一些事情。以辛善寇為例，他可不只是說速食業者造成消費者肥胖，他是在「抱怨」或「抗議」（protest）速食業者使人發胖，他是在「質疑」（challenge）、「斥責」（chastise）並「控訴」（indict）這些業者。《美國獨立宣言》不只是在談論（talk about），而是在「抗議」（protest against）英國如何對待殖民地。

要公正提出所援引的內容，我們會建議，盡量**使用鮮明而精確的示意動詞**（signal verb）。雖然有時候使用 he "says"、she "believes" 是最符合情況的，但若能使用更貼切的動詞，你的論文會更正確且生動。

範本 7：提出概述和引述

▶ **She advocates** _____ .

她主張_____。

▶ **They celebrate the fact that** _____ .

他們頌揚_____這件事情。

▶ _____ , **he admits.**

他承認_____。

範本 7-1：適合用來概述和引述的動詞

▶ **提出主張**

argue 主張、認為

assert 主張、斷言

believe 相信

claim 主張、聲稱

emphasize 強調

insist 堅持、堅決認為

observe 察覺到、注意到

remind us 提醒我們

report 報告；描述

suggest 暗示；意味著

▶ **表示同意、認同**

acknowledge 承認、認可

admire 讚賞、誇讚

agree 同意、贊成

endorse 贊同

extol 讚揚、讚頌

praise 稱讚、表揚

▶ 表示質疑或不認同

complain 抱怨

complicate 使複雜化、使更難懂

contend 聲稱、斷言

contradict 駁斥、反駁

deny 否認

deplore the tendency to 強烈譴責……

qualify 補充說明；提出但書

question 質疑、懷疑

refute 駁斥、反駁

reject 拒絕、駁回

renounce 宣布放棄

repudiate 否認、駁斥

▶ 提出建議

advocate 提倡、主張

call for 呼籲、要求

demand 強烈要求

encourage 鼓勵

exhort 敦促、規勸

implore 懇求、哀求

plead 懇求、請求

recommend 建議

urge 促請、力勸

warn 警告、告誡

練習

1. 為了體驗艾爾博所提出的「信任遊戲」，請寫一則概述，說明某個你強烈反對的理念，接著再寫一則概述，表達你對此議題所持的真正立場。請一兩位同學幫你看過這兩篇概述，看是否能辨識出你支持哪一個立場。假如你寫得很成功，他們是辨識不出來的。

2. 請針對辛善寇的文章〈別怪吃的人〉（見本書 268-271 頁）撰寫兩則概述。第一則概述和辛善寇相反的立場，主張除了速食餐廳之外，還是有既便宜又方便的選擇。第二則則質疑過胖其實是醫療問題，而非文化刻板印象。比較你寫的兩則概述，雖然都是針對同一篇文章而寫，但是內容應該會截然不同。

第 **3** 堂　引述的技巧

"As he himself puts it..."
「誠如他所言……」

　　本書的一項主旨是，若要提出有效的論證，得先述說他人的論點。除了概述他人說了什麼之外，還可以直接引述（quote）他確切的說法。**引述別人的話可以大幅提升立論可信度**，確保論文公允、正確。換言之，引述的功能就像是拿出證據，告訴讀者：「看吧，這不是我編造的，她的確有此主張，她就是這麼說的。」

　　只不過，寫作者在引述時可能會犯下多種錯誤，其中一種不小的錯誤是，引述不夠充分。有些人引述得太少，或許是因為他們懶得回去查證原文，也有可能自認為憑記憶就可以重現作者的想法。有人則是相反，引述得過多，以致於最後文章裡幾乎沒有自己的論述。這可能是出於缺乏信心，認為自己沒有能力評論別人的論點，或者是由於沒有全盤了解所引述的話，因此無法解釋這些話的意思。

　　然而，有些寫作者假設這些引述本身已經不言而喻，這才是最大的問題。很多寫作者自己覺得引述的論點相當明顯，就假設讀者也有相同理解，而實際上往往並非如此。會犯這種錯誤的人，往往以為只要選出引用的句子，插進文章中，就大功告成。他們草擬一篇論文、塞幾段引述進去，嗽呴！大功告成。

這些寫作者並不明白，引述不僅是把別人說的話放進引號裡這麼簡單。就某種意義來看，引述句就像孤兒一樣，它們脫離了原生的背景，需要融入新的文本環境。本課將提供兩種引述句融入論文的方法：(1) **慎選引述內容**，並清楚知道它們對你文章中的某個特定部分，支持作用有多大。(2) **在每段主要引述前後建立架構**，說明其出處與意義，以及它和你的文本之間的關聯。我們要強調的是，引述別人的論點，一定要和你自己的論點產生連結。

引述相關的語段

在選擇適當的引述內容之前，你必須先知道你想拿它們做什麼。當你在某個位置插入引述時，你必須知道它們是否能**支持你的論點**。請注意，引述的目的，不是只為了顯示自己讀過該作者的作品；引述的語段要能真正支持你的論點，才有意義。

然而，要找到這樣適用的引述並不容易。即使你所引述的內容在一開始的確和你的論點有關，可是在寫作修改過程中，由於內容改變，那則引述也可能變得越來越不相關。有鑒於寫作本來就是逐步成形、十分繁複的過程，有時候你以為已經找到能支持論證的完美引述，然而隨著文章鋪陳下去，沒多久就發現焦點已經轉移，原先的引述又不合用了。因此，如果將論文主題論述和安插相關引述看成一前一後的兩個分離步驟，並不妥當。**撰寫修改論文時，必須在自己論點和所選用引述之間，來回不斷檢視。**

為每則引述組織架構

找到適用的引述只是部分工作。引用這些引述時，還得讓讀者清楚看出引述的意義，以及與你的論文內容的相關性。引述無法自己為自己發聲，你要為引述做好前後文架構，顯示它們的意義。

若缺少前後文架構，將引述與文本整合，這樣的狀況有時會稱為「孤懸引述」（dangling quotation），因為引述缺乏前後文與解釋，就這樣被孤零零懸在那裡。曾與我們共事的一位教師史提夫・班頓（Steve Benton）把這種情況叫做「撞了就跑」（hit-and-run）的引述，這種引述就像有人撞了你的車，卻加速逃逸，罔顧你被撞凹的擋泥板和碎落一地的車尾燈。

以下舉一個典型的「撞了就跑」的引述，該引述是要回應女權主義哲學家蘇珊・博爾朵（Susan Bordo）所寫的一篇論文。博爾朵感嘆媒體對年輕女性造成壓力，促使她們節食，而這種現象已經蔓延到斐濟這種原本遺世獨立的地區。

Susan Bordo writes about women and dieting. "Fiji is just one example. Until television was introduced in 1995, the islands had no reported cases of eating disorders. In 1998, three years after programs from the United States and Britain began broadcasting there, 62 percent of the girls surveyed reported dieting."

I think Bordo is right. Another point Bordo makes is that....

蘇珊・博爾朵寫到了關於女性和節食的問題。「斐濟僅是其中一例，1995 年電視引進之前，當地從沒有過飲食障礙的案例。到了 1998 年，美國與英國節目在那裡播放三年之後，受訪的女孩裡面有 62% 表示她們在節食。」

　　我認為博爾朵是對的，她還提出了一點，就是……

　　作者沒有適當引述博爾朵的話，也沒有說明引述的理由，讀者不容易理解博爾朵的論點是什麼。作者沒說明博爾朵是誰，甚至引述的句子是不是她所寫的也沒交代，這些引述和作者自己的任何論點之間有些什麼關聯也不清不楚。我們甚至不知道作者覺得博爾朵的論點哪一部分是「對的」。他只是拋出這段引述，就急忙往下一個論點推進。

　　要好好安置一段引述，就必須把它放進所謂的「**引述三明治**」（quotation sandwich）中間。引述句就是中間的夾心，上層麵包是引導它的文字，下層麵包則是後續說明。引述句出現前，要先說明這是誰講的，替引述的內容做好鋪陳；引述句之後，則要解釋你為何認為這段引述重要，以及你認為它在說什麼。

範本 8：介紹引述內容

▶ X states, "_____."
　X 表示：「_____。」

▶ As the prominent philosopher X puts it, "_____."
　誠如知名哲學家 X 所言：「_____。」

▶ According to X, "_____."
　根據 X 的說法：「_____。」

▶ X himself writes, "_____."

X 自己說：「_____。」

▶ In her book, _____, X maintains that "_____."

X 在她的著作《_____》裡，堅持「_____。」

▶ Writing in the journal _____, X complains that "_____."

X 在《_____》雜誌撰文，埋怨「_____。」

▶ In X's view, "_____."

X 的觀點，是認為：「_____。」

▶ X agrees when she writes, "_____."

X 是同意的，她說：「_____。」

▶ X disagrees when he writes, "_____."

X 是不同意的，他說：「_____。」

▶ X complicates matters further when she writes, "_____."

X 說：「_____」，這使得問題更複雜了。

範本 9：解釋引述內容

　　我們的學生表示，有關引述最受用的一個建議就是：養成在每個主要引述後面加以解釋的習慣。下列範本，都可用來解釋引述句：

▶ Basically, X is warning _____.

基本上，X 是在警告，_____。

▶ **In other words, X believes** _____.

換言之，X 認為_____。

▶ **In making this comment, X urges us to** _____.

X 用這個說法，是要促使我們_____。

▶ **X is corroborating the age-old adage that** _____.

X 證實了這句亙古名言：_____。

▶ **X's point is that** _____.

X 的論點是_____。

▶ **The essence of X's argument is that** _____.

X 的論證本質在於_____。

　　解釋引述語時，使用的語詞要能貼切地表現引述語的立場。在引用博爾朵關於斐濟的說法時，寫 Bordo "states/asserts"（表示／主張）已經足夠。但是，如果考量到媒體影響力竟已遠達斐濟，這種情況顯然讓博爾朵憂心忡忡，則可以改用更精確的字詞來反應其憂心，如 Bordo "is alarmed that / is disturbed by / complains"（對……憂心不已／感到不安／有所抱怨）。

　　運用剛剛建議的寫作範本，對於博爾朵的引述段落可以修改如下：

The feminist philosopher Susan Bordo **deplores** Western media's obsession with female thinness and dieting. **Her basic complaint** is that increasing numbers of women across the globe are being led to see themselves as fat and in need of a diet. Citing the islands of Fiji as a case in point, **Bordo notes that** "until television was introduced in 1995, the

參考範本 7-1（p. 50）的示意動詞。

islands had no reported cases of eating disorders. In 1998, three years after programs from the United States and Britain began broadcasting there, 62 percent of the girls surveyed reported dieting" (149-50). **Bordo's point is** that the Western cult of dieting is spreading even to remote places across the globe. Ultimately, **Bordo complains,** the culture of dieting will find you, regardless of where you live.

Bordo's observations ring true to me because, now that I think about it, many women I know, regardless of where they are from, worry about their weight...

女權主義哲學家蘇珊‧博爾朵強烈譴責西方媒體對女性身材苗條和節食的執念。她主要批評的是，世界各地有越來越多的女性受到影響，認為自己太胖、需要節食。博爾朵舉斐濟群島為例，指出「1995 年電視引進之前，當地從沒有過飲食障礙的案例。到了 1998 年，美國與英國節目開始在那裡播放三年之後，受訪的女孩裡面有 62% 表示她們在節食。」（頁149-50）博爾朵的重點在於，西方的節食風潮竟已跨越全球，蔓延到偏遠地區。最後，博爾朵還抱怨說，不管你住在哪裡，都逃不出節食文化的掌控。

在我看來，博爾朵的言論確實沒錯，因為我想了一下，我認識的很多女性不管是哪裡人，都在擔心自己的體重……

這個引述架構不僅較能把博爾朵的話融入寫作者的文本，同時也讓我們看到作者如何詮釋博爾朵的論點。文中說明被引述者背景是「女性主義哲學家」（feminist philosopher），並用「博爾朵指出」（Bordo notes）帶出引述，提供了讀者需知道的訊息。引述句之後的幾個句子，則將博爾朵和作者的論點加以連接。裡面提到62%的斐濟女孩正在節食，聽起來也不再只是個刻板的數據，而是「西方節食狂潮如何蔓延全球」的量化例證。同樣重要的是，作者用自己的話來解釋對博爾朵的引述。這麼一來，寫作者引述的目的就變得相當清楚，他打算用引述來提出自己的論點，而不只是為了擴充字數，或者讓參考文獻的列表好看而已。

▍讓原作者和你的話融為一體

剛剛修改後的引述方式較佳，另一原因是，除了正確呈現博爾朵論點，也默默帶進了作者的觀點。請注意，這個段落不只一次提到「節食」（dieting）這個關鍵概念，也巧妙運用「文化」（culture）一詞，並進一步指明是「西方」（western）文化，來呼應博爾朵所講的「電視」（television）以及「播放英美節目」（U.S. and British broadcasting）。引述句後面的句子，不是一字不漏重複博爾朵的話，而是一方面恰到好處解釋博爾朵的說法，一方面將討論導向寫作者的論點。換言之，這個架構完整融合了博爾朵和作者的觀點。

▍對引述內容會過度詮釋嗎？

我們有沒有可能對引述內容過度詮釋、過猶不及呢？又如何知道自己對引述的解釋充分、恰到好處呢？畢竟，並非所有引述都需要相同份量的說明架構，也沒有明確的規則指出需要多少解釋。以通則來看，讀者不容易消化的引述內容往往需要最詳盡的解釋架構，如引述太長或太複雜、或該引述充滿細節和專業術語，或含有隱藏訊息。

雖然解釋引述語的時機與篇幅長短，要視個別情況而定，但有一個原則：**沒有把握時，寧可說清楚。**我們寧可鉅細靡遺說明某個引述，也不要讓它懸而未決，陷讀者於五里迷霧。甚至，即使讀者對所引述的作者已經很熟悉，有能力自行理解這些引述內容，我們仍然鼓勵你提供一段說明。就算在這種情況下，讀者都要知道身為作者的你如何詮釋這段引述，因為言詞——尤其是爭議人物的言詞——有各種不同的解讀方法，相同的言詞有時甚至可以被用來支持不同、甚至對立的論點。讀者要知道你是怎麼看待這些引述內容。唯有這樣，讀者與作者之間才能確保雙方對這份資料的解讀是一致的。

▎「不」該用哪些方式來介紹引述內容

本堂課最後，我們談談不適用來介紹引述內容的方式。引述時，不要寫 Orwell asserts an idea that（歐威爾主張一個想法）或 a quote by Shakespeare says（莎士比亞引述的一句話說）這樣的句子。這種引述冗贅，也有誤導之虞。第一個例子中，你可以寫 Orwell asserts that（歐威爾主張）或 Orwell's assertion is that（歐威爾的主張是），就是不要把兩種用法組合在一起，那樣是累贅的用法。第二個例子容易誤導讀者，以為被引述的人不是莎士比亞，而是作者。a quote by Shakespeare 暗示是莎士比亞在引用別人的話。

本堂課提供的範本可以幫助你避免犯下這種錯誤，一旦你熟練了如 **as X puts it**（如 X 所言）、**in X's own words**（以 X 的話來說）這種引述寫法，之後連想都不用想就可以得心應手運用。這樣一來，你就能透過這些範本協助建構出較困難複雜的觀點。

練習

1. 找一篇已經發表的論文，找出引述之處。作者是如何把引述內容整合到自己的文本中呢？他是怎麼引述的？他說了些什麼（一點點都好）來解釋引述內容，並且讓引述內容和自己的文本結合？根據你從這一課所讀到的方法，有沒有任何想建議作者修改的地方？

2. 找一份你寫過的課堂報告。你有引用任何資料來源嗎？如果有的話，你是怎麼把它融入你的文本呢？你是怎麼介紹引述內容的？有說明它的意義嗎？有指出它和你的文本之間的關聯嗎？假如你沒有全部做到，就修改一下。你可以參考〈範本 8：介紹引述內容〉（第 55-56 頁）和〈範本 9：解釋引述內容〉（第 56-57 頁）這兩個小節，使用裡面的句型。如果你寫的報告都沒有引述內容，就稍作修改，加進一些引述。

» PART II «

I Say
我說

第一部分說明學術寫作中聆聽的重要性之後，

本部分接著說明如何提出自己論點作為回應。

第四堂課說明三種回應的方式，

接著探討如何在「他人意見」和「自身論點」之間轉換，

並活用反對論點鞏固自身論點。

最後，第七堂課提醒寫作者在論文中必須回答的兩個問題：

「那又有什麼重要？」（So what?）與

「誰在意這個議題？」（Who cares?）。

Three Ways to Respond

第 **4** 堂 　回應的三種方式

> "Yes" 「是」
>
> "No" 「不是」
>
> "Okay, but" 「好的，但是」

前三堂課探討了學術寫作的第一階段，將焦點放在其他人或團體的論點（they say）。本課要進入第二階段，提出自己的論點（I say），以回應他人的論點。

想到要在學術上「提出自己論點」，可能令人卻步，彷彿你得是某個領域的專家，才能提出論點。很多學生告訴我們，在大學或研究所參與一些高深對話時，他們感到困難重重，因為他們對於要討論的主題了解不夠深入。不過，他們如有機會深入研究某些學者在專門領域所發表的文章時，看法就可能有所轉變，他們會說：「我可以理解為什麼她有這種想法，我知道她是如何以其他學者的論點為基礎來闡述自己的觀點。要是多花點時間研究，我也可以說出類似的道理。」

這些學生終於明白，好的論證並非來自某些領域少數專家獨有的知識，而是來自**良好的思維習慣**，這是人人都看得到、辨識得出、也運用得了的。當然，專業知識無可取代，盡可能知悉論述主題也是絕對必要，但是，最終獲得別人支持的論點，其基礎是建立在非常基本的論述方法上面，是我們多數人每天都在使用的。

要回應別人的觀點有很多種方式，在本堂課裡，我們會集中在三種最常見也最容易辨認的回應上：**同意、不同意、兩者參半**。雖然每種回應都有無限多的再細分方式，但我們之所以聚焦在這三種，是因為讀者閱讀任何文本時，都要快速掌握作者的立場，而方法就是將文本放到由一連串熟悉選項所組成的腦海地圖上檢視：**作者對他所回應的論點是否同意？抑或他是部分同意、部分不同意？**

作者如果做了太多鋪陳，然後才針對他所概述或引述的論點表明自己的立場，讀者會一頭霧水：「這個人是同意還是不同意？他是贊成那個人說的話還是反對？不然是什麼來著？」基於這個原因，本課所提出的建議不僅適用於寫作，亦適用於閱讀，尤其是遇到艱深的文本時。一來，你要能看出作者所回應的論點 ── 也就是「他人論點」 ── 是什麼；再者，你也要能判斷作者對此，是同意、質疑還是疑信參半。

▎只有三種回應方式嗎？

或許你會擔心，只從這三種類別當中擇一來做回應，會不會使你的論點過度簡化，減損了它的複雜性、縝密性或原創性。治學嚴謹的學者關切論文過度簡化、缺失不全，對之感到疑慮，是理所當然的。然而，我們要強調的是，你的論證越是複雜而縝密，越不符合一般人的傳統思維模式，讀者就必須一直不斷把你的論證置入腦海地圖，不斷分析這些錯綜複雜的細節。因此，如果讀者能對你所引述的論點有個基本概念，你所撰寫的內容的複雜性、縝密性或原創性才更有可能突顯出來。

透過這一堂課，希望你會了解，我們所探討的同意、不同意與兩者參半這三種回應形式，足以處理高階創意和複雜思維，絕不會過於簡化或缺乏深度。

不要劈頭就洋洋灑灑談一堆細節，應該要**先清楚表明你到底是同意、不同意或兩者參半**，這才是展開回應的好策略。運用直接、乾淨俐落的說法，如 I agree（我同意）、I disagree（我不同意）或 I am of two minds. I agree that _____, but I cannot agree that _____.（我覺得各有道理。我同意_____，但是我不同意的是，_____。）一旦你寫出這種直截了當的語句，讀者就能明確掌握你的立場，有餘力去欣賞你在鋪陳回應時所呈現的細緻思維。

儘管如此，你可能還是會反對，說這三種基本方式並沒有涵蓋所有的可能回應型態 —— 譬如可能忽略了解釋和分析等類型的回應方式。你或許會認為，解讀一份文學作品的時候，未必有什麼好同意或不同意的，無非就是說明作品的意義、風格或體裁。有人會說，許多關於文學和藝術的論文都是採用這種模式 —— 闡釋作品的意義，至於同不同意倒是無關緊要。

然而，用同意與否或正反參半的方式來做闡釋，往往才是最有趣的。最好的闡釋方法不是自說自話，而是要對於他人的詮釋展現自己的立場。事實上，如果不是為了去回應他人已經做出的詮釋，也沒有道理去解釋一份文學或藝術作品。就算你從一份藝術作品當中點出了別人沒發現的特色或性質，你也是在默默反對其他詮釋者所說的話，因為你點出了他們遺漏的某些部分，而你認為這是很重要的。

要做出有效的闡釋，不僅要說明你認為這個藝術作品的意義何在，還要比對其他讀者的詮釋，這些讀者可能是專業學者、老師、同學，甚至是假想的讀者，像是你可以寫：**Although some readers might think that this poem is about _____, it is in fact about _____.**（雖然有些讀者可能認為這首詩是在講_____，但它其實是關於_____。）

● 參考 p. 31 在開頭預告自己立場的方式。

表示不同意，並解釋原因

對於寫作者而言，對某個觀點表示不同意是比較簡單的寫作方式，這個方法常常會讓人聯想到所謂「批判性思考」。抱持不同意觀點也是提出論述的最簡單途徑：針對你的論述主題，從別人說過或可能說的話當中找出你可以不同意的部分，先將對方論點做概述，然後加以論辯。不過，這其實也會帶來隱藏的挑戰，你不能只說你不同意某個觀點，還必須提出有說服力的理由，說明你為什麼不同意。畢竟，不同意不是在別人的言論前面加個 not 就了事，不能只是說「雖然他們說女權正在進步，我卻要說女權**沒有**在進步。」（Although they say women's rights are improving, I say women's rights are **not** improving.）這種回應只是反駁要回應的觀點，卻沒有補充任何有趣或新穎的想法。如果你要讓它成為一種論證，就要提出支持的理由，例如：因為對方的論點並沒有考量到相關因素；因為它的證據不可靠或不完整；因為它立基在不確定的假設上；因為它的邏輯錯誤或自相矛盾，或因為它忽略了你認為是真正的議題所在。為了讓你與對方的對談順利進行（也是寫論述的基本目的），你必須提出自己的論點。

甚至於，你的不同意還可以用近似冷笑（duh）的口氣來表示。此時你反對的不是針對該立場本身，而是發覺對方說法了無新意，頗感失望。以下段落就是這種語氣的示範，這是篇討論美國學校現狀的論文的第一段：

> According to a recent report by some researchers at Stanford University, high school students with college aspirations "often lack crucial information on applying to college and on succeeding academically once they get there."

> Well, duh... It shouldn't take a Stanford research team to tell us that when it comes to "succeeding academically," many students don't have a clue.

根據史丹佛大學部分研究人員的最新報告指出，想上大學的高中生「通常缺乏申請學校的重要資訊，也不曉得進入大學後要如何在學術上取得成功。」

唉……用不著史丹佛大學的研究團隊來說，我們也知道很多學生根本不知如何「在學術上成功」。

—— 杰拉德‧葛拉夫，〈涓滴模糊處理〉（Trickle-Down Obfuscation）

冷笑口氣的回應和本書中所提供的其他範本一樣，你可以根據自己的寫作情況修改。如果你覺得用這種語氣會顯得太自負，你也可以改成其他寫法，如：**It is true that _____, but we already knew that.**（_____，確實如此；但是我們早就知道了。）

範本 10：表示不同意並說明理由

▶ **X is mistaken because she overlooks _____.**
X 錯了，她忽略了_____。

▶ **X's claim that _____ rests upon the questionable assumption that _____.**
X 主張_____，這是立基在_____這個不確定的假設上。

▶ **I disagree with X's view that _____ because, as recent research has shown, _____.**
我不同意 X _____的觀點，因為最新的研究已經顯示_____。

▶ **X contradicts herself/can't have it both ways. On the one hand, she argues _____. On the other hand, she also says _____.**

X 是自我矛盾的／不可能兩面兼顧。一方面，她主張_____；另一方面，她又說_____。

▶ **By focusing on _____, X overlooks the deeper problem of _____.**

X 的論點聚焦在_____，卻忽略了_____這個更深的問題。

　　你也可以用我們稱之為「扭轉」（twist it）的寫作方法來表示不同意。這種情況下，你雖然同意對方提出的證據，但是透過邏輯上的轉換，讓這個證據轉而支持你的不同意立場，如下面這個例子：

> X argues for stricter gun control legislation, saying that the crime rate is on the rise and that we need to restrict the circulation of guns. I agree that the crime rate is on the rise, **but that's precisely why I oppose** stricter gun control legislation. We need to own guns to protect ourselves against criminals.

> 　　X 主張槍枝管制立法應該要更嚴格，他說犯罪率一直在攀升，我們需要限制槍枝的流通。我同意犯罪率一直在攀升，但那正是我反對更嚴格立法管制槍枝的原因，我們需要擁槍自保以對抗罪犯。

　　在這個運用「扭轉」寫法的段落當中，寫作者先是同意某人主張的犯罪率攀升，但是接著就提出論證，說這樣高漲的犯罪率正是反對槍枝管制條例的主要理由。

有時，因為種種原因，你不願意表態不同意別人的意見──不想讓人感到不舒服、不想傷害別人的感情、不想讓自己反過來淪為箭靶。我們在第一堂一開始描述的那位會議演講者，可能就是出於上述原因之一，才不想提到他與其他學者意見不一致之處，一直到演講結束後的討論會上，有聽眾質疑他才提出來。

我們都了解這種害怕衝突的心境，也都親身經歷過，但是比起避而遠之，坦誠委婉說出不認同，才是比較好的做法。如果將質疑異議壓抑不表，它並不會消失，只會累積，無法化解。不過，你不必用貶低別人的方式表現不認同。此外，全盤推翻別人的觀點也沒什麼意義，只須針對其中有疑慮的部分去評論就好，其他該認同的還是要認同──只不過，這樣會需要更複雜的寫作方法，也就是同意和不同意參半，在本堂課後段會討論。

以不同的方式表達同意

如同表達不同意一樣，表達同意也不像表面上那麼簡單。表達不同意的時候，不可以只把該觀點反過來說一遍。表達同意也是如此，不能只是把他人的話重複講一遍。即便你同意他們的看法，還是得拿出新意來、補充一些內容，好跟對方形成充分對談。

即使是同意某人論點，也有許多方法能讓自己的發言有所貢獻，不只是空言附和。你可以提出原作者尚未注意到的證據、或者是原作者未使用的論證方法；也可以引用一些有助於佐證的個人經驗，或者某一狀況，來幫助讀者的更清楚了解。如果作者的論述艱澀難懂，非一般人所能理解，你可以提供通俗易懂的解釋──為那些尚未了解的讀者做解讀。換言之，只要點出某些沒有人注意到的細節，或者解釋某些內容增進理解，你與原作者的對談就別具意義。

不論你選擇哪一種贊同模式，重要的是，你和對方的立場要**同中有異**、產生反差，而不僅是模仿對方再說一次。

範本 11：表示贊同，但補充一點不同的看法

▶ I agree that ＿＿＿＿ because my experience ＿＿＿＿ confirms it.
我同意＿＿＿＿，因為我＿＿＿＿的經驗證實了這一點。

▶ X is surely right about ＿＿＿＿ because, as she may not be aware,
recent studies have shown that ＿＿＿＿.
X 對＿＿＿＿的見解絕對是正確的，因為最新的研究顯示＿＿＿＿，只是她可能還沒注意到這一點。

▶ X's theory of ＿＿＿＿ is extremely useful because it sheds light on
the difficult problem of ＿＿＿＿.
X 的＿＿＿＿理論極為有用，因為有了它，要解決＿＿＿＿這個難題，就有了相當樂觀的前景。

▶ Those unfamiliar with this school of thought may be interested to know
that it basically boils down to ＿＿＿＿.
對這個學派不熟悉的人，可能樂於知道它基本上可歸結為＿＿＿＿。

許多寫作者不想對別人的論點表示贊同，程度就和那些避免表達不同意的人一樣嚴重。寫作者有時不太願意承認已有人提出過相同的論點，彷彿是被捷足先登了。然而，只要你能夠對別人的論點提出支持點，而不是單純複述一遍，就無須擔心「缺乏原創性」的問題。甚至，你大可以對你同意別人的看法

感到高興，這代表他們可以幫你的論證背書。你當然不想只抄襲別人的觀點，但總不能只在荒野裡孤鳴。

你也一定要知道，你同意一個人的看法，勢必就可能反對另一個人，很難說你選定了一個立場卻絲毫不會牴觸其他人。心理學家凱蘿‧姬莉甘（Carol Gilligan）的一篇論文就屬於這樣的例子。她在論文中同意某些科學家的論點，說人類大腦設計「與生俱來」就以合作為目的；在此同時，她也就是在反對另一派說法，那些深信人生來就自私自利、相互競爭的看法。

> These findings join a growing convergence of evidence across the human sciences leading to a revolutionary shift in consciousness... If cooperation, typically associated with altruism and self-sacrifice, sets off the same signals of delight as pleasures commonly associated with hedonism and self-indulgence; if the opposition between selfish and selfless, self vs. relationship biologically makes no sense, then a new paradigm is necessary to reframe the very terms of the conversation.
>
> 這些發現與人文社會學科各領域的研究證據匯集一起，導致對意識研究的革命性轉變……如果合作（通常與利他主義與自我犧牲相關）能產生如享樂主義與自我放縱所觸發的喜悅感；如果自私與無私之間、自我與人際之間的對立關係已不存在生理上的根本差異，那麼就有必要建立一個新典範來重新架構對話方式。
>
> ——凱蘿‧姬莉甘，〈姊妹情是愉快的：一場心理學的無聲革命〉
> （Sisterhood is Pleasurable: A Quiet Revolution in Psychology）

姬莉甘在同意某些科學家所說「如果自私與無私……已不存在生理上的根本差異」的同時，正暗示了她不贊同這兩者是生理上對立的關係。姬莉甘的這段言論可以簡化成下列範本：

▶ I agree that _____, a point that needs emphasizing since so many people still believe _____.
我同意_____，這一點是需要強調的，因為太多人仍舊相信_____。

▶ If group X is right that _____, as I think they are, then we need to reassess the popular assumption that _____.
如果 X 團隊提出_____是對的，此點我也同意，那麼對於一般的看法_____，我們就要重新考慮。

以上這樣的範本能讓你在同意一個論點的同時，質疑另一個論點——由此，也將進入下一節的討論，對同一論點表達既同意也不同意。

既同意也不同意

最後這個項目是我們最喜愛的回應方式，我們偏好同時表示同意與不同意。幼兒爭執或是電視名嘴強辯時，常出現「不是你對就是我錯」的激烈對話模式，我們現在要談的，正有助於我們超越這樣的模式。

Yes and no.（是，也不是。）、**Yes, but...**（是，但是……）、**Although I agree up to a point, I still insist...**（雖然我大致贊同，我仍然堅持……），這些寫法能讓論證發展得更細緻入微，同時又維持結構清晰易讀。使用像是 **Yes and no.** 或 **on the one hand I agree, on the other I disagree**（一方面我同意，一方面我不同意）這樣的**平行結構**，能協助讀者把你的論點放到判斷立場的地圖上快速檢視，而且論證不失周密。

我們喜歡這個方式的另一個原因是，你還可以利用這個方式將你的論點微妙地導向同意或不同意。

範本 12：正反參半，傾向不同意

如果在正反參半的觀點中，你傾向於不同意，就可以用「對，但是……」（yes, but...）這個範本：

▶ **Although I agree with X up to a point, I cannot accept his overriding assumption that _____ .**
雖然我某種程度同意 X 的觀點，我無法接受他認為_____的全面觀點。

▶ **Though I concede that _____, I still insist that _____ .**
雖然我承認_____，我仍堅持_____。

▶ **X is right that _____, but she seems on more dubious ground when she claims that _____ .**
X 說_____，這是對的，但她主張_____，好像有點說不通。

範本 13：正反參半，傾向同意

反之，如果你是同意多於不同意，可以用「不對，但是……」（no, but...）寫法：

► Although I disagree with much that X says, I fully endorse his final conclusion that _____.

雖然 X 所說的我多半不贊同，我倒是完全支持他的最後結論，就是

_____。

► While X is probably wrong when she claims that _____, she is right that _____.

X 主張_____，這可能並不正確，但是她說_____，這是沒有錯的。

► Whereas X provides ample evidence that _____, Y and Z's research on _____ and _____ convinces me that _____ instead.

儘管 X 對於_____ 提出充分證據，Y 和 Z 在_____和_____ 上面的研究卻令我轉而相信_____。

範本 14：正反意見並存

另一個同時表示同意與不同意的典型方法，就是採行所謂的「正反並存」（I'm of two minds）或「猶豫不決」（mixed feelings）的寫法：

► I'm of two minds about X's claim that _____. On the one hand, I agree that _____. On the other hand, I'm not sure if _____.

關於 X 所主張的_____，我覺得各有道理。一方面，我同意_____，另一方面，我不確定是否_____。

▶ My feelings on the issue are mixed. I do support X's position that
_____, but I find Y's argument about _____ and Z's research
on _____ to be equally persuasive.

我對於這個議題有點猶豫。我的確是支持 X_____的立場，但是我發現
Y 關於_____的論點和 Z 對於_____的研究也都同樣有說服力。

假如你要回應一個剛發表的論點，或難度特別高的文本，而你尚未確定自
己的立場，以上套句範本就特別好用。它也適合作為一種試探性的調查，讓你
先權衡一個論點的正反兩面，以便以後再做判斷。但是我們還是要說，如同前
面所建議的，不管你是同意也好、不同意也好，或者兩種立場都有，你都要盡
可能表達清楚，坦誠說出你還沒有定論，也是表達清楚的一種方式。

真的可以沒有定論嗎？

儘管如此，寫作者在表達內心的矛盾時，擔憂的程度並不亞於明確表達同
意或不同意。有人會擔心，如果自己沒有定論，會讓人覺得是在含糊其辭、對
自己沒信心，或是會因而造成讀者的困擾，因為讀者通常需要果斷而明確的結
論。

這些擔憂的確是合情合理的。寫作者猶豫不決有時會讓讀者失去信心，覺
得你沒有盡到說明的義務。然而在某些狀況下，直言該議題不可能有明確的解
答，反而能展現你身為寫作者的審慎老練。在一個看重複雜思維的學術文化
裡，如果排除他人單向片面式論點，直言你還沒有定論，更會使人認同。追根
究底，你的論文可否不做定論、到什麼程度，其實是很主觀的。要考量的因
素，可以包括不同讀者對文稿的反應、你對讀者的了解程度，以及你的論點和
立場所承受的挑戰。

練習

1. 請自本書後面所提供的論文當中選擇一篇來閱讀，也可以上 theysayiblog. com網站挑選文章。辨識出文章中作者表達同意、不同意或正反參半之處。

2. 針對前一題你所挑選的論文，寫篇回應的文章。你需概述或引述作者的論點，然後清楚表達你是同意、不同意或正反意見各半。本書的範本可以幫助你下筆：第一到三堂的範本用來提出別人的觀點，本堂課的範本可以幫助你寫出自己的回應。

第 5 堂　區分自己和他人的論點

"And yet"

「然而」

　　好的學術論文就是進行一場對談，在每個寫作環節，讀者都要能看得出哪些是你自己的看法，哪些是別人的意見。在這一堂課中，我們將繼續探討，如何在不造成讀者混淆的前提下，從「他人論點」（they say）轉移到「自身論點」（I say）。

▎判斷文本中的言論是誰說的

　　要在論文寫作中標示（signal）出什麼人說了什麼話，我們不妨先以讀者身分，從閱讀文本過程中辨識出這些「標記」（signal）── 進行特別困難的閱讀作業時，這種技巧特別重要。讀者看不懂文本，不僅是因為裡面含有不熟悉的論點或用詞，更是因為文本用很含糊細緻的方式，來說明某特定觀點是屬於寫作者本身，還是他人。在閱讀觀點交流的文本時，一定要留意這些含糊細微的標記，才能判斷寫作者在以誰的聲音說話。

　　社會評論家暨教育家葛瑞格里・孟修斯（Gregory Mantsios）有一篇論文討論美國社會階級不平等。我們來看看，他如何運用這些「**發言標記**」（voice marker）來區分不同的觀點。

"We are all middle-class," **or so it would seem**. Our national consciousness, as shaped in large part by the media and our political leadership, provides us with a picture of ourselves as a nation of prosperity and opportunity with an ever expanding middle-class life-style. As a result, our class differences **are muted** and our collective character **is homogenized**.

Yet class divisions **are real** and arguably the most significant factor in determining both our very being in the world and the nature of the society we live in.

「我們人人都是中產階級」，或者，看起來似乎是如此。我們的民族意識——大致是由媒體和政治領袖所塑造的——讓我們自認是一個欣欣向榮、充滿機會的國家，我們的中產階級形態也不斷擴張。結果，我們的階級差異沒有人談論，我們的集體角色都看似同質了。

然而，階級劃分卻是千真萬確的，而且註定了個人在世界上的生存方式，以及我們所處的社會本質。

——葛瑞格里・孟修斯，〈報酬與機會：美國的階級政治學與經濟學〉
（Rewards and Opportunities: The Politics and Economics of Class in the U.S.）

儘管孟修斯寫得淺顯易懂，實際上他運用好幾個細緻的修辭技巧，將他所反對的一般觀點和自己的立場區分開來。

舉例來說，在第一段當中，孟修斯把作為開場的觀點用引號標示，代表這不是他講的話。他用了「或者，看起來似乎是如此」（or so it would seem），可見他不盡然同意前面的論點。寫作者一般不會形容自己的理念僅僅「似乎」（seem）是真的。孟修斯接著指出第一段所概述的論點的來源：我們的民族意識大致是「由媒體和政治領袖所塑造的」（as shaped in large part by the media and our political leadership），進一步拉開自己與該論點的距離。他指出這個負面「結果」（result）來自「民族意識」（consciousness），而結果導致「我們的階級差異」（our class differences）「沒有人談論」（muted）、「我們的集體角色」（our collective character）都看似「同質」（homogenized），其多元性和特殊性都蕩然無存。因此，在第二段孟修斯說明自己的立場之前，讀者早就清楚得知他的態度。

再來，第二段用 "yet"（然而）開頭，表示孟修斯正轉移到自己的論點（就是反對他到現在為止所描述的普遍論點）。他在這兩段之間建立起對比的關係——第一段說階級差異並不存在，第二段則說存在——這樣的對比做法，也強烈凸顯出兩種論點的反差。最後，孟修斯在第二段用了直接、權威、宣告式的口吻，這也暗示著聲音轉換了。雖然他沒有用到 I say 或 I argue 的字眼，依然清楚表示出自己的觀點，因為他不是說「似乎」（seem）是真的，也不是「別人告訴我們」（others tell us）的，而「就是」（are）真的，而且是「千真萬確」（real）的。

注意這些發言標記是閱讀理解的關鍵，無法辨識這些標記的讀者，經常會把作者概述別人的觀點當成作者本身的論點。我們在講授孟修斯的論文時，總有部分學生以為 "We are all middle-class." 是孟修斯的立場，而不是他反對的觀點。他們看不出來孟修斯在寫這幾個字的時候，有點像是用腹語在模仿別人說話，而非表達自己的想法。

為了讓大家了解發言標記有多麼重要，我們把發言標記拿掉，看看孟修斯的段落會變成什麼樣子。

We are all middle-class... We are a nation of prosperity and opportunity with an ever expanding middle-class life-style...

Class divisions are real and arguably the most significant factor in determining both our very being in the world and the nature of the society we live in.

我們人人都是中產階級……我們是一個欣欣向榮、充滿機會的國家，我們的中產階級形態也不斷擴張……

階級劃分是千真萬確的，而且註定了個人在世界上的生存方式，以及我們所處的社會本質。

孟修斯的原文仔細劃分這兩者的發言，相對之下，這個沒有發言標記的版本讓我們很難看出從哪裡開始是他的發言，哪裡是別人的發言。一旦把標記拿掉，讀者無法分辨 "We are all middle-class."（我們人人都是中產階級。）是作者不認同的觀點，而 "Class divisions are real."（階級劃分是千真萬確的。）是作者自己的想法。更何況，如果沒有標記，尤其是少了 "Yet" 這個字，讀者很有可能無法會意第二段的 "Class divisions are real." 是在反駁第一段所說的 "We are all middle-class."

範本 15：標示出誰在說什麼

為了避免讀者混淆，一定要讓讀者在每個環節都明確看出這是誰說的、在說什麼。前面各課提供的許多範本都有發言標記的作用，可以參考利用。

▶ **Although X makes the best possible case for _____, I am not persuaded.**

雖然 X 的_____立論甚佳，但我仍無法苟同。

▶ **My view, however, contrary to what X has argued, is that _____.**

然而，我的觀點和 X 所主張的相反，我認為_____。

▶ **Adding to X's argument, I would point out that _____.**

為了補充說明 X 的論點，我想指出_____。

▶ **According to both X and Y, _____.**

根據 X 和 Y 雙方的看法，_____。

▶ **Politicians, X argues, should _____.**

X 認為政治人物應該_____。

▶ **Most athletes will tell you that _____.**

大部分的運動員會跟你說_____。

可是有人說不要用第一人稱「我」

剛剛列出的前三個範本都使用了第一人稱「我」、「我的」、「我們」（I、my 或 we），本書所列舉的許多其他範本也是如此，違背了一般學術寫作書建議避免第一人稱的寫法。儘管有人告訴你，用「我」這個字會容易讓我們表達意見顯得主觀又自以為是，論證不夠持平，然而，是否使用「我」的文本都是一樣的，都可以提出充分的客觀論點；或者，也可以反過來看──也可能都是主觀又自以為是。持平論證靠的是令人信服的的理由和證據，而不在於是否使用某個特定的代名詞。

假如你的論文一直避免使用第一人稱，你就很難落實本堂課所強調的寫作方法：區別你的和他人的論點；甚至，在你一開始提出自己論點時就會出現問題。不過，即使你暫不同意也無妨，你可以先參閱本書所引用的範文，看看作者如何自由運用第一人稱，也可以看看你的閱讀教材中，作者是怎麼寫的。

儘管如此，某些狀況應避免使用第一人稱。例如可以直接說「她是對的」，不必說「我認為她是對的。」此外，假如通篇文章讀起來都是毫無變化地使用「我」，可能就太單調了，所以一個辦法，是把第一人稱和以下的範本交替使用。

範本 16：取代第一人稱「我」

▶ **X is right that** _____.
X 認為_____，他說得沒錯。

▶ **The evidence shows that** _____.
證據顯示_____。

▶ **X's assertion that** _____ **does not fit the facts.**
X 主張_____，這與事實不符。

▶ **Anyone familiar with** _____ **should agree that** _____.
熟悉_____的人應該都會同意_____。

甚至你可以照著孟修斯的引言來寫，如下面範本所示：

▶ But _____ are real, and are arguably the most significant factor in _____.

然而_____是真的，而且可能是_____的最大因素。

───── 整體而言，目前的學術論文寫作已經大量使用第一人稱的敘述，即便是科學或社會科學的領域也是如此。

表現是誰在說話的另一個技巧

任何時候，如果你要提醒讀者某論點是由誰提出，不必一直用 **X argues**（X 主張）這樣明顯直接的發言標記，你也可以在你的句子裡，將他人論點嵌入，指出發言者是誰。因此，下面這句話：

Liberals believe that cultural differences need to be respected. I have a problem with this view, however.

自由主義者認為需要尊重文化差異，不過我對這個觀點相當質疑。

可以改寫成：

I have a problem with what liberals call cultural differences.

自由主義者所說的文化差異，我相當質疑。

There is a major problem with the liberal doctrine of so-called cultural differences.

參考運用第一人稱作敘述的範文（pp. 280-287）。

自由主義所謂的文化差異有一個很大的問題。

你還可以把自己先前說過的話嵌入句子中。因此，不必寫兩句冗贅的文字：

Earlier in this chapter we coined the term "voice markers." We would argue that such markers are extremely important for reading comprehension.

我們在這一堂課的前面使用了「發言標記」這個詞。我們會主張這種標記對於閱讀理解非常之重要。

你可以這樣改寫：

We would argue that "voice markers," as we identified them earlier, are extremely important for reading comprehension.

我們主張，先前所提出的「發言標記」，對於閱讀理解非常重要。

這種嵌入式的方法可以節省你的思路，還可以流暢提出別人的觀點。

範本 17：嵌入發言標記

▶ **X overlooks what I consider an important point about _____.**
關於_____，X 忽略了我認為的一個重點。

▶ My own view is that what X insists is a _____ is in fact a

_____.

我個人的觀點是，X 所堅持是_____的問題，事實上是_____。

▶ I wholeheartedly endorse what X calls _____.

我完全支持 X 所稱的_____。

▶ These conclusions, which X discusses in _____, add weight to the argument that _____.

X 在_____所探討的這些結論，進一步證明了_____的論證。

　　如果寫作者在概述別人的論點時，沒有使用發言標記，就很容易讓讀者誤會該論點是作者自己的論點，或是將寫作者的論點誤以為是他人論點。讀者很容易因為無法辨識寫作者是在表述自己的論點，或是在支持別人某個說法，而被迫停下來遲疑：「且慢，我以為作者是反對這個主張的，難道她一直是支持的嗎？」或者「咦？我以為她會反對這種說法，莫非她是贊成的？」習慣使用發言標記，就不會寫出讓讀者混淆的文章，你自己閱讀艱深的文本時，也會去留意類似的標記。

練習

1. 閱讀下面這段由社會歷史學家茱莉・查莉普（Julie Charlip）所寫的段落，觀摩她在主張自己的論點和概述別人的論點時，是如何標示的。閱讀時，請辨識哪些地方是指別人的論點，找出她用了哪些標記來區分自己與他人的論點。

Marx and Engels wrote: "Society as a whole is more and more splitting up into two great hostile camps, into two great classes directly facing each other—the bourgeoisie and the proletariat" (10). If only that were true, things might be more simple. But in late twentieth-century America, it seems that society is splitting more and more into a plethora of class factions—the working class, the working poor, lower-middle class, upper-middle class, lower uppers, and upper uppers. I find myself not knowing what class I'm from.

In my days as a newspaper reporter, I once asked a sociology professor what he thought about the reported shrinking of the middle class. Oh, it's not the middle class that's disappearing, he said, but the working class. His definition: if you earn thirty thousand dollars a year working in an assembly plant, come home from work, open a beer and watch the game, you are working class; if you earn twenty thousand dollars a year as a school teacher, come home from work to a glass of white wine and PBS, you are middle class.

How do we define class? Is it an issue of values, lifestyle, taste? Is it the kind of work you do, your relationship to the means of production? Is it a matter of how much money you earn? Are we allowed to choose? In this land of supposed classlessness, where we don't have the tradition of English society to keep us in our places, how do we know where we really belong? The average American will tell you he or she is "middle class." I'm sure that's what my father would tell you. But I always felt that we were in some no man's land, suspended between classes, sharing similarities with some and recognizing sharp, exclusionary differences from others. What class do I come from? What class am I in now? As an historian, I seek the answers to these questions in the specificity of my past.

—— Julie Charlip, *A Real Class Act: Searching for Identity in the Classless Society*

2. 找一篇你自己寫的論文來研究一下，看看你一共說明了多少論點，有沒有好好區分自己和別人的發言。思考下列問題：

　　a. 你一共提到了幾個人的論點？

　　b. 你還可以補充哪些其他的論點？

　　c. 你是如何區分自己的看法和所概述的他人論點？

　　d. 你有沒有運用明確的發言標記用語？

　　e. 你可以選擇哪些手法來釐清是誰在說什麼？

　　f. 這些手法當中，哪一種最適合你這份文本？

若是你發現自己並沒有引用多方觀點，或者並未明確區隔自己與他人的論點，請做適當的修改。

第 6 堂　將反面論點納入文中

"Skeptics may object..."
「懷疑的人可能說……」

作家珍‧湯普琴絲（Jane Tompkins）曾說，她每次在寫書或文章時，總會經過以下的循環模式。剛開始的幾個禮拜，進展得相當順利；然而過了幾週之後，她會在夜半時分冒著一身冷汗驚醒，驚覺她某些論點必然會受到一些重大批評，怎麼沒有想到？這時，她直覺的反應總是，打消計畫吧，或者捨棄已寫的內容、重新來過。接著她又會領悟一個道理：「這個懷疑與恐慌的瞬間，才是我文章真正的開始。」於是她去修改前面的內容，納入預期會受到的批評，使她的文章因此論述更有力、也更具趣味。

這個小故事對於新手與老練的寫作者，都是一個重要教訓：大多數人一想到作品會被批評，都難免心煩意亂，但其實這些批評往往是對我們有利的。雖然我們很想當作沒聽到，但是如果忽略了這些批評，可是大錯特錯。唯有傾聽反對的聲音，給它們充分表達的機會，我們的寫作才會改進。甚至可以說，要**快速改善論文品質**，最好辦法就是**將反面論點納入文中**，也就是用這樣的說法：「儘管有些讀者可能會反對」（although some readers may object）你的某個論點，你「會回答說＿＿＿＿＿＿」（would reply that ＿＿＿＿＿＿）。

預測會遭遇哪些異議

但是你會說，將他人的批評論點納入，難道不會破壞論文的可信度、削弱自身的論點嗎？你努力論證、表明立場，而我們卻要你讓讀者聽到所有可能反對的看法？

沒錯，我們就是在力勸你，把可能反對的說法都讓讀者知道。這麼做不會減弱論點，反而會提升論文的可信度。本書中，我們一直在說，好的寫作不能忽視環境、只敘述毫無爭議的事實，而是要與其他人展開對談和辯論——因此，不僅要如第一堂課所建議的，寫作開始先概述別人已經說過的話，還要隨著論證的發展，想像別人可能提出的異議。一旦你將寫作視為與人對談，就會明白，相反論點對你是助力，而非阻力。

神奇的是，你**越是把批評者的反對意見說出來，越是容易削弱其殺傷力**，特別是你的論述要具有說服力的話。納入反面意見就是先發制人，搶在別人批評之前，先找出自己論點裡的問題。再來，納入反面意見也是尊重讀者的表現，不把他們當作可以愚弄蒙蔽的人，要尊重他們能獨立思考並做出明確判斷；且知道在此主題上，有其他不同的觀點。除此之外，提出他人可能的不同論點，讀者會認為你很包容、有度量，並且有足夠的自信願意接受辯論。

反之，如果你都不考慮反面意見，會顯得思想封閉，彷彿自認理念沒有爭議，也容易造成重要的問題沒有充分論述，一些疑義也未澄清。再者，若不納入反面意見，你會發現，很快就沒什麼好寫的了。學生常說，把反面意見納入文中，比較容易寫出足夠的內容，達到作業規定的頁數。

在論文中納入反面意見是個相當簡單的寫作方法，從下列取自作家芹・齊爾寧（Kim Chernin）書中的一段文字就可以看得出來。齊爾寧花了約三十頁埋怨美國女性承受身材纖瘦的壓力，並插入了一個名為〈持懷疑態度的人〉

（The Skeptic）的章節，一開頭的段落是這樣寫的：

At this point I would like to raise certain objections that have been inspired by the skeptic in me. She feels that I have been ignoring some of the most common assumptions we all make about our bodies and these she wishes to see addressed. For example: "You know perfectly well," she says to me, "that you feel better when you lose weight. You buy new clothes. You look at yourself more eagerly in the mirror. When someone invites you to a party you don't stop and ask yourself whether you want to go. You feel sexier. Admit it. You like yourself better."

現在，我想提出一些反面的意見，是我內心的懷疑者告訴我的。她覺得我忽略了我們對自己身體常有的態度，希望我能說說這些問題。舉個例子，她跟我說：「妳明明就清楚得很，體重減輕心情就是比較好。妳會買新衣服、更喜歡照鏡子。有人邀請你去參加派對，妳不用多想就答應了。妳覺得自己變得性感了。承認吧，妳更喜歡自己了。」

—— 芹・齊爾寧，《執念：反思身材苗條的束縛》
（ *The Obsession: Reflections on the Tyranny of Slenderness* ）

齊爾寧在下文中都在回應心中懷疑者的問題。面對懷疑者針對書中核心論點的質疑（減肥的壓力嚴重影響了女性的生活），齊爾寧回應的方式不是去壓制阻攔，也不是讓步、放棄自己的立場。她反而大方地把這個質疑想法寫進文章裡。同時請注意，她並沒有草草打發這種質疑（我們很多人就容易這麼做），而是騰出一整段的篇幅，將它完整地敘述。我們借用齊爾寧的部分用語得到以下範本，你可以用來陳述任何一種反面意見。

範本 18：納入反對意見

▶ At this point I would like to raise some objections that have been inspired by the skeptic in me. She feels that I have been ignoring _____.

現在，我想提出一些反面的意見，是我內心的懷疑者告訴我的。她覺得我忽略了_____。

▶ Yet some readers may challenge my view by insisting that _____.

然而，有些讀者可能會質疑我的觀點，堅持說_____。

▶ Of course, many will probably disagree on the grounds that _____.

當然，很多人或許會不同意，理由是_____。

　　請留意，上述範本都未指明反對意見來自哪些具體的人或團體，只用了「質疑的人」（skeptics）、「讀者」（readers）、「很多人」（many）。用不指名的方式列出反對意見，並無問題。但是，產生爭論和反對意見的思想，是源自於哪個具體的思想體系或學派（如自由主義者、基督教基要派、新實用主義者），也可以，甚至應該加以說明。換句話說，**請將論文裡的反對論點歸類**，如果能夠表明這些反方意見屬於哪個派系，你的論文會更精準、更有影響力。

範本 19：指出反對者的身分

▶ Here many feminists would probably object that _____.

許多女權主義者可能會反對_____這件事。

▶ But social Darwinists would certainly take issue with the argument that
_____.

但是社會達爾文主義人士一定會對_____的論點提出異議。

▶ Biologists, of course, may want to question whether _____.

當然了，生物學家可能會質疑是否_____。

▶ Nevertheless, both followers and critics of X will probably suggest otherwise and argue that _____.

不過，X 的支持者和批評者雙方都可能有不同看法，主張說_____。

不可否認，有些人不喜歡這種標識身分的方式，也很討厭被加上標籤。他們認為，用標識會將人侷限在某群體框架內，忽略了個人獨特之處。的確沒錯，標識使用不當，可能抹殺個人特色，加深刻板印象。不過，思想（即使是最私密的想法）是透過群組和分類才能進行交流，不是零星分散的。因此，知識的交流需要靠標識將概念加以定義，方便記載。如果你完全拒絕使用標識，就是放棄了一項重要的資源，使讀者以為你和他人觀點毫無關連；而你也會錯失機會，無法將你的作品在一個更大的對談架構中，展現重要性和關聯性。

當你指名你所概述的是哪一種立場，比方說是自由主義或歷史唯物主義，你論述的就不再只是你的個人觀點，而是更廣泛的思想和思維習慣的交集，這些可能都是讀者原本就在關注的。

若要避免產生刻板印象，並不是完全避免使用標識，而是在使用時，力求精確、貼切，如同下列範本所示：

▶ Although not all Christians think alike, some of them will probably dispute my claim that _____.

雖然並非所有的基督徒想法都一致，其中一部分人可能會質疑我的主張，說 _____。

▶ Non-native English speakers are so diverse in their views that it's hard to generalize about them, but some are likely to object on the grounds that _____.

非以英語為母語人士之間的想法差異太大，很難一概而論，但是其中一些人可能會反對，理由是 _____。

另一種避免刻板印象的方法，就是採取謹慎的態度，要提供完整的標識，例如說「公益服務律師」（pro bono lawyers），而不是通稱「律師」（lawyers），或者指出是「量化社會學家」（quantitative sociologists），而不是所有的「社會學家」（social scientists）。

範本 20：以非正式方法帶出反面意見

你也可以用較不拘謹的方法來帶出反面意見，譬如說，你可以用**提問**的方式來組織反面論點。

▶ But is my proposal realistic? What are the chances of its actually being adopted?

但是我的提議可行嗎？它被真正採納的機會有多少？

▶ Yet is it necessarily true that _____? Is it always the case, as I have been suggesting, that _____?

然而_____必定是正確的嗎？真的一直如我所認為的那樣，_____嗎？

▶ However, does the evidence I've cited prove conclusively that _____?

然而，我所援引的證據可以確實證明_____嗎？

你也可以直接讓反對者開口說話：

▶ "Impossible," some will say. "You must be reading the research selectively."

有人會說：「不可能，你的解讀以偏概全。」

這種寫作方法讓你直接引入表示異議的論點。創作歌手喬・傑克森（Joe Jackson）在下面這段文字中就是採用這種寫法，這是從他發表在《紐約時報》（New York Times）上的文章所摘錄的段落，他抗議紐約市在餐廳和酒吧等公共場所禁止吸菸的規定。

I like a couple of cigarettes or a cigar with a drink, and like many other people, I only smoke in bars or nightclubs. Now I can't go to any of my old haunts. Bartenders who were friends have turned into cops, forcing me outside to shiver in the cold and curse under my breath... It's no fun. Smokers are being demonized and victimized all out of proportion.

"Get over it," say the anti-smokers. "You're the minority." I thought a great city was a place where all kinds of minorities could thrive... "Smoking kills," they say. As an occasional smoker with otherwise healthy habits, I'll take my chances. Health consciousness is important, but so are pleasure and freedom of choice.

我喜歡一邊小酌順便抽上幾根菸，和多數人一樣，我只在酒吧或夜店裡面抽菸。現在，這些常去的地方都不能去了，以前還把我當朋友的酒保們，搖身變成警察攆我出去，放我在寒天中打哆嗦、低聲咒罵……這很沒意思，抽菸的人被當成妖魔，糟蹋到這種地步。

反菸人士說：「看開一點吧，誰叫你是少數。」我還以為既然是偉大的城市，應該讓各種少數人士都可以生存……他們說：「抽菸會要了你的命。」但是我的生活習慣很健康，不過偶爾來根菸而已，我有本錢冒這個險。健康意識很重要，但是快樂和選擇的自由也同樣重要。

——喬·傑克森〈想抽菸？去漢堡吧〉
（Want to Smoke? Go to Hamburg）

第二段開頭，傑克森把自己的發言轉移給虛構的反對者時，也可以用比較正式的語氣，如：

Of course anti-smokers will object that since we smokers are in the minority, we should simply stop complaining and quietly make the sacrifices we are being called on to make for the larger social good.

當然反菸人士會對此提出異議，畢竟我們抽菸的人是少數，我們應該就停止抱怨，為了社會公益著想，照著要求默默犧牲。

或者說：

Anti-smokers might insist, however, that the smoking minority should submit to the non-smoking majority.

然而反菸人士可能會堅稱，吸菸的少數應該服從不吸菸的多數。

不過，傑克森選擇了比較口語的形式，我們認為這使得敘事更加生動活潑。傑克森借用了劇作家和小說家的寫作方法，直接切入反對者的觀點，再加以反駁，然後又回到反對者的觀點，又再加以反駁。以此方式，在自己的文章裡營造成一場對談或者一個微劇場。這種寫作方法效果很好，也是因為他使用了引號和其他發言標記，讓我們清楚明白是誰在發言。

▋ 持平呈現反對的意見

一旦你決定在寫作中納入一個不同或相反的論點，你的工作才正要開始而已，因為你還需要用持平、寬大的心胸來呈現並解釋該論點。雖然我們巴不得對不同的意見輕描淡寫、草草帶過或嘲弄一番，但是這樣做通常會產生反效果。寫作者要能全力將批評者的論點完整說明（也就是玩艾爾博的「信任遊戲」），讀者對他們的信賴不減反增，讀者會認為這位作者值得信賴。

所以我們建議，在寫作中提到不同論點時，一定要以幾個句子甚至幾個段落的篇幅，來盡量認真敘述討論它們。我們也建議，你對相反論點進行概述時，要站在反對者的角度，問問自己：如果反對意見的人來看，是否會確認那真的就是他的主張？他會認為你確實認真地，用合理態度了解他的論點理念嗎？抑或是，他會覺得你評論他的主張時，語帶嘲諷，或者過度簡化了呢？

請參考第 5 堂更多使用發言標記的建議。

參考 p. 43 有關信任遊戲的說明。

不可否認，一定有些反對的看法是你認為不值得一提的，甚至不值得尊重，讓人不禁想揶揄一番。但是請記住，假如你真的去嘲弄你反對的意見，可能會讓那些還沒有站在你這邊的讀者離你而去──他們很可能正是你想要爭取的讀者。同時也要知道，嘲弄別人的觀點可能會助長敵對的論證文化，這種情況下，別人可能也會嘲弄你作為反擊。

回應反對的意見

　　說明了相反論點後，還要做出有力的回應。畢竟，一旦把相反論點寫進文章裡，就得承擔風險：讀者可能會發覺這些相反論點比你的論證更有說服力。以我們上面引用的社論文章為例，傑克森冒的風險是，讀者可能會比較認同他所引述的禁菸論點，而不認同他贊成抽菸的立場。

　　這正是富蘭克林（Benjamin Franklin）在其《富蘭克林自傳》（*The Autobiography of Benjamin Franklin*）中描述發生在自己身上的事情。他回憶，自己在讀了反對自然神論（Deism，推崇理性超過靈性的宗教信仰）的一些書籍之後，反而成為自然神論的信徒。富蘭克林解釋說，當他看到反對自然神論的作者們，盡用負面語氣描述自然神論者的觀點時，反而發覺自然神論者的立場比較有說服力。為了避免造成這種反效果，你所提出的任何相反論點，絕不能比你自己的論證還有說服力。在論文中提及相反論點是好事，但你要有能力駁倒它。

　　有一種駁斥相反論點的方法絕對會失敗，那就是**不加思索就予以駁斥**，例如說 That's just wrong.（那就是不對。）這種回應方式（沒有提出任何支持性的理由）和本書一直倡導的細膩回應，一個就像在霸凌讀者，而另一個才是在說服讀者。

要駁倒一個相反論點，最好的方法通常是不全盤推翻，而是部分表示同意，**僅針對有疑慮之處提出異議**。換言之，在回應反論時，最好是說 yes, but（沒錯，但是……）或 yes and no（是，也不是），把這些相反的觀點視為**修正、斟酌自我立場**的機會。與其試圖將你的論點築成牢不可破的堡壘，倒不如堅守基本立場，卻稍所退讓。在下面這個段落中，齊爾寧針對前面她所引述的相反論點，提出了回應。當她用「懷疑者」的聲音說話時，她寫道：「承認吧，減肥之後妳更喜歡自己了。」（Admit it. You like yourself better when you've lost weight.）然後，她的回應如下：

> Can I deny these things? No woman who has managed to lose weight would wish to argue with this. Most people feel better about themselves when they become slender. And yet, upon reflection, it seems to me that there is something precarious about this wellbeing. After all, 98 percent of people who lose weight gain it back. Indeed, 90 percent of those who have dieted "successfully" gain back more than they ever lost. Then, of course, we can no longer bear to look at ourselves in the mirror.

> 我可以否認這些事嗎？減肥成功的女人，沒有一個會對這種事有所爭論。大部分的人變苗條之後，自我感覺會更好。但是經過審慎思考之後，我覺得這種幸福感似乎有點不牢靠。畢竟有 98% 的人減肥之後又復胖，甚至，這些節食「成功」的人有 90% 胖回來的體重比減掉的還多。那麼，我們當然不敢再照鏡子。

齊爾寧利用相反論點作為讓步，改進並琢磨自己的整體論證。她先承認減肥在短時間能帶來快樂，但她接著說，就長期看來，體重還是會恢復，節食的人只會更痛苦而已。

範本 21：讓步之餘仍堅持立場

▶ **Although I grant that _____ , I still maintain that _____ .**
雖然我承認_____ ，我仍然堅信_____ 。

▶ **Proponents of X are right to argue that _____ . But they exaggerate when they claim that _____ .**
X 的擁護者說得沒錯：_____ ，但是他們主張_____ 是有點言過其實了。

▶ **While it is true that _____ , it does not necessarily follow that _____ .**
_____ 是事實沒錯，但未必能由此推斷_____ 。

▶ **On the one hand, I agree with X that _____ . But on the other hand, I still insist that _____ .**
一方面，我同意 X 說的_____ ，但是另一方面，我仍然堅持_____ 。

你可以從以上的範本看到，回應異議不一定要走到極端 —— 全然否定或全然被否定。處理不同的論點最理想的結果是，你最後會得到能涵蓋兩方的綜合洞見。

然而，如果你已經嘗試過各種想得到的方式來回應一個相反論點，卻仍然覺得惶惶不安，深怕這個相反論點比你的論證還要有說服力，那該怎麼辦？倘若遇到這種情況，最好的辦法就是回過頭去，從基礎上修改你的論證；必要的話，甚至要徹底翻轉你的立場。雖然，到了後面才發現連自己都沒辦法說服自己是很痛苦的事，但實際上，你最後的定稿會因而更有誠信，內容會更嚴謹有深度。歸根究柢，寫作的目標並非在於不斷證明自己一開始的立論就是正確的，而是在於擴充思考的範圍。因此，如果在論文中納入相反論點，反而使你改變心意，倒也不是什麼壞事。有人會說，學術界就是這麼一回事。

練習

1. 閱讀下面由文化評論家艾瑞克・施洛瑟（Eric Schlosser）所寫的一段文字。你會發現他在文中並沒有納入任何相反論點，請幫他加上相反論點。請針對他的論點，插入一段簡短的文字說明一個相反論點，接著以他的立場做出回應。

> The United States must declare an end to the war on drugs. This war has filled the nation's prisons with poor drug addicts and smalltime drug dealers. It has created a multibillion-dollar black market, enriched organized crime groups and promoted the corruption of government officials throughout the world. And it has not stemmed the widespread use of illegal drugs. By any rational measure, this war has been a total failure.

> We must develop public policies on substance abuse that are guided not by moral righteousness or political expediency but by common sense. The United States should immediately decriminalize the cultivation and possession of small amounts of marijuana for personal use. Marijuana should no longer be classified as a Schedule I narcotic, and those who seek to use marijuana as medicine should no longer face criminal sanctions.

We must shift our entire approach to drug abuse from the criminal justice system to the public health system. Congress should appoint an independent commission to study the harm-reduction policies that have been adopted in Switzerland, Spain, Portugal, and the Netherlands. The commission should recommend policies for the United States based on one important criterion: what works.

In a nation where pharmaceutical companies advertise powerful antidepressants on billboards and where alcohol companies run amusing beer ads during the Super Bowl, the idea of a "drug-free society" is absurd. Like the rest of American society, our drug policy would greatly benefit from less punishment and more compassion.

—— Eric Schlosser, A People's Democratic Platform

2. 檢視自己的一份報告。檢查你是否有加入預期的相反論點並加以回應。如果沒有，請修改。如果有，你是否有將所有可能的相反論點都考慮進去？如果這些相反論點有確切的來源，你有沒有指明是誰？你有沒有持平地呈現這些相反論點？你有沒有充分地回應，或者你認為有必要再把自己的論證補充完善？你能夠運用本課所建議的範本嗎？引用反對者的意見是否強化了你的論點呢？是的話，原因為何？否的話，原因又為何？

第 7 堂　說明論點有什麼重要

"Who cares?"　　「誰在乎？」

"So what?"　　「那又如何？」

棒球是美國全民娛樂、貝尼尼（Bernini）是巴洛克時期最優秀的雕刻家、所有的寫作都是在進行對談。那又如何呢？誰在乎？這些有什麼重要？

你有幾次認真地問過這些問題呢？不管主題對身為作者的你是多麼有趣，必須讓讀者知道文章內容有什麼重要，他們為什麼要注意。然而，這些問題卻往往沒有回答，因為寫作者或演講者認為讀者或聽眾早就知道答案，或者讓他們自己動動腦筋想一想也就知道了。結果，許多學生聽完老師講課離開，對於剛剛聽到的內容，感覺像事不關己，就好像我們聽完演講之後，仍然心有存疑一般。問題不盡然是演講者的論點不清楚或沒有重點，或者支持論點的證據不足，而是演講者並沒有回答以下這個關鍵問題：**「我的論點有什麼重要？」**

這個問題經常被忽略，實在很可惜，因為事實上，演講者是可以講出既有趣又引人關注的答案。舉例來說，大部分學者被追問時，會說得出，他們的演講或文章之所以重要，是因為有些理念需要修正或更新，而他們的論點會對其產生一些重要、實際的結果。然而，多數學者沒有在演講或寫作之中，表明這些理由或結果。寫作者要在文中及早說明**「誰在乎這個論點？」**（Who cares?）和**「那又如何？」**（So what?）這兩點，不要以為讀者就該自己知道這些論點如何重要。所謂重要，不是說人人都要聲稱找到治療癌症的方法，或者能完全解決貧窮問題。但是，如果寫作者未能表明為何應該關心這個論點，或是有人已經在關心，讀者與聽眾終究會失去興趣。

本堂課中將說明一些寫作方法，讓你在寫作中用來回答「誰在乎這個論點？」和「那又如何？」就某種意義上來說，這兩個問題處理的是同一件事：你的論點有何關聯性和重要性。不過它們的處理手法是不同的。「誰在乎這個論點？」是要**說明哪個人或團體會注意你的主張**；「那會如何？」問的則是**這些論點的現實應用和後果**──假如這個論點被接受，會造成什麼結果。我們首先來看如何說明「誰在乎」。

誰在乎這個論點？

要看寫作者如何回答「誰在乎這個論點？」的問題，請思考下面這段由科學作家狄妮絲‧葛蕾笛（Denise Grady）所寫的文字。此文發表於《紐約時報》，說明了關於肥胖細胞的最新研究。

> Scientists used to think body fat and the cells it was made of were pretty much inert, just an oily storage compartment. But within the past decade research has shown that fat cells act like chemical factories and that body fat is potent stuff: a highly active tissue that secretes hormones and other substances with profound and sometimes harmful effects...
>
> In recent years, biologists have begun calling fat an "endocrine organ," comparing it to glands like the thyroid and pituitary, which also release hormones straight into the bloodstream.

科學家過去認為，體脂肪和組成體脂肪的細胞是惰性的，不過就是一個油膩的儲藏間。但是過去十年來的研究顯示，脂肪細胞的作用就像化工廠，而體脂肪是活性的東西：是非常活躍的組織，會分泌荷爾蒙，以及其他可能有重大影響、甚至不良作用的物質……

　　近年來，生物學家開始把脂肪稱為「內分泌器官」，拿它與甲狀腺、腦垂體等腺體相提並論，因為這些器官也會直接將荷爾蒙排放到血液裡。

——狄妮絲‧葛蕾笛，〈一個功能細胞的祕密生活〉
（The Secret Life of a Potent Cell）

　　葛蕾笛的文章印證了本書的核心建議，她不僅提出了明確的主張，在組織架構時也藉著回應別人的論點，來提出自己主張。接著，葛蕾笛立刻表明，至少有一群人參與新研究，認為脂肪「很活躍」、是「活性的東西」，這個團體就是原本認為脂肪是惰性的科學界。葛蕾笛提到這些科學家，就在暗示，這篇文章屬於一個大對談的一部分，也點出除了她自己之外，對她的論點有興趣的還有哪些人。

　　然而，如果葛蕾笛把「科學家過去認為……」（Scientists used to think...）這句話刪除，只單獨解釋科學上的新發現，想一想這段文字讀起來會是什麼感覺。

Within the past decade research has shown that fat cells act like chemical factories and that body fat is potent stuff: a highly active tissue that secretes hormones and other substances. In recent years, biologists have begun calling fat an "endocrine organ," comparing it to glands like the thyroid and pituitary, which also release hormones straight into the bloodstream.

在過去十年間，研究已經顯示，脂肪細胞的作用就像是化工廠，體脂肪是活性的東西：是非常活躍的組織，會分泌荷爾蒙和其他物質。近年來，生物學家開始把脂肪稱為「內分泌器官」，拿它與甲狀腺、腦垂體等腺體相提並論，因為這些也會直接釋放荷爾蒙到血液裡。

雖然這段陳述清楚易懂，卻沒有指出誰該聽聽這段話。好，有人會一邊讀這段文字、一邊點頭，脂肪是一個活躍、活性的東西，聽起來甚是有理，沒有懷疑的理由。但是誰要關心這件事？誰會有興趣知道這件事？

範本 22：點出在乎這個論點的人

為了回答「誰在乎這個論點？」的問題，我們建議用下列的寫作範本，這些範本仿效自葛蕾笛的寫法，與過去的論點形成對比。

▶ **Parents used to think _____. But recently [or within the past few decades] experts suggest that _____.**
家長們過去認為_____，但是最近（或者在過去數十年間）專家指出_____。

▶ **This interpretation challenges the work of those critics who have long assumed that _____.**
這個解釋挑戰了某些批評者的論點，他們長久以來認定_____。

▶ **These findings challenge the work of earlier researchers, who tended to assume that _____.**
這些發現挑戰了早期研究者的研究成果，他們多傾向於認定_____。

▶ Recent studies like these shed new light on _____, which previous studies had not addressed.

諸如此類的新近研究重新釐清了_____，而先前的研究未能處理到這部分。

要是葛蕾笛更明確一點，她也可以在文章裡直接寫出「誰在乎這個論點？」（Who cares?）這個問句，如下列這個範本：

▶ But who really cares? Who besides me and a handful of recent researchers has a stake in these claims? At the very least, the researchers who formerly believed _____ should care.

但是有誰真的關心？除了我和近來的少數相關研究人員之外，還會有誰？起碼過去相信_____的那些研究者應該關心吧。

若要提高論點的說服力，也可以把相關的特定人士或團體名稱寫出來，並且稍微詳細說明他們的論點。

▶ Researchers have long assumed that _____. For instance, one eminent scholar of cell biology, _____, assumed in _____, her seminal work on cell structures and functions, that fat cells _____. As _____ herself put it, "_____" (2012). Another leading scientist, _____, argued that fat cells "_____" (2011). Ultimately, when it came to the nature of fat, the basic assumption was that _____.

But a new body of research shows that fat cells are far more complex and that _____.

研究人員長期以來一直認定＿＿＿＿＿。舉例來說，一名聲譽卓著的細胞生物學者＿＿＿＿＿在其關於細胞結構和功能的開創性研究＿＿＿＿＿當中，就認為脂肪細胞＿＿＿＿＿。如＿＿＿＿＿本人所言：「＿＿＿＿＿」（2012 年）。另一位頂尖的科學家＿＿＿＿＿則主張脂肪細胞「＿＿＿＿＿」（2011 年）。最後，說到脂肪的本質，過去的基本看法是＿＿＿＿＿。但是多項新的研究顯示，脂肪細胞比原本以為複雜許多，而且＿＿＿＿＿。

此外，你也可以點出，哪些特定人士或團體應該關心你的論點。

▶ **If sports enthusiasts stopped to think about it, many of them might simply assume that the most successful athletes ＿＿＿＿＿. However, new research shows ＿＿＿＿＿.**
如果愛好運動者思考這個問題，其中許多人或許會單純認為，最成功的運動員都＿＿＿＿＿。然而新的研究顯示，＿＿＿＿＿。

▶ **These findings challenge neoliberals' common assumption that ＿＿＿＿＿.**
這些發現挑戰了新自由主義者的普遍假設，那就是＿＿＿＿＿。

▶ **At first glance, teenagers might say ＿＿＿＿＿. But on closer inspection ＿＿＿＿＿.**
乍看之下，青少年可能會說＿＿＿＿＿，但是更仔細一看，其實是＿＿＿＿＿。

如同這些範本所示，要回答「誰在乎這個論點？」的問題，得在別人和自己的言論之間建立起一種對比，這也是本書的核心。終歸到最後，這些範本可以協助你在論文中**營造戲劇張力**或意見衝突，讀者會感覺投入、想要看到你怎麼解決這些衝突。

那又如何？

回答「誰在乎這個論點？」是非常重要的，但是許多情況下，光是回答這個問題還不夠，尤其如果目標讀者是一般大眾，他們對於你所設定的特殊觀點衝突未必鑽研得很透徹。以葛蕾笛關於脂肪細胞的論點為例，讀者可能還是會納悶，有些研究者認為脂肪細胞是活性的、有些認為是惰性的，這有什麼好說的？我們來看看另一個不同的研究領域：美國文學。馬克吐溫在小說《頑童歷險記》（*Adventures of Huckleberry Finn*）裡面，描述了哈克和逃跑的奴隸吉姆之間的情誼，要是有學者對此不認同的話，那又如何？若不是該領域的專家學者，何必關心這些爭論呢？它們如果有影響，會是什麼樣的影響呢？

這些問題都會影響到你的論點發展，要回答這樣的問題，最好就是**訴諸於讀者已經關心的事情**。要回答「誰在乎這個論點？」這個問題，你需要找出對這個論點有興趣的某人或某團體。而要回答「那又如何？」這個問題，則需要將你的論點**連結到某個讀者已經很重視的更大議題上**。因此，寫作者在分析《頑童歷險記》的時候，可能會主張，故事主人翁和吉姆之間情誼看似小事，其實解釋了馬克吐溫這本廣為流傳的經典小說，原是一部批判美國種族主義的作品；也可能主張，這本小說因為隱含種族歧視而光芒受損。

我們看看葛蕾笛在其關於脂肪細胞的文章中，如何喚起廣泛的關注。她首先將研究者對於脂肪細胞的關注，連結到一般大眾對於肥胖和健康的關注。

Researchers trying to decipher the biology of fat cells hope to find new ways to help people get rid of excess fat or, at least, prevent obesity from destroying their health. In an increasingly obese world, their efforts have taken on added importance.

研究人員試圖破解脂肪細胞的生物特質，以期能發現新的方式消除多餘脂肪，或至少預防因肥胖而失去健康。肥胖問題日益嚴重，他們的努力更顯重要。

接下來，葛蕾笛證明這個議題的關聯性和急迫性，提醒讀者為何要關心。

Internationally, more than a billion people are overweight. Obesity and two illnesses linked to it, heart disease and high blood pressure, are on the World Health Organization's list of the top 10 global health risks. In the United States, 65 percent of adults weigh too much, compared with about 56 percent a decade ago, and government researchers blame obesity for at least 300,000 deaths a year.

世界各國有超過十億人口體重過重。肥胖以及兩個相關疾病 —— 心臟病與高血壓 —— 已被世界衛生組織列為全球十大健康風險。全美有 65% 的成人體重過重，十年前則為 56%，政府研究人員認為每年至少有三十萬人的死亡是由肥胖所造成。

葛蕾笛在這段文字中暗指的是：

Look, dear reader, you may think that these questions about the nature of fat cells I've been pursuing have little to do with everyday life. In fact, however, these questions are extremely important—particularly in our 'increasingly obese world' in which we need to prevent obesity from destroying our health.

親愛的讀者，你們可能會認為，我所談的脂肪細胞本質的問題和日常生活毫無關係；其實，這些問題至關重要——尤其『肥胖問題日益嚴重』，我們要防止肥胖危及我們的健康。

請注意葛蕾笛使用的句型：**in an increasingly _____ world**（在一個日益_____的世界裡），我們也可以拿來應用在其他領域，作為回答「那又如何？」的一個範本。舉例來說，社會學家在分析過去三十年中的回歸自然運動時，可採用下面的陳述方式：

> **In a world increasingly** dominated by cellphones and sophisticated computer technologies, these attempts to return to nature appear futile.

> 在一個生活日益被手機和精密電腦科技掌控的世界裡，想要回歸大自然的努力彷彿都是徒然。

這個寫作方法可以應用在其他學科，因為各門學科儘管差異甚多，共同點都是要你證明所關注的事項有其重要性。

範本 23：表明你的主張何以重要

▶ _____ **matters / is important because** _____
_____之所以重要，是因為_____。

▶ **Although X may seem trivial, it is in fact crucial in terms of today's concern over** _____.
雖然 X 看似微不足道，事實上，以今日人們對於_____的關心來看，它極其重要。

▶ **Ultimately, what is at stake here is _____.**
最後，真正事關重大的是_____。

▶ **These findings have important implications for the broader domain of**
_____.
這些發現對於更廣泛的_____領域有著重大的意義。

▶ **If we are right about _____, then major consequences follow for**
_____.
如果我們對於_____的看法是正確的，那麼在_____方面將產生重大的後果。

▶ **These conclusions / This discovery will have significant applications in**
_____ as well as in _____.
這些結論／發現不僅在_____方面有著重大的影響，在_____方面也是。

　　最後，你還可以將「那又如何？」和「誰在乎這個論點？」這兩個問題作連結。

▶ **Although X may seem of concern to only a small group of _____,**
it should in fact concern anyone who cares about _____.
即便可能只有一小群_____人士關心 X 這件事，實際上任何在意_____的人，都該對此關心。

　　以上這些範本都有助於吸引讀者的注意。用這些範本，來說明你的論點在現實世界中的實用性，你不僅指出已經有人關心你的論點，同時也告訴讀者他們為什麼也應該關心。我們不厭其煩地再三叮嚀，只是陳述和證明自己的論點是不夠的，你要好好規劃架構，吸引讀者來關心這個論點。

有些讀者已經知道論點的重要性

你或許會納悶，每件事都要回答「誰在乎這個論點？」和「那又如何？」這兩個問題嗎？假如你提出的論點具有極大的影響力，且眾所皆知，比方說自閉症的療法，或者是掃盲計畫，那還有必要回答這些問題嗎？大家都關心這樣的問題，不是嗎？抑或是，你知道讀者對這個論點很有興趣，也相當清楚其重要性，還需要多說嗎？換言之，每次都要回答「誰在乎這個論點？」和「那又如何？」嗎？

答案很簡單，是的，每次都需要。當然，你也不能解釋個沒完沒了，到了某個程度就得打住。縱然有個鍥而不捨的懷疑者無止境地問這有什麼重要——「我為什麼要在乎工作賺錢？我為什麼要在乎養家活口？」——你回答到一個程度，還是不得不停止。不論如何，我們建議，對於這類的問題，要盡可能充分回答。假如你認為讀者理所當然憑直覺大概也能知道答案，不須加以著墨，你原本精采的文章必會失色不少，而且讀者還可能認為，你的文章跟他們沒關係、不重要、不值得一讀。

反之，當你詳細說明了誰在乎、為什麼要在乎，就像是請啦啦隊幫你的文章助陣。即使有些專家讀者早就明白你的主張哪裡重要，你還是需要再次提醒。因此，最保險的方法就是，盡可能明確回答「那又如何？」的問題，對已知情的讀者也不要怠慢。當你從正文中抽離、解釋一下其重要性，就是在敦促讀者繼續閱讀、不要分心、**繼續關注**。

練習

1. 找幾篇文章（學術論文、報紙文章、電子郵件、備忘錄、部落格文章等），看看作者們是否回答了「誰在乎這個論點？」和「那又如何？」這兩個問題。有些有，有些或許沒有。這兩種文章給你的感受差別在哪裡？回答這些問題的作者們是運用了什麼方法？有沒有哪些策略或技巧是你可以借用到自己論文裡的呢？本堂課所建議的策略和技巧，或是你自己發現或研究出的策略或技巧當中，有沒有你想推薦給這些作者的呢？

2. 找一份你自己寫的東西，檢查一下。你有沒有點出「誰在乎這個論點？」和「那又如何？」這兩個問題？沒有的話請修改一下。你可以用下面的範本起頭。

   ▶ **My point here (that _____) should interest those who _____ . Beyond this limited audience, however, my point should speak to anyone who cares about the larger issue of _____ .**
   我的論點（_____）應該會讓那些_____的人產生興趣。不過除了這些有限的讀者之外，任何關心_____這個更大議題的人，希望都能聽聽我的論點。

PART III

Tying It All Together
使文章前後連貫

本部分介紹銜接「他人論點」與「自身論點」的寫作技巧，

首章介紹銜接句子與通篇一致性的寫作技巧，

接下來介紹正式與非正式用語，

說明學術論文和日常使用的非正式語言並無二致。

最後以說明後設評論技巧的章節做終，

告訴讀者如何透過後設評論引導讀者理解文本。

第 **8** 堂 銜接前後句子

"As a result"

「因此」

班上有位學生叫做比爾，他寫文章時，最常寫出這樣的句子：

Spot is a good dog. He has fleas.

小花是隻乖狗狗。他有跳蚤。

「你要把句子銜接起來。」我們在他的作業旁邊寫下這樣的評語。「小花是隻乖狗狗和他有跳蚤有什麼關聯？」「這兩句話不太相關，可以找出合理的連接方式嗎？」這些評語無法奏效，我們只好提供他一些建議的銜接方式，例如：

Spot is a good dog, **but** he has fleas.

小花是隻乖狗狗，但是他有跳蚤。

Spot is a good dog, **even though** he has fleas.

小花是隻乖狗狗，儘管他有跳蚤。

但是比爾還是不懂我們的意思，直到學期結束，他寫的句子都沒有連結。

儘管如此，比爾倒是能將重心集中在特定主題上。他在一個句子裡面提到狗狗小花（或者柏拉圖等其他主題），下一個句子也一定是在講小花（或柏拉圖）。這一點有些其他同學就做不到，他們句與句之間的主題變來變去，甚至一個句子裡幾個子句之間主題都不一樣。然而，因為比爾不善於銜接句子，他的文章和其他同學一樣不好讀。這種情況下，我們閱讀的時候，得仔細思考這些句子或段落之間有什麼關係，或是根本找不到關係。

換言之，這種寫作者的文章之所以不好閱讀，是因為他們沒有承接先前所說的話，也沒有預告接下來打算說什麼。他們可能奉行「永不回頭」的座右銘，把寫作的過程看作是想到什麼就寫什麼，接著再想出些相關的內容、再寫下來，持續這個步驟直到寫滿規定的頁數為止。每個句子基本上都各自獨立，而非承襲前一個句子的思路。

比爾承認自己從不回頭看前面寫過的東西。他甚至說，他只用電腦軟體檢查拼字，確定時態一致就交作業了，連重看一遍也沒有。我們從比爾的描述中彷彿看到，閱讀和寫作是不相干的兩件事；寫作是坐在電腦前面所做的事情，而閱讀則是手上拿書、窩在舒服的椅子上才做的活動。他從來沒有想過，寫出一個好句子必須承上啟下，反覆推敲，融入上下文。比爾寫出的每一個句子，都好像存在各自獨立的隧道裡，和其他句子隔絕。他從未下功夫去整合文中的各部分，因為對他來說，寫作只是堆砌資料或言論，而非持續進行論證。因此，本堂課所要提出的建議就是，寫作不僅是與別人對談，也是和自己對談。更重要的是，你必須用明確的方法，將各個論點一一連結。

本堂課所討論的主題是銜接文章的各個部分。好的文章在不同單位之間有明確的連結，藉此**產生一種動力和方向感**；因此，每個句子（或段落）會引導出後面的內容，也會清楚承接前文。你寫出的每一個句子，都會使讀者心裡產生預期，預期下一句會做某種程度的重複或延伸。就算你的論點從下一句開始轉到新方向，這種心理預期也一樣重要。

你可以想像，每個句子都像是長了一雙手臂，一隻往前、一隻往後。你的句子像這樣前後延伸，就可以建立連結，讓文章流暢易懂。反之，如果缺乏這樣的連結，斷斷續續，讀者勢必得反覆閱讀，自行猜測其中的連結。為了避免中斷，行文流暢，我們建議，要遵循「自己做」（do it yourself）的原則，也就是說，銜接句子是寫作者的工作，不應該像比爾一樣，讓讀者去傷腦筋。

以下是幾個可以協助你連結句子或段落的技巧：

(1) **利用轉接語**（transition，源自拉丁字根 trans，「跨越」的意思。如 **therefore**、**as a result**）。

(2) **加上指示詞**（pointing word，如 **this**、**such**）。

(3) 文章內**使用一套特定詞彙和用語**。

(4) **換個方式重述一次** —— 這種方法是要你重複自己說過的話，但是加以足夠的變化，才不會顯得累贅。

這些方法都要你不斷回顧先前所寫的內容，加以思考。

截至目前為止，你可以看看本文是如何運用這些連結手法的。舉例來說，本文的第二段開頭，用一個轉接語「儘管如此」（And yet）作為開頭，標示著方向有所轉變；第三段的第一句以「換言之」（in other words）開頭，告訴讀者我們正要重述剛才的論點。在整本書裡，你會發現，許多句子都使用特定字詞或片語，來銜接前文，或是引導後文，或是同時承前啟後。而本課通篇文字，更是一直重複幾個字詞，來強調銜接的概念，像是：「連結」（connect）、「切分」（disconnect）、「連接」（link）、「關聯」（relate）、「承前」（backward）、「啟後」（forward）。

利用轉接語

為了讓讀者跟上你的思路，不僅句子與段落之間要有連結詞語，更要發揮連結的作用。要做到這一步，最簡單的方式就是利用轉接語，幫助你從文章的一處跨越到另一處。轉接語通常位於句首或靠近句首的位置，以便提示讀者文章的走向，是繼續朝同一個方向發展，抑或是轉向新的方向。更具體來說，轉接語是告訴讀者，接下來的文字是針對前一個句子或段落進行重複說明（使用 in other words「換句話說」）、補充說明（使用 in addition「除此之外」）、歸納結論（使用 as a result「結果」），還是表示轉折（使用 and yet「然而」）。

以下是依照功能分類的常用轉接語：

範本 24：常用轉接語

▶ **補充**

also 再者；此外
and 而且；然後
besides 此外
furthermore 此外；再者
in addition 除此之外

indeed 甚至；而且
in fact 事實上
moreover 此外
so too 也是如此

▶ **詳述**

actually 實際上
by extension 進而；乃至於
in other words 換而言之
in short 簡而言之
that is 也就是說

to put it another way 換而言之
to put it bluntly 恕我直言
to put it succinctly 簡而言之
ultimately 歸根究柢

▶ 舉例

after all 畢竟；終究
as an illustration 作為例子
consider 考慮
for example 例如

for instance 例如
specifically 具體來說
to take a case in point 舉一個實例

▶ 因果

accordingly 因此
as a result 結果
consequently 結果
hence 因此
since 既然；因為

so 所以
then 那麼；於是
therefore 因此
thus 因此

▶ 比較

along the same lines 以相同的方式
in the same way 以相同的方式

likewise 同樣地
similarly 類似地

▶ 對比

although 雖然；儘管
but 但是
by contrast 相較之下
conversely 反過來說
despite 儘管
even though 即使；縱然
however 然而
in contrast 相比之下

nevertheless 儘管如此；然而
nonetheless 儘管如此；然而
on the contrary 相反地
on the other hand 在另一方面
regardless 不管怎樣地
whereas 然而
while yet 然而

▶ 退讓

admittedly 不可否認地；誠然
although it is true 雖然沒錯
granted 誠然；的確

naturally 自然；當然
of course 當然
to be sure 不可否認地

▶ 結論

as a result 結果
consequently 結果
hence 因此
in conclusion 最後；總之
in short 總而言之

in sum 總而言之
therefore 因此
thus 因此
to sum up 總而言之
to summarize 總而言之

理想的情況是，轉接語在文章中不能太顯眼，而是要退居幕後，讓讀者感覺不到它們的存在。有點像是汽車駕駛在轉彎之前會先打方向燈，其他駕駛幾乎是無意識地注意到燈號閃爍。所以讀者在處理轉接語時，不需要過度斟酌思考。然而，即便這類轉接語在文章中不顯眼，卻是你最強而有力的字彙。試想，假如有個人對你讚美了一番，緊接著說出「但是」（but）、「然而」（however），你的內心肯定涼了半截。不管接下來他要說什麼，你都知道不會是好話。

有些轉接語的作用，不只是從一個句子移動到下一個句子，還能把兩個以上的句子結合在一起。當你把太多短句放在一起，就會產生語意不連貫、斷斷續續的問題，但是你如果用轉接語結合句子，就能避免這種情況。舉例來說，如果要把比爾的兩個不連貫句子 Spot is a good dog. 與 He has fleas. 組成較流暢的一個句子，我們建議他寫成 Spot is a good dog, **even though** he has fleas.（小花是隻乖狗狗，儘管他有跳蚤。）

這樣的轉接語可以引導讀者思路隨你的論點發展；更重要的是，能讓你確認自己確有論點存在。事實上，我們可把 but、yet、nevertheless、besides 等字稱做議論詞（argument words），因為若不是議論，是不太會用到這些字的。以 therefore（因此）為例，這個字就是要確保前面的主張能順理成章導出後面的結論。for example（舉例來說）也代表一種議論，表示你所引用的資料能作為前面泛論的實例或證據。於是，轉接語用得越多，不僅能把句子和段落銜接得越好，而且最重要的是，可以使論證更有力。只要經常運用轉接語，終會習慣成自然。

　　不可否認，轉接語也可能有使用得過猶不及的情況，因此，初稿應該仔細讀過，將不必要的轉接語刪除。不過，你總得先學會論證的方法，熟練了才能知道哪些用語可以省略，因此，在你尚未嫻熟使用轉接語之前，還是盡量明確使用為佳。我們多年的教學經驗裡，看過無數篇論文轉接語用得太少，或者根本沒有轉接語，還想不起有哪一篇是用得過多的。熟練的作家有時不用明確的轉接語，是因為他們大量運用了其他類型的銜接方式，接下來我們將會討論這部分。

　　我們要提醒一件事：轉接語的意義如沒有確認，不能隨意使用。如果論證上應該使用 nevertheless 或 however，你卻用了 therefore，就會使文意大不相同，所以一定要小心。選擇轉接語時務必費點心思，所以要用轉接語，就是為了令讀者更好閱讀，而不是讓閱讀更困難。閱讀比爾寫的 Spot is a good dog. He has fleas. 這種文字已經夠讓人頭痛了，假如用錯轉接語，寫成 Spot is a good dog. For example, he has fleas.（小花是隻乖狗狗，例如說，他有跳蚤。）讀起來更是折磨。

使用指示詞

另一種銜接句子的方法，是使用指示詞。顧名思義，指示詞就是指向前面句子的某個概念，最常用的包括 this、these、that、those、their、such。另外也包括簡單的代名詞，如 his、he、her、she、it、their。這類用語可以營造流暢感，讀者在閱讀過程中才會暢行無阻。就某種意義上來說，這些用語就好像一隻無形的手，從一個句子伸到前面的句子裡，抓住它所需要的成分，一起往下走。

不過指示詞和轉接語一樣，需要謹慎使用。我們很容易把指示詞放入文中，卻沒有定義其指涉的對象，因為寫作者本身相當清楚所指涉的對象，就容易假設讀者也應該很清楚。舉個例子，請思考下列段落中 this 的用法：

> Alexis de Tocqueville was highly critical of democratic societies, which he saw as tending toward mob rule. At the same time, he accorded democratic societies grudging respect. **This** is seen in Tocqueville's statement that...

> 亞歷西斯・托克維爾嚴厲批判民主社會，認為極可能流於暴民政治。與此同時，他對民主社會仍有少許肯定。這一點從托克維爾以下言論中可以看出。

上面句中「這一點」（this）的指涉模稜兩可，讀者無法判斷「這一點」是指托克維爾對民主社會的批判態度，或是對民主社會的勉強肯定，還是兩者都有。讀者一邊嘟噥著「這一點是什麼啊？」（This what?），一邊得回顧這段文字，試圖找出答案。有些寫作者也會想用指示詞來欺騙讀者，希望用來掩飾或彌補自己論點中可能潛藏的模糊概念，想用簡單的 this 或 that，使某一含糊論點看似清楚。

想解決指示詞指涉不明的問題，就必須確保指示詞要有指涉的對象，且是唯一對象。另一作法是點明指涉的對象。例如，你可以把上述示例裡面孤零零的「這一點」（this）改成更具體的詞語，如「這種對民主社會的矛盾心理」（this ambivalence toward democratic societies...）或「這點勉強的肯定」（the grudging respect...）。

重複使用特定詞語

能讓論證前後連貫的第三個策略，就是使用一套特定詞彙和用語，包括各種同義詞和反義詞，然後反覆提及，貫穿全文。如能有效運用特定詞語，讀者就能在文章中特別注意這些詞語，進而清楚了解文章的主旨。善用特定詞語，也是設定論文題目和章節標題的好方法。

請閱讀下面這段小馬丁·路德·金恩在〈來自伯明罕監獄的一封信〉當中所寫的首段。請留意他如何多次提及「批評」（criticism）、「聲明」（statement）、「回覆」（answer）、「書信」（correspondence）這幾個主要字詞。

Dear Fellow Clergymen:

While confined here in the Birmingham city jail, I came across your recent **statement** calling my present activities "unwise and untimely." Seldom do I pause to **answer criticism** of my work and ideas. If I sought to **answer** all the **criticisms** that cross my desk, my secretaries would have little time for anything other than such correspondence in the course of the day, and I would have no time for constructive work. But since I feel that you are men of genuine good will and that your **criticisms** are sincerely set forth, I want to try to **answer** your **statement** in what I hope will be patient and reasonable terms.

親愛的牧師同仁們：

　　我在伯明罕市監獄身陷囹圄，閱讀了各位的最新聲明，稱我當前的活動「不明智且不合時宜」。我對批評我的工作和思想的言論鮮少回覆，倘若我要回覆桌上所有的批評書信，我的祕書一整天將不用做別的事，光是處理這些書信就忙不完，而我也沒時間做建設性的工作。但是既然我感受到各位的善意，各位的批評亦是發自真誠，因此我願訴諸耐心理性之文字，回覆各位的聲明。

　　　　　　　　　　　——小馬丁‧路德‧金恩，〈來自伯明罕監獄的一封信〉

　　即使金恩使用了三次的「批評」（criticism）和「回覆」（answer）、兩次的「聲明」（statement），卻沒有過度重複的感覺，反而營造出段落的動力感，把整段文字凝聚在一起。

　　再來看下面這段文字，這是另一個有效運用主要詞彙的例子。歷史學家蘇珊‧道格拉斯（Susan Douglas）在文中，使用了一套對比鮮明的詞彙，來討論「文化精神分裂症患者[1]」（cultural schizophrenics）的概念。道格拉斯文中所指的「文化精神分裂症患者」，是像她這樣的女性，對於媒體所加諸的理想女性形象存在著矛盾心理。

In a variety of ways, the mass media helped make us the **cultural schizophrenics** we are today, women who rebel against yet submit to prevailing images about what a desirable, worthwhile woman should

---

1　譯註：schizophrenic 現譯「思覺失調症患者」，本文不探討醫療範疇，故暫採舊譯。

be... [T]he mass media has engendered in many women a kind of cultural **identity crisis**. We are **ambivalent** toward femininity on the one hand and feminism on the other. Pulled in opposite directions—told we were equal, yet told we were subordinate; told we could change history but told we were trapped by history—we **got the bends** at an early age, and we've never gotten rid of them.

When I open *Vogue*, for example, I am simultaneously infuriated and seduced... I adore the materialism; I despise the materialism... I want to look beautiful; I think wanting to look beautiful is about the most dumb-ass goal you could have. The magazine stokes my desire; the magazine triggers my bile. And this doesn't only happen when I'm reading *Vogue*; it happens all the time... On the one hand, on the other hand—that's not just me— that's what it means to be a woman in America.

To explain this **schizophrenia**...

大眾媒體透過各種方式，讓我們女性陷入現在這樣的文化精神分裂症。對於那種令人喜愛、受到肯定的女性傳統形象，我們是既反抗卻又屈服……大眾媒體讓女性產生一種文化認同危機。我們游移在女性氣質和女權主義之間，不知何去何從。我們受到兩股相反力量拉扯，一方面學到人皆平等，一方又聽到我們屬於次等；一方面學到可以改變歷史，一方面卻又感覺我們被歷史所禁錮 —— 我們有如從小就壓力不適，永遠也擺脫不了。

舉例來說，當我一翻開《時尚》雜誌，既是憤怒又受誘惑……我崇拜物質主義，我也鄙夷物質主義……我想要美麗動人，又覺得追求美貌膚淺愚蠢；這本雜誌激起我的欲望，這本雜誌也燃起我的怒火。我不是看《時尚》雜誌才有這樣感受；這種感受一直都在。一方面這樣，另一方面又——不是只有我這樣——在美國身為一名女性就是如此。

為了解釋這種精神分裂的現象……

——蘇珊·道格拉斯，《女孩們在哪裡：隨大眾媒體成長的女性》
（*Where the Girls Are: Growing Up Female with the Mass Media*）

道格拉斯在這段文字當中，把「精神分裂症」（schizophrenia）當作主要概念，再透過同義詞如「認同危機」（identity crisis）、「不知何去何從」（ambivalent）、「壓力不適」（got the bends）來重複這個概念——甚至用一系列的對比字詞或片語來表現這個概念，像是：

rebel against 反抗／ submit 屈服

told we were equal 學到人皆平等／
told we were subordinate 聽到我們屬於次等

told we could change history 學到可以改變歷史／
told we were trapped by history 感覺我們被歷史所禁錮

infuriated 憤怒／ seduced 受誘惑

I adore 我崇拜／ I despise 我鄙夷

I want 我想要／
I think wanting... is about the most dumb-ass goal 我覺得……膚淺愚蠢

stokes my desire 激起我的欲望／ triggers my bile 燃起我的怒火

on the one hand 一方面／ on the other hand 另一方面

道格拉斯用這些對比片語，形容女人被往兩方向拉扯，鮮活生動；同時也把整段文字凝為一體，即使文字複雜細膩，卻能始終維持焦點。

重述你的說法 —— 但稍作變化

最後一個銜接文章各部分的技巧，是把自己的說法重述一次，但要有所變化 —— 也就是，換句話說以避免單調。為求有效銜接論點的各個部分，並使論點發展下去，要小心不要從一個論點跳接到另一個論點，或者無預警地導入一個新想法。你必須重複先前的話，同時引導文章邁向新方向，並在前後論點之間搭起橋樑。

本課所討論的前三種銜接手法，其實也都可以算是在重述。使用特定詞彙、指示詞、甚至許多轉接語，都可以達到延續前句語意，同時稍做修改的作用。舉例來說，道格拉斯採用了一個主要字詞 ambivalent（不知何去何從）來重複先前提及的精神分裂症狀，但是略作變化 —— 用不同的措辭重述同樣的概念，產生新的聯想。

除此之外，使用 in other words 和 to put it another way（換句話說）這樣的轉接語時，也是在換一種方式重述，因為這些片語是用不同的口氣，重述先前的主張。你在句首用了 in other words，就是在告訴讀者，萬一他們無法全然了解前一個句子的意義，你現在會從另一個角度再說一次；又或者因為你自認論點十分重要，不宜草草帶過，而是要繼續深究，確保讀者能全盤理解。

我們甚至會建議你，在第一個句子之後，差不多每寫一個句子都需要某種程度回應前面的陳述。不管是用 furthermore（此外）來補充說明剛才說過的話，或者用 for example 來解釋剛才說過的話，每個句子都應該回應前一個句子當中的某一點，而且是要看得出的某一點。即使你改變了論述方向，仍然需要用到 in contrast（相形之下）、however、but 這類的轉接語與前面的句子做連結，標示出這種轉變，如下面範例所示：

Cheyenne loved basketball. **Nevertheless,** she feared her height would put her at a disadvantage.

> 夏安熱愛籃球。儘管如此，她擔心自己身高上是吃虧的。

這兩句話意思清楚，第二句雖然話鋒已轉，且對第一句做了限制，但它仍然重述了第一句的主要概念。"she" 和 "Cheyenne" 指的是同一個人，彼此有呼應關係；"feared" 和 "loved" 在 "nevertheless" 的作用下，也有顯著對比關係。因此，句子裡使用 nevertheless 不是就完全改變主題，還是需要透過重複的方式，帶領讀者跟著你一起調整思緒，讓他們能跟上你的思路。

簡而言之，重述是將文章從論點 A 轉移到論點 B 的核心技巧。我們再做最後一個比喻，想像攀岩高手如何爬上陡峭的山壁，他們不會貿然從一個手點（handhold）跳到另一個手點，好的攀岩者會在已經穩固的位置上找到牢固的手點，才往下一個平台（ledge）前進。同樣的道理也適用於寫作，為了順暢地自一個論點移往下一個論點，你必須以先前說過的話為堅實的基礎，來提出接下來要說的話，如此方能讓你的文章維持焦點，同時又繼續發展。

「且慢，」你可能會這樣想：「老練的寫作者不正是應該避免贅語重複嗎？這樣的寫法豈不是太過簡化，對顯而易見的事還喋喋不休？」這麼說，也對，也不對。一方面來說，如果寫作者只是一再重複、了無新意，當然可能會遇上麻煩；另一方面來說，重複是使寫作維持連貫的關鍵。如果你通篇完全不重複自己的論點，就很難維持一貫的思路。再者，假如寫作者對主要論點重述不夠，就無法鞏固這些論點，使它們突顯於次要論點之上；如此一來，絕對沒辦法對讀者產生影響。因此技巧不在於避免重複，而是在重複當中要有足夠的變化、要有趣，才能夠一邊鋪陳論點，又不顯得乏味。

1. 閱讀下面這段節自喬治・歐威爾《通往威根碼頭之路》（*The Road to Wigan Pier*）一書第二章的起始段落，請標示出這段文字中所運用到的連結手法：將轉接語畫底線、主要詞彙畫圓圈、指示詞畫方框。

Our civilisation... is founded on coal, more completely than one realises until one stops to think about it. The machines that keep us alive, and the machines that make the machines, are all directly or indirectly dependent upon coal. In the metabolism of the Western world the coal-miner is second in importance only to the man who ploughs the soil. He is a sort of grimy caryatid upon whose shoulders nearly everything that is not grimy is supported. For this reason the actual process by which coal is extracted is well worth watching, if you get the chance and are willing to take the trouble.

When you go down a coal-mine it is important to try and get to the coal face when the "fillers" are at work. This is not easy, because when the mine is working visitors are a nuisance and are not encouraged, but if you go at any other time, it is possible to come away with a totally wrong impression. On a Sunday, for instance, a mine seems almost peaceful. The time to go there is when the machines are roaring and the air is black with coal dust, and when you can actually see what the miners have to do. At those times the place is like hell, or at any rate like my own mental picture of hell. Most of the things one imagines in hell are there—heat, noise, confusion, darkness, foul air, and, above all, unbearably cramped space.

Everything except the fire, for there is no fire down there except the feeble beams of Davy lamps and electric torches which scarcely penetrate the clouds of coal dust.

When you have finally got there—and getting there is a job in itself: I will explain that in a moment—you crawl through the last line of pit props and see opposite you a shiny black wall three or four feet high. This is the coal face. Overhead is the smooth ceiling made by the rock from which the coal has been cut; underneath is the rock again, so that the gallery you are in is only as high as the ledge of coal itself, probably not much more than a yard. The first impression of all, overmastering everything else for a while, is the frightful, deafening din from the conveyor belt which carries the coal away. You cannot see very far, because the fog of coal dust throws back the beam of your lamp, but you can see on either side of you the line of half-naked kneeling men, one to every four or five yards, driving their shovels under the fallen coal and flinging it swiftly over their left shoulders...

—— George Orwell, *The Road to Wigan Pier*

2. 找一份你寫過的報告，留意裡面用了哪些方法來銜接句子，將所有的轉接語、指示詞、主要詞彙和重述論點的地方都畫上底線。你有沒有看出什麼模式？你運用這種手法是否比其他人更多？有沒有哪些段落不好閱讀？如果有的話，你可以用本課所提到的其他方法來改寫嗎？

第 **9** 堂　**學術論文用自己的話
來寫也通喔**

"Ain't so"
「不是這樣吧」

　　你是否有過這種想法：要寫出成功的學術著作，就必須摒棄自己日常所使用的那種語言。你必須使用艱澀的詞彙、很長的句子以及複雜的句型，好令指導老師印象深刻。如果真的這麼想，我們現在要告訴你，沒有這個必要。相反地，學術論文寫作可以 —— 在我們看來也應該如此 —— 很輕鬆、好閱讀，甚至帶點趣味。我們不是要阻止你在學術寫作中使用複雜的專業術語，而是要鼓勵你，把在日常生活中和親朋好友談天傳訊的那些語句和用詞，運用到學術寫作上。我們在這堂課將告訴你，如何提出有力學術論證，卻又**不失去自己的風格**。

　　這一點很重要。假如你發現，你每天所使用的語言都不能帶進教室裡，那你就很有可能排斥寫作。你可能跟我們班上的一個學生一樣，我們問她對課堂上寫的小論文有什麼感覺，她回答：「我是不得已才寫的，那根本不是我的風格！」

這不是說你和朋友聊天所用的任何語言都可以用在學術寫作上，也不代表你可以只會口語用法，拿這個當作藉口，不學習更嚴謹的表達方式。畢竟，學習嚴謹的表達方式、培育出更高智識的自我，才是接受教育的主要用意。然而，我們希望提出來的是，輕鬆口語化的語言能令學術寫作更**活潑生動，甚至更為嚴密精準**。這種非正式的語言能讓你和讀者產生智識上，也是人際關係的連結互動。因此，在我們看來，如果說學術用語和日常用語完全不同、絕對不能混用，這種說法，完全不對。

▌混合學術與口語風格

許多成功的寫作者會將學術專業用語和大眾用語混合使用。舉例來說，下面這段文字出自一篇學術文章，談論的是老師對於學生寫作錯誤該如何回應。

Marking and judging formal and mechanical errors in student papers is one area in which composition studies seems to have a **multiple-personality disorder**. On the one hand, our **mellow**, **student-centered**, **process-based** selves tend to condemn marking formal errors at all. Doing it represents **the Bad Old Days**. Ms. Fidditch and Mr. Flutesnoot with sharpened red pencils, spilling innocent blood across the page. Useless detail work. Inhumane, perfectionist standards, making our students feel stupid, wrong, trivial, misunderstood. Joseph Williams has pointed out how **arbitrary and context-bound** our judgments of formal error are. And certainly our noting of errors on student papers gives no one any great joy; as Peter Elbow says, English is most often associated either with grammar or with high literature—"two things designed to make **folks** feel most out of it."

要批改並找出學生報告裡的形式錯誤，讓寫作研究似乎出現了多重人格的症狀。一方面，我們溫和親切、以學生為中心、以過程為本位的本性，傾向反對挑剔形式錯誤，認為這是「沒好時代」的不當作法。嚴厲的費老師和傅老師，拿著削尖的紅色鉛筆，在作業上隨意下手，血光片片。這種瑣細要求毫無意義。不近人情地追求完美標準，只會讓學生自認愚蠢、錯誤百出、無能且受盡誤會。約瑟夫‧威廉斯曾指出，我們判斷寫作形式錯誤，標準常是主觀隨興。況且，我們在學生作業上只會標註錯誤，任誰看到都歡喜不起來。彼德‧艾爾博說過，英文常常使人聯想到文法或高級文學——而「這兩樣東西就是設計來讓大夥兒感覺格格不入的」。

　　——羅伯特‧康諾斯與安德莉雅‧郎斯福德（Robert Connors & Andrea Lunsford），
〈現今大學寫作形式錯誤之頻率，或者凱托老爹老媽做研究〉
（Frequency of Formal Errors in Current College Writing, or Ma and Pa Kettle Do Research）

　　這段文字混用多種寫作風格。首先，作者摻雜使用輕鬆的口語用詞，像是「溫和親切」（mellow）、「沒好時代」（the Bad Old Days）、「大夥兒」（folks），也使用比較正式的學術用語像是「多重人格症狀」（multiple-personality disorder）、「以學生為中心」（student-centered）、「以過程為本位」（process-based）、「主觀隨興」（arbitrary and context-bound）。甚至文章標題〈Frequency of Formal Errors in Current College Writing, or Ma and Pa Kettle Do Research〉也很特別，逗號前面是正式學術用語，後面則是大眾文化用語。Ma and Pa Kettle 是一系列電影[1]裡的虛構角色。其次，兩位作者在討論批改作業的嚴師時，為了賦予鮮明具體的形象，他們如魔法般地召喚出兩位經典的假想人物，也就是老古板又守舊的嚴師費老師和傅老師[2]。兩位作者的表

1　譯註：《Ma and Pa Kettle》是美國四〇到五〇年代期間非常流行的卡通角色，後來也被拍成同名電影。

2　譯註：Ms. Fidditch 是語言學家 Martin Joos 在其著作《The Five Clocks》中所創造的角色，指過於鑽研文法的英文老師。Mr. Flutesnoot 則是四〇年代漫畫《Archie》裡面的一個虛構角色，是名瘦削的老化學老師。

達方式非常有創意，替原本可能枯燥、學究式的文體增添了活力。

這樣將正式與非正式用語交互使用的情況，在無數論文中都可以看得到，不過，人文領域比自然科學用得多，而新聞報導用得更是頻繁。下面這段文字，取自文化評論家艾瑞克·施洛瑟探討美國速食業的暢銷書，請注意他如何描述科羅拉多泉市的一些改變。

> The **loopiness** once associated with Los Angeles has come full blown to Colorado Springs—the strange, creative energy that crops up where the future's consciously being made, where people walk the fine line separating a visionary from **a total nutcase**.

> 這種瘋昏現象一度在洛杉磯出現，如今在科羅拉多泉市發展成熟──這種奇怪又充滿創意的能量在此發揮；或許這地方正要刻意打造未來，人們在這地方也得小心翼翼，區別誰有真知灼見，誰是瘋得沒救。

> ──艾瑞克·施洛瑟，《速食王國》（*Fast Food Nation*）

施洛瑟本可以保守一點，不把這種現象稱為「瘋昏」（loopiness），而稱為「怪異」（eccentricity），不要形容是「瘋得沒救」（a total nutcase）而是「精神錯亂」（a lunatic）。然而他決定冒險嘗試，運用色彩更強烈的字詞，為他的寫作注入更多活力，如果採用了比較保守的字詞，可能就沒辦法達到這樣的效果。

另外還有一篇文章也是混合了正式和非正式用語，這是文學評論家茱蒂絲·斐特利（Judith Fetterley）所寫的論文，內容是關於美國小說家薇拉·凱瑟（Willa Cather）。她探討的主題是「凱瑟在控制我們對她的看法上，做得是多麼成功」，她以另一位學者的理論為基礎，做了如下的論述：

As Merrill Skaggs has put it, "She is **neurotically controlling** and **self-conscious** about her work, but she knows at all points what she is doing. Above all else, she is self-conscious." Without question, Cather was a **control freak**.

誠如梅里爾‧史卡格斯所言:「她對自己的作品進行神經性控制,有充分自我意識,然而她完全知道自己在做什麼。最重要的一點是,她有充分自我意識。」毫無疑問,凱瑟就是個控制狂。

— 茉蒂絲‧斐特利,〈薇拉‧凱瑟與同情的問題:非官方版本〉
（Willa Cather and the Question of Sympathy: The Unofficial Story）

　　這段文字做了很好的示範,讓我們看到心理學的專業術語像是「有自我意識」（self-conscious）和「神經性控制」（neurotically controlling）,和日常的流行語像是「控制狂」（control freak）是可以並用的;也讓我們看到,把一種說法轉換成另一種說法,也就是把專業術語改寫成日常用語,對於釐清論點是有幫助的。她把史卡格斯描述凱瑟的超長片語「她對自己的作品進行神經性控制,有充分自我意識」（neurotically controlling and self-conscious）改寫成雖直接但卻簡明扼要的主張:「毫無疑問,凱瑟就是個控制狂」（Without question, Cather was a control freak.）。她表明了,寫作並不需要在精簡的學術語文和日常的閒談用語之間二擇其一。甚至,這段文字示範了一個可以雅俗並存的簡單技巧:**先用專業領域的語言陳述你的論點,再用日常用語重複一遍** —— 這的確是進行論述的高明訣竅。

　　這種混合語氣的方式,除了可以讓寫作更活潑有力,也可以用來表達一種**政治態度**。舉例來說,假如社會各種方言地位不平等,某些受重視,其他受貶抑,就可以用這種方式來傳達你的政治理念。如語言學家潔奈瓦‧史密瑟曼（Geneva Smitherman）的兩本著作,分別是《說話與證實:黑人美國的

參考 p. 272 混合口語和學術風格的範文。

語言》（*Talkin and Testifyin: The Language of Black America*）和《黑人語言：從貧民區到教堂前座的詞彙和片語》（*Black Talk: Words and Phrases from the Hood to the Amen Corner*），書中混合了非裔美國人的通俗說法和比較學術性的用語，她想表達，黑人通俗英語和各種被視為「標準」英語的語言一樣是正當合宜的。以下節錄其中三個經典段落：

> In Black America, the **oral tradition** has served as a **fundamental vehicle** for **gittin ovuh**. That tradition preserves the Afro-American heritage and reflects the collective spirit of the race.

> 在黑人美國，口語傳統一直是話講清楚的基本媒介，這個傳統保存了非裔美國人的文化資產，反映出民族的集體精神。

> Blacks are quick to ridicule "educated fools," people who done gone to school and read all **dem** books and still don't know nothin!

> 黑人老愛嘲弄那些「受過教育的傻子」，那些人去上學、讀卡多屁書，然後還是啥米攏瞴知！

> ... it is a socially approved verbal strategy for black rappers to talk about **how bad they is**.

> ……黑人饒舌歌手談論自己有夠踐，是社會認可的語言策略。

> —— 潔奈瓦·史密瑟曼，《說話與證實：黑人美國的語言》

在這幾段範例當中，史密瑟曼混合了標準的英文書面用語，像是「口語傳統」（oral tradition）、「基本工具」（fundamental vehicle），以及黑人通俗口語，像是「話講清楚」（gittin ovuh）、「屁書」（dem books）、「他們有夠跩」（how bad they is）。甚至她還穿插使用黑人的變體拼字，如 "dem"、"ovuh" 等，來表現黑人英語發音特色。雖然有些學者並不贊成這種不合常規的做法，但這正是史密瑟曼想要傳達的重點：我們要放寬習以為常的語言習慣，讓更多人參與學術對話。

無獨有偶，作家暨行動家葛蘿莉亞・安札杜瓦（Gloria Anzaldúa）也是將標準英語和德墨語（Tex-Mex）混合使用。這是一種特殊方言，由英語、卡斯提亞西班牙語、北墨西哥方言以及印第安人的納瓦特爾語（Nahuatl）等融合而成。她藉此提出一個政治觀點，表達西班牙語在美國所遭受的壓抑。

> From this racial, ideological, cultural, and biological cross-pollinization, an "alien" consciousness is presently in the making—a new mestiza consciousness, *una conciencia de mujer*.
>
> 在這場種族、意識形態、文化與生物的異花授粉當中，一種「外來」的意識正逐漸成形 —— 麥士蒂索人的一種新意識：una conciencia de mujer。
>
> —— 葛蘿莉亞・安札杜瓦，《邊境：新麥士蒂索人》
> （*Borderlands / La Frontera: The New Mestiza*）

安札杜瓦和史密瑟曼一樣，她不僅透過說的內容，也透過說的方式來表達她的論點，說明她所描述的這種新混血民族，或者說麥士蒂索人，他們的意識「正逐漸成形」（presently in the making）。最後，以上幾個段落也暗示著，這樣混合語言的出現，即維尚・阿善提・楊（Vershawn Ashanti Young）所謂的「語碼齧合」（code meshing），讓人開始檢討質疑，語言真是各自獨立、互不相屬的嗎？

何時該使用混合形式？視目標讀者和寫作目的而定

寫作時用字遣辭可以有許多選擇，不必畫地自限，一成不變。你可以將各種措辭嘗試變化，再求改進。你可以詞藻華美也可以輕鬆隨興，更可以採取混搭風格。舉例來說，假如你選擇輕鬆隨興的用語，你可以不說某人「未及注意」（fail to notice），而改用某事物「逃過他的法眼」（fly under the radar）；你要形容一個人「沒意識到」某件事時，可以不要寫 be unaware of，而改用 be out to lunch（心不在焉）。你甚至可以把本書的英文書名《They Say / I Say》用年輕人的話來改寫，如《She Goes / I'm Like》。

但是，何時該循規蹈矩、遵守標準用語，何時又應該大膽一點，混合使用呢？換言之，何時該寫 fail to notice，何時又可以寫 fly under the radar，甚至說這樣寫更有力呢？採用混合文體都不用看場合嗎？如果你採用了混合文體，又該如何拿捏分寸？

不管是哪一種情況，都要仔細考慮你的讀者和寫作目的。舉個例子，假如你在寫求職信，或者提出一份申請補助企畫書，這些內容會由正式審核機構進行評估，那麼使用過於口語或俚語的寫法，可能會讓你錯失機會。這種情況下，我們寧可保守，盡可能遵循標準書面英語的傳統寫法。然而，假設你的讀者是其他人，你就有機會發揮創意，如本書就是這種情況。總而言之，要判斷各種情況的適合用語，務必把可能的讀者和你的寫作目的都考量進去。

現在許多學科的學術寫作，早已不再是一場西裝筆挺的語言盛宴。因此，要在學術寫作上獲得成功，你不須使用極為正式的用語。雖然學術寫作確實常用複雜句型和專業詞彙，但是利用一些街頭流行文化或日常的用語，也是相當常見。當各種用語交融使用，所謂的「標準」英文也隨著時間改變，學術寫作者所能夠發揮運用的彈性亦越來越大了。

練習

1. 從本書中選出一個段落，把它變得輕鬆隨興一點，用非正式的口氣改寫。接著針對同一個段落，雕琢其中的辭藻，把它變得正式一點。最後再改寫一次，這次採用混合文體。找一位同學分享你寫的三段文字，討論哪一個版本較為有力，並說出原因。

2. 找一份你寫過的課堂作業，研究看看是否有用到日常用語，哪些詞彙和句型不屬於「學術」用語。萬一都沒有，試著把一些地方以輕鬆的用語或意想不到的措辭改寫，能夠有助於闡述你的論點並吸引讀者注意，或至少能讓文章活潑起來。務必要考量目標讀者和寫作目的，選擇同時符合兩種考量的用語。

第 10 堂　後設評論的技巧

"But don't get me wrong."

「請別誤會我的意思。」

　　我們跟人說要介紹後設評論寫作技巧時，他們多半是一臉茫然，問我們什麼是「後設評論」。他們會說：「我知道評論（commentary），但是『後設』（meta）是什麼？」我們會回答，認識這個字也好，不認識也好，但是後設評論是我們每天都在運用的技巧。我們特意**解釋自己說過或寫過的話**，就是在做後設評論，譬如說：「我剛才的意思是＿＿＿＿＿。」「我剛才的意思不是＿＿＿＿＿，而是＿＿＿＿＿。」「我等一下要說的話或許不中聽，但是我還是要說＿＿＿＿＿。」在這種情況下，我們並沒有要提出新論點，只是告訴對方，我們剛才說過或接下來要說的話，究竟意思是什麼。因此簡單來說，後設評論是在評論自己的說法，是要**告訴別人該如何理解你的說法**。

　　不妨把後設評論想成是古希臘戲劇裡面的歌隊（chorus），當舞台上的戲劇正在演出時，他們會在一旁述說，把劇情解釋給觀眾聽。後設評論也像電影或影集裡面解釋情節的旁白。你也可以將後設評論看作是配合主文的次要文字，用來解釋主文的意思。主文提出了一些論點，再利用後設文字引導讀者，加以理解消化。

　　因此我們建議，把你的文章看成兩組關係緊密的文字；一個是主文，用來提出論點，另一個則是用來「打理」你的思想、區別容易混淆的論點、預測和回應反對意見、連結各項論點、解釋你的論點為何可能具爭議性，諸如此類。

使用後設評論澄清並詳述論點

為什麼需要後設評論來告訴讀者意思，並且引導讀者閱讀文章呢？不能在一開始就解釋清楚嗎？答案在於，你寫得再清楚、再精確，讀者看不懂的情況還是非常多。即便是頂尖的作家，也可能得到讀者意料之外的反應；即便是再優秀的讀者，都有可能迷失在複雜的論證裡，無法看出論點之間的關聯。讀者可能無法明白你的論點將導出什麼結論；或者，他們看得懂你的推論和舉證，卻不知道你從中得到什麼更大的結論；他們也可能無法領會你論點的整體重要性，或者誤把你的話和他們聽過的其他論點混為一談，所以必須澄清。因此，不管你的寫作風格是多麼簡明扼要，讀者還是需要你的協助，才能掌握文中真正的意義。書面文字容易產生太多是非，也可以有千百種解讀方式，因此我們需要後設評論，來**防止錯誤解讀**和其他**溝通失誤**。

另外一個必須掌握後設評論技巧的原因在於，它可以幫助你擴充思路，並產出更多文字。假如你擔心寫不到作業所規定的頁數，後設評論可以幫助你增加文章的長度和內容深度。我們曾經看過，有學生要寫五頁的論說文，才寫了兩三頁就洩氣地停下筆來，抱怨這個主題已經沒什麼好寫的了。學生說：「我已經提出我的論點，理由和證據都寫上了。」「我已經江郎才盡了。」他們明明已經發想出一個論點，卻不知要如何發揮。然而，要是學會使用後設評論，他們可以從自己的理念中延伸出更多想法，寫出更長、內容更充實的文章。簡而言之，後設評論可以把你的論點中所蘊藏的內涵完全發揮出來、找出可能的重大意義、從不同角度解釋觀點，還有很多其他的效用。

因此，即使你認為自己已經針對某論點進行了相當充分的說明，但你可以試著用下列的寫作範本，在文中加入後設評論。

▶ **In other words,** _____.
換言之，_____。

▶ **What** _____ **really means is** _____.
_____的真正意思是_____。

▶ **My point is not** _____ **but** _____.
我的重點不是_____而是_____。

▶ **Ultimately, then, my goal is to demonstrate that** _____.
那麼最後，我的目標是要證明_____。

最理想的情況是，後設評論應該能夠幫你看出自己論點的特別意涵，而這是你起初沒有察覺到的。

下面這段文字出自文化評論家尼爾‧波茲曼（Neil Postman），我們來看看他是如何運用後設評論的。這段文字描述美國文化從報紙書刊，發展到電視電影，這之間所歷經的轉變。

It is my intention in this book to show that a great... shift has taken place in America, with the result that the content of much of our public discourse has become dangerous nonsense. **With this in view, my task in the chapters ahead** is straightforward. I **must, first, demonstrate** how, under the governance of the printing press, discourse in America was different from what it is now—generally coherent, serious and rational; **and**

then how, under the governance of television, it has become shriveled and absurd. **But to avoid the possibility that my analysis will be interpreted as** standard-brand academic whimpering, a kind of elitist complaint against "junk" on television, **I must first explain that**... I appreciate junk as much as the next fellow, **and I know full well that** the printing press has generated enough of it to fill the Grand Canyon to overflowing. Television is not old enough to have matched printing's output of junk.

我寫這本書的用意，是想讓大家看到，美國已經發生一個重大的轉變，結果是絕大多數的大眾言論內容都是危險的胡言亂語。有鑑於此，在接下來的章節中，我的目的很明確。首先，我必須說明，過去在報業的主導之下，大眾言論和現在是如何的不同——當時普遍是有條理、嚴謹、理智的；接著，我會說明如今在電視的主導之下，大眾言論如何變得貧乏而荒謬。但是為了避免我的分析被解讀成標準學究式的怨嘆，好像帶著優越感在抱怨電視上的「垃圾」，我必須先解釋一下……我跟任何人一樣都愛看垃圾節目，我充分了解報業所製造出來的垃圾內容多到連大峽谷都不夠填。以電視年代之短，它製造的垃圾量還不能跟報界相比。

——尼爾·波茲曼，《娛樂至死：追求表象、歡笑和激情的媒體時代》
（*Amusing Ourselves to Death: Public Discourse in the Age of Show Business*，
副書名原意為「演藝時代的大眾談話」）

為了讓各位了解所謂的後設評論，請看上述段落的粗體字部分。基本上，波茲曼先撇開主要概念不談，而先幫助讀者理解他的主張是什麼，他採取了下列方法：

- 先預告會提出什麼主張：It is my intention in this book to show...（我寫這本書的用意是想讓大家看到……）

- 詳述將如何提出論證：With this in view, my task in these chapters...is. ... I must, first, demonstrate... and then...（有鑒於此，在接下來的章節中，我的目的很明確。……首先，我必須說明……接著……）

- 把自己的論點和其他易混淆論點做出區隔：But to avoid the possibility that my analysis will be interpreted as... I must first explain that...（但是為了避免我的分析被解讀成……我必須先解釋一下……）

把書名當作後設評論

甚至連波茲曼的這本書名《Amusing Ourselves to Death: Public Discourse in the Age of Show Business》都可以看做一種後設評論，因為所有的書名都一樣，都是將內文放一邊，先告訴讀者本書的宗旨：當代演藝界所提供的娛樂危害極大。

事實上，書名是最重要的一種後設評論形式，它的作用有點像在園遊會場外招攬遊客，讓路過的人知道進到裡面可以看到些什麼。副書名的功能也是後設評論，進一步解釋主書名。本書的英文副書名，不僅說明了這本書是關於「學術論文寫作之關鍵技巧」（*the moves that matter in academic writing*），還點出主書名《They say / I say》就是其中一個技巧。如果你把書名看作後設評論，就能發想出更清楚的書名，波茲曼的書名就是很好的例子，可以讓讀者對你的論點有個概念。把這種標題和一些不著邊際、沒什麼作用的標題，像「莎士比亞」（Shakespeare）、「類固醇」（Steroids）、「英文論文」（English Essay），或者根本無題的論文拿來對比一下就知道了。論文的題目如果含糊不清（或根本沒有題目），會傳達出一個訊息，就是寫作者並不願意費心去回想他所寫的內容，對於引導讀者理解也是意興闌珊。

其他後設評論技巧

　　本書的許多寫作方法都可以產生後設評論的作用，例如納入反對意見、使用轉接語、為引述句組織架構，還有對「那又如何？」和「誰在乎我的論點？」這樣的問題找答案。納入反對意見的時候，暫時不要考慮正文，先想像批評者會怎麼說；使用轉接語的時候，要說明各種論點之間的關係；回答「那又如何？」和「誰在乎我的論點？」這類問題的時候，也是先放下核心論點，去說明論點與誰有關，為何值得關注。

範本 25：後設評論的用法

避免誤解

　　下列範本有助於區別容易混淆的觀點：

▶ **Essentially, I am arguing not _____, but that we should _____.**
基本上，我所主張的並非_____，而是我們應該_____。

▶ **This is not to say _____, but rather _____.**
這並不代表_____，而是_____。

▶ **X is concerned less with _____ than with _____.**
X 對於_____關注得較少，對於_____則較多。

詳細說明先前的論點

下列範本可用來詳細說明前面提到的論點，告訴讀者：「怕你第一次沒看懂，我換個方式再說一次。」

▶ **In other words, _____.**
換言之，_____。

▶ **To put it another way, _____.**
換句話說，_____。

▶ **What X is saying here is that _____.**
X 在這裡所說的意思是_____。

提供文章指引

這裡的範本是導引讀者方向，釐清文章前面探討的內容、引出後面即將探討的內容，讓讀者更容易消化理解文章。

▶ **Chapter 2 explores _____, while Chapter 3 examines _____.**
第二章探討的是_____，而第三章則檢視_____。

▶ **Having just argued that _____, I want now to complicate the point by _____.**
方才我們已經提出了_____的論點，現在我想要透過_____的方式，把這個論點說得更複雜一點。

從泛論到實例

下列範本有助於闡釋一個普遍論點，透過具體實例說明你的論點。

▶ **For example,** _____ .

舉例來說，_____ 。

▶ _____ **, for instance, demonstrates** _____ .

比方說，_____ 就顯示出_____ 。

▶ **Consider** _____ **, for example.**

舉例來說，試想_____ 的情況。

▶ **To take a case in point,** _____ .

舉一個典型的例子，_____ 。

指出某主張的重要性

下列範本可以表現出某主張的相對重要性，拿該主張與前面提到的主張相比，說明它是比較重要、不重要或一樣重要。

▶ **Even more important,** _____ .

更重要的是，_____ 。

▶ **But above all,** _____ .

然而最重要的是，_____ 。

▶ **Incidentally, we will briefly note,** _____ .

附帶一提，我們將略為談到_____ 。

▶ **Just as important,** _____ .

同樣重要的是，_____ 。

▶ **Equally, _____.**

同樣地，_____。

▶ **Finally, _____.**

最後，_____。

預期可能的反對，並據理回應

這個範本可以幫助你預測可能出現的反對意見，並加以回應。

▶ **Although some readers may object that _____, I would answer that _____.**

雖然有些讀者可能會反對說_____，我的回答是_____。

總結論點

下列方法是用來總結你的論點，把先前提到的各種次要論點做一個總整理。

▶ **In sum, then, _____.**

因此，總而言之，_____。

▶ **My conclusion, then, is that _____.**

因此，我的結論是_____。

▶ **In short, _____.**

簡言之，_____。

> 參考第 **6** 堂更多用來預測反對意見的範本。

本堂課告訴各位，最有力的寫作要常反思評論自己的論點，以幫助讀者思索並消化這些論點。寫作高手，不能只將論點一一堆疊，而要「精心策畫」如何呈現每個論點，好讓讀者順利吸收。的確，論文要有說服力，必須提出堅實的論點。但是，再有力的論點也可能鋪陳不易，還是得靠寫作者運用後設評論來避免讀者誤解，才能將論證寫得精采出色。

練習

1. 閱讀一篇論文或文章，找出作者用哪些不同方式表現後設評論。利用本堂課範本作為指引。例如說，你可以圈出轉接語，並且在旁邊空白處寫上「轉」（trans）；用方括弧標示出詳細說明前面句子的語句（elaboration），並且標註為「詳」（elab）；把總結論點（sum up）的句子劃上底線，標註為「總」（sum）。

   作者是如何運用後設評論的？他有沒有一字不差地遵循本書所提出的範本呢？你有沒有發現其他本課沒提到的後設評論形式？如果有的話，你能將它們辨識出來、說出是什麼樣的手法，或者以之為基礎發展出新的範本，以備將來寫作之用嗎？最後，你認為作者所運用的後設評論，對他的寫作產生什麼樣的加分（或扣分）效果呢？

2. 在以下空格處填入文字，完成下列的後設評論範本。

   ▶ **In making a case for the medical use of marijuana, I am not saying that**

   _____.

   我支持大麻用於醫療用途，意思並不是說_____。

▶ But my argument will do more than prove that one particular industrial chemical has certain toxic properties. In this article, I will also _____.

但是我的論點不只是要證明某個特定的工業化學物質具有毒性，我也將 _____。

▶ My point about the national obsessions with sports reinforces the belief held by many _____ that _____.

我所提出關於全民瘋運動的論點，可以印證許多_____所持的想法，也就是_____。

▶ I believe, therefore, that the war is completely unjustified. But let me back up and explain how I arrived at this conclusion: _____. In this way, I came to believe that this war is a big mistake.

因此我相信這場戰爭毫無道理可言。但是請容我回過頭去，重新解釋我是如何得到這個結論的： _____。因為這樣，我才相信這場戰爭是一大錯誤。

第 11 堂　運用範本修改文稿

"He says ~~says~~ contends"

「他說堅稱」

　　寫作過程中最重要的步驟之一就是修改。你得閱讀初稿，檢查自己的論述是否充分，並且看看還有哪些地方需要改進。修改難處在於，要找出哪裡需要修改，以及到底該怎麼修改。

　　有時候，指導教授會給你明確的評語和建議，比方說，你的立場要更明確一點、你的論點不夠清楚、或是你做的概述誤解了原作者等等。但是，假如沒有人從旁指導，或者你並不知道該怎麼改，該怎麼辦呢？下面列有一些指引，帶你回顧本書的建議和相關範本，協助你檢查並修改自己的寫作。

　　你有沒有針對別人的言論，用自己的論點作為回應呢？除了自己的論點之外，有沒有提到別人的論點呢？你有沒有使用發言標記，讓讀者能清楚區別你的論點和他人論點呢？為了讓你的論點具有說服力，是否運用了「對，但是……」範本，對一些反論稍做讓步呢？

　　問問自己這些大的架構問題，可以知道，本書核心「人們說／我說」的架構是否已運用得很好，也可以發覺需要進一步修改的地方。以下依照本書順序，列出各項檢查清單。

你有沒有好好提出別人的看法？

■ 文章起頭，你是否有先提出他人的論點？沒有的話就朝此方向修改。可參考本書第 34-36 頁的範本。

■ 你是否有概述或轉述他人的看法？如果是的話，有沒有正確且充分地呈現他們的觀點？

■ 你是否引述了別人的話？有沒有將每段引述置放在妥善的位置，與本文整合？這段引述是否能支持你的論點？每一段引述是否做了適度解釋，並寫明出自何人（並說明其身分）？你是否有用自己的話解釋這段引述的意義呢？是否有寫明這段引述和你的論點之間有何關聯？可參考本書第 55-57 頁關於製作「引述三明治」的訣竅。

■ 檢查你用了什麼動詞來作概述引述，這些動詞是否精確表達出原作者者的意思？假如你用的是中性的示意動詞，如 X "said" 或 Y "believes"，有沒有其他動詞可以更精確地反映出原文的意思？請參考本書第 50-51 頁，可用來作概述和引述的動詞。

■ 所有的概述和引述內容是否都有註明文獻出處？有沒有在正文中說明資料來源，並且提供參考文獻列表？

■ 是否有在全文中時時提醒讀者，哪些是他人論點呢？如果沒有的話，請參考本書第 39-40 頁進行修改。

你自己的看法是什麼？

- 對於你所回應的他人論點，你是同意、反對，抑或是既同意也反對？你有沒有明確表態？

- 假如你是持反對意見，是否有提出反對的理由？假如你是持贊同意見，你補充了什麼論證？假如你是部分同意、部分反對，有沒有讓讀者一目了然，還是含糊其辭？

- 你有沒有把自己的立場和所回應的立場整合在一起呢？

- 針對你自己的立場，也就是「我說」（I say）的部分，你用哪些理由和證據作為支持？你的論點和你所回應的論點（they say），所探討的是否為同一主題或議題？還是說其中有所轉折，導致你已經離題，而讓讀者看得一頭霧水呢？

- 有一個方法可以確保你的論點和他人論點密切配合，而不是像兩個擦肩而過的陌生人，就是兩者要使用相同的主要詞彙。請參考第八堂所提供的訣竅。

- 讀者是否可以區別出你的和他人的說法？請參考第五堂，使用發言標記清楚區隔出你和別人的說法，尤其當你正在兩方說法之間來回切換時。

你是否加入了反對者的意見？

- 你是否預期自己的論點可能會遭遇到反對？如果是，你是否公平客觀地說明了可能的反對論點，並且有力地回應呢？請參考第六堂所提供的技巧。如果沒有的話，請思考，對你的主題還有哪些不同的觀點存在，並把它們納入你的文中。

你是否運用後設評論澄清意思？

- 不管你自認論點已說明得多麼清楚，都建議再用「換言之」（in other words）或「別誤解我的意思」（don't get me wrong），來補充說明你的本意是什麼，或不是什麼。請參考第十堂的範例說明。

- 你的論文有沒有題目？有的話，這個題目是否能讓讀者明白你的主要論點或議題？它的表現方式活不活潑？是否該加上副標題來補充說明呢？

你的文章是否連貫？

- 你的句子、段落之間語意是否連貫，好讓讀者能看懂你的論點、明白每個連續的論點如何支持你的整體論述呢？

- 檢查所使用的轉接語，像是 however 和 therefore，這類字詞是用來釐清觀點之間的關係。假如你需要使用轉接語，可參考本書第 121-123 頁的完整列表。

- 檢查所使用的指示詞。你是否運用了常見的指示詞如 this 和 that，引導讀者從一個句子前往下一個句子呢？如果有的話，this 和 that 所指涉的對象是否清楚呢？或者你需要在後面加上名詞以免混淆呢？請參考本書第 125-126 頁關於使用指示詞的說明。

- 你是否運用了我們所謂的「重述你的說法 —— 但稍作變化」的技巧，來連結論點的各個部分呢？請參考本書第 130-131 頁的範例說明。

你有沒有說明你的論點何以重要？

■ 切勿假設讀者自會明白你的論點為何重要，或者自會明白他們為什麼該關心你的論點。請確認向他們說清楚。可參考第七堂的說明。

一篇修改過的學生論文

　　以下將提供一篇範例文章，各位會看到一位叫安東妮雅・皮蔻克（Antonia Peacocke）的學生運用本書的建議修正論文。原文是皮蔻克在高中校刊上面所發表，她依照本書的建議修改之後，便成為一篇大學程度的學術論述。皮蔻克的原文旨在介紹自己喜歡的卡通影集《蓋酷家庭》（*Family Guy*）的原因。修改時，她簡明扼要以「他人論點」開頭，再帶入「自己論點」，開宗明義表明她的整體主張。儘管她在原本的版本中承認許多人對這部卡通感到「反感」，卻沒有說出這些人的名字，也沒有說明他們反感的理由。在修正版中，皮蔻克做了進一步的調查，指出了她不認同的是哪些人，並且充分予以回應。

　　除此之外，皮蔻克加強了原文中的轉接語，更增加了一些轉接語，並闡明了自己論點的重要性。此外，更具體說明《蓋酷家庭》的是非好壞為何值得關心。皮蔻克運用並修改本書好幾個範本，表現出自己的風格。

　　我們在她的論文旁邊加上註解，標出所用到的範本在本書出現的章節。透過她的論文和我們的註解，各位會更清楚知道，可以用什麼方式來撰寫並修改論文。

Family Guy and Freud: Jokes and Their Relation to the Unconscious

Antonia Peacocke

While slouching in front of the television after a long day, you probably don't think a lot about famous psychologists of the twentieth century. Somehow, these figures don't come up often in prime-time—or even daytime—TV programming. Whether you're watching *Living Lohan* or the *NewsHour*, the likelihood is that you are not thinking of Sigmund Freud, even if you've heard of his book *Jokes and Their Relation to the Unconscious*. I say that you should be.

What made me think of Freud in the first place, actually, was *Family Guy*, the cartoon created by Seth MacFarlane. (Seriously—stay with me here.) Any of my friends can tell you that this program holds endless fascination for me; as a matter

Antonia Peacocke 安東妮雅・皮蔻克

　　這篇論文是皮蔻克高中畢業之後、進入哈佛之前的那年暑假所寫的，她目前是加州大學柏克萊分校（University of California at Berkeley）哲學系的博士生。

聽聽別人怎麼說（第 1 堂）

回應他們說的話（第 4 堂）

of fact, my high school rag-sheet "perfect mate" was the baby Stewie Griffin, a character on the show. Embarrassingly enough, I have almost reached the point at which I can perform one-woman versions of several episodes I know every website that streams the show for free, and I still refuse to return the five *Family Guy* DVDs a friend lent me in 2006. Before I was such a devotee, however, I was adamantly opposed to the program for its particular brand of humor.

It will come as no surprise that I was not alone in this view; many still denounce *Family Guy* as bigoted and crude. *New York Times* journalist Stuart Elliott claimed just this year that "the characters on the Fox television series *Family Guy*... purposely offen[d] just about every group of people you could name." Likewise Stephen Dubner, co-author of *Freakonomics*, called *Family Guy* "a cartoon comedy that packs more gags per minute about race, sex, incest, bestiality, etc. than any other show [he] can think of." Comparing its level of offense to that of Don Imus's infamous comments about the Rutgers women's basketball team in the same year, comments that threw the popular CBS radio talk-show host off the air, Dubner said he wondered why Imus couldn't get away with as much as *Family Guy* could.

Dubner did not know about all the trouble *Family Guy* has had. In fact, it must be one of the few television shows in history that has been canceled not just once, but twice. After its premiere in April 1999, the show ran until August 2000, but was besieged by so many complaints, some of them from MacFarlane's old high school headmaster, Rev. Richardson W. Schell, that Fox shelved it until July 2001 (Weinraub). Still afraid of causing a commotion, though, Fox had the cartoon censored and irregularly scheduled; as a result, its ratings fell so low that 2002 saw

採用後設評論避免可能的懷疑（第 **10** 堂）

引述和概述別人的話（第 **2**、**3** 堂）

its second cancellation (Weinraub). But then it came back with a vengeance—I'll get into that later.

Family Guy has found trouble more recently, too. In 2007, comedian Carol Burnett sued Fox for 6 million dollars, claiming that the show's parody of the Charwoman, a character that she had created for *The Carol Burnett Show*, not only violated copyright but also besmirched the character's name in revenge for Burnett's refusal to grant permission to use her theme song ("Carol Burnett Sues over *Family Guy* Parody"). The suit came after MacFarlane had made the Charwoman into a cleaning woman for a pornography store in one episode of *Family Guy*. Burnett lost, but U.S. district judge Dean Pregerson agreed that he could "fully appreciate how distasteful and offensive the segment [was] to Ms. Burnett" (qtd. in Grossberg).

I must admit, I can see how parts of the show might seem offensive if taken at face value. Look, for example, at the mock fifties instructional video that features in the episode "I Am Peter, Hear Me Roar."

[*The screen becomes black and white. Vapid music plays in the background. The screen reads "WOMEN IN THE WORKPLACE ca. 1956," then switches to a shot of an office with various women working on typewriters. A businessman speaks to the camera.*]

BUSINESSMAN : Irrational and emotionally fragile by nature, female coworkers are a peculiar animal. They are very insecure about their appearance. Be sure to tell them how good they look every day, even if they're

公正持平呈現反對觀點（第 6 堂）

homely and unkempt. [*He turns to an unattractive female typist.*] You're doing a great job, Muriel, and you're prettier than Mamie van Doren! [*She smiles. He grins at the camera, raising one eyebrow knowingly, and winks.*]

And remember, nothing says "Good job!" like a firm open-palm slap on the behind. [*He walks past a woman bent over a file cabinet and demonstrates enthusiastically. She smiles, looking flattered. He grins at the camera again as the music comes to an end.*]

Laughing at something so blatantly sexist could cause anyone a pang of guilt, and before I thought more about the show this seemed to be a huge problem. I agreed with Dubner, and I failed to see how anyone could laugh at such jokes without feeling at least slightly ashamed.

Soon, though, I found myself forced to give *Family Guy* a chance. It was simply everywhere: my brother and many of my friends watched it religiously, and its devoted fans relentlessly proselytized for it. In case you have any doubts about its immense popularity, consider these facts. On Facebook, the universal forum for my generation, there are currently 23 separate *Family Guy* fan groups with a combined membership of 1,669 people (compared with only 6 groups protesting against *Family Guy*, with 105 members total). Users of the well-respected Internet Movie Database rate the show 8.8 out of 10. The box-set DVDs were the best-selling television DVDs of 2003 in the United States (Moloney). Among the public and within the industry, the show receives fantastic acclaim; it has won eight awards,

表達同意，但補充其他看法（第 **4** 堂）

預測反對者可能的懷疑（第 **6** 堂）

including three primetime Emmys (IMDb). Most importantly, each time it was cancelled fans provided the brute force necessary to get it back on the air. In 2000, online campaigns did the trick; in 2002, devotees demonstrated outside Fox Studios, refused to watch the Fox network, and boycotted any companies that advertised on it (Moloney). Given the show's high profile, both with my friends and family and in the world at large, it would have been more work for me to avoid the Griffin family than to let myself sink into their animated world.

With more exposure, I found myself crafting a more positive view of *Family Guy*. Those who don't often watch the program, as Dubner admits he doesn't, could easily come to think that the cartoon takes pleasure in controversial humor just for its own sake. But those who pay more attention and think about the creators' intentions can see that *Family Guy* intelligently satirizes some aspects of American culture.

Some of this satire is actually quite obvious. Take, for instance, a quip Brian the dog makes about Stewie's literary choices in a fourth-season episode, "PTV." (Never mind that a dog and a baby can both read and hold lengthy conversations.)

[*The Griffins are in their car. Brian turns to Stewie, who sits reading in his car seat.*]

BRIAN: *East of Eden*? So you, you, you pretty much do whatever Oprah tells you to, huh?
STEWIE: You know, this book's been around for fifty years. It's a classic.

利用「引述三明治」引述對話（第 **3** 堂）　　區分他人和自己的言論（第 **5** 堂）

學術和口語風格並用（第 **9** 堂）

BRIAN: But you just got it last week. And there's a giant Oprah sticker on the front.

STEWIE: Oh—oh—oh, is that what that is? Oh, lemme just peel that right off,

BRIAN: So, uh, what are you gonna read after that one?

STEWIE: Well, she hasn't told us yet—damn!

Brian and Stewie demonstrate insightfully and comically how Americans are willing to follow the instructions of a celebrity blindly—and less willing to admit that they are doing so.

The more off-color jokes, though, those that give *Family Guy* a bad name, attract a different kind of viewer. Such viewers are not "rats in a behaviorist's maze," as *Slate* writer Dana Stevens labels modern American television consumers in her article "Thinking Outside the Idiot Box." They are conscious and critical viewers, akin to the "screenagers" identified by Douglas Rushkoff in an essay entitled "Bart Simpson: Prince of Irreverence" (294). They are not—and this I cannot stress enough, self-serving as it may seem—immoral or easily manipulated people.

Rushkoff's piece analyzes the humor of *The Simpsons*, a show criticized for many of the same reasons as *Family Guy*. "The people I call 'screenagers,'" Rushkoff explains, "... speak the media language better than their parents do and they see through clumsy attempts to program them into submission" (294). He claims that gaming technology has made my generation realize that television is programmed for us with certain intentions; since we can control characters in the virtual world, we are more aware that characters on TV are similarly controlled.

區分他人和自己的言論（第 5 堂）

"Sure, [these 'screenagers'] might sit back and watch a program now and again," Rushkoff explains, "but they do so voluntarily, and with full knowledge of their complicity. It is not an involuntary surrender" (294). In his opinion, our critical eyes and our unwillingness to be programmed by the programmers make for an entirely new relationship with the shows we watch. Thus we enjoy *The Simpsons*' parodies of mass media culture since we are skeptical of it ourselves.

Rushkoff's argument about *The Simpsons* actually applies to *Family Guy* as well, except in one dimension: Rushkoff writes that *The Simpsons*' creators do "not comment on social issues as much as they [do on] the media imagery around a particular social issue" (296). MacFarlane and company seem to do the reverse. Trusting in their viewers' ability to analyze what they are watching, the creators of *Family Guy* point out the weaknesses and defects of U.S. society in a mocking and sometimes intolerant way.

Taken in this light, the "instructional video" quoted above becomes not only funny but also insightful. In its satire, viewers can recognize the sickly sweet and falsely sensitive sexism of the 1950s in observing just how conveniently self-serving the speaker of the video appears. The message of the clip denounces and ridicules sexism rather than condoning it. It is an excerpt that perfectly exemplifies the bold-faced candor of the show, from which it derives a lot of its appeal.

Making such comically outrageous remarks on the air also serves to expose certain prejudiced attitudes as outrageous themselves. Taking these comments at face value would be as foolish as taking Jonathan Swift's "Modest Proposal" seriously. Furthermore, while they put bigoted words into the mouths of their

用轉接語銜接句子（第 **8** 堂）

characters, the show's writers cannot be accused of portraying these characters positively. Peter Griffin, the "family guy" of the show's title, probably says and does the most offensive things of all—but as a lazy, overweight, and insensitive failure of a man, he is hardly presented as someone to admire. Nobody in his or her right mind would observe Peter's behavior and deem it worth emulation.

Family Guy has its own responses to accusations of crudity. In the episode "PTV," Peter sets up his own television station broadcasting from home and the Griffin family finds itself confronting the Federal Communications Commission directly. The episode makes many tongue-in-cheek jabs at the FCC, some of which are sung in a rousing musical number, but also sneaks in some of the creator's own opinions. The plot comes to a climax when the FCC begins to censor "real life" in the town of Quahog; officials place black censor bars in front of newly showered Griffins and blow foghorns whenever characters curse. MacFarlane makes an important point: that no amount of television censorship will ever change the harsh nature of reality—and to censor reality is mere folly. Likewise, he puts explicit arguments about censorship into lines spoken by his characters, as when Brian says that "responsibility lies with the parents [and] there are plenty of things that are much worse for children than television."

It must be said too that not all of *Family Guy*'s humor could be construed as offensive. Some of its jokes are more tame and insightful, the kind you might expect from the *New Yorker*. The following light commentary on the usefulness of high school algebra from "When You Wish Upon a Weinstein" could hardly be accused of upsetting anyone—except, perhaps, a few high school math teachers.

[*Shot of Peter on the couch and his son Chris lying at his feet and doing homework.*]

CHRIS: Dad, can you help me with my math? [My teacher] says if I don't learn it, I won't be able to function in the real world.

[*Shot of Chris standing holding a map in a run-down gas station next to an attendant in overalls and a trucker cap reading "PUMP THIS." The attendant speaks with a Southern accent and gestures casually to show the different road configurations.*]

ATTENDANT: Okay, now what you gotta do is go down the road past the old Johnson place, and you're gonna find two roads, one parallel and one perpendicular. Now keep going until you come to a highway that bisects it at a 45-degree angle. [*Crosses his arms.*] Solve for x.

[*Shot of Chris lying on the ground next to the attendant in fetal position, sucking his thumb. His map lies abandoned near him.*]

In fact, *Family Guy* does not aim to hurt, and its creators take certain measures to keep it from hitting too hard. In an interview on *Access Hollywood*, Seth MacFarlane plainly states that there are certain jokes too upsetting to certain groups to go on the air. Similarly, to ensure that the easily misunderstood show doesn't fall

用轉接語銜接句子（第 8 堂）

into the hands of those too young to understand it, Fox will not license *Family Guy* rights to any products intended for children under the age of fourteen (Elliott).

However, this is not to say that MacFarlane's mission is corrective or noble. It is worth remembering that he wants only to amuse, a goal for which he was criticized by several of his professors at the Rhode Island School of Design (Weinraub). For this reason, his humor can be dangerous. On the one hand, I don't agree with George Will's reductive and generalized statement in his article "Reality Television: Oxymoron" that "entertainment seeking a mass audience is ratcheting up the violence, sexuality, and degradation, becoming increasingly coarse and trying to be... shocking in an unshockable society." I believe *Family Guy* has its intelligent points, and some of its seemingly "coarse" scenes often have hidden merit. I must concede, though, that a few of the show's scenes seem to be doing just what Will claims; sometimes the creators do seem to cross—or, perhaps, eagerly race past—the line of indecency. In one such crude scene, an elderly dog slowly races a paraplegic and Peter, who has just been hit by a car, to get to a severed finger belonging to Peter himself ("Whistle While Your Wife Works"). Nor do I find it particularly funny when Stewie physically abuses Brian in a bloody fight over gambling money ("Patriot Games").

Thus, while *Family Guy* can provide a sort of relief by breaking down taboos, we must still wonder whether or not these taboos exist for a reason. An excess of offensive jokes, especially those that are often misconstrued, can seem to grant tacit permission to think offensively if it's done for comedy—and laughing at others' expense can be cruel, no matter how funny. Jokes all have their origins, and the

表示部分同意、部分反對，一方面堅守立場，一方面有所退讓（第 **4**、**6** 堂）

總結文章：說明誰應關心其論點，以及論點為何重要（第 **7** 堂）

funniest ones are those that hit home the hardest; if we listen to Freud, these are the ones that let our animalistic and aggressive impulses surface from the unconscious. The distinction between a shamelessly candid but insightful joke and a merely shameless joke is a slight but important one. While I love *Family Guy* as much as any fan, it's important not to lose sight of what's truly unfunny in real life—even as we appreciate what is hilarious in fiction.

Works Cited

"Carol Burnett Sues over *Family Guy* Parody." CBC, 16 Mar. 2007. ww.cbc.ca/news/entertainment/carol-burnett-sues-over-family-guy-parody-1.693570. Accessed 14 July 2008.

Dubner, Stephen J. "Why Is *Family Guy* Okay When Imus Wasn't?" *Freakonomics Blog*, 3 Dec. 2007, freakonomics.com. Accessed 14 July 2008.

Elliott, Stuart. "Crude? So What? These Characters Still Find Work in Ads.*" New York Times*, 19 June 2008, nyti.ms/2bZWSAs. Accessed 14 July 2008.

Facebook search for *Family Guy* under "Groups." www.facebook.com. Accessed 14 July 2008.

Freud, Sigmund. *Jokes and Their Relation to the Unconscious*. 1905. Translated by James Strachey, W. W. Norton, 1989.

Grossberg, Josh. "Carol Burnett Can't Stop Stewie." *E! News*, Entertainment Television, 5 June 2007, www.eonline.com. Accessed 14 July 2008.

"I Am Peter, Hear Me Roar." *Family Guy*, season 2, episode 8, 20th Century Fox, 28 Mar. 2000. *Hulu*, www.hulu.com/watch/171050. Accessed 14 July 2008.

"Family Guy." *IMDb*, IMDb, 1999-2016, www.imdb.com/title/tt0182576. Accessed 14 July 2008.

MacFarlane, Seth. Interview. *Access Hollywood*, NBC Universal, 8 May 2007. *YouTube*, www.youtube.com/watch?v=rKURWCicyQU. Accessed 14 July 2008.

Moloney, Ben Adam. "*Family Guy*." *BBC.com*, 30 Sept. 2004. www.bbc.com. Accessed 14 July 2008.

"Patriot Games." *Family Guy*, season 4, episode 20, 20th Century Fox, 29 Jan. 2006. *Hulu*, www.hulu.com/watch/171089. Accessed 22 July 2008.

"PTV." *Family Guy*, season 1, episode 14, 20th Century Fox, 6 Nov. 2005. *Hulu*, www.hulu.com/watch/171083. Accessed 14 July 2008.

Rushkoff, Douglas. "Bart Simpson: Prince of Irreverence." *Leaving Springfield: The Simpsons and the Possibility of Oppositional Culture*, edited by John Alberti, Wayne State UP, 2004, pp. 292–301.

Stevens, Dana. "Thinking Outside the Idiot Box." *Slate*, 25 Mar. 2005, www.slate.com/articles/news_and_politics/surfergirl/2005/04/thinkingoutside_the_idiot_box.html. Accessed 14 July 2008.

Weinraub, Bernard. "The Young Guy of 'Family Guy': A 30-Year-Old's Cartoon Hit Makes an Unexpected Comeback." *New York Times*, 7 July 2004, nyti.ms/1lEBiUA. Accessed 14 July 2008.

"When You Wish Upon a Weinstein." *Family Guy*, season 3, episode 22, 20th Century Fox, 9 Nov. 2006. *Hulu*, www.hulu.com/watch/171136. Accessed 22 July 2008.

"Whistle While Your Wife Works." *Family Guy*, season 5, episode 5, 20th Century Fox, 12 Nov. 2008. *Hulu*, www.hulu.com/watch/171160. Accessed 14 July 2008.

Will, George F. "Reality Television: Oxymoron." *Washington Post*, 21 June 2001, p. A25.

《蓋酷家庭》與佛洛伊德：
《笑話及其與潛意識之關係》

漫長的一天過去，你窩在電視前面，大概不怎麼會想到二十世紀的心理學大師們。不知怎地，這些大師不常出現在黃金時段 —— 甚至白天時段 —— 的電視節目裡。不管你正在看《蘿涵實境秀》還是《新聞一小時》，你都不太可能聯想到佛洛伊德，就算你有聽過他的著作《笑話及其與潛意識之關係》也是一樣。我覺得你應該要想一下。

事實上，第一個讓我想起佛洛伊德的是賽斯‧麥克法蘭製作的卡通《蓋酷家庭》。（我是講真的，請聽我慢慢道來。）問我朋友就知道，他們隨便一個都會跟你說，這節目對我真是魅力無窮。事實上，劇中小嬰兒葛屁可是我高中的「完美伴侶」。說起來真有點不好意思，但我對這齣影集的瘋狂程度，幾乎到了我可以單獨一人將好幾集的內容全部演出來的地步。我對所有免費播放這齣影集的網站瞭若指掌。一位朋友在 2006 年借我的五片 DVD，我到現在都不肯歸還。然而，在我成為這樣一個迷妹之前，我曾對這齣影集極度抗拒，原因是它獨特的幽默。

有這種態度的人可不只我一個，這絕不令人意外。許多人到現在依舊譴責《蓋酷家庭》是粗俗難耐的影集。就在今年，《紐約時報》記者史都華‧艾略特（Stuart Elliott）指出：「福斯的電視影集《蓋酷家庭》裡面的角色……故意冒犯了差不多你想得到的任何一類人」。《蘋果橘子經濟學》的作者之一，史蒂芬‧杜伯納（Stephen Dubner）也稱《蓋酷家庭》這部卡通「每一分鐘都在拿種族、性別、亂倫、人獸交等話題開玩笑，其程度超過任何其他節目」。杜伯納納悶，《蓋酷家庭》節目中大肆冒犯社會各族群，不受譴責，但同年一度當紅的 CBS 廣播節目主持人唐‧伊姆斯（Don Imus）對羅格斯大學女籃隊做了不當評論，結果節目遭到停播，無法像《蓋酷家庭》那樣輕易脫身。

杜伯納並不知道，《蓋酷家庭》可是把各種麻煩都給惹遍了。它被停播不只一次而是兩次，這種例子史上少有。《蓋酷家庭》自 1999 年 4 月開播至 2000 年 8 月的期間，觀眾怨聲載道；其中麥克法蘭就讀的高中校長理查森‧謝爾神父的抗議，導致福斯公司停播《蓋酷家庭》，直到 2001 年 7 月才又恢復（資料來源：Weinraub）。只不過，福斯公司很怕又引起騷動，因而將節目送審，並且改為不定時播出。結果卻因收視率太低，導致 2004 年第二度停播（資料來源：Weinraub）。但是而後它捲土重來，我稍後會說明這個情況。

近幾年《蓋酷家庭》仍然爭議不斷。2007 年，喜劇演員卡蘿‧柏奈特控告福斯公司並求償六百萬美元，聲稱該節目惡搞她在《卡蘿‧柏奈特秀》裡面的清潔女工角色。《蓋酷家庭》某一集裡頭，麥克法蘭將這清潔女工變成色情書店店員。這不僅侵犯原節目的著作權，也敗壞該角色的名聲，原因是《蓋酷家庭》為了報復柏奈特拒絕授權使用主題曲（資料來源：Grossberg）。這起訴訟雖然柏奈特並未勝訴，但是美國地方法官迪恩‧普雷格森說，他可以「完全體會柏奈特女士對這段節目有多麼反感與不舒服」（資料來源：Grossberg）。

我必須承認，如果就其表面來看的話，這個節目的某些橋段的確是很粗鄙。比方說，在〈我是彼德，聽我咆哮〉一集裡，有一段模仿五〇年代的教學影片：

（螢幕轉為黑白畫面，播放著乏味的背景音樂，螢幕上寫著「工作場所中的女性，約末為 1956 年」。接著畫面帶到一間辦公室，有好幾名女性正在打字。一位企業家對著攝影機說話。）

企業家：女性同事真是種奇特的動物，她們生性就不講理，又很玻璃心。她們對外貌超沒安全感，就算她們長得很抱歉又不打扮，你還是得每天稱讚她們太美了。

（他面朝一位其貌不揚的女打字員。）

妙瑞兒，你做得真是太好了，而且你比瑪咪·范多倫還要美啊！

（她微笑了。企業家對著鏡頭咧嘴一笑，挑了眉，一副「你看吧」，還使了個眼色。）

而且要記得，要讚美她們「做得好！」，最好就是紮紮實實地拍一下屁股了。

（他經過一名彎腰趴在檔案櫃上的女子，熱情滿滿地示範一次。女子微笑著，一臉受寵若驚。企業家再度對著鏡頭咧嘴一笑，背景音樂終止。）

要是看了這段性別歧視的露骨演出，還笑得出來的人，肯定會被唾棄。在深入思考這部影集之前，我也覺得是很嚴重的問題。我同意杜伯納的看法，我實在不明白有誰會因這種笑話發笑，而且絲毫不覺得可恥。

然而沒過多久，我就不得不重新審視這個影集，給它一次平反的機會。當時我身邊的人都在瘋迷《蓋酷家庭》。我的兄弟和好多朋友都會固定收看，這群忠實影迷不斷地宣揚它有多好看，叫你也一起加入。如果你對它的火紅程度懷疑的話，請看看下面的這些資料。以當代全球論壇臉書為例，目前共有23個《蓋酷家庭》的粉絲專頁，粉絲共有 1669 人（相比之下，反《蓋酷家庭》的粉絲專頁只有 6 個，粉絲共 105 人）。備受推崇的網路電影資料庫的用戶滿分 10 分給了它 8.8 的評分。其套裝 DVD 名列全美 2003 年最暢銷的電視 DVD（資料來源：Moloney）。不管是民眾還是業界都對它讚譽有加；它八度獲獎，其中包含三次黃金時段艾美獎（資料來源：IMDb）。最關鍵的來了，每次一停播都會引發粉絲力爭，迫使節目復播。2000 年的網路聯合運動奏效；2002 年，影迷齊聚在福斯公司門口示威，表示要拒看福斯電視網的節目，而且凡是福斯播出的廣告商品，他們一律抵制拒買（資料來源：莫隆尼）。以《蓋酷家庭》如此備受矚目，舉凡我的親朋好友乃至於全世界都在關注，要我抗拒葛里芬家族的魅力，倒不如投身其中。

我接觸得越多，發現自己對《蓋酷家庭》的觀感逐漸轉向正面。那些不常收看節目的人，像杜伯納自己就承認不常看，很容易認為該節目純粹出於私利，製作一些爭議性幽默。但如果你稍加注意，想想製作者的用意，就會明白《蓋酷家庭》是發揮機智去諷刺美國文化的一些層面。

有些諷刺很明顯，例如在第四季的〈PTV〉這一集裡，狗狗來西對於葛屁選擇文學讀物的方式發表了一串妙語。（先別管狗狗和小嬰兒為什麼都會說話，而且還對話連連。）

（葛家一家子坐在車內，來西轉朝坐在汽車座椅上看書的葛屁。）

來西：《伊甸之東》？你，你，你，該不會歐普拉說什麼你就做什麼唄？

葛屁：嘿，這本書大概有五十年了，是經典呢。

來西：可是你上個禮拜才買的，封面還貼了大大的歐普拉貼紙。

葛屁：喔，喔，喔，有嗎？喔，我馬上撕了它。

來西：那你接下來還要看哪一本書？

葛屁：這個嘛，她還沒有說耶 —— X 的！

來西和葛屁用其獨到但搞笑的方式，點出美國人盲從影視名人的程度 ——

而且還死不承認。

　　然而，有一些令《蓋酷家庭》染上惡名的低級笑話，吸引的是一群特殊觀眾。這類觀眾並不是「行為主義迷宮裡的老鼠」，這個詞彙是《石板》雜誌作家黛娜・史蒂文斯（Dana Stevens）用在其〈跳脫白癡的框架思考〉一文中，所指的現代一般美國電視觀眾。相反地，他們是有意識、善於思辨的觀眾，類似道格拉斯・羅許寇夫（Douglas Rushkoff）在其〈霸子・辛普森：沒禮貌大王〉論文中所說的「螢幕世代」（頁 294）。我這麼說即使有點偏私之嫌，但他們並不是道德淪喪、容易被操縱的人。

　　羅許寇夫在這篇論文中分析了《辛普森家庭》裡的幽默，這個節目被抨擊的許多原因和《蓋酷家庭》是一樣的。羅許寇夫解釋說：「我稱之為『螢幕世代』的這些人……對媒體語言的掌握遠勝過他們父母那一輩，任何想愚弄欺瞞他們的拙劣手法都會被識破。（頁 294）」他主張，電玩科技讓我們這個世代明白，電視節目是出於某些目的而設計出來給我們看的；既然我們可以控制虛擬世界的人物，自然更可以意識到電視角色也受到類似的控制。羅許寇夫繼續解釋：「當然，這些『螢幕世代』可能偶爾會坐下來看個電視節目，但是他們是出於主動才這麼做，也完全知道自己觀賞的立場，而不是被動地任其擺布。（頁 294）」以他的觀點來看，我們帶著審慎的眼光，不願任憑節目製作人操縱；我們已經和節目之間建立起一種全新的關係。因此，我們喜歡看《辛普森家庭》惡搞大眾媒體文化，因為連我們自己都對其抱持懷疑的態度。

　　羅許寇夫對《辛普森家庭》的論點其實也適用於《蓋酷家庭》，唯有一項差異：羅許寇夫說，《辛普森家庭》的製作者「對社會議題的直接評斷較少，對相關的媒體意象評斷較多（頁 296）」。麥克法蘭製作群作法似乎恰好相反。《蓋酷家庭》製作者相信觀眾有能力分析自己在看什麼，於是他們用嘲弄或是毫不留情的方式，指出美國社會的弱點和缺失。

如果以這種觀點來看，我們前面引用的「教學影片」就不只是搞笑，而是富有洞見了。在《蓋酷家庭》的嘲諷中，觀眾透過劇中人如何隨時趁機取利，就可以看穿五〇年代那種病態的甜蜜，以及虛偽敏感的性別主義。這段影片所要傳達的訊息是對性別歧視的譴責和揶揄，而非姑息，並在以上橋段中粗鄙地表達出來，而這就是其魅力所在。

　　透過影集用詼諧而粗鄙的評論，正好可以揭發某些同樣粗鄙的態度。如果只看了這些影集中的粗鄙言論的表面，就直接信以為真，就好像閱讀強納森・史威夫特（Jonathan Swift）〈一個小小的建議〉[1]一文時，只看文字表面意義一樣愚蠢。再者，既然編劇為劇中人物寫出充滿偏見的台詞，你就不能指責他們是在肯定這些角色。本影集英文片名「居家男人」（Family Guy）指的就是彼得（Peter Griffin），他差不多把所有瞎事做盡、瞎話說盡了。但是這麼一個懶惰、肥胖又遲鈍的失敗男人，絕不是編劇創造來讓人尊重的角色。只要是神智還清醒的人，都不會想仿效他的行為。

　　對於指其粗俗的控訴，《蓋酷家庭》也有所回應。在〈PTV〉一集當中，彼德在家裡安裝了自己的電視台播放系統，結果葛家就槓上了美國聯邦通訊委員會。這一集有很多情節都在挖苦美國聯邦通訊委員會，其中有些還是以激昂的歌曲唱出來的，而創作者也在其中加入了一些自己的看法。劇情的高潮是，美國聯邦通訊委員會要開始對他們居住的下港鎮進行「現實生活」審查。委員拿著黑色的審查板，等彼德一洗完澡就遮住他的正面，並且只要有人一飆粗口就鳴喇叭警告。這裡，麥克法蘭指出了很重要的一點：電視審查再怎麼執行，都改變不了現實生活的粗俗本質——更遑論審查現實生活這件事本身就是愚

1　譯註：強納森是十八世紀的愛爾蘭作家，其著作〈一個小小的建議〉大量運用反諷手法，針對當時英國對愛爾蘭的剝削進行揭露與批判。其中一句話充分代表了其作品精神：「將愛爾蘭十二萬嬰兒中的十萬嬰兒提供富家人士當成桌上佳餚」，該反諷暗示這樣做可以讓貧苦父母獲得解脫。

蠢。同樣地，他把審查制度的論點寫成台詞，由劇中角色口中說出，就像來西曾說的，「責任應該由家長承擔，況且對小孩子來說，比電視還糟糕的事情多得是」。

還有一點一定要提，並不是所有《蓋酷家庭》的幽默都是有意冒犯，有些笑話是溫和、具有深知灼見的，就像那些只在《紐約客》雜誌上才看得到的笑話。以下這段出自〈當你指望一個韋恩斯坦〉一集，評論高中代數沒什麼用處，這個橋段可以說沒有任何冒犯意味 —— 如果有，大概也是少數高中數學老師才感覺得到吧。

（鏡頭裡，彼德坐在沙發上，他的兒子葛馬藍躺在他腳邊做功課。）

葛馬藍：老爹，你幫我算數學好不好？老師說如果不好好學，我在社會上就沒法生活。

（鏡頭轉到葛馬藍手裡拿著地圖，站在一間破舊的加油站裡面，旁邊是一名身穿工作服的服務生，還有一頂卡車司機帽上面寫著「在這加油」。服務生操著一口南方腔，漫不經心地用手比劃著不同的道路走法。）

服務生：好的，現在你要做的事，就是沿著這條路走，經過老強森他家，然後會發現兩條路，一條是平行的，一條是垂直的。這時候你就繼續走，直到有一條公路以 45 度角把它切成兩半。（他把雙手交叉）求解 x 為何。

（鏡頭轉到葛馬藍以胎兒姿勢躺在服務生旁邊的地上，吸著大拇指，地圖被丟在一邊。）

事實上，《蓋酷家庭》並不想傷害任何人，創作者麥克法蘭採取一些措施，避免節目產生過於嚴重的影響。他接受新聞節目《走進好萊塢》訪問時，就說得很清楚，有些笑話不適合特定觀眾，因此只好捨棄不播。同樣地，為避免影響缺乏判斷能力的兒童接觸，福斯公司也不會把《蓋酷家庭》商標授權給十四歲以下兒童使用的商品（資料來源：Elliott）。

然而，這並不是說，麥克法蘭具有想矯正社會亂象的高尚使命感；提醒大家，他一心只以娛樂為目的，而這也使他飽受其母校羅德島設計學院幾名指導教授的抨擊（資料來源：Weinraub）。因此之故，他的幽默還是可能會造成危險。一方面，我並不認同喬治‧威爾在其〈真人實境秀：矛盾修辭法〉一文中所做的簡化而籠統的論述，他說：「娛樂表演為追求大量觀眾，充斥著越來越多的暴力、性愛、墮落，越來越粗俗，試圖……讓一個不會感到震驚的社會震驚。」我相信《蓋酷家庭》有其智慧所在，有些看似「粗鄙」的情節往往有其隱藏價值。然而我不得不承認，該節目的部分情節確實是威爾所說的那個樣子，有時候製作者的表現流於低級 —— 或者就是刻意想表現得很低級。其中有這樣沒水準的一幕：一隻行動緩慢的老狗、一位半身不遂人士，以及剛出車禍的彼德，這三人為了爭奪彼德的斷指而進行賽跑（〈當你的老婆工作時請吹口哨〉一集）。還有一幕，葛屁為了搶奪賭金，把來西揍得頭破血流，這我也不覺得有什麼好笑的（〈愛國者遊戲〉一集）。

因此，儘管《蓋酷家庭》以打破禁忌的方式，為我們提供了生活上的調劑，但我們仍須思考，這些禁忌的存在是否有其原因。過多不雅的笑話，尤其是那些扭曲事實的說法，有時會導致人們以為可以隨時像鬧劇一樣，用不雅方式思考。而且，不管再怎麼好笑，嘲笑別人的不幸就是殘忍的，最好笑的笑話，大概也是傷人最深的。照佛洛伊德的話來說，這些笑話就是把我們的動物衝動和攻擊衝動從潛意識裡顯露出來。一個低俗坦率卻具深知灼見的笑話，和一個純粹低俗的笑話之間僅一線之隔，然此差別卻至關重要。雖然我對《蓋酷家庭》的熱愛不亞於任何一位影迷，但是在我們欣賞虛構影片裡的滑稽之處時，也絕不能忽視那些在現實生活中絕對稱不上有趣的情況。

PART IV

In Specific
Academic Contexts
應用在其他學術領域

本部分說明如何參與不同學術領域的對話，
分別說明口頭討論、網路寫作、閱讀文本，
以及文學、科學、社會科學領域之論文寫作。

Entering Class Discussions

第 12 堂 參與口頭討論

"I take your point"

「我明白你的觀點」

　　參與口頭討論時，你是否曾有過這種感覺：大家不是真的在進行心智交流，倒像是人人滔滔不絕，各講各的、互不連貫？比方說，你提出了一個你覺得頗有見地的論點，但是接著發言的同學卻對此隻字不提，反而另起一個全新的話題。然後，接在他後面發言的同學，也沒有提到你或其他人，好似這場對話中的每個人，都只在乎自己的看法，完全不想要與他人討論。

　　在討論中越是能積極回應別人，我們的意見就越有力、越能讓人信服；再者，課堂討論不該只是建構自己的主張，更要能回應其他人的意見。說到這裡，一場優質的面對面討論（或線上交流）不可能自然產生，就跟寫作一樣，要週全的規劃及練習，以確定你是對誰回應、回應什麼論點。接下來將提出的原則，希望能改善課堂討論乃至各種線上交流的效果。

▋ 回應他人，再提出自己的論點

　　參與討論時最重要的一件事，就是將你所要發表的意見，連結到別人已提出的意見，如：

▶ I really liked Aaron's point about ＿＿＿＿＿. I'd add that ＿＿＿＿＿.

我很贊同亞倫所說，＿＿＿＿＿，我想補充的是，＿＿＿＿＿。

▶ I take your point, Nadia, that ＿＿＿＿＿. Still...

娜蒂雅，你說＿＿＿＿＿，我明白你的意思。不過……

▶ Though Sheila and Ryan seem to be at odds about ＿＿＿＿＿, they may actually not be all that far apart.

雖然席拉和萊恩對於＿＿＿＿＿似乎有不同的看法，他們其實沒有到截然不同的地步。

　　用這種方式論述的時候，最好能同時說出你所回應的人是誰，以及他的觀點是什麼。假如只說出人名（如：I agree with Aaron because ＿＿＿＿＿. 我同意亞倫的看法，因為＿＿＿＿＿。）大家或許並不清楚你指的是亞倫的哪一個看法。反之，假如你只概述亞倫的言論，卻沒有說出是誰講的，大家可能不知道你是說的是誰的論點。

　　然而，如果你在口頭討論時，把其他同學提到的觀點重複一遍，聽起來會不會嫌生硬冗長？畢竟以剛剛提到的第一個範本來看，全班同學剛剛才聽到亞倫說，雙方關係比表面上來得密切，你何必重複一遍？

　　我們同意，在一般交談的情況下，把別人才剛說過的話一字不漏重複一次，確實顯得不太自然，因為他們也才剛說而已。假如在吃午餐的時候，有人請你把鹽遞給他，你卻回答：「如果我的理解沒錯，你請我把鹽遞給你。好，沒問題，拿去吧。」這樣的確是很奇怪。然而，在討論複雜的議題時，因為會產生多種的解讀方式，我們有必要把別人的話大概重述一次，才能確定每個人的思考是一致的。再者，亞倫發言的時候可能提出了好幾個論點，在他後面也有別的同學發言，因此你可能要向全班同學大致說明，你指的是他的哪一點。

即使亞倫只有提出一個論點，重述一遍也有幫助，一方面提醒大家他的論點是什麼（畢竟可能有人沒聽到或忘記了），另一方面也是**確保你、亞倫和其他人，對他的論點解讀一致**。

轉換話題前，先作表明

要改變討論方向是可以的，唯須注意，要讓聽者知道你即將改變話題，例如：

▶ **So far we have been talking about _____. But isn't the real issue here _____?**
到目前為止，我們一直在討論_____。但是真正重點應是_____吧？

▶ **I'd like to change the subject to one that hasn't yet been addressed.**
我想要談一個尚未討論到的主題。

你可能會不做說明，就直接轉換話題。但這樣可能會讓聽者認為你離題，這樣的發言無助於討論進行。

要比寫作時表明得還清楚

口頭討論的時候，聽者無法回頭重讀一遍你說過的話，因此，比起文本的讀者，他們更容易產生記憶超載的情況。因此，口頭討論時，最好還是多花幾個步驟，幫助聽者跟上你的思路。(1) 發表意見的時候，**一次提出一個論點**就好，但可以把這個論點儘量敘述得詳盡一點，並且補充一些實例和證據。假如非得提出兩個論點不可，要不就是把它們整合在一個總論之下，要不就是先論述其一，另一個留待稍後再談。如果想將兩個以上的論點一次講出來，只會造成兩個都失焦。(2) **利用後設評論來強調重點**，好讓聽眾容易掌握。

▶ In other words, what I'm trying to get at here is _____.
　換言之，我所要說的是_____。

▶ My point is this: _____.
　我的論點是： _____。

▶ My point, though, is not _____, but _____.
　然而我的論點並不是_____，而是_____。

▶ This distinction is important because _____.
　這個差別非常重要，因為_____。

第 **13** 堂 網路交流是好是壞，抑或好壞參半？

"IMHO"
「個人淺見」

也許你會納悶，本書中關於學術對話的建議，和世上最重大的創新之一——網路科技——有什麼關聯。你大概聽過家長和記者們抱怨，說那些已經離不開我們生活的智慧手機、平板電腦等電子裝置，正在摧毀我們思考、溝通、與人互動的能力。同時你也聽過相反的論調，聲稱這些數位科技可以增進心智能力、加強人際溝通，甚至讓我們成為更好的寫作者。

以上論點，都是當今一系列有關於網路科技爭論的一部分。這些爭論有時出現在部落格圈（blogosphere），有時出現在新聞界、學術界、和其他論述中。爭論中，讚揚數位科技的人認為，今日的網路科技讓我們變得更聰明，因為我們得以廣泛接觸多元觀點，即時獲得大量的新資訊。從前我們得花上數小時，在滿是灰塵的圖書館架上翻來翻去，尋找我們所需要的資訊，而今我們只需要舒舒服服地待在家裡，滑鼠一點就可以獲得同樣的資訊。多虧了網路，我們的可能獲取的知識量比起以往增加了千萬倍。如此之進展對於任何一位寫作人士來說，何嘗不是一大利多？

然而批評者卻反駁，網路科技非但沒有讓我們更聰明，反而讓我們更笨，連我們的寫作能力都因而下降。根據這些批評者的說法，許多利用網路做研究的人，點進 Google 搜尋出現的第一個條目（通常是維基百科）之後，調查就算完成。而且在電子郵件、簡訊傳送、推特推文的限制之下，我們不得不用三言兩語和愚蠢的縮寫（像是 OMG!「我的老天啊！」、LOL「哈哈大笑」、IMHO「個人淺見」）來溝通，連完整的字詞都不寫。批評者進一步指控，網路讓我們太容易獲得過多的新知識，令我們難以負荷，也無法仔細思考。以電子方式取得的資料多到也快到我們不能再像以往一樣，好好思考或將我們的想法寫下來。批評者表示，我們的指尖上累積的資訊越多，就越難從中找到最有價值、最有用的部分，讓我們難以專注並予以回應。這導致了以下這樣的結果：根據研究員克里弗德‧納斯（Clifford Nass）的評論，由於網路和其他數位科技鼓勵我們一心多用，使得寫作的學生不太能在論文中維持一個「大想法」，容易寫得「零星而片段」（出處：Nass）。

　　不過也有許多人不認同這種悲觀的看法。修辭與寫作教授安德莉雅‧郎斯福德（Andrea Lunsford）便駁斥「Google 正讓我們變笨」這種想法，也反對「臉書讓我們的腦子快炸掉了」，她也不認為網路正讓學生失去表達意見的能力（出處：引用自 Haven）。郎斯福德就一項為期五年的《史丹佛寫作研究》（*Stanford Study of Writing*）提出了報告。根據她的說法，現在寫作的學生非常「擅於寫出能吸引目標讀者群的訊息，正因為他們經常使用社群媒體之故」（出處：Lunsford）。也就是說，現在的學生很擅長「修辭學家所謂的『把握對的時機』（kairos）——他們會評估讀者群，然後調整敘事的口吻和技巧，好傳達他們的看法」（出處：Thompson）。

　　網路技術對於人際對話和社群交流，究竟是促進或破壞，仍無定論。一方面，有人推崇網路科技能拉近人們的距離，網路也讓他們得以透過電子郵件、部落格、視訊聊天和社群網站，更容易與人互動。持此看法的人，看到本書所建議，以回應他人論點來提出個人論點，可能同意此一作法適用於網路交流。畢竟網路讓我們得以發表言論，而且很快，甚至立刻就得到回應。網路也讓我們更容易取得關於任何主題的多方觀點，我們可以直接把別人的意見以連結形式放入文章中，讀者只要點擊就能觀看。

另一方面，批評者質疑網路對談的品質，認為這些對談稱不上是真正的思想交流，他們指出網文作者經常是各說各話，不顧對談的對象。由於網文作者可能未經深思熟慮就按下「送出」鍵，不像一般使用較慢、較慎重的印刷媒體的作者比較可以好好思考，因此這些評論家指責說，各方確實傾聽彼此意見的那種真正論辯，在網路上少之又少。換言之，用網路溝通往往無法達到真正的討論，因為寫作的人太容易漠視或忽略其他觀點，很容易變成以自我為中心發表長篇大論，只稍微用別人的論點開場，目的是要闡述自己的看法。

以上正反兩方的看法，都是關於網路科技對思考以及溝通行為（包括寫作在內）的影響。雖然我們同意網路讓我們得以獲取過去無法想像的大量資訊，並且大為拓展溝通範圍——也同意這可能擴展視野——我們卻也認為，批評者有一點說得有道理，他們提到，許多網路對話與其說是交換意見，倒不如說是個人獨白。這些對話漠視彼此，一點交集也沒有。我們發表在網路上的文章就曾經出現這樣開頭的留言評論：「我還沒有讀葛拉夫和柏肯斯坦的文章，不過我的看法是……」，讓我們相當錯愕。在我們看來，要改善這種溝通失敗的情況，最好的辦法就是提升本書所強調的聆聽和概述技巧，無論在網路上也好、網路外也好，都要勵行，連石器時代都該如此。

至於這些數位科技對學生寫作的影響是如何，依我們兩個加起來七十年教學經驗所看過的作文來看，我們認為這種影響並不如批評者所擔心的是場災難，卻也不是擁護者所說的超級革命。和納斯的看法正好相反，早在網際網路出現之前，學生就覺得很難有所謂的一個「全面想法」。但與郎斯福德不同的是，我們也看不出任何證據，顯示社群媒體上推文和發文的網文作者更擅於吸引讀者。就我們看到的情況，寫作者吸引不了讀者的困境，在網路科技時代也是持續上演著。一名寫作人士在一個媒體上面吸引不到讀者，就算換一個媒體也是一樣。舉例來說，我們有位學生要發文給課程群組上面的同學，他用下面的方式開頭：

"Going off what Meg said, I would argue…"

「先不談梅格所言，我認為……」

收到的人都非常困惑，因為沒有人記得梅格說過什麼話，連梅格自己也不記得了。這件事告訴我們，網路書寫——不只是在課程群組上，還包含電子郵件、社群媒體等——的即時性非常類似口頭交流，使我們忘記這依然是種寫作形式，還是需要掌握正式的傳統寫作手法。這個例子缺乏的就是概述別人說過的話。我們前面提過，每個寫作者都需要努力發揮論述技巧，從概述、說明、引述別人的言論，到加以回應，以及其他技巧。

然而在這短短的一堂課中，我們的目的並不是要解決這些爭論，而是要請各位以讀者和作者的身分想想，數位科技對你的工作有什麼影響。數位科技有沒有讓你更容易參與對談？它們讓你的思考和寫作能力提升還是下降？你有什麼看法，原因為何？為了幫助你回答這些問題，我們在本課最後提供幾個練習，讓你延續這一段討論——以肯尼斯・柏克的話來說：「親手試試吧」（put in your own oar）。

本章參考文獻

Haven, Cynthia. "The New Literacy: Stanford Study Finds Richness and Complexity in Students' Writing." *Stanford Report*, Stanford University, 12 Oct. 2009, news.stanford.edu/pr/2009/pr-lunsford-writing-101209.html. Accessed 14 Nov. 2013.

Lunsford, Andrea. "Everyone's an Author." W. W. Norton Sales Conference, 5 Aug. 2012, Park City.

Nass, Clifford. Interview. *Frontline*, WGBH, Boston, 1 Dec. 2009. *PBS*, www.pbs.org/wgbh/pages/frontline/digitalnation/interviews/nass.html. Accessed 14 Nov. 2013.

Thompson, Clive. "Clive Thompson on the New Literacy." *Wired*, 24 Aug. 2009, www.wired.com/2009/08/st-thompson-7. Accessed 14 Nov. 2013.

練習

1. 關於這個具爭議性的議題，你覺得本課的說明實不實用？有沒有遺漏哪些重點？請你寫一篇論文，要概述一些書中的評論，作為你文章中的「他人論點」的部分，接著提出自己的回應。你可以表示反對，也可以表示同意但有其他意見，或者用某種方式重新說明這些議題。

2. 這裡提供一個案例，讓大家思考本文前面所提到的幾個問題，請到本書的部落格 theysayiblog.com 上面，瀏覽其中一些意見的交流，並且評估這些回覆的優劣。譬如說，參與意見交流的人在提出自己的看法之前，有沒有概述別人的主張？你會怎麼描述其中任何一組的討論？他們真的是在交流思想，還是有時在挖苦作者、把作者看成稻草人，不當一回事？這些網路討論和你們課堂上的面對面討論比較起來怎麼樣？兩者各自有哪些優點？也請看看其他你感興趣的部落格，思考同樣的問題。

第 **14** 堂　仔細閱讀，準備對談

"What's motivating this writer?"
「作者的動機是什麼？」

「這位作者的論點是什麼？他想說些什麼？」多年來，我們在討論閱讀作業之前，都會先問全班同學這個問題。結果討論總是零零落落、斷斷續續，因為大家掌握不到作者的論點；不過經過一番尷尬的折騰之後，同學總能慢慢說出一些內容，找出認可的作者論點。然而，即便我們越過了這個障礙，接著的問題讓人更傷腦筋。這個問題就是：在弄清楚作者說什麼之後，**我們自己要說些什麼？**

以前，我們對這種凌亂不順的討論情況不太在意，我們會告訴自己，這都是因為指定的閱讀作業太難、挑戰性太高。直到數年前，我們開始撰寫這本書，並開始將寫作視為一種參與對談關係的藝術，才想到該採用各種問題來引導討論，例如：「這位作者是在回應哪些其他的論點？」「作者有沒有針對某件事表達反對或同意？有的話是什麼事？」「作者提出該論點的動機是什麼？」「你在這堂課或其他地方有沒有聽到哪些相關的說法？」結果成效相當顯著，引起的討論比以往要熱烈得多，也吸引了更多學生參與。我們還是一樣會請學生找出文中主要論點，但不同的是，我們要學生將該論點看作是受到其他論點啟發所做的回應，給它一個存在的理由，讓我們明白為何應該關心這個論點。

我們發現，我們改變提問方式之後，也連帶改變了學生的閱讀方式，或多或少也改變了他們對學術寫作的看法。他們不再將文本中的論點視為孤立的個體，而看出它是在回應並引發其他論點。他們現在必須處理的論點不是一個，而是至少兩個（即作者的論點與其所回應的論點），自然就得從不同的角度去看這個主題。也就是說，學生不只是學著去了解作者的論點，也要能夠運用智識去質疑該論點，去參與象徵著大學教育的那種討論和論辯。我們的課堂討論，如果有一部分學生認為作者的論點很有說服力，另一部分學生卻較為認同相對的論點的時候，就會引起一番熱烈的論辯。論辯得精采的時候，其他學生會質疑正反雙方各自極端的立場，認為兩邊都將問題過於簡化了，其實雙方可能都有部分道理，或者可能還有第三種說法。也可能還有其他學生會抗議說，討論到這裡根本已經離題了，建議大家回到文本上，認真看一下作者到底說了些什麼。

我們終於明白，我們如果把閱讀技巧不只看成找出作者個別論點，而是探討作者如何將論點與其他人交流，才能幫助讀者積極主動、慎思明辨，而不是被動接受知識。就某種層面來說，閱讀時，找出作者說了什麼，並不困難，難的是，找出內容所蘊含的對談關係。你不只要判斷作者在想什麼，還要判斷作者的想法與其他人的想法有何異同，最終與你自己的想法有何異同。而就另一種層面來說，用這種方式閱讀，比尋找主旨要來得單純得多也熟悉得多，因為這等於是把寫作回歸到日常生活中我們很常在做的事，就是和別人談論真實的議題。

察覺對談關係

因此我們會建議，做老師所指定的閱讀作業時，要想像作者並不是獨自坐在房間裡，趴在桌上或盯著電腦螢幕，而是在一個人潮眾多的咖啡廳裡和其他人說話，別人提出主張，他正忙著回應。換言之，要想像作者正在參與一個持續進行的多方觀點對談，每個人都試圖說服別人同意自己的看法，或至少認真思考自己的看法。

　　若要找出其中所包含的對談關係，技巧在於，要找出**作者在回應哪些論點，以及作者自己的論點是什麼**——或者用本書的術語來說，就是要決定 they say 的部分是什麼，而作者又是如何回應。但是要讀出文中的 they say 和 I say 可能會面臨一些挑戰，其中之一就是要區分哪些是 they say、哪些是 I say。作者哪些時候是在概述別人的論點、哪些時候是在陳述自己的意見，區別未必很明顯。讀者必須留意每個語氣轉換的時機，因為作者未必會使用明確的指示片語，如 although many believe（雖然許多人相信），他們可能直接就陳述他們所要回應的觀點，只隱約表示那不是他們的意見。

　　我們再看一次收錄在本書第 268 頁大衛・辛善寇的論文第一段：

> If ever there were a newspaper headline custom made for Jay Leno's monologue, this was it. Kids taking on McDonald's this week, suing the company for making them fat. Isn't that like middle-aged men suing Porsche for making them get speeding tickets? Whatever happened to personal responsibility?
>
> I tend to sympathize with these portly fast-food patrons, though. Maybe that's because I used to be one of them.

　　假如真有報紙標題是為了登上傑・雷諾的脫口秀而特意製作的，那就非此莫屬了。本週兒童迎戰麥當勞，控告該企業害他們發胖。這豈不就像是中年男子控告保時捷害他們被開超速罰單？個人責任感到哪裡去了？

不過呢，我倒是相當同情這些肥胖的速食常客，或許因為我也曾是其中一員吧。

——大衛・辛善寇，〈別怪吃的人〉

我們每次講解這段文字時，總是有些學生認為，辛善寇自己在第一段已經展現支持的態度，亦即：控告麥當勞是很荒謬的。如果有其他同學質疑，他們總是指著課本說：「你們看，就在這裡，辛善寇自己寫的，他的確是這麼說的。」這些學生覺得，只要出現在論文裡的內容，就一定是作者認同的。但事實上，我們常會說出一些自己並不相信，甚至實際上是極力反對的論點。本文中，辛善寇反對第一段論點的關鍵線索出現在第二段，他在這裡才以第一人稱發言，並且使用了對比的轉接語 though，完全解答了他的立場的問題。

如果文中未明白列出他人論點

我們會面臨的另外一個挑戰是，如果作者沒有明白指出「他人論點」，那該如何辨識。辛善寇在一開始就概述了他所要回應的論點，然而，其他寫作者可能會覺得讀者已經很熟悉這些觀點，因此不指名道姓或多做說明。在這種情況下，身為讀者的你就必須透過推論的方式，重現沒有在文中出現的「他人論點」。

下面這個例子，是塔瑪拉・杜蘿特（Tamara Draut）的論文〈日益擴大之大學差距〉（The Growing College Gap）第一段，請試著指出杜蘿特所質疑的論點。

"The first in her family to graduate from college." How many times have

請見第 6 堂更多描述反對意見的說明。

we heard that phrase, or one like it, used to describe a successful American with a modest background? In today's United States, a four-year degree has become the all-but-official ticket to middle-class security. But if your parents don't have much money or higher education in their own right, the road to college—and beyond—looks increasingly treacherous. Despite a sharp increase in the proportion of high school graduates going on to some form of postsecondary education, socio-economic status continues to exert a powerful influence on college admission and completion; in fact, gaps in enrollment by class and race, after declining in the 1960s and 1970s, are once again as wide as they were thirty years ago, and getting wider, even as college has become far more crucial to lifetime fortunes.

「她是家族裡第一個大學畢業的人。」這句話，或是類似的話，用來描述一個出身寒微卻終得成功的美國人，我們早已聽過不知多少次。在今日的美國，讀四年大學，拿到學位，幾乎就是躋身中產階級的非正式入門票。但是如果你的父母並不富裕，沒有受過高等教育，那麼你的大學之路——以及未來前途——似乎將日益坎坷。儘管高中畢業生高等教育的比例已有顯著提升，他們是否能進入大學並完成學業，仍相當受到家庭社經地位的影響。事實上，因階級與種族所造成的入學差距，在六〇和七〇年代縮小後，如今卻又拉大到三十年前的差距，甚至日漸惡化，然而大學對於人的一生際遇已經更加重要。

——塔瑪拉·杜蘿特，〈日益擴大之大學差距〉

你可能會認為，這裡的「他人論點」是暗藏在第三句話：有人說（或者我們都認為）一個四年的學位是「躋身中產階級的非正式入門票」（the all-but-official ticket to middle-class security），而且你可能會判斷杜蘿特接著是要提出反對。

假如你是這樣解讀這段文字，那就錯了。杜蘿特質疑的，不是大學學位是否已成為「躋身中產階級的非正式入門票」，而是大部分美國人是否能獲得這張門票，以及大部分美國家庭是否都能負擔大學學費。這個句子先是說大學已經成為躋身中產階級的先決條件，但接著出現的 "but" 可能就把你給迷惑了。然而，這裡的 "but" 和辛善寇所使用的 though 並不一樣。這個 "but" 並不是說杜蘿特不同意「躋身中產階級的非正式入門票」這個觀點，她其實把該觀點視為一個已知的事實。這張非正式入門票，對於中產階級和勞工階級來說仍然很容易取得的這個論點，才是杜蘿特所無法苟同的。

想像有一群人對這個主題持有強烈的意見，而杜蘿特正與他們齊聚一室高談闊論，這時候你應該要想像，她質疑的不是大學等於經濟保障（這件事她是同意的，並且也認為確實是如此），而是大學之門正隨時為任何有心上進的人敞開這件事。因此，杜蘿特所質疑的觀點並未出現在這段開頭文字裡；她假設這個觀點眾所周知，因此無須說明。

從杜蘿特的例子可以看到，一旦文中沒有即時點出「他人論點」，你就必須根據文本提供的線索勾勒出來。你必須先找出作者的論點，接著想像可能會出現的反論。大家會以什麼說法反對這個論點？以杜蘿特的例子來看，建立一個反論是很容易的，也就是：提到進大學，大家就想到如同美國夢一樣人人機會平等。思考反論不僅能夠知道杜蘿特的寫作動機，也能讓你作一個主動探索、觀察敏銳的讀者，去回應她的論文。構思出反論也能讓你明白，你的哪些思考會受到杜蘿特的刺激，好檢視你原本認為理所當然的想法。

▋如果文中的「他人論點」無人提過

在閱讀並找出文中的對談關係時，會遭遇的另一個困難在於，有時作者的論點並不存在對談的對象。寫作者並不是在和現存的論點爭論（例如對美國夢的信心，或者我們須為自己的體重負責這個看法），而是直指別人所忽略之處。如同寫作評論家約翰‧史威爾斯（John M. Swales）及克麗絲汀‧斐克（Christine B. Feak）所言，要在學術界「創造研究空間」和「建立利基」的最有效方法，就是「指出過去研究的缺口」。很多科學和人文領域的研究都會採用這種 Nobody has noticed X（尚未有人注意到……）的寫法來發表意見。

在這種情況下，寫作者可能是在回應科學家，認為他們忽略了一種影響全球暖化甚鉅的不知名植物；或者是在回應文學批評家，認為他們念茲在茲探討一齣戲劇的主人翁，卻未注意到其他小角色的某種重要性。

閱讀特別艱澀的文本

有時要釐清作者所回應的觀點非常困難，並不是因為他們沒有指明，而是因為他們的用語特別艱澀，所申論的概念也特別難懂。以《性別麻煩：女權主義與認同顛覆》（Gender Trouble: Feminism and the Subversion of Identity）一書頭兩句話為例，作者是女權主義哲學家與文學理論家茱蒂絲‧芭特勒（Judith Butler），她是眾所公認文章特別難懂的學術作者。

> Contemporary feminist debates over the meaning of gender lead time and again to a certain sense of trouble, as if the indeterminacy of gender might eventually culminate in the failure of feminism. Perhaps trouble need not carry such a negative valence.

> 當代女權主義對性別意義之爭論屢屢招致一種困擾，彷彿終可能因性別不確定而宣告女權主義失敗。或許不用讓困擾背負著這麼一個負面評價。

> —— 茱蒂絲‧芭特勒，《性別麻煩：女權主義與認同顛覆》

短短一段文字卻讓人讀得結結巴巴，其中有很多原因，最大的一點在於芭特勒沒有清楚界定她的觀點從哪裡開始、她所回應的觀點到哪裡結束。芭特勒不像辛善寇使用了第一人稱和 in my own view 這樣的片語，來告訴讀者第二個句子是她的觀點。她也沒像是辛善寇運用清楚的轉接語，在第二句的一開始加上 but 或 however，告訴大家她的第二句是在質疑第一句所概述的論點。最後，她和許多學術作者一樣，使用了抽象、罕見的詞彙，導致讀者可能要查一下才能理解，例如 "gender"（性別認同、男人或女人）、"indeterminacy"（無法定義或不確定）、"culminate"（最終造成）、"negative valence"（負價，此為化學術語，借指「負面意義」）。基於這些原因，我們可以想像，許多讀者還沒讀到書中的第三句，就已經卻步。

　　但是讀者如果把這段文字分解成幾個重要部分，就會發現它符合本書的標準寫作格式：「人們說／我說」。雖然要在這兩個句子中找出衝突點並不容易，但仔細分析之後會發現，第一個句子提出了女權主義政治界裡看待一種「困擾」（trouble）的方式，第二個句子則對此加以質疑。

　　若要理解這種艱澀的段落，就得把它改寫成自己的語言。換言之，在文本中出現的罕見術語和你所習慣的語言之間搭起橋樑，如此你才能將作者的意見跟已知的事實連結起來，並進一步幫助你閱讀理解、進而寫作，讓你知道需要使用何種語言來對原文作概述。然而，改寫作者文字時，會面臨的一大挑戰就是，要忠於作者本義，避免發生所謂的「近陳腔濫調症」，亦即誤把一個普遍觀點套用在作者的複雜觀點上（譬如說，誤以為芭特勒對「女性」的概念的評論，就是認為女性必須享有平權的一般觀念）。像芭特勒這種心思縝密的作家時常挑戰傳統思維，他們的作品不可能都和大眾一般見識。因此當你在改寫時，不能企圖讓他們的看法符合你既有的想法，你要**讓自己接受挑戰**。在你和作者之間搭起橋樑時，放下成見，遷就他們，往往是必要的。

請見第 2 堂關於「近陳腔濫調症」之說明。

那芭特勒的這段開頭文字到底在說什麼？用淺顯易懂的方式來改寫，第一句就是在說，對於今天的許多女權主義者而言，「性別不確定」——無法定義性別認同的本質——意味著女權主義走上絕路；對於許多女權主義者而言，無法定義「性別」代表著女權主義政治遭遇嚴重的「困擾」，畢竟這可說是女權運動的基石。相對之下，第二句表示不需要用這些「負面」詞語來形容這種「困擾」，並且表示沒有能力定義女性氣質，或者如其書名所形容的，「性別困擾」未必是件壞事——她在後續內容中有說明，女權主義運動者甚至有可能從中得利。換言之，芭特勒認為，女性主義者反而可以強調男子氣概和女性氣質之間的不確定性，把它當作一個有力的武器。

綜合這些推論，她的開頭句子可以這麼改寫：

While many contemporary feminists believe that uncertainty about what it means to be a woman will undermine feminist politics, **I, Judith Butler, believe that** this uncertainty can actually help strengthen feminist politics.

儘管許多當代的女權主義者認為，無法確定身為女性的意義會阻礙女權主義政治的發展，我，茱蒂絲·芭特勒，卻認為這種不確定性其實有助於鞏固女權主義政治。

把她的論點用本書的基本寫作方法來改寫，就是：

They say that if we cannot define 'women', feminism is in big trouble. **But I say** that this type of trouble is precisely what feminism needs.

有人說倘若我們無法定義『女性』，女權主義的麻煩就大了。但是我說這種麻煩正是女權運動所需要的。

雖然芭特勒的這段文字並不好懂，假如你繼續讀下去，我們希望你會認同，這段文字起先雖叫人望而生畏，但的確是有道理的。

思辨性閱讀是一條雙向道，一方面，你要敞開心胸，讓作者挑戰你、甚至顛覆你的理念。另一方面，你也要質疑作者的觀點，兩者缺一不可。假如你在閱讀過程中需要把作者的論點改寫成自己的話，務必要容許文本帶你跳脫自己的框架去思考、帶你認識新的詞語和概念。即便到最後你還是不認同作者，也得先表現出你真的聽完他說的話、徹底掌握他的論點，而且可以正確無誤地描述出來。倘若沒有如此深入、專注的傾聽，你的任何評論都會流於表面且絕對沒有思辨力，會變成是講自己比講作者還要多，或比你該回應的觀點還要多。

我們在本課說明，透過閱讀找出文中的對談關係，不僅要找出作者的論點，還要知道是哪個或哪些觀點促使這個論點產生 —— 即「他人論點」的部分。透過閱讀找出文中的對談關係，也意味著你須留意作者運用了哪些不同策略，來處理這些促使他們寫作的他人論點，畢竟每位作者處理他人論點的方式都不盡相同。有些作者會在文章一開始明確指出他所回應的論點，並且加以概述，隨文章的發展不時回顧該論點。有些作者不會直指啟發他們寫作的論點，因為他們假設讀者可以自己構築出來。有些作者不會用我們都覺得清楚的方式，明確區分自己和對方的論點，因此有些讀者會感到納悶，到底某個論點是作者自己的，還是他要質疑的。有些作者則慣用艱澀的學術用語，來描述啟發他們寫作的他人論點，使得讀者要將其文字改寫為易懂的日常用語。簡而言之，雖然大部分議論文的作者確實遵循對談關係的「人們說／我說」的寫作模式，但卻有著各式各樣的變體。這些對談關係未必總是顯而易見，讀者必須具備各種閱讀技巧，才能察覺。

第 15 堂　文學領域的學術寫作

"On closer examination"

「仔細檢視之後」

In Chinua Achebe's novel *Things Fall Apart*, Okonkwo, the main character, is a tragic hero.

在奇努瓦‧阿契貝的小說《分崩離析》中，主人翁歐康闊是一個悲劇英雄。

那又怎樣？誰在乎呢？

這種探討文學作品的論文的典型開場白，常常令讀者納悶：「你為什麼要告訴我這件事？」我們認為，這種寫法令人不解的原因在於：其他人會有別的看法嗎？有人不同意阿契貝小說裡的主角是個悲劇英雄嗎？作者是在回應這個主題的某個其他觀點嗎？因為文中沒有提到其他的可能解讀方式，讀者會想：「好吧，歐康闊是一個悲劇英雄──那他不是什麼呢？」

現在，把這段開場白改寫，比較一下：

Several members of our class have argued that Okonkwo, the main character of *Things Fall Apart*, is a hateful villain. My own view, however, is that, while it is true that Okonkwo commits villainous acts, he is ultimately a tragic hero—a flawed but ultimately sympathetic figure.

班上有些同學認為《分崩離析》的主角歐康闊是個內心充滿仇恨的惡棍。然而我的看法是，歐康闊的惡行惡狀雖是事實，卻終究是名悲劇英雄——是個有缺陷卻終叫人同情的人物。

希望你的看法和我們相同。第二個版本回應了別人對歐康闊的看法，比起第一個來得有吸引力。第一個版本不是對同主題的其他觀點做回應，讀者可能會感到突兀，不知道何必要談到這件事。

如本書所強調的，因為先有別人的論點存在，而我們想要回應這些論點，才會產生寫作動機，讀者也才能理解，為什麼要在乎我們的看法、為什麼我們要關心、為什麼我們在文章開始就要先提出這一點。在本課中，我們要提出，這個原則也適用於文學論文寫作。畢竟文學評論家不會無端對作品發表意見。相反地，一定是該文學作品的意義和重要性引發討論和爭論，他們才會發表意見，其中有些討論和爭論甚至已經持續多年甚至好幾世紀。

再者，這樣的討論會讓多數文學課程變得較活潑，學生先在課堂上針對指定作品進行討論和辯論，接著才著手撰寫論文。與老師同學的切磋，讓我們對作品有更多發現，這是我們獨自一人閱讀作品所沒有的收穫。

我們建議你把文學論文寫作當作是這種課堂討論的自然延伸，仔細傾聽別人的意見，以之建立和啟發你自己的論點。

先聽聽別人怎麼說

在文學寫作上，要回應的「他人論點」從哪裡來呢？來源非常多，已發表的文學評論隨手可得，例如你可以這樣寫：

▶ **Critic X complains that Author Y's story is compromised by his _____ perspective. While there's some truth to this critique, I argue that Critic X overlooks _____.**
評論家 X 抱怨作者 Y 從_____的角度敘事，顯得不夠精采。雖然這篇評論不無道理，但我認為評論家 X 忽略了_____。

▶ **According to Critic A, novel X suggests _____. I agree, but would add that _____.**
根據評論家 A 的說法，X 小說暗示了_____。我同意這個看法，但要補充的是_____。

不過，撰寫文學類的論文時，回應的對象可以近在身邊，不一定要捨近求遠，搜尋正式發表的文學評論。我們前面提供的範例便說明，回應的對象可以是同學或老師的論點：

▶ **Several members of our class have suggested that the final message of play X is _____. I agree up to a point, but I still think that _____.**
班上的幾位同學提出，戲劇 X 最終所要傳遞的訊息是_____。我大致是同意的，但仍然認為_____。

另一種展開文章的技巧，是寫出你原本對該作品的想法，然而再三思考後卻有了改觀，例如：

▶ On first reading play Z, I thought it was an uncritical celebration of
_____. After rereading the play and discussing it in class, however,
I see that it is more critical of _____ than I originally thought.

初次讀到戲劇 Z 時，我以為它只是不經深思一味頌揚_____。然而，經過重新閱讀並在班上討論之後，我發現它對_____的分析比我原本想得要深刻得多。

你甚至可以拿一個沒有人說過、但假設可能有人會說的言論，當作回應的對象，例如：

▶ It might be said that poem Y is chiefly about _____.
But the problem with this reading, in my view, is _____.

可能有人會說 Y 這首詩主要是關於_____，但我認為這樣解讀的問題在於_____。

▶ Though religious readers might be tempted to analyze poem X as a
parable about _____, a closer examination suggests that the
poem is in fact _____.

儘管宗教讀者可能想把 X 這首詩解讀成一個關於_____的寓言，但仔細閱讀之後會發現這首詩其實是_____。

有時，在撰寫文學論文時，你所要回應的「他人論點」就存在於該作品本身，而不是評論者或其他讀者針對該作品所發表的意見。許多偉大的文學評論是直接回應文學作品本身，先對該作品的某種形式或內容進行概述，接著加以評論，這種方式和你回應一篇論說文是一樣的道理，例如：

▶ Ultimately, as I read it, *The Scarlet Letter* seems to say _____.
I have trouble accepting this proposition, however, on the grounds that

_____.

最後，以我的解讀，《紅字》似乎是要說_____。然而我不大同意這個
立場，理由是_____。

還有一種更強而有力回應文學作品的方式，就是去探討其中的矛盾之處，
如：

▶ At the beginning of the poem, we encounter the generalization,
seemingly introducing the poem's message, that "_____." But this
statement is then contradicted by the suggestion made later in the
poem that "_____." This opens up a significant inconsistency in the
text: is it suggesting _____ or, on the contrary, _____?
這首詩的一開始，我們讀到一個整體的概念，似乎是在傳達這首詩的訊息，
這個概念是「_____」。然而這個說法又與詩中後來暗示的「_____」
產生矛盾。這顯示出此文本有個重大的前後矛盾之處： 到底它是在暗示
_____，或者恰好相反，是在暗示_____？

▶ At several places in novel X, Author Y leads us to understand that
the story's central point is that _____. Yet elsewhere the text
suggests _____, indicating that Y may be ambivalent on this issue.
在 X 這部小說中有多處，作者 Y 讓我們以為_____是故事的核心，然而
文本在其他地方又暗示了_____，這說明 Y 對此議題態度可能是模稜兩
可的。

你再看一次上面這些套句範本，會發現每個都符合好對話、好演講、好論文的條件，即：針對一個作品可能引發的多重解讀發表論點。它們不是僅對某作品提出主張——譬如只說 X 這個角色是悲劇英雄、Y 這首十四行詩是描述失去摯愛——而是回應他人主張，以帶出自己的論點，好清楚顯示論點的緣起。它們就像是展開對談的人，會邀請或甚至激發讀者，也用自己的解讀和判斷來對某一論點做回應。

思考一部文學作品的「意義」

要參與文學方面討論和論辯時，一個長久存在的挑戰，就是要有能力閱讀並了解作品，要能分析並理解文本。一方面，跟本書一直強調的學術對談一樣，文學作品也是在傳達作者的論點，像是贊成或反對某事，或是支持或批判某論點；另一方面，要找出一部文學作品的「論點」——它在「說」什麼——也相當不易。文學作品跟論說文不同，文學作家通常不會明言自己的論點。儘管詩人、小說家、劇作家信念堅強不亞於論說文作者，但他們卻鮮少從文本後面走出來說：「好的，各位，這就是它的意義。簡單一句話，我想要說的就是＿＿＿＿＿。」也就是說，文學作品通常不會有明確的論點陳述讓你直接明白主旨，而是要讀者自行去思考。

由於文學作品往往缺乏這樣的明確性，讀者通常得透過文本中所提供的線索，如角色之間的對話、故事情節、意象和象徵，以及作者所使用的語言找出意義。而也正因為文學作品的論點隱晦不明，針對文學作品的論辯才可以無止盡進行下去，而這個現象，正好與學生在課堂上參與的討論狀況相當類似。

難以捉摸的文學作家

甚至，文學作品中所使用的第一人稱 "I" 也不能代表作者的立場，而這點和其他類型的論文相當不同。舉例來說，辛善寇在〈別怪吃的人〉（見本書第268-270頁）一文當中，提到某些速食常客對業者提出了控告，他寫道：「我倒是同情這些肥胖的速食常客。」（I tend to sympathize with these portly fast-food patrons.）我們可以確定這裡的「我」就是指辛善寇本人，他所表達的就是自己的立場，而且這個立場在整篇論文中都前後一致。但是小說或詩歌裡對我們說話的 I 就不能解讀為作者本人，因為他們是虛構的角色，說法未必可靠也不能信賴。

我們來看愛倫坡（Edgar Allan Poe）的短篇小說《一桶阿蒙提亞多酒》（*The Cask of Amontillado*）中的第一個句子：

> The thousand injuries of Fortunato I had borne as best I could, but when he ventured upon insult I vowed revenge.
>
> 弗杜納託對我百般傷害我已能忍則忍，然他竟斗膽侮辱我，我便發誓非報仇雪恨不可。

我們立刻明白在這個故事中，敘事的 "I" 不是作者愛倫坡本人，而是個一心想報仇的殺人兇手，我們必須穿透他的話語才能直達故事的中心思想。

文學作品不會提供容易辨識的論點，而是經常透過許多不同角色來傳達論點，由讀者自行判斷哪一個代表作者的立場，當然也有可能每個都不是。因此，像《哈姆雷特》（*Hamlet*）裡面意味深長的這麼一句話：「你必對自己忠實，你才不會對人虛假。」（To thine own self be true / And thou shalt not be false to any man.）假如這句話是出現在一篇論文裡，也許可以假設是作者的觀點，但這裡卻不能這樣假設。這句話是出自莎翁筆下的角色普羅涅斯（Polonius）之口，莎士比亞筆下，他是一個油腔滑調、廢話連篇的無聊傢伙──根本不值得信賴。畢竟，哈姆雷特的部分問題就在於，他自己也不清楚怎麼做才是對自己「忠實」。

文學文本這種捉摸不定的特質，說明了為什麼有些學生會抱怨，很難在其中找到所謂的「隱義」（hidden meaning），更別提要在作業中概述這個意義。有些學生表示，如果閱讀文學作品當作消遣，當然樂意，但在學校裡分析文學作品的「意義」或「象徵」，可另當別論。有些學生甚至說，要找出作品中的意義和象徵，根本糟蹋了文學的趣味。

事實上，越來越多學生漸漸明白，分析意義、象徵和其他元素，非但不會減少文學閱讀的趣味，反而應該是增加。不過，文學作品的意義確實可能晦澀難解。畢竟，文學作家不同於辛善寇這類的論文作家，不會明確告訴我們他想說什麼。這時候，讀者該如何判斷一則故事或一首詩的中心思想？要怎麼從一個小說事件或詩歌圖像（譬如一個發狂男人行兇的事件、林中兩條岔路的圖像）或小說人物間的對話（譬如「老實說，親愛的，我一點也不在乎。」）聯想到其中的意義？

找出作品裡的矛盾

要找出文學作品的含義沒有捷徑，不過有個策略會有幫助，就是找出文學作品中蘊含的矛盾或爭議，並想一想：這個文本希望我們如何看待這個矛盾？換言之，作品中是否顯示什麼矛盾，而如果確實有矛盾存在的話，我們應該站在哪一邊？這些問題有助於思考作品的含義並形成你自己的立場。而這些不同論點通常是文學研究者所爭論的重點。因此，思考文學作品中的矛盾，往往可以讓你加入該作品的相關討論和論辯，然後加以回應。文學作家不會把文本的意義明白告訴我們，因此永遠沒有定論 —— 你的寫作任務就是為你自己的看法據理力爭。要回應別人的詮釋，可用下面這兩個範本起頭：

▶ **It might be argued that in the clash between character X and Y in play Z, the author wants us to favor character Y, since she is presented as the play's heroine. I contend, however, that _____.**
也許有人認為在 Z 這部戲劇裡，X 和 Y 這兩個角色矛盾，作者是要我們支持 Y，因而將她塑造成劇中英雄。然而我確信_____。

▶ **Several critics seem to assume that poem X endorses the values of discipline and rationality represented by the image of _____ over those of play and emotion represented by the image of _____. I agree, but with the following caveat: that the poem ultimately sees both values as equally important and even suggests that ideally they should complement one another.**
幾位評論家似乎都假設 X 這首詩認同_____形象所代表的紀律和理性的價值觀，超過認同_____形象所代表的玩樂和情感的價值觀。這點我同意，但是我要附帶一提：這首詩終歸還是將兩種價值觀等同視之，甚至暗示了最理想應該要互補才是。

尋找文學作品裡的矛盾（conflict），是研究文學長久以來使用的一種思辨方式，認為矛盾就是文學作品的核心。在古希臘時期，亞里斯多德就曾提出，人物或強權間的矛盾是諸如《伊底帕斯王》（*Oedipus*）等悲劇的情節基礎。古希臘文 agon 一字有「敵對、矛盾、爭辯」的意味，在 protagonist 一字中仍可見到它的痕跡，意指「一部敘事作品的主角，並且將與其他角色或命運發生矛盾」。柏拉圖發現文學作品裡充滿著矛盾的現象，他以作品描繪的盡是矛盾與分裂為由，把詩人逐出他的理想國。

這種強調文學作品以矛盾為核心的觀念，也受到現代理論家，如四〇、五〇年代興起的新批評派（New Critics）的推崇。他們專注於這種張力，如善與惡、純真與經驗等悖論。到了更近期還受到後結構主義論者及政治評論家的附和，他們認為文學和社會一樣充斥著這種兩極性，像是男性與女性、同性戀與異性戀、黑人與白人，諸如此類。今日的寫作人士持續認為有矛盾才能寫出好故事，誠如好萊塢編劇勞勃‧麥基（Robert McKee）所言：「唯有矛盾能讓故事裡的一切進展。」

基於矛盾為文學之核心這個觀念，可以利用下列四個問題，幫助你了解任何一部文學作品，並建立論點：

1. 該文本的核心矛盾為何？
2. 該文本如果傾向支持矛盾的某一方，是哪一邊？
3. 你可以提出什麼支持的證據？別人對這些證據可能有什麼其他解讀？
4. 你對該文本的看法為何？

該文本的核心矛盾為何？

不同類型的文學作品，往往以不同的方式表現矛盾。採用敘事體或故事體的作品（如小說、短篇故事、戲劇）通常會透過角色間的爭執來表現核心矛盾。這些角色之間的爭執，反映的是當時社會或時代裡存在的重大問題和爭議，內容涵蓋統治者的責任、資本主義與消費主義所帶來的後果、爭取兩性平等的努力等等。有時，這些爭執會以單一角色的內心戲呈現，表現在一個人陷入矛盾或兩難時的內心掙扎。無論以哪種形式呈現，從這些爭執都可以看到作品提出的議題、作品的歷史背景、作者的世界觀。

富蘭納瑞・歐康納（Flannery O'Connor）在 1961 年發表的短篇故事〈凡興起之一切必將匯合〉（Everything That Rises Must Converge）便是很適合採用這種手法的敘事作品，本書也在第 302-323 頁收錄了這則故事。該故事描述一名母親與其子朱立安之間的一場持續的爭執，內容是關於當時美國南方為爭取種族平等而爆發的民權運動，朱立安極力維護民權運動的理念，其母則為南方傳統種族階級制度辯護。這則故事引發了一個可議之處，究竟我們該支持哪一個角色：朱立安？他母親？雙方都支持？雙方都不支持？

▍該文本如果傾向支持矛盾的某一方，是哪一邊？

我們教這篇故事時，大部分學生一開始都假設故事是支持朱立安的觀點，以二十一世紀北方都市大學生的角度來看，顯然這種態度才是開明的。誰看不出，這名母親的觀點既落後又充滿種族偏見？然而，當我們開始討論後，多數學生開始放棄這種想法，認為自己解讀錯誤，原來那只是自己的想法，而非故事的本意。漸漸地，陸續有學生以批判方式描述朱立安。文中多處他對種族融合所展現的同情共感，表面上看似走在時代前端，卻是建立在空泛不切實際的想法上，偽善、且毫無自知之明；相形之下，他的母親卻是發自內心忠於自己的根。討論到最後，出現了另外一種詮釋的聲音：這兩個角色都是社會弊病的受害者，他們活在內心的泡沫世界裡，看不見真實的自己。

我們給學生的寫作作業通常以此課堂討論為基礎，並提供下面這個範本，讓他們思考該文本希望他們支持哪一個角色 —— 如果有的話：

▶ Some might argue that when it comes to the conflict between Julian and his mother over _____, our sympathies should lie with _____. My own view is that _____.

也許有人會認為，就朱立安與他母親對_____這件事的矛盾上，我們應該要支持_____。我個人的看法卻是_____。

你可以提出什麼證據支持？

以上面範本的方式參與對話和論辯時，要如何決定「該支持哪一邊」？說得更清楚一點，要如何詮釋一個文學文本的意義，且證明這樣詮釋是對的呢？

答案就在作品所提供的證據，例如意象、對話、情節、歷史出處、語氣、文體細節等等。

然而有一點務必牢記，這些證據並非絕對。學生們有時會認為，分析文義、象徵、意象和其他證據時，會有固定的規範可供依循。一個角色死了？想必是受到責難的一方。出現了一座階梯？這是往上移動的象徵。有一座花園？肯定是性暗示。

不過，證據是容許各方詮釋的，因此也適於開放討論。以歐康納故事中的母親之死為例，或許說明了我們應該駁斥她的種族觀念落後過時。但另一方面，她的死也可象徵她成為一名英勇的殉道者，這個殘酷苛刻的世界不適合這樣的完人生存。因此，一個角色之死到底意味著什麼，要看他在作品中如何被描述，是正面還是負面，不過這也是另一個具爭議的話題。

如我們於本書中一再強調，別人經常會反對你的看法，並且拿同樣的證據做出相反的解讀。文學作品就如同那張既是鴨也是兔的圖，端看你從哪個角度來看。

既然文學作品裡的同一個證據常可用來支持不同甚至相反的看法，你就需要**據理說明**你怎麼看這證據，也要接受別人可能有不同的詮釋角度。

因此在寫作文學類的論文時，必須證明援引的證據可支持你的詮釋，也要預測其他可能的詮釋角度，例如：

▶ Although some might read the metaphor of _____ in this poem as evidence that, for Author X, modern technology undermines community traditions and values, I see it as _____.
雖然有人可能將此詩中_____的比喻當作證據，認為對作者 X 來說，現代科技會破壞社區傳統和價值觀，我卻將之視為_____。

如果要把證據用「人們說／我說」範本表現，就須留意別人會用什麼不同角度看待——甚至是把這個證據拿來支持一個相反的詮釋。

▶ Some might claim that evidence X suggests _____, but I argue that, on the contrary, it suggests _____.
有些人也許主張 X 這個證據暗示了_____，但是我認為正好相反，它暗示著_____。

▶ I agree with my classmate _____ that the image of _____ in novel Y is evidence of childhood innocence that has been lost. Unlike _____, however, I think this loss of innocence is to be read not as a tragic event but as a necessary, even helpful, stage in human development.
我同意同學_____的看法，在 Y 這部小說中的_____形象代表的是失落的童真。然而我和_____看法不同的地方在於，我認為這種純真的失落不應被視為一場悲劇，而是人類發展的一個必然，甚至有益的階段。

如果有些解讀就是錯的呢？

無論證據有多麼大的解讀空間、多麼可以開放討論，絕不是說，因而產生的各種詮釋同樣有理。有些詮釋根本不能立基於這項證據，我們將就此說明。

如我們先前所提，有些學生起初偏向支持朱立安而非其母親。其中一位學生，我們姑且叫她南西，引用了故事前段的一段文字作為證據，這段文字將朱立安比作基督教的一位殉道者聖塞巴斯蒂安（Saint Sebastian），據知他在極大的痛苦與迫害之下，仍展現堅定的信念。當母親正站著整理東西，朱立安等著帶她前往每週的游泳課時，故事描述朱立安佇立著，彷彿「被釘在門框上，如聖塞巴斯蒂安等待萬箭穿心一般」。

南西認為這段文字證明朱立安是比較值得同情的一方，並且還找出其他證據，例如下面這個段落：

[Julian] was free of prejudice and unafraid to face facts. Most miraculous of all, instead of being blinded by love for [his mother] as she was for him, he had cut himself emotionally free of her and could see her with complete objectivity. He was not dominated by his mother. (412)

朱立安沒有種族偏見也不怕面對現實。最不可思議的是，他對母親的愛沒有蒙蔽他的眼，這就和他母親不同，情感上他早已不受母親束縛，可以完全客觀地看待她。他並不受母親的支配。（頁 412）

南西在論文中引用了類似這樣的段落，總結說：「朱立安代表的是未來社會，是一個非種族主義者、一個受過教育的思想者。」

然而當她把故事重讀一遍，並且聽過其他同學的觀點之後，她逐漸明白她所援引的這幾個段落——把朱立安比作聖人、暗示他種族思想進步、他「不受母親束縛」、「客觀」看待母親 —— 全都是用來諷刺。朱立安自以為有聖人情操、沒有種族偏見、公正客觀，但是這個故事根本是暗示他在欺騙自己。

支持以諷刺角度來解讀朱利安的人，是如何說服南西改變看法呢？首先，他們指出，朱立安和聖塞巴斯蒂安的情況和承受的痛苦截然不同。他們說，不過是被迫等個幾分鐘前往基督教青年會這麼普通的事，有誰會拿來跟一個殉道者為信仰而死相提並論？他們確信，誰也不會。因此他們認為，把這麼懸殊的事件拿來相比，可見這段文字其實是將朱立安描繪成不耐煩、不知感恩、不孝順的兒子，絕非什麼聖人。除此之外，學生還指出，朱立安自我定位為一個「完全客觀」、「面對現實」、「不受（母親）束縛」的進步人士，到了故事結尾卻是個滿懷「罪惡與傷悲」、哽咽哭喊「媽媽！媽媽！」的青年，這樣的反差，暗示朱立安自我定位的正直高尚只是表面形象而已。

此時也許你會納悶，我們怎麼可以說某些文學詮釋觀點是錯的？相較於科學或歷史文本，文學詮釋最大的好處不就是沒有錯誤答案嗎？我們是打算說解讀文學作品有一個「正確」方法 —— 該作品要我們「應該」這樣看的嗎？

不是的，我們不是要說文學作品只有一種解讀法。假如我們是這麼認為，就不會提出一個以**多重解讀**和**開放討論**為基礎的文學分析法。但是的確，承認文學解讀可以開放討論，不代表一個作品的含義可以任由我們發揮，好似無論怎麼詮釋都一樣好。依我們及多數文學老師看來，有些詮釋確實比其他來得好 —— 推論上比較有說服力，從文本的證據看來也比較有根據。

如果我們認定任何的詮釋都說得通，就可能造成讓原文作者觀點和我們觀點之間混淆不清，這就如同那些學生一樣，把自己對六〇年代民權運動的觀點和歐康納的觀點混為一談。這種誤解讓人聯想到我們所說的「近陳腔濫調症」，在這種情況下，我們所概述的並非作者真正想表達的想法，而是一個極很接近的陳腔濫調 —— 或者以歐康納的例子來說，是一種社會理念 —— 寫作的

見 p. 44 關於「近陳腔濫調症」之說明。

人自己這麼相信，就錯誤地假設原作者亦然。如果過度強調文學詮釋沒有錯誤答案，會助長「唯我論」（solipsism）的心態，以為我的想法可以代表別人，把我們看到的一切全轉換成我們自己的版本。

誠如文學理論家勞勃・史寇爾斯（Robert Scholes）所言，閱讀「首先得想像成順應別人的意圖」來了解文學作品含義。「若我們不承認文本背後有一個作者存在」，我們「只是把自己的主觀思維模式和願望投射在文本上」。換而言之，除非盡量去理解作者的話，否則永遠無法真正明白作者的想法，我們看到的只是自己的版本。史寇爾斯承認，好的詮釋往往需要超越作者的意圖，指出矛盾之處和意識形態上的盲點，但是在此之前，我們必須先找出作者的意圖，才能嘗試以這些方式做更多的詮釋。

你對文本的看法為何？

秉持著必須先嘗試理解文本意圖才能加以回應的原則，我們在這堂課裡一直著重在如何了解與說明文學文本在說什麼和做什麼。了解它們在說什麼的方法，包含找出核心矛盾，然後自問作者如何運用各種證據（如角色、對話、意象、事件、情節等）引導你思考該矛盾。最後，作為一名文學讀者，你的工作就是要對作品敞開心胸，接受作者所呈現出來的樣貌，詮釋上才不至於忽略值得閱讀和思考的地方。

一旦理解相當透徹之後，就可以加入自己的見解。提出你對作品的詮釋，並且接受別人的回應，這是所有文學分析的重要步驟，但這樣還不算完成。還有最後一個步驟，就是對作品以及它的見解，做透徹的分析與評論。以你為標準，評斷它在道德上是合情合理還是值得懷疑、內容一致或有所矛盾，並從歷史發展角度看來是進步還是落伍，諸如此類。舉例來說：

Though she is one of the most respected Southern authors of the American literary canon, Flannery O'Connor continually denigrates the one character in her 1961 story who represents the civil rights movement, and in so doing disparages progressive ideas that I believe deserve a far more sympathetic hearing.

雖然富蘭納瑞·歐康納是美國文豪當中最受推崇的南方作家之一，她在 1961 年所撰寫的故事中，對代表民權運動的一個角色一再貶低；她的這種作法，對於應該受到理解尊重的進步思想，也是表現一種貶抑。

然而，評論未必是要挑剔批評，譬如說：

Some criticize O'Connor's story by suggesting that it has a politically regressive agenda. But I see the story as a laudable critique of politics as such. In my view, O'Connor's story rightly criticizes the polarization of political conflicts—North vs. South, liberal vs. conservative, and the like—and suggests that they need to come together: to "converge," as O'Connor's title implies, through religious love, understanding, and forgiveness.

有人批評歐康納的故事，認為某些看法在政治意識上落伍。但我認為，該故事本身就是一篇政治評論佳作。依我來看，歐康納的故事對政治矛盾的兩極對立 —— 南北對立、自由與保守對立等等 —— 做了合理評論，也提出它們需要藉由宗教之愛、體諒和寬恕而向彼此靠攏；就如同書名所暗示的，要「匯合」。

我們知道，一談到評論文學作品，多數人會感到氣餒，甚至只是要你說說作者在講什麼，都可能令人膽怯，因為這意味著你將在無人支持的情況下，設法維護自己對文學大師的某個主張 —— 而其作品往往錯綜複雜、相互矛盾、和更大的歷史運動有關聯。然而，一旦能克服這些挑戰，你會發現思考文學作品的含義、提出意見、與人對談和論辯，才是文學的重要精神。只要做得好，你說的話也會成為別人回應的對象：你的 I say 會成為別人口中的 they say，對談也會不斷地繼續下去。

第 **16** 堂　科學領域的學術寫作

"The data suggest"
「資料顯示」

克里斯多夫・季倫（Christopher Gillen）

　　達爾文（Charles Darwin）形容《物種起源》（*On the Origin of Species*）是「一個長久的爭論」。伽利略（Galileo Galilei）在《關於兩大世界體系的對話》（*Dialogue Concerning the Two Chief World Systems*）一書中，把自己太陽中心說的太陽系理論用一系列的對談形式呈現。這些例子顯示，科學論文寫作基本上是議論式的。科學家和所有學術作家一樣，提出並捍衛主張。他們解決

Christopher Gillen 克里斯多夫・季倫

　　凱尼恩學院（Kenyon College）生物學系教授，也是凱尼恩生物醫學暨科學寫作學會（Kenyon Institute in Biomedical and Scientific Writing）的會長，開設的課程包含動物生理學、運動生物學、生物學概論，全都強調對重要研究論文（primary research article）的審慎閱讀。

歧見、探索尚未解答的問題；他們提出新機制或新理論；他們提出一些解釋、推翻其他解釋。雖然科學作家使用的詞彙更專業，也更強調數字，然而論述技巧與其他領域作家並無二致。

下面這個段落節錄自一本談論物理定律的書，請思考這個範例：

The common refrain that is heard in elementary discussions of quantum mechanics is that a physical object is in some sense both a wave and a particle, with its wave nature apparent when you measure a wave property such as wavelength, and its particle nature apparent when you measure a particle property such as position. But this is, at best, misleading and, at worst, wrong.

量子力學的初級討論中，有一種老掉牙的說法，就是說，物體某種意義上既是波也是粒子。測量波長等屬於波的特性時，波動性就較為顯著，測量位置等屬於粒子特性時，粒子性就較為顯著。但是這充其量只能說是誤解，嚴格來說則是完全錯誤。

——維克多・史坦格（V. J. Stenger），《可理解的宇宙》
（*The Comprehensible Cosmos*）

這段文字裡的「有人說／我說」架構很清楚：**有人說**物體同時具有波和粒子性質，**我說**他們是錯的。這個範例並不是從該篇非議論文裡精挑細選出的唯一一段議論式文字，相反地，史坦格整本書都在維護一個論點，也就是書名所預示的《可理解的宇宙》：儘管有人認為宇宙複雜得難以理解，基本上還是可以理解的。

再舉一個議論式的段落為例，這段文字出自一篇研究論文，探討乳酸對肌肉疲勞的作用：

In contrast to the often suggested role for acidosis as a cause of muscle fatigue, it is shown that in muscles where force was depressed by high [K$^+$]o, acidification by lactic acid produced a pronounced recovery of force.

酸中毒經常被認為是肌肉疲勞的一個肇因，然而證據卻顯示出相反的結果，在因鉀離子累積導致肌力下降的肌肉裡，乳酸所引起的酸化作用反倒使肌力明顯恢復。

—— 奧列·倪爾森、法蘭克·德保力，與克里斯汀·奧維嘉
（O. B. Nielsen, F. de Paoli, and K. Overgaard），
〈乳酸對老鼠骨骼肌之肌力產生之保護作用〉
（Protective Effects of Lactic Acid on Force Production in Rat Skeletal Muscle），
《生理學期刊》（*The Journal of Physiology*）

換個方式來講就是：

Many scientists think that lactic acid causes muscle fatigue, **but our evidence shows** that it actually promotes recovery.

許多科學家認為乳酸是肌肉疲勞的肇因，但我們的證據顯示它其實有助於恢復疲勞。

注意作者們如何稍加修改「有人說／我說」範本來組織論點：

▶ **Although previous work suggests** _____, **our data argue** _____.
雖然過去的研究認為_____，我們的資料卻顯示_____。

這個基本架構以各種型態廣泛運用在科學論文中。本書中所教導的寫作技巧各學科都適用，科學當然也不例外。本課所提供的套句範本與示例皆出自職業科學家之筆，但是裡面出現的技巧都可用於任何關於科學議題的寫作。

儘管議論在科學寫作上有其重要性，但對於剛接觸這種體裁的人，往往只拿來表現一些無爭議的客觀事實。我們可以理解為何會有這種心態。採用客觀語氣可以淡化科學寫作的議論性，許多教科書只介紹公認的結論，對於持續存在的爭議僅輕描淡寫，這也加深了科學毋庸置疑的形象。況且，由於科學作者的論點是根據實驗數據而來，許多科學文章大部分的確是在傳達無爭議的事實。

然而，科學寫作的目的不只是報導事實。科學議論中資料很重要，但絕不是唯一條件。科學家取得重要的新資料之後，必須評估它們的性質、從中得到結論，並且思考可能產生的影響。他們必須將新資料與既有資料結合，提出創新理論，然後設計後續的實驗。簡單來說，科學進展靠的是科學家以洞察力和創造力來使用資料。科學研究和科學寫作最讓人振奮的地方，正在於不斷努力運用資料，增進對世界的理解。

從研究資料開始

資料就是科學論證的基本貨幣。科學家從既有資料發展出假說（hypothesis），再把他們的預測跟實驗資料進行比較，藉此檢驗這些假說。因此，概述資料就成了科學論文寫作的基本方法之一。資料通常可以有不同的解讀方式，因此，由描述資料可以進而審慎分析，也有機會去評論過去的解釋、發展出新的解釋。

描述資料所要求的，不只是報告數字和結論那麼簡單。不能一下子就跳到關鍵處——跳到某人的結論——而必須先描述導致該結論的研究假說、研究方法（method）和研究結果（result），例如：**To test the hypothesis that _____, X measured and found that _____. Therefore, X concluded _____.**（為了驗證_____這個假說，X測量後發現_____。因此，X做出了_____的結論。）在下面的小節裡，我們將分段探討專門用來描述支持科學論證資料的三大論述技巧：**提出普遍的理論、說明研究方法、總結研究結果**。

提出普遍的理論

　　讀者必須先了解該項研究要回應的是哪些主流理論，才能充分理解該研究的細節。因此，寫作者在全心投入細節之前，必須先描述主流理論和假說，讓大家了解這項研究的背景。下面這個段落出自一篇探討昆蟲呼吸的期刊文章，在這段文字中，作者們提出了關於間歇式呼吸（discontinuous gas exchange, DGC）的一個解釋，這是昆蟲週期性關閉呼吸管上的氣孔的現象。

> Lighton (1996, 1998; see also Lighton and Berrigan, 1995) noted the prevalence of DGC in fossorial insects, which inhabit microclimates where CO_2 levels may be relatively high. Consequently, Lighton proposed the chthonic hypothesis, which suggests that DGC originated as a mechanism to improve gas exchange while at the same time minimizing respiratory water loss.

請見 pp. 280-287 物理學家如何以描述數據作為論文的開頭。

賴登（1996 年、1998 年；另參考賴登和貝里根，1995 年）注意到掘地昆蟲普遍有間歇式呼吸的現象，它們居住的特有氣候環境中，二氧化碳濃度可能相當高。因此賴登提出了地底假說，認為間歇式呼吸這種的機制的發生，是為了改善呼吸同時降低呼吸水分流失。

—— 艾倫‧季布斯與勞勃‧江森（A. G. Gibbs and R. A. Johnson），
〈間歇式呼吸在昆蟲身上的作用：地底假說站不住腳〉
（The Role of Discontinuous Gas Exchange in Insects:
The Chthonic Hypothesis Does Not Hold Water），
《實驗生物學期刊》（The Journal of Experimental Biology）

請注意，季布斯和江森不只敘述了賴登的假說，同時扼要說明了該假說的支持證據。他們之所以提出這個證據，是為了探討賴登的見解，所以先做好鋪陳。譬如說，他們可能會指出資料的不足或解讀的謬誤，來質疑地底假說，也可能提出可證明該假說的新方法。重點是，他們在撰寫賴登假說的摘要時，加入了一段關於實驗結果的討論，這便開啟了與賴登的對談。

下列範本可用來提出支持普遍見解：

▶ Experiments showing ＿＿＿＿＿ and ＿＿＿＿＿ have led scientists to propose ＿＿＿＿＿.
有些實驗顯示＿＿＿＿以及＿＿＿＿，這使得科學家提出了＿＿＿＿。

▶ Although most scientists attribute ＿＿＿＿＿ to ＿＿＿＿＿, X's result ＿＿＿＿＿ leads to the possibility that ＿＿＿＿.
雖然多數科學家把＿＿＿＿歸因於＿＿＿＿，但 X 的研究結果＿＿＿＿顯示有＿＿＿＿的可能性。

說明研究方法

　　儘管我們已經提過，科學論證是取決於資料，但仍然必須注意一件事：**資料的品質**會因取得方式而有所不同。透過粗糙或設計不良的實驗所取得的資料，可能會導致錯誤的結論。因此，說明研究方法是非常重要的。為了讓讀者得以評估一個研究方法，寫作者必須說明採用這種方法的目的為何，如下面從一篇期刊文章中節錄的段落，內容是在談論鳥類消化系統的演化：

> To test the hypothesis that flowerpiercers have converged with hummingbirds in digestive traits, we compared the activity of intestinal enzymes and the gut nominal area of cinnamon-bellied flowerpiercers (Diglossa baritula) with those of eleven hummingbird species.
>
> 　　為了驗證刺花鳥和蜂鳥之消化特徵趨於一致的假說，我們比較了桂紅腹刺花鳥和十一種不同品種蜂鳥的腸酶活性及腸道名義面積。

——霍爾赫・尚度貝與馬丁尼茲・德里歐
（ J. E. Schondube and C. Martinez del Rio ），
〈刺花鳥與蜂鳥之糖與蛋白質消化：關於適應趨同的一個比較試驗〉
（ Sugar and Protein Digestion in Flowerpiercers and Hummingbirds:
A Comparative Test of Adaptive Convergence ），
《比較生物學期刊》（ *Journal of Comparative Physiology* ）

　　無論是描述你自己的或別人的研究，都必須指出研究目的，請參考下列範本：

▶ Smith and colleagues evaluated ＿＿＿＿＿ to determine whether
＿＿＿＿＿ .
史密斯與同僚評估了＿＿＿＿＿，以決定是否＿＿＿＿＿。

▶ Because _____ does not account for _____,
we instead used _____.
由於_____無法說明_____，我們改採_____。

總結研究結果

　　科學資料通常以數字的形式表現。提出一項數據時，你的責任就是提供背景資料讓讀者理解數據，譬如提供輔助資料（supporting information）還有進行比較。下面這段文字摘錄自史考特‧透納（J. S. Turner）探討生物體與環境互動的一本著作，他利用數據來印證太陽能對地球的作用。

　　The potential rate of energy transfer from the Sun to Earth is prodigious—about 600 W m^{-2}, averaged throughout the year. Of this, only a relatively small fraction, on the order of 1-2 percent, is captured by green plants. The rest, if it is not reflected back into space, is available to do other things. The excess can be considerable: although some natural surfaces reflect as much as 95% of the incoming solar beam, many natural surfaces reflect much less (Table 3.2), on average about 15-20 percent. The remaining absorbed energy is then capable of doing work, like heating up surfaces, moving water and air masses around to drive weather and climate, evaporating water, and so forth.

　　從太陽到地球的潛在能量轉換率是相當驚人的──全年平均約為每平方公尺分之一（m^{-2}）有 600 瓦特。其中只有約 1-2% 的極少部分會被綠色植物接收，其餘能量若沒被反射回太空，就能產生其他作用。這些多餘的能量相當龐大：儘管部分天然地表會反射高達 95% 的入射太陽光束，不過許多天然地表的反射量卻相對低得多（表 3.2），約為 15-20%。其餘被地表吸收的能量就能夠產生作用，例如提高地面溫度、使水團和氣團四處移動而產生天氣和氣候變化、使水分蒸發等等。

——史考特・透納，《延伸的生物體》（*The Extended Organism*）

透納的論點是，大量的太陽能可以直接轉換並作用於地球，於是他引用了一個帶有度量單位（W m^{-2}）的實際數值（600）來支持他的論點。讀者需要知道單位才能評估這個數值，每平方英寸 600 瓦特和每平方公尺分之一（m^{-2}）600 瓦特，兩者是天差地遠的。接著他用百分比來進行比較，表示接觸地球的總能量只有 1-2% 被植物接收。最後，他把比較結果用區間範圍（1-2% 和 15-20%）而非單一數據表示，利用這種方式表達數據的變異性（variability）。

輔助資料，如度量單位、樣本數（sample size，以 n 表示）、變異量等，能幫助讀者評估數據。一般來說，樣本數增加、變異量減少，資料的可信度就會增加。輔助資料可用下列公式精確地表現：

▶ （平均值） ± （變異量） （單位），n =（樣本數）.

譬如你可以這樣寫：

Before training, resting heart rate of the subjects was 56 ± 7 beats per minute, n = 12.

訓練前受試者的靜止心率為每分鐘 56±7 次，受試者人數 12 人。

另一種提出輔助資料的方式如下：

▶ We measured _____ (sample size) subjects, and the average response was _____ (mean with units) with a range of _____ (lower value) to _____ (upper value).

我們測試了_____（樣本數）受試者，平均反應為_____（平均值附單位），介於_____（較低值）到_____（較高值）之間。

為了幫助讀者理解數據，可以拿同一研究或其他類似研究中的數據一起比較。

下列是可用來表示比較的範本：

▶ Before training, average running speed was _____ ± _____ kilometers per hour, _____ kilometers per hour slower than running speed after training.

訓練前之平均跑步速度為每小時_____±_____公里，比訓練後慢了_____公里。

▶ We found athletes' heart rates to be _____ ± _____ % lower than nonathletes'.

我們發現運動員的心率比非運動員低了_____±_____%。

▶ The subjects in X's study completed the maze in _____ ± _____ seconds, _____ seconds slower than those in Y's study.

X 研究中的受試者在_____±_____秒之內走完迷宮，比 Y 研究中的受試者慢了_____秒。

有時候，作者會需要提出質性資料（qualitative data），像是從圖片或照片中所觀察到的資料。這些無法簡化為數字，而必須用文字精準描述。下列段落節錄自一篇探討細胞蛋白質分布和細胞成長之間關係的論文，其中作者便描述了三種蛋白質 Scrib、Dlg、Lgl 的確切分布位置。

Epithelial cells accumulate different proteins on their apical (top) and basolateral (bottom) surfaces. ... Scrib and Dlg are localized at the septate junctions along the lateral cell surface, whereas Lgl coats vesicles that are found both in the cytoplasm and "docked" at the lateral surface of the cell.

上皮細胞將不同蛋白質堆積在頂端和基底側邊的細胞表面……Scrib 蛋白和 Dlg 蛋白分布在細胞側面的間壁連接組織上，而 Lgl 蛋白則包覆著在小囊泡上，這些囊泡或位於細胞質內，或「附著」在細胞側面。

── 馬克‧佩弗（M. Peifer），〈交通快報 ── 交通堵塞引發腫瘤〉（Travel Bulletin—Traffic Jams Cause Tumors），《科學》（Science）

▍解釋資料的意義

一旦概述完實驗和結果之後，便需要解釋資料的含義。思考下面從一份研究報告中節錄出的段落，文中可以看到科學家用氮（N）和／或磷（P）為幾塊熱帶雨林的土地施肥。

Although our data suggest that the mechanisms driving the observed respiratory responses to increased N and P **may be** different, the large CO_2 losses stimulated by N and P fertilization **suggest** that knowledge of such patterns and their effects on soil CO_2 efflux is critical for understanding the role of tropical forests in a rapidly changing global C [carbon] cycle.

雖然我們的資料顯示，面對氮、磷增加所觀察到的呼吸反應，其驅動機制可能不同，但是施以氮、磷所引發的二氧化碳大量流失，大致顯示，了解這種模式及其對土壤二氧化碳流失之影響，對於了解熱帶雨林在快速變化的全球碳循環上的作用，有密切關係。

—— 柯瑞・克里夫蘭與艾倫・湯森（C. C. Cleveland and A. R. Townsend），
〈為熱帶雨林添加養分致使大量土壤二氧化碳往大氣中流失〉
（Nutrient Additions to a Tropical Rain Forest Drive Substantial Soil
Carbon Dioxide Losses to the Atmosphere），《美國國家科學院院刊》
（*Proceedings of the National Academy of Sciences*）

請留意，克里夫蘭和湯森在討論他們的資料可能產生的影響時，使用了一些象徵他們對資料解釋的信賴水準（level of confidence）的詞彙，包括了動詞 "suggest"（大致顯示）和 "may be"（可能）。

無論是概述別人對資料的解釋，或是提出自己的解釋，都要注意所挑選來連結資料和解釋的動詞。

表示中等信賴水準的動詞有：

▶ **The data suggest / hint / imply _____ .**
這份資料大致顯示／似可顯示_____。

表示確定性更高的動詞有：

▶ **Our results show / demonstrate _____ .**
我們的結果顯示／表示_____。

我們幾乎不會用 prove（證明）這個動詞來描述單一研究，因為再強大的證據通常都不足以證明什麼，除非有其他研究支持同樣的結論。

當多項研究指向同樣的結論，就會產生科學共識（scientific consensus）；反之，研究之間的矛盾往往代表研究上有問題，有待進一步解決。基於這些理由，你可能需要把一項研究的結果拿來跟另一項研究的結果進行比較。這種情況下也要慎選動詞，例如：

▶ **Our data support / confirm / verify the work of X by showing that** _____.

　我們的資料證實 X 的研究，因為它顯示_____。

▶ **By demonstrating** _____**, X's work extends the findings of Y.**

　藉由顯示_____，X 的研究延伸了 Y 的研究結果。

▶ **The results of X contradict / refute Y's conclusion that** _____.

　X 得到的結果與 Y 的_____結論相反。

▶ **X's findings call into question the widely accepted theory that** _____.

　X 的研究結果造成人們開始懷疑_____這個廣為接受的理論。

▶ **Our data are consistent with X's hypothesis that** _____.

　我們的資料與 X 的_____假說是一致的。

提出自己的論點

現在我們要來談科學寫作中**表達個人意見**的部分。這裡會遇到的一個挑戰是，你通常必須接受其他科學家對他們的研究方法和結果的陳述，例如你可能無法主張說：「X 和 Y 聲稱他們研究了六頭大象，但我認為他們實際上只研究了四頭。」然而倒是可以說：「X 和 Y 只研究了六頭大象，這麼少的樣本數令人對他們的結果感到懷疑。」後面這個句子並沒有質疑科學家所做或發現的事，只是在檢視該研究結果該如何解讀。

發展個人論點，也就是 I say 的部分時，通常會從評估其他科學家的解釋開始。請看下面這則範例，這段文字來自一篇探討有益馴化假說（beneficial acclimation hypothesis, BAH）的評論文章，這個假說提出了一個觀念：暴露在特定環境中的生物體，會比未暴露的生物更能適應該環境。

> To the surprise of most physiologists, all empirical examinations of the BAH have rejected its generality. However, we suggest that these examinations are neither direct nor complete tests of the functional benefit of acclimation.

> 令多數生理學家驚訝的是，所有對於有益性馴化假說的實證研究都否定了它的普遍性。然而，我們認為這些研究既未直接也未完全檢驗到馴化作用的有益功能。

—— 羅比・威爾森與克雷格・法蘭克林（R. S. Wilson and C. E. Franklin），
〈檢驗有益馴化假說〉（Testing the Beneficial Acclimation Hypothesis），
《生態與演化趨勢》（*Trends in Ecology & Evolution*）

威爾森與法蘭克林採用的寫作技巧是「扭轉」技巧：先認可其他生理學家所收集的資料，但是質疑這些資料的解釋方法，因此創造機會提出自己的解釋。

見 p. 69 關於「扭轉」寫作技巧的說明。

也許你會問，我們是否該質疑別的科學家如何解釋他們自己的研究。他們是執行研究的人，不是最有資格評估結果的嗎？也許是如此，但是從上面的範例看來，其他科學家可能從不同的觀點，或比較客觀的角度來看這項研究。事實上，科學文化靠的就是激烈的論辯，科學家捍衛自己的研究結果，也質疑別人的研究結果——這是一場你來我往的思想交流，科學的可靠性也會因此而提升。因此，對別人的研究提出一個審慎思辨觀點，是科學進展裡不可或缺的一部分。以下一些基本寫作方法，在參與科學對談時可以使用：表示同意並提出不同的看法、表示反對並說明原因、既有同意也有反對、預測反對意見、說明為何重要。

表示同意並提出不同的看法

科學研究在正式發表之前，會經過一層又一層的質疑思辨。科學家和同僚進行內部討論、在會議上提出研究結果、收到別人對他們手稿的評論時，都可以取得回饋意見。換言之，最重大的爭論很有可能在發表之前就已經解決，因此，我們很難在已發表的文獻當中找到可以反對的論點。即便如此，我們還是可以並且必須找出方法參與對談。

一個方法就是提出仍有進一步研究的空間，例如：

▶ Now that _____ has been established, scientists will likely turn their attention toward _____.
既然_____已經確立，科學家很有可能將注意力轉向_____。

▶ X's work leads to the question of _____. Therefore, we investigated _____.
X 的研究導致產生_____的疑問，因此我們對_____進行了調查。

▶ **To see whether these findings apply to _____, we propose to _____.**

為了了解這些研究結果是否適用於_____，我們打算_____。

　　另一種表達同意卻又能同時參與對談的方法，是先對一項研究結果表示認同，接著提出一種解釋方法。下面這個句子是出自一篇關於膳食營養缺乏的評論文章，作者同意先前的一項研究結果，並且提出了可能的解釋。

Inadequate dietary intakes of vitamins and minerals are widespread, most likely due to excessive consumption of energy-rich, micronutrient-poor, refined food.

　　膳食維他命和礦物質攝取不足的情況十分普遍，最有可能是食用過多含有高能量、低營養素的精緻食物所造成。

—— 布魯斯・艾姆斯（B. Ames），〈低微量營養素攝取量可能因利用篩檢產生的稀少微量營養素分配而加速老化退化性疾病〉（Low Micronutrient Intake May Accelerate the Degenerative Diseases of Aging through Allocation of Scarce Micronutrients by Triage），《美國國家科學院院刊》

　　下列範本，可以用來解釋實驗結果：

▶ **One explanation for X's finding of _____ is that _____.**
An alternative explanation is _____.

針對 X _____的研究結果，有一個解釋是_____，
另一個可能的解釋則是_____。

▶ **The difference between _____ and _____ is probably due to _____ .**

_____ 和 _____ 之間的差別很有可能是 _____ 所造成。

表示反對並說明理由

儘管科學界常有共識，但合理的意見分歧也一樣常見。由不同科學家團隊在同樣條件下所進行的測量，照理來說應該產生一樣的結果。然而，對於何種實驗方法最適當、某種實驗設計對某個假說的測試效果如何、實驗結果該如何解釋，科學家經常抱持不同的意見。為了說明這種分歧，讓我們回到乳酸在運動期間是否對身體有益這個爭論。在下面這段文字中，蘭姆和史蒂芬森正在回應克里斯坦森與同僚所做的一項研究，文中提到乳酸可能對靜止肌肉有好處，對活動肌肉卻是沒有的。

The argument put forward by Kristensen and colleagues (12)... is not valid because it is based on observations made with isolated whole soleus muscles that were stimulated at such a high rate that > 60% of the preparation would have rapidly become completely anoxic (4)... Furthermore, there is no reason to expect that adding more H+ to that already being generated by the muscle activity should in any way be advantageous. It is a bit like opening up the carburetor on a car to let in too much air or throwing gasoline over the engine and then concluding that air and gasoline are deleterious to engine performance.

由克里斯坦森及其同僚所提出的論點（頁 12）……是不足採信的，因為這個論點所根據的資料，是觀察獨立的整塊比目魚肌受到過度強烈的刺激，導致超過 60% 的準備系統早已迅速進入無氧狀態（頁 4）……此外，肌肉活動產生氫離子時，再添加更多氫離子能有助益的這個論點是沒有根據的。這就有點像是打開汽車的化油器讓太多空氣進來，或者在引擎上倒汽油，然後下結論說空氣和汽油會危害引擎效能一樣。

—— 葛拉罕·蘭姆與喬治·史蒂芬森（G. D. Lamb and D. G. Stephenson），
〈論點：乳酸堆積是肌肉活動期間的一個有利因素〉
（Point: Lactic Acid Accumulation Is an Advantage during Muscle Activity），
《應用生理學期刊》（*Journal of Applied Physiology*）

蘭姆和史蒂芬森舉出實驗細節來反駁克里斯坦森及其同僚的論點，首先是批評他們的研究方法，認為他們用如此高強度的肌肉刺激創造出無氧的狀態，也批評實驗設計的邏輯不通，認為把更多酸（氫離子）加到已經正在產生酸的肌肉中並沒有意義。另外值得注意的是，他們把該實驗方法比做是讓引擎充滿空氣和汽油，藉此將自己的論點講得更透徹。因此，即便是在科學寫作上，也不必完全迴避使用自己熟悉的語言。

在思考別人的研究時，可以看看其實驗設計和方法是否不足以驗證假說：

▶ **The work of Y and Z appears to show that _____,**
but their experimental design does not control for _____.
Y 和 Z 的研究表面上顯示出_____，但是他們的實驗設計並沒有
控制_____。

另外，也可以考慮，有些研究結果可能不會導致聲稱的結論：

▶ While X and Y claim that _____ , their finding of _____
actually shows that _____ .
X 和 Y 雖主張_____，他們的研究結果_____事實上顯示
_____。

好的，但是……

科學通常是漸進式的進展，新的研究也許會改進或延伸過去的研究，但往往不會全盤推翻。因此，**科學作家經常會表示某種程度同意，接著提出部分異議**。下面這段範例出自一篇評論文章，文中對評估蛋白質如何交互作用的研究方法表達評論，作者承認雙雜交研究的價值，同時也指出一些缺失。

The two-hybrid studies that produced the protein interaction map for D. melanogaster (12) provide a valuable genome-wide view of protein interactions but have a number of shortcomings (13). Even if the protein-protein interactions were determined with high accuracy, the resulting network would still require careful interpretation to extract its underlying biological meaning. Specifically, the map is a representation of all possible interactions, but one would only expect some fraction to be operating at any given time.

雙雜交研究讓我們得到黑腹果蠅的蛋白質交互作用圖（頁 12），為蛋白質的交互作用提供了一個寶貴的全基因觀點，但此仍有些缺失（頁 13）。即便蛋白質交互作用可以準確地判定，其造成的網絡仍有待詳細解釋，才能找出潛在的生物意涵。具體而言，該作用圖表現出所有可能的交互作用，但只能在某些特定時間才能在某個部分產生作用。

—— 傑洛米・萊斯、亞隆・柯申邦與古斯塔沃・史托洛維茲奇
（J. J. Rice, A. Kershenbaum, and G. Stolovitzky），
持續的印象：蛋白質交互作用圖之圖案可能提供演化事件的足跡〉
（Lasting Impressions: Motifs in Protein-Protein Maps May Provide
Footprints of Evolutionary Events.），《美國國家科學院院刊》

勾勒出一項研究的範圍和限制，是表示某種程度同意的一個好方法，可運用下列範本：

▶ **While X's work clearly demonstrates** _____, _____
   will be required before we can determine whether _____.
   雖然 X 的研究清楚顯示出_____，還是需要_____才能決定
   是否_____。

▶ **Although Y and Z present firm evidence for** _____, **their data**
   can not be used to argue that _____.
   雖然 Y 和 Z 提出有力證據證明_____，他們的資料卻不足以主張
   _____。

▶ **In summary, our studies show that** _____, **but the issue of**
   _____ **remains unresolved.**
   簡而言之，我們的研究顯示_____，但是_____的議題仍懸而
   未決。

預測反對意見

　　質疑是科學過程裡的一項關鍵要素。在一項解釋被接受之前，科學家需要有力的證據，並且評估其他可能的解釋是否皆已徹底探討過。因此，科學家在

提出自己的論點之前，必須要考慮到其他可能反對的理由。下面段落節自一本關於宇宙起源的書，作者泰森與葛德史密斯首先承認，有些人可能質疑物理學家所提出的「暗物質」（dark matter）是否真的存在，目前人們對暗物質的了解並不多，接著他們便對這些懷疑論者做出回應。

Unrelenting skeptics might compare the dark matter of today with the hypothetical, now defunct "ether," proposed centuries ago as the weightless, transparent medium through which light moved... But dark matter ignorance differs fundamentally from ether ignorance. While ether amounted to a placeholder for our incomplete understanding, the existence of dark matter derives from not from mere presumption but from the observed effects of its gravity on visible matter.

鍥而不捨的懷疑論者也許會將今天的暗物質，拿來跟已推翻的假想物質「乙太」相提並論，乙太的概念在幾個世紀前曾被提出，是一種無重量的透明介質，光在其中移動⋯⋯但是人們對暗物質的不了解和乙太基本上不同。乙太象徵的是我們的一知半解，然而暗物質的存在並非源於單純的假設，而是在可見物質上觀察到它的重力作用，才衍生出的理論。

—— 尼爾·泰森與唐納·葛德史密斯（N. D. Tyson and D. Goldsmith），
《萬物起源：宇宙一百四十億年演化史》
（*Origins: Fourteen Billion Years of Cosmic Evolution*）

預測自己論文可能遭遇的反對意見，有助於釐清和應付可能的批評。你整體的論證方法和特定的解釋都可能遭受的異議，這都必須考慮在內。下列是一些可套用的範本：

▶ Scientists who take a _____ (reductionist / integrative / biochemical / computational / statistical) approach might view our results differently.

採用 _____（還原／整合／生化／計算／統計）方法的科學家，對我們的結果可能會有不同的看法。

▶ This interpretation of the data might be criticized by X, who has argued that _____.

X 可能會批評這項資料的解讀，他曾主張_____。

▶ Some may argue that this experimental design fails to account for _____.

也許有人會認為這個實驗設計無法說明_____。

說明論點的重要性

儘管單一研究所著眼的範圍不大，但科學最終的目的還是要回答重要問題以及創造實用的技術。因此，在參與科學對談時，很重要的便是說明這項研究——以及你的論點——的價值。下面這段文字是從一篇評論文章中節錄而來，內容是在評論一篇研究文章，並提出這項評估電子軌域（electron orbital）形狀的研究可能產生的兩大影響。

The classic textbook shape of electron orbitals has now been directly observed. As well as confirming the established theory, this work may be a first step to understanding high-temperature superconductivity.

電子軌域的標準形狀現在已經可以直接觀察。除鞏固了確立的理論之外，這項研究可能是了解高溫超導現象的第一步。

—— 柯林‧漢弗萊斯（C. J. Humphreys），〈繞行軌道中的電子樣貌〉（Electrons Seen in Orbit），《自然》

漢弗萊斯認為這項研究鞏固了既有的理論，並可能幫助理解另一範疇。思考一項研究的重要意義時，可以同時考量它的實用性，以及對未來科學研究的影響。

▶ **These results open the door to studies that _____.**
這些結果為_____的研究開啟了大門。

▶ **The methodologies developed by X will be useful for _____.**
X 所發展出來的研究方法將對_____有所助益。

▶ **Our findings are the first step toward _____.**
我們的研究結果是邁向_____的第一步。

▶ **Further work in this area may lead to the development of _____.**
這個領域的深入研究可能導致_____的發展。

解釋以便參與科學對談

科學領域如同其他學科一樣，通常要從別人完成的研究開始討論，因此要以質疑辯論的態度來評估這些研究。為了達到這個目的，你需要思索他們的資料如何支持解釋，如此也有助於發展出你自己的解釋——這就是你的入場券，可以加入一場持續進行的科學對談。下列問題可以幫助你解讀和回應科學研究：

這些方法對試驗假說的效果如何？

■ 樣本數足夠嗎？

■ 這個實驗設計是否有效度？
　實驗是否控制得宜？

■ 此研究方法有什麼侷限性？

■ 有其他可運用的技術嗎？

研究結果的解釋是否平實客觀？

■ 研究結果是否能支持所陳述的結論？

■ 是否已充分考慮資料的變異性？

■ 其他研究結果證明（或反駁）這個結論嗎？

■ 還有哪些實驗可以測試這個結論？

該研究可產生哪些更廣泛的意涵（implication），它的重要性何在？

■ 該研究結果能否應用到這個研究本身之外呢？

■ 該研究可產生什麼實際的影響？

■ 該研究引發了什麼問題？

■ 接下來應該進行什麼實驗？

　　本堂課所提供的範例在在顯示，科學家的工作不僅只是收集事實，也要解釋這些事實並論述其意義。科學前線是我們探測問題的地方，這些問題都是我們目前能力所不及、無法解答的，此時資料必然不全、爭議也在所難免。科學論文寫作讓你有機會在一場持續進行的討論中，把自己的論點加入。

第 17 堂　社會科學領域的學術寫作

"Analyze this"

「分析這一點」

愛琳・艾克曼（Erin Ackerman）

　　社會科學是研究人的學問 —— 研究人的行為和人際關係，以及促進這些互動的組織和機制。人是非常複雜的，因此任何關於人類行為的研究再怎麼樣都是片面的，只能考慮部分行為及其原因，但是不一定能做出決定性的解釋。正因如此，社會科學是一門持續對談與爭辯的學科。

Erin Ackerman 愛琳・艾克曼

　　新澤西學院（College of New Jersey）的社會科學圖書館員，曾於紐約市立大學約翰傑學院（John Jay College, City University of New York）教授政治學。其研究與教學興趣包含女性與美國法律、生殖衛生之法律與政治，以及社會科學的資訊素養（information literacy）。

試想，社會科學研究的一些議題，如最低工資法、移民政策、健康照護、就業歧視等，你對這些議題有意見嗎？人人都有意見。不過作為一名社會科學的學生，寫作時不能只是寫出自己的意見。如同其他學科，好的社科寫作必須讓人看到你的想法是經過深思熟慮的。為了達到這個目的，最好讓你的觀點和別人的觀點產生交流，並比對相關資料，來檢視你們的看法。換言之，要先聽聽別人怎麼說，再提出你的想法作為回應。

　　下面的示例來自一本講述當代美國政治文化的書，請思考這段文字：

> Claims of deep national division were standard fare after the 2000 elections, and to our knowledge few commentators have publicly challenged them. ... In sum, contemporary observers of American politics have apparently reached a new consensus around the proposition that old disagreements about economics now pale in comparison to new divisions based on sexuality, morality, and religion, divisions so deep as to justify fears of violence and talk of war in describing them.

> This short book advocates a contrary thesis: the sentiments expressed in the previously quoted pronouncements of scholars, journalists, and politicos range from simple exaggeration to sheer nonsense. ... Many of the activists in the political parties and various cause groups do, in fact, hate each other and regard themselves as combatants in a war. But their hatreds and battles are not shared by the great mass of the American people. ...

> 　　2000 年的選舉過後，聲稱國家嚴重分裂的說法已經司空見慣，且據我們所知，幾乎無人對此公開質疑……簡單來說，當代美國政治的觀察家顯然已經達成新共識，就是過去在經濟上的分歧，要是與新近一些因為

性、道德、宗教而產生的分裂現象相比，已經算不上什麼了。這種分裂之深，使得人們談到此一現象時，直指疑懼暴力和戰爭發生的可能。

本書提出一個相反的論點：前述學者、記者、政客的激烈言論，根本是單純誇大，甚至一派胡言……事實上，政黨和各種社團中的許多激進分子確實互相仇視，並且自詡為戰爭裡的鬥士。然而那都只是他們自己的仇恨和戰爭，廣大的美國人民並不打算參與。

—— 莫里斯・費奧里娜（Morris P. Fiorina），
《文化戰爭？一個分化的美國之迷思》
（*Culture War? The Myth of a Polarized America*）

換言之，「有人」（記者、專家、其他政治學家）說美國民眾是嚴重分裂的，費奧里娜卻質疑他們對證據的解釋並不正確 —— 尤其這是他們從少數特例（激進分子）所歸納出來的結論。甚至，本書的書名也在質疑別人所持的一個觀點，費奧里納娜將之歸為一種「迷思」（myth）。

本堂課將探討社會科學作家所採用的一些基本寫作技巧。此外，社會科學領域的論文大致包含幾個核心成分：一段強有力的緒論（introduction）和論點、一段文獻探討（literature review），與寫作者的個人分析，此分析包含提出資料並思考可能產生的影響。你的論文主要內容就是上述這些成分的全部或部分。緒論的部分闡述全篇的主旨，簡單扼要地說明文章的內容，以及此論點在已進行的對談中如何定位。文獻探討的部分概述關於這個主題的各家看法。個人分析的部分則提出資料 —— 將你評量或檢視人類行為的相關資料與他人論點比對 —— 並說明根據你的調查得到什麼結論。你同意或不同意別人的看法，還是部分同意部分反對？你的理由何在？那又如何呢？誰應該關心你的看法，為什麼？

緒論與論點：「本研究質疑……」

　　緒論中，你必須提出即將討論的內容。你可檢視以往學者的研究或某些普遍的看法，以新資料對照後發現它們並不正確。或者，你可指出一個作者的研究大抵正確，但是還可以加上一些限制條件或以某種方式延伸。又或者，你可能發現了一個知識缺口——我們對 X 主題很了解，對另一個密切相關的主題卻幾乎一無所知。不管在哪一種情況下，緒論都必須涵蓋「有人說」和「我說」兩種觀點。如果概述完「有人說」的部分就停止，讀者不知道你要為這段對談帶來什麼見解。同理，如果你直接跳到「我說」部分，讀者可能不知道這段談所為何來。

　　有時候你加入對談時，相關討論似已經塵埃落定。某個話題的各種觀點，已經由相關學者或整個社會上廣泛接受，成為該主題的普遍思維方式。你或許想對此論點提出新的支持理由，或許你想加以質疑。為了達到目的，就必須先指明並簡述這些已有普遍共識的說法，接著提出自己的看法。事實上，社會科學領域的寫作常是在對我們自認為已知的事物質疑。請思考下面這段節自《經濟展望期刊》（*The Journal of Economic Perspectives*）的示例：

> Fifteen years ago, Milton Friedman's 1957 treatise *A Theory of the Consumption Function* seemed badly dated. Dynamic optimization theory had not been employed much in economics when Friedman wrote, and utility theory was still comparatively primitive, so his statement of the "permanent income hypothesis" never actually specified a formal mathematical model of behavior derived explicitly from utility maximization ... [W]hen other economists subsequently found multiperiod maximizing models that could be solved explicitly, the implications of

those models differed sharply from Friedman's intuitive description of his "model." Furthermore, empirical tests in the 1970s and 1980s often rejected these rigorous versions of the permanent income hypothesis in favor of an alternative hypothesis that many households simply spent all of their current income.

Today, with the benefit of a further round of mathematical (and computational) advances, Friedman's (1957) original analysis looks more prescient than primitive...

十五年前，米爾頓‧傅利曼 1957 年出版的專著《消費函數理論》看似已嚴重過時。在傅利曼寫作之時，動態最佳化理論尚未廣泛應用在經濟學上，效用理論也仍然在起步階段，因此他對「恆常所得假說」的陳述從未實際提出一個數學模式，來解釋因效用極大化所產生的行為……後來其他經濟學家發現了可明確解決的多期極大化模式，這些模式的含義和傅利曼對其「模式」的直覺描述大相逕庭。再者，於 1970 和 1980 年代所進行的實證研究，往往駁斥了恆常所得假說的各個嚴謹版本，而偏向另一個假說，主張許多家庭會花光現有收入。

今天，隨著數學（和電算科技）進一步的發展，傅利曼（1957 年）的最早分析看起來反倒是很有先見之明，不能說是原始……

—— 克里斯多夫‧卡羅（Christopher D. Carroll），
〈消費函數理論，有與無流動性限制〉（A Theory of Consumption Function, With and Without Liquidity Constraints），《經濟展望期刊》

這段緒論清楚顯示，卡羅要為傅利曼辯護，駁斥一些對他研究的主要批評。卡羅先提出別人對傅利曼的研究有什麼批評，接著說明這些批評結果證明是錯誤，並再度認為傅利曼的研究是有說服力的。卡羅的範本類似這樣：

▶ Economics research in the last fifteen years suggested Friedman's 1957 treatise was _____ because _____. In other words, they say that Friedman's work is not accurate because of _____, _____, and _____. Recent research convinces me, however, that Friedman's work makes sense.

過去 15 年內的經濟研究大致顯示，傅利曼於 1957 年所發表的專著 _____，原因在於_____。換言之，他們認為傅利曼的研究不正確，理由是_____、_____，以及_____。然而近來的研究則令我相信，傅利曼的研究是有意義的。

不過，在部分情況下，專家之間對一個主題未必有強烈共識。你可以藉由支持某方說法或提出另一種觀點，來參與這種類型的持續爭論。在下列示例中，莎里·柏曼（Shari Berman）針對二十世紀人們如何解釋世界事件，指出兩種互相爭論的說法，接著提出第三種觀點。

Conventional wisdom about twentieth-century ideologies rests on two simple narratives. One focuses on the struggle for dominance between democracy and its alternatives... The other narrative focuses on the competition between free-market capitalism and its rivals... Both of these narratives obviously contain some truth... Yet both only tell part of the story, which is why their common conclusion—neoliberalism as the "end of History"—is unsatisfying and misleading.

What the two conventional narratives fail to mention is that a third struggle was also going on: between those ideologies that believed in the primacy of economics and those that believed in the primacy of politics.

傳統對於二十世紀意識形態的觀念以兩種簡單的論述為基礎，一個著重在民主體系與其他體系之間的主權鬥爭……一個則側重於自由市場資本主義和其他意識形態之間的競爭……兩種論述顯然都有其真實性……不過兩種論述都不夠周全，也因此他們的共同結論——作為「歷史終結」的新自由主義——不僅說服力不足，亦使人產生誤解。

兩種傳統論述皆未提及第三種鬥爭亦在進行：發生在兩種意識形態之間，一方認為經濟優先，另一方則相信政治優先。

—— 莎里·柏曼，〈經濟優先與政治優先：了解二十世紀的意識形態動力學〉（ The Primacy of Economics versus the Primacy of Politics: Understanding the Ideological Dynamics of the Twentieth Century ），《政治觀點》（ Perspectives on Politics ）

柏曼先是指出兩種互相競爭的論述，接著提出第三種觀點，而在後續文章中，她表態認為第三種觀點解釋了當前關於全球化的爭論。這種緒論所採用的範本大致是這樣：

▶ In recent discussions of ＿＿＿＿＿, a controversial aspect has been ＿＿＿＿＿. On the one hand, some argue that ＿＿＿＿＿. On the other hand, others argue that ＿＿＿＿＿. Neither of these arguments, however, considers the alternative view that ＿＿＿＿＿."
近來關於＿＿＿＿＿的討論中，一直有個爭議之處在於＿＿＿＿＿。一方面，有人認為＿＿＿＿＿。另一方面，又有人主張＿＿＿＿＿。然而這兩種論點都未考慮到另一個觀點，也就是＿＿＿＿＿。

然而，有鑑於社會科學領域所探討的議題相當複雜，有時你對各項觀點可以表示部分同意、部分反對，也就是一方面指出你認為正確或有價值的地方，

更多回應的方式請參考第 4 堂。

一方面反對或修正其他論點。在下面的範例中，人類學家莎莉‧恩格爾‧梅麗（Sally Engle Merry）同意一位學者說某個現象是現代社會的關鍵特徵，但是主張該特徵的來源與該學者所指的不同。

> Although I agree with Rose that an increasing emphasis on governing the soul is characteristic of modern society, I see the transformation not as evolutionary but as the product of social mobilization and political struggle.

> 儘管我同意蘿絲的意見，日益強調統治靈魂是現代社會的特徵，然而我不認為這種轉變是一種進化，這只是社會動員和政治鬥爭的產物。

> ——莎莉‧恩格爾‧梅麗，〈權利、宗教和社區：全球化環境下解決針對女性之暴力行為的方法〉（Rights, Religion, and Community: Approaches to Violence against Women in the Context of Globalization），《法律與社會評論》（Law and Society Review）

下列是可同時表達同意和反對的範本：

▶ **Although I agree with X up to a point, I cannot accept his overall conclusion that _____.**
儘管我某種程度同意 X 的說法，我不能接受他的整體結論_____。

▶ **Although I disagree with X on _____ and _____, I agree with her conclusion that _____.**
雖然我在_____和_____方面並不認同 X 的看法，但我認同她的結論_____。

▶ Political scientists studying _____ have argued that it is caused by _____ . While _____ contributes to the problem, _____ is also an important factor.

研究_____的政治科學家主張這是由_____所造成，雖然_____確實是問題的起因之一，_____亦是一個重要因素。

在從不同角度檢視人類的過程中，社會科學家有時會發現缺口（gap），亦即過去研究未曾探索之處。在一篇探討非裔美國人社區的文章中，社會學家瑪麗・帕堤洛（Mary Pattillo）便指出了這樣的缺口。

The research on African Americans is dominated by inquiries into the lives of the black poor. Contemporary ethnographies and journalistic descriptions have thoroughly described deviance, gangs, drugs, intergender relations and sexuality, stymied aspiration, and family patterns in poor neighborhoods (Dash 1989; Hagedorn 1988; Kotlowitz 1991; Lemann 1991; MacLeoad 1995; Sullivan 1989; Williams 1989). Yet, the majority of African Americans are not poor (Billingsley 1992). A significant part of the black experience, namely that of working and middle-class blacks, remains unexplored. We have little information about what black middle-class neighborhoods look like and how social life is organized within them... this article begins to fill this empirical and theoretical gap using ethnographic data collected in Groveland, a middle-class black neighborhood in Chicago.

　　針對非裔美國人的研究以貧窮黑人生活的調查為主。當代的人誌研究和新聞報導都在描述貧窮社區裡的偏差行為、幫派、毒品、性別關係和性行為、生平不得志和家庭模式等（達許，1989；哈格多恩，1988；科洛威茨，1991；李曼，1991；麥克勞德，1995；蘇利文，1989；威廉斯，1989）。然而，大多數的非裔美國人並不貧窮（比林斯利，1992），有一個重要部分沒有被探討，亦即就業中產階級黑人的生活經驗。我們對於黑人中產階級社區的樣貌，以及他們的社會生活型態所知甚少……本文的緣起，就是要利用我們在格羅夫蘭這個芝加哥中產階級黑人社區所收集到的人誌研究資料，來填補這個實證和理論缺口。

——瑪麗·帕堤洛，〈慈母與幫派分子：中產階級黑人社區之犯罪管理〉
（Sweet Mothers and Gangbangers: Managing Crime in a Black "Middle-Class Neighborhood），《社會力》（Social Forces）

帕堤洛表示，關於貧窮非裔美國人的言論已經很多，然而，我們對於其就業和中產階級社區的生活卻所知甚少——這正是她將在文中填補的缺口。

下列範本可用來指出現有研究的缺口：

▶ **Studies of X have indicated _____ . It is not clear, however, that this conclusion applies to _____ .**
X 的研究已經指出_____，然而，這項結論是否可應用於_____並不清楚。

▶ **_____ often take for granted that _____ . Few have investigated this assumption, however.**
_____經常把_____視為理所當然，然而很少有人對這個假設進行調查。

▶ X's work tells us a great deal about _____ . Can this work be generalized to _____ ?

X 的研究對於 _____ 做了很多說明。這份研究是否能推論到 _____ 上面呢？

再說一次，一段好的緒論是以別人的言論為背景，表明自己的看法。在緒論之外，整篇論文都必須在「有人說」和「我說」之間來回切換，補充更多細節。

文獻探討：「先前研究指出……」

在文獻探討的部分，要把「有人說」和「我說」的話解釋得更詳細，針對欲回應的觀點加以概述、轉述或引述，須在別人的言論和你的焦點之間取得平衡。要持平、正確地描述別人的研究，但也要有選擇性，藉由選擇與你的觀點和觀察結果相關的細節，為個人論點做好準備。

社會科學寫作很常見的一種手法，就是同時概述好幾個論點，用一個段落指出他們的主要論點和研究結果，例如下面這個段落：

> How do employers in a low-wage labor market respond to an increase in the minimum wage? The prediction from conventional economic theory is unambiguous: a rise in the minimum wage leads perfectly competitive employers to cut employment (George J. Stigler, 1946). Although studies in the 1970's based on aggregate teenage employment rates usually confirmed this prediction, earlier studies based on comparisons of

employment at affected and unaffected establishments often did not (e.g., Richard A. Lester, 1960, 1964). Several recent studies that rely on a similar comparative methodology have failed to detect a negative employment effect of higher minimum wages. Analyses of the 1990-1991 increases in the federal minimum wage (Lawrence F. Katz and Krueger, 1992; Card, 1992a) and of an earlier increase in the minimum wage in California (Card, 1992b) find no adverse employment impact.

低薪勞力市場的雇主如何因應最低薪資的調漲？傳統經濟理論的預測很明確：最低薪資調漲會令完全競爭型的雇主減少僱用（喬治·史提格樂，1946）。儘管 1970 年代，依據青少年總就業率所做的一些研究，證實了此一預測，然而更早期的研究，將受影響與不受影響企業之僱用情形進行比較，卻往往無法證實此一預測（如：理查·萊斯特，1960、1964）。最近幾個類似之比較研究，也沒有發現最低薪資調高會對僱用行為產生負面效應。分析 1990 到 1991 年間的聯邦最低薪資調升（勞倫斯·卡茨與克魯格，1992；卡爾德，1992a），以及更早加州實施的最低薪資調升（卡爾德，1992b），也都沒有發現對僱用行為產生不利影響。

——大衛·卡爾德與艾倫·克魯格（David Card and Alan Krueger），
〈最低薪資與僱用行為：一項新澤西州與賓州速食業之個案研究〉
（Minimum Wages and Employment: A Case Study of the Fast-Food
Industry in New Jersey and Pennsylvania），《美國經濟評論》
（*The American Economic Review*）

卡爾德和克魯格舉出一些研究的重要結果和結論，這些研究都與他們正在調查的問題及所要提出的論點息息相關，他們先問：「低薪勞力市場的雇主如何因應最低薪資的調漲？」繼而回答這個問題。過程中他們回顧了其他曾回答過此問題的人，說明這個問題曾有不同、甚至相反的答案。

這種摘要很簡潔，把多位學者的相關論點放在一起，綜覽一個特定主題的學術研究。在寫這種摘要時，你必須自問，假如是你是那些學者的話，會如何描述自己立場，同時也要考慮其研究有哪些部分和你想建立的論點有關聯。若是你手上有某一主題的豐富相關研究資料，想要為一場爭論理出頭緒，或者你想要指出某作者的研究是如何立基於其他人的研究，這種摘要方式就非常適合。下列範本可用來概述論文提要：

► **In addressing the question of _____, political scientists have considered several explanations for _____. X argues that _____. According to Y and Z, another plausible explanation is _____.**

在處理_____的問題上，政治學家已經考慮過_____的幾種解釋。X 認為_____，而根據 Y 和 Z 的看法，另一可信的解釋則為_____。

► **What is the effect of _____ on _____? Previous work on _____ by X and by Y and Z supports _____.**

_____對於_____的效應為何？過去針對_____，由 X 以及 Y 和 Z 的研究皆主張_____。

有時候你要對文中所引用的研究加以解釋，譬如在期中考或期末考時，你可能需要展現對一份研究已有深入了解。社會科學領域有部分學科，標準寫作法會要求較長且較詳細的文獻探討。你可以請問老師，或者看看老師指定閱讀的文章，就知道文獻探討需要的長度和詳細程度。此外，有時某些作者的研究對你的論點特別重要，因此你需要提出更多的細節來說明他們的看法。在下面的示例中，瑪莎·德西克（Martha Derthick）概述了一個對其著作很重要的論點，她的這本書是在討論菸草管制的政治意義。

The idea that governments could sue to reclaim health care costs from cigarette manufacturers might be traced to "Cigarettes and Welfare Reform," an article published in the *Emory Law Journal* in 1977 by Donald Gasner, a law professor at the University of Southern Illinois. Garner suggested that state governments could get a cigarette manufacturer to pay the direct medical costs "of looking after patients with smoking diseases." He drew an analogy to the Coal Mine Health and Safety Act of 1969, under which coal mine operators are required to pay certain disability benefits for coal miners suffering from pneumoconiosis, or black lung disease.

認為政府可透過訴訟向香菸製造商追討健康照護成本的想法，或許是起源自〈香菸與福利改革〉一文，這是南伊利諾大學法律教授唐納·賈斯納 1977 年發表於《埃默里法律期刊》的文章。賈斯納提出州政府大可要香菸製造商支付「照顧菸疾病患」的直接醫療成本。他拿 1969 年的《煤礦健康安全法》做比較，在該法案的規範下，煤礦業者須為罹患肺塵症或稱黑肺症的礦工，支付一定的傷殘撫卹金。

—— 瑪莎·德西克，《付之一炬：菸草政治上從立法到訴訟》
（*Up In Smoke: From Legislation to Litigation in Tobacco Politics*）

德西克指出了她所要概述的論點，亦直接引用了作者的論述，接著加上一個關於先例的細節。你可能想要效法她直接引用一段言論，逐字如實引述該作者的話，以表現你的公正持平。你不能只是插入一句引述句，還必須向讀者解釋它對你的論點有何意義。下面這個示例節自一本探討侵權改革（tort reform）的書，請思考這段文字：

The essence of agenda setting was well enunciated by E. E. Schattschneider: "In politics as in everything else, it makes a great difference whose game we play" (1960, 47). In short, the ability to define or control the rules, terms, or perceived options in a contest over policy greatly affects the prospects for winning.

謝茨耐德把議題設定的涵義闡釋得很好:「政治,跟世上其他事情一樣,關鍵是,我們玩的是誰的遊戲。」(1960,頁 47)。簡而言之,在一場政治競賽中,擁有能定義或控制規則、規定,或是其他可能選項的能力,就掌握了獲勝的關鍵。

——威廉·霍爾頓與麥克·麥康(William Haltom and Michael McCann),
《曲解法律:政治、媒體與訴訟危機》
(*Distorting the Law: Politics, Media, and the Litigation Crisis*)

注意,霍爾頓和麥康先是引用了謝茨耐德的言論,再用自己的話解釋一遍,說明為什麼議題設定可被視為一場遊戲,有輸家也有贏家。

概述、引述或改述別人的研究時,務必要使用正確的文獻引用格式(style)。即便是用自己的話敘述,如內容是源自別人的想法,還是必須指明出處。撰寫資料來源的格式有很多種,請向你的老師請教,選擇正確的文獻引用格式。

▌研究分析

文獻探討敘述別人對於研究主題的論點,研究分析則提出你的回應,並舉證支持。在緒論當中,你已說明對別人的意見是同意、反對或兩者都有。你會想要詳細解釋自己如何產生這個看法,以及別人為何應該關心這個主題。

「研究資料指出……」

社會科學利用資料來發展和驗證各種解釋。資料可以是量化的也可以是質性的，也可以有非常多的來源。你可以採用國內生產毛額成長、失業情況、投票率、人口統計資料的相關資料，或可使用調查報告、訪談記錄或其他第一人稱敘述資料。

先不論你使用的資料類型為何，有三件事情務必做到：**定義資料、說明資料來源、並解釋你對資料做了哪些研究**。政治學家約書亞・威爾森（Joshua C. Wilson）在一篇期刊文章中，檢視了一起關於墮胎診所抗議的訴訟案件，並且提問，爭議雙方的行為是否符合他們自己認知的言論自由。

> [T]his paper relies on close readings of in-person, semi-structured interviews with the participants involved in the real controversy that was the Williams case.

> Thirteen interviews ranging in length from 40 minutes to 1 hour and 50 minutes were conducted for this paper. Of those interviewed, all would be considered "elites" in terms of political psychology / political attitude research—six were active members of Solano Citizens for Life...; two were members of Planned Parenthood Shasta-Diablo management; one was the lawyer who obtained the restraining order, temporary injunction, and permanent injunction for Planned Parenthood; one was the lawyer for the duration of the case for Solano Citizens for Life; two were lawyers for Planned Parenthood on appeal; and one was the Superior Court judge who heard arguments for, and finally crafted, the restraining order and injunctions against Solano Citizens for Life. During the course of

the interviews, participants were asked a range of questions about their experiences and thoughts in relation to the Williams case, as well as their beliefs about the interpretation and limits of the First Amendment right to free speech—both in general, and in relation to the Williams case.

　　本論文採取的方法，是針對曾真正涉及威廉斯案糾紛的人士，進行親自訪談和半結構式訪談。

　　本研究共進行 13 次訪談，時間從 40 分鐘到 1 小時 50 分鐘不等。就政治心理學或政治態度研究的角度來看，所有的受訪人士都算是「菁英分子」——其中 6 位是索拉諾居民維護生命組織的活躍分子，2 位是沙斯塔暨迪亞布洛生育計畫公司的成員，1 位是申請對索拉諾居民維護生命組織發出禁止令、暫時禁制令與永久禁制令的律師，1 位是索拉諾居民維護生命組織的辯護律師，2 位是為計畫生育社團提出上訴的律師，1 位是高等法院的法官，他聽取了對索拉諾居民維護生命組織申請禁止令和禁制令的理由，最終核准。在訪談過程中，受訪者被問及許多關於威廉斯案的經驗和想法，也被問到第一修正案裡所保障的言論自由，認為應如何解讀、有何限制——不管是針對一般情況，或者只就威廉斯案而言。

——約書亞‧威爾森，〈當權利相抵：反墮胎抗議行動以及沙斯塔暨迪亞布洛計畫生育公司與威廉斯之間的意識形態兩難〉（When Rights Collide: Anti-Abortion Protests and the Ideological Dilemma in Planned Parenthood Shasta-Diablo, Inc. v. Williams），《法律、政治與社會研究》（Studies in Law, Politics, and Society）

　　威爾森指出並描述了他的質性資料——涉及此衝突的關鍵雙方所進行的訪談——也解釋了他所提出的問題本質是什麼。

　　假設你採用的是量化資料，也必須用類似的方法加以解釋。請看政治學家布萊恩·阿爾博（Brian Arbour）如何解釋一份量化資料，這是他發表在《論壇》（*The Forum*）中的論文所使用的資料，該文是在探討，假如規則改變，那麼 2008 年的民主黨初選結果，希拉蕊和歐巴馬勝負是否會翻盤。

I evaluate these five concerns about the Democratic system of delegate allocation by "rerunning" the Obama-Clinton contest with a different set of allocation rules, those in effect for the 2008 Republican presidential contest. ... Republicans allow each state to make their own rules, leading to "a plethora of selection plans" (Shapiro & Bello 2008, 5)... To "rerun" the Democratic primary under Republican rules, I need data on the results of the Democratic primary for each state and congressional district and on the Republican delegate allocation rules for each state. The Green Papers (www.thegreenpapers.com), a website that serves as an almanac of election procedures, rules, and results, provides each of these data sources. By "rerunning" the Democratic primaries and caucuses, I use the exact results of each contest.

我「重作」歐巴馬和希拉蕊的競選統計，以評估民主黨代表分配制度的五個關切點，但是使用的是不同的代表分配規則，用的是 2008 年共和黨總統競選時實際採行的規則……共和黨員允許各州制訂自己的規則，產生「過多的選擇方案」（夏皮羅與貝羅，2008，頁 5）……為了用共和黨的規則「重作」民主黨初選，我需要民主黨各州及國會選區的初選結果資料，也需要共和黨各州黨代表分配規則的資料。綠皮書（資料來源：www.thegreenpapers.com）這個網站是記錄選舉過程、規則與結果的年鑑，作為上述兩項資料的來源。為了「重作」民主黨初選及黨團會議，我用了每一場競選活動的切實結果。

—— 布萊恩・阿爾博，〈更接近、更漫長：假如 2008 年民主黨初選採用共和黨規則，會是什麼結果？〉（Even Closer, Even Longer: What If the 2008 Democratic Primary Used Republican Rules?），《論壇》

請注意，阿爾博指明他用的資料是初選投票結果和共和黨的初選規則。在後文中，阿爾博用這兩份資料解釋，有人認為，如果當初採用共和黨規則，能讓歐巴馬和希拉蕊之間的激烈競爭明朗化，其實這種想法是錯的，而且競爭可能反而會「差距更接近、過程更漫長」。

下列是可用來討論資料的範本：

▶ **In order to test the hypothesis that　　　　　, we assessed　　　　　.**
Our calculations suggest　　　　　.
為了驗證　　　　　這一假說，我們估算了　　　　　。計算結果顯示
　　　　　。

▶ **I used to investigate　　　　　. The results of this investigation**
indicate　　　　　.
我曾經調查過　　　　　。這項調查的結果顯示　　　　　。

▍「但是其他人可能會反對……」

無論你的資料如何強力支持你的論點，也不得不承認幾乎必然有其他觀點（因而有其他資料）存在。請先考慮你的論點可能遭遇哪些反對意見，並且認真面對這些意見，如此你可以展現出你的努力，也讓讀者知道有其他觀點存在。最重要的是，這可以證明你的論點是一場持續對談的一部分。

請看經濟學家克里斯多夫·卡羅（Christopher Carroll）如何承認有人可能會反對他的論點，該論點是關於人們的收入中，消費和儲蓄如何分配。

I have argued here that the modern version of the dynamically optimizing consumption model is able to match many of the important features of the empirical data on consumption and saving behavior. There are, however, several remaining reasons for discomfort with the model.

我已經說明過，現代版的動態最佳化消費模式能吻合消費與儲蓄行為實證資料的許多重要特徵。然而，還有幾個原因讓人對此模式不甚放心。

——克里斯多夫·卡羅，〈消費函數理論，有與無流動性限制〉（A Theory of Consumption Function, With and Without Liquidity Constraints），《經濟展望期刊》（*The Journal of Economic Perspectives*）

卡羅在後文中便指出他的模式可能有哪些侷限性。

有人提出異議，理由可能是你的分析沒解釋到某相關現象，或者你對問題沒有用正確的資料調查，或者是不認同你論點的假設，也可以是不贊成你處理資料的方法。下列範本可用來納入反對者的意見：

▶ _____ **might object that** _____.
　　　_____可能會反對_____。

▶ **Is my claim realistic? I have argued** _____, **but readers may question** _____.
我的主張是否務實？我主張了_____，但讀者也許會懷疑_____。

▶ **My explanation accounts for** _____ **but does not explain**
_____ **. This is because** _____ .

我的解釋說明了_____但並未說明_____，這是因為_____。

「為何我們應該關心？」

你的研究誰該關心？為什麼？既然社會科學是要解釋人類的行為，寫作者就必須考慮，自己的研究如何影響我們對人類行為的假設。此外，你也可以對其他科學家提出建議，如可以怎麼繼續探索某個議題、或建議決策者應採取什麼行動。

社會學家黛瓦‧裴哲（Devah Pager）研究了有犯罪記錄如何影響一個人求職，在下列範例中，她指出了這項研究可能產生的影響。

[I]n terms of policy implications, this research has troubling conclusions. In our frenzy of locking people up, our "crime control" policies may in fact exacerbate the very conditions that lead to crime in the first place. Research consistently shows that finding quality steady employment is one of the strongest predictors of desistance from crime (Shover 1996; Sampson and Laub 1993; Uggen 2000). The fact that a criminal record severely limits employment opportunities—particularly among blacks—suggests that these individuals are left with few viable alternatives.

就政策上的影響來說，這項研究的結論讓人憂心。我們的「犯罪控制」政策只是一股腦兒把人關起來，實際上可能反而使導致犯罪的條件更加惡化。研究一致顯示，防止犯罪的最主要的可預知因素之一，就是找到穩定的好工作（蕭弗，1996；山普森與勞勃，1993；阿根，2000）。犯罪記錄嚴重限制就業機會這項事實——尤其對於黑人——顯示出這些人除了犯罪幾乎沒有生存餘地。

> ——黛瓦·裴哲，〈犯罪記錄留下的汙點〉（The Mark of a Criminal Record），《美國社會學期刊》（*The American Journal of Sociology*）

裴哲下了一個結論，犯罪記錄給就業機會帶來不利影響，這將產生一種惡性循環，她認為穩定的工作能遏止再犯的情況發生，但是犯罪記錄卻讓人難以找到工作。

回答「那又怎樣？」這個問題的時候，需要說明讀者應該關心的理由。雖然，有時研究結果的影響面也許太廣，但點出哪些人該重視你的研究，總是好事。這些範本可以用來證明你的主張為何很重要：

▶ **X is important because** _____.
　X 很重要，因為_____。

▶ **Ultimately, what is at stake here is** _____.
　歸根究柢，重要的是_____。

▶ **The finding that** _____ **should be of interest to** _____
　because _____.
　研究結果發現_____，_____應該會感興趣，因為_____。

如本堂課一開始所提到的，正因為人的複雜，才令我們得以從許多不同視角看待人的行為。人類是如何產生那些所作所為，又是出於什麼原因，很多都已經討論過，也將會繼續討論下去。因此，社會科學的寫作可視為一場持續的對談。要加入這場對談時，便可利用「人們說／我說」架構，去思考有哪些已經存在的論點（they say），以及你可以補充的內容（I say）。本課所提出的社會科學寫作要素，都是可用來參與對談的好工具。

PART V

Readings
範文集

本部分收錄不同學術領域的五篇佳作論文，
並標上應用本書寫作範本的註記，
讓讀者能進一步作為應用參考：

01 社科

Don't Blame the Eater
別怪吃的人

David Zinczenko

If ever there were a newspaper headline custom-made for Jay Leno's monologue, this was it. Kids taking on McDonald's this week, suing the company for making them fat. Isn't that like middle-aged men suing Porsche for making them get speeding tickets? Whatever happened to personal responsibility?

5　　I tend to sympathize with these portly fast-food patrons, though. Maybe that's because I used to be one of them.

I grew up as a typical mid-1980s latchkey kid. My parents were split up, my

---

David Zinczenko 大衛・辛善寇

　　曾擔任多年健康雜誌《男士健康》（*Men's Health*）主編，目前則是全球健康媒體公司 Galvanized Brands 的總裁。本文是他於 2002 年 11 月 23 日初次發表在《紐約時報》社論對頁專欄（op-ed page）的文章。

dad off trying to rebuild his life, my mom working long hours to make the monthly bills. Lunch and dinner, for me, was a daily choice between McDonald's, Taco Bell, Kentucky Fried Chicken or Pizza Hut. Then as now, these were the only available options for an American kid to get an affordable meal. By age 15, I had packed 212 pounds of torpid teenage tallow on my once lanky 5-foot-10 frame. 5

Then I got lucky. I went to college, joined the Navy Reserves and got involved with a health magazine. I learned how to manage my diet. But most of the teenagers who live, as I once did, on a fast-food diet won't turn their lives around: They've crossed under the golden arches to a likely fate of lifetime obesity. And the problem isn't just theirs—it's all of ours. 10

Before 1994, diabetes in children was generally caused by a genetic disorder—only about 5 percent of childhood cases were obesity-related, or Type 2, diabetes. Today, according to the National Institutes of Health, Type 2 diabetes accounts for at least 30 percent of all new childhood cases of diabetes in this country.

Not surprisingly, money spent to treat diabetes has skyrocketed, too. The 15 Centers for Disease Control and Prevention estimate that diabetes accounted for $2.6 billion in health care costs in 1969. Today's number is an unbelievable $100 billion a year.

Shouldn't we know better than to eat two meals a day in fast-food restaurants? That's one argument. But where, exactly, are consumers—particularly teenagers— 20 supposed to find alternatives? Drive down any thoroughfare in America, and I guarantee you'll see one of our country's more than 13,000 McDonald's restaurants. Now, drive back up the block and try to find someplace to buy a grapefruit.

參考第 **7** 堂，說明你的論點為何重要。

Complicating the lack of alternatives is the lack of information about what, exactly, we're consuming. There are no calorie information charts on fast-food packaging, the way there are on grocery items. Advertisements don't carry warning labels the way tobacco ads do. Prepared foods aren't covered under Food and Drug Administration labeling laws. Some fast-food purveyors will provide calorie information on request, but even that can be hard to understand.

For example, one company's Web site lists its chicken salad as containing 150 calories; the almonds and noodles that come with it (an additional 190 calories) are listed separately. Add a serving of the 280-calorie dressing, and you've got a healthy lunch alternative that comes in at 620 calories. But that's not all. Read the small print on the back of the dressing packet and you'll realize it actually contains 2.5 servings. If you pour what you've been served, you're suddenly up around 1,040 calories, which is half of the government's recommended daily calorie intake. And that doesn't take into account that 450-calorie super-size Coke.

Make fun if you will of these kids launching lawsuits against the fast-food industry, but don't be surprised if you're the next plaintiff. As with the tobacco industry, it may be only a matter of time before state governments begin to see a direct line between the $1 billion that McDonald's and Burger King spend each year on advertising and their own swelling health care costs.

And I'd say the industry is vulnerable. Fast-food companies are marketing to children a product with proven health hazards and no warning labels. They would do well to protect themselves, and their customers, by providing the nutrition information people need to make informed choices about their products. Without such warnings, we'll see more sick, obese children and more angry, litigious parents.

I say, let the deepfried chips fall where they may.

02 教育

Hidden Intellectualism
隱藏的唯智主義

Gerald Graff

Everyone knows some young person who is impressively "street smart" but does poorly in school. What a waste, we think, that one who is so intelligent about so many things in life seems unable to apply that intelligence to academic work. What doesn't occur to us, though, is that schools and colleges might be at fault for missing the opportunity to tap into such street smarts and channel them into good

5

Gerald Graff 杰拉德 · 葛拉夫

　　本書作者之一,現任伊利諾大學芝加哥分校(University of Illinois at Chicago)英文與教育學院之教授,曾任美國現代語言學會(Modern Language Association of America, MLA)之會長,該學會的成員皆是大學學者與教師,是全球最大的專業學會。這篇論文是從他 2003 年出版的著作《茫茫學海:學校教育如何蒙蔽了心智生活》中節選出來。

academic work.

Nor do we consider one of the major reasons why schools and colleges overlook the intellectual potential of street smarts: the fact that we associate those street smarts with anti-intellectual concerns. We associate the educated life, the life of the mind, too narrowly and exclusively with subjects and texts that we consider inherently weighty and academic. We assume that it's possible to wax intellectual about Plato, Shakespeare, the French Revolution, and nuclear fission, but not about cars, dating, fashion, sports, TV, or video games.

The trouble with this assumption is that no necessary connection has ever been established between any text or subject and the educational depth and weight of the discussion it can generate. Real intellectuals turn any subject, however lightweight it may seem, into grist for their mill through the thoughtful questions they bring to it, whereas a dullard will find a way to drain the interest out of the richest subject. That's why a George Orwell writing on the cultural meanings of penny postcards is infinitely more substantial than the cogitations of many professors on Shakespeare or globalization (104-16).

Students do need to read models of intellectually challenging writing—and Orwell is a great one—if they are to become intellectuals themselves. But they would be more prone to take on intellectual identities if we encouraged them to do so at first on subjects that interest them rather than ones that interest us.

I offer my own adolescent experience as a case in point. Until I entered college, I hated books and cared only for sports. The only reading I cared to do or could do was sports magazines, on which I became hooked, becoming a regular reader

見第 6 堂表達論點為何重要的方法。

of *Sport* magazine in the late forties, *Sports Illustrated* when it began publishing in 1954, and the annual magazine guides to professional baseball, football, and basketball. I also loved the sports novels for boys of John R. Tunis and Clair Bee and autobiographies of sports stars like Joe DiMaggio's *Lucky to Be a Yankee* and Bob Feller's *Strikeout Story*. In short, I was your typical teenage anti-intellectual—or so I believed for a long time. I have recently come to think, however, that my preference for sports over schoolwork was not anti-intellectualism so much as intellectualism by other means.

In the Chicago neighborhood I grew up in, which had become a melting pot after World War II, our block was solidly middle class, but just a block away—doubtless concentrated there by the real estate companies—were African Americans, Native Americans, and "hillbilly" whites who had recently fled postwar joblessness in the South and Appalachia. Negotiating this class boundary was a tricky matter. On the one hand, it was necessary to maintain the boundary between "clean-cut" boys like me and working-class "hoods," as we called them, which meant that it was good to be openly smart in a bookish sort of way. On the other hand, I was desperate for the approval of the hoods, whom I encountered daily on the playing field and in the neighborhood, and for this purpose it was not at all good to be book-smart. The hoods would turn on you if they sensed you were putting on airs over them: "Who you lookin' at, smart ass?" as a leather-jacketed youth once said to me as he relieved me of my pocket change along with my self-respect.

I grew up torn, then, between the need to prove I was smart and the fear of a beating if I proved it too well; between the need not to jeopardize my respectable future and the need to impress the hoods. As I lived it, the conflict came down to a choice between being physically tough and being verbal. For a boy in my neighborhood and elementary school, only being "tough" earned you complete legitimacy. I still recall endless, complicated debates in this period with my closest pals over who was "the toughest guy in the school." If you were less than negligible as a fighter, as I was, you settled for the next best thing, which was to be inarticulate, carefully hiding telltale marks of literacy like correct grammar and pronunciation.

In one way, then, it would be hard to imagine an adolescence more thoroughly anti-intellectual than mine. Yet in retrospect, I see that it's more complicated, that I and the 1950s themselves were not simply hostile toward intellectualism, but divided and ambivalent. When Marilyn Monroe married the playwright Arthur Miller in 1956 after divorcing the retired baseball star Joe DiMaggio, the symbolic triumph of geek over jock suggested the way the wind was blowing. Even Elvis, according to his biographer Peter Guralnick, turns out to have supported Adlai over Ike in the presidential election of 1956. "I don't dig the intellectual bit," he told reporters. "But I'm telling you, man, he knows the most" (327).

Though I too thought I did not "dig the intellectual bit," I see now that I was unwittingly in training for it. The germs had actually been planted in the seemingly philistine debates about which boys were the toughest. I see now that in the interminable analysis of sports teams, movies, and toughness that my friends and I engaged in—a type of analysis, needless to say, that the real toughs would never have stooped to—I was already betraying an allegiance to the egghead world. I was practicing being an intellectual before I knew that was what I wanted to be.

It was in these discussions with friends about toughness and sports, I think, and in my reading of sports books and magazines, that I began to learn the rudiments of the intellectual life: how to make an argument, weigh different kinds of evidence, move between particulars and generalizations, summarize the views of others, and enter a conversation about ideas. It was in reading and arguing about sports and toughness that I experienced what it felt like to propose a generalization, restate and respond to a counterargument, and perform other intellectualizing operations, including composing the kind of sentences I am writing now.

Only much later did it dawn on me that the sports world was more compelling than school because it was *more intellectual than school*, not less. Sports after all was full of challenging arguments, debates, problems for analysis, and intricate statistics that you could care about, as school conspicuously was not. I believe that street smarts beat out book smarts in our culture not because street smarts are nonintellectual, as we generally suppose, but because they satisfy an intellectual thirst more thoroughly than school culture, which seems pale and unreal.

They also satisfy the thirst for community. When you entered sports debates, you became part of a community that was not limited to your family and friends, but was national and public. Whereas schoolwork isolated you from others, the pennant race or Ted Williams's. 400 batting average was something you could talk about with people you had never met. Sports introduced you not only to a culture steeped in argument, but to a public argument culture that transcended the personal. I can't blame my schools for failing to make intellectual culture resemble the Super Bowl, but I do fault them for failing to learn anything from the sports and entertainment worlds about how to organize and represent intellectual culture, how to exploit its gamelike element and turn it into arresting public spectacle that might have competed more successfully for my youthful attention.

For here is another thing that never dawned on me and is still kept hidden from students, with tragic results: that the real intellectual world, the one that existed in the big world beyond school, is organized very much like the world of team sports, with rival texts, rival interpretations and evaluations of texts, rival theories of why they should be read and taught, and elaborate team competitions in which "fans" of writers, intellectual systems, methodologies, and -isms contend against each other.

To be sure, school contained plenty of competition, which became more invidious as one moved up the ladder (and has become even more so today with the advent of high-stakes testing). In this competition, points were scored not by making arguments, but by a show of information or vast reading, by grade-grubbing, or other forms of one-upmanship. School competition, in short, reproduced the less attractive features of sports culture without those that create close bonds and community.

And in distancing themselves from anything as enjoyable and absorbing as sports, my schools missed the opportunity to capitalize on an element of drama and conflict that the intellectual world shares with sports. Consequently, I failed to see the parallels between the sports and academic worlds that could have helped me cross more readily from one argument culture to the other.

Sports is only one of the domains whose potential for literacy training (and not only for males) is seriously underestimated by educators, who see sports as competing with academic development rather than a route to it. But if this argument suggests why it is a good idea to assign readings and topics that are close to students' existing interests, it also suggests the limits of this tactic. For students who get excited about the chance to write about their passion for cars will often write as poorly and unreflectively on that topic as on Shakespeare or Plato. Here is the flip side of what I pointed out before: that there's no necessary relation between the degree of interest a student shows in a text or subject and the quality of thought or expression such a student manifests in writing or talking about it. The challenge, as college professor Ned Laff has put it, "is not simply to exploit students' nonacademic interests, but to get them to see those interests through academic eyes."

To say that students need to see their interests "through academic eyes" is to say that street smarts are not enough. Making students' nonacademic interests an object of academic study is useful, then, for getting students' attention and overcoming their boredom and alienation, but this tactic won't in itself necessarily move them closer to an academically rigorous treatment of those interests. On the other hand, inviting students to write about cars, sports, or clothing fashions does not have to be a pedagogical cop-out as long as students are required to see these interests "through academic eyes," that is, to think and write about cars, sports, and fashions in a reflective, analytical way, one that sees them as microcosms of what is going on in the wider culture.

If I am right, then schools and colleges are missing an opportunity when they do not encourage students to take their nonacademic interests as objects of academic study. It is selfdefeating to decline to introduce any text or subject that figures to engage students who will otherwise tune out academic work entirely. If a student cannot get interested in Mill's *On Liberty* but will read *Sports Illustrated* or *Vogue* or the hip-hop magazine *Source* with absorption, this is a strong argument for assigning the magazines over the classic. It's a good bet that if students get hooked on reading and writing by doing term papers on *Source*, they will eventually get to *On Liberty*. But even if they don't, the magazine reading will make them more literate and reflective than they would be otherwise. So it makes pedagogical sense to develop classroom units on sports, cars, fashions, rap music, and other such topics. Give me the student anytime who writes a sharply argued, sociologically acute analysis of an issue in *Source* over the student who writes a lifeless explication of *Hamlet* or Socrates' *Apology*.

Works Cited

Cramer, Richard Ben. *Joe DiMaggio: The Hero's Life*. Simon & Schuster, 2000.

DiMaggio, Joe. *Lucky to Be a Yankee*. Bantam, 1949.

Feller, Bob. *Strikeout Story*. Bantam, 1948.

Guralnick, Peter. *Last Train to Memphis: The Rise of Elvis Presley*. Little, Brown, 1994.

Orwell, George. *A Collection of Essays*. Harcourt, 1953.

03 科學

Nuclear Waste
核廢料

Richard A. Muller

As people recognize the dangers of fossil fuel plants—especially the risk of global warming from carbon dioxide production—nuclear power begins to look more attractive. But what about the waste—all that highly radioactive debris that will endure for thousands of years? Do we have the right to leave such a legacy to our children?

Nuclear waste is one of the biggest technical issues that any future president

Richard A. Muller 理查・穆勒

加州大學柏克萊分校（University of California at Berkeley）物理系教授，曾獲頒麥克阿瑟天才獎。這篇文章原本是他為非科學系學生所開設的物理課的一次講課內容，後來收錄在他 2008 年出版的課程演講選集《給未來總統的物理課》（*Physics for Future Presidents*）。

is likely to face. The problem seems totally intractable. Plutonium—just one of the many highly radioactive waste products—has a half-life of 24,000 years. Even in that unimaginable amount of time, its intense radioactivity will decrease by only half. After 48,000 years it will still emit deadly radiation at a quarter of its original level. Even after 100,000 years the radiation will still be above 10% of the level it had when it left the reactor. What if it leaks into the ground and reaches human water supplies? How can we possibly certify that this material can be kept safe for 100,000 years?

Still, the US government persists in its pursuit of "safe" nuclear waste disposal. It has created a prototype nuclear waste facility buried deep within Yucca Mountain, Nevada as shown in the figure below. To keep the waste safe, the storage rooms are 1000 feet below the surface. To store even part of the present nuclear waste requires a vast area, nearly 2 square miles. The cost of the facility is expected to reach $100 billion, with hundreds of billions of dollars more in operating costs.

To make matters worse, the Yucca Mountain region is seismically active. More than 600 earthquakes of magnitude 2.5 and higher have occurred within 50 miles in the last decade alone. Moreover, the region was created by volcanic activity. Although that was millions of years ago, how sure can we be that the waste facility won't be torn apart by another eruption?

Many alternatives have been suggested for nuclear waste storage. Why not just send the waste into the sun? Well, maybe that's not such a good idea, since on launch some rockets do crash back down on the Earth. Some scientists have proposed that the waste be put in vessels and sunk under the oceans, in a region where the movement of the Earth's crustal plates will subduct the material, eventually burying it hundreds of miles deep. Yet just the fact that scientists make such suggestions seems to emphasize how severe the problem really is.

Here is the worst part. We have already generated more than enough nuclear waste to fill up Yucca Mountain. That waste won't go away. Yet you, a future president, are considering more nuclear power? Are you insane?

My Confession

The furor against nuclear power has been so intense that I felt compelled to reproduce the anti-nuke viewpoint in the opening of this chapter, including at least part of their passion. These are the arguments that you will hear when you are president. Yet it hardly matters whether you are pro-nuke or anti-nuke. The waste is there, and you will have to do something with it. You can't ignore this issue, and to do the right thing (and to convince the public that you're doing the right thing) you must understand the physics.

When I work out the numbers, I find the dangers of storing our waste at Yucca Mountain to be small compared to the dangers of not doing so, and significantly smaller than many other dangers we ignore. Yet the contentious debate continues. More research is demanded, but every bit of additional research seems to raise new questions that exacerbate the public's fear and distrust. I have titled this section "My Confession" because I find it hard to stand aside and present the physics without giving my own personal evaluation. Through most of this book I've tried to present the facts, and just the facts, and let you draw the conclusions. In this section, I confess that I'll depart from that approach. I can't be evenhanded, because the facts seem to point strongly toward a particular conclusion.

I've discussed Yucca Mountain with scientists, politicians, and many concerned citizens. Most of the politicians believe the matter to be a scientific issue, and most of the scientists think it is political. Both are in favor of more research—scientists because that is what they do, and politicians because they think the research will answer the key questions. I don't think it will.

Here are some pertinent facts. The underground tunnels at Yucca Mountain are designed to hold 77,000 tons of high-level nuclear waste. Initially, the most dangerous part of this waste is not plutonium, but fission fragments such as strontium-90, an unstable nucleus created when the uranium nucleus splits. Because these fission fragments have shorter half-lives than uranium, the waste is about 1000 times more radioactive than the original ore. It takes 10,000 years for the waste (not including plutonium, which is also produced in the reactor, and which I'll discuss later) to decay back to the radioactive level of the mined uranium. Largely on the basis of this number, people have searched for a site that will remain secure for 10,000 years. After that, we are better off than if we left the uranium in the ground, so 10,000 years of safety is probably good enough, not the 100,000 years that I mentioned in the chapter introduction.

Ten thousand years still seems impossibly long. What will the world be like 10,000 years from now? Think backward to appreciate the amount of time involved: Ten thousand years ago humans had just discovered agriculture. Writing wouldn't be invented for another 5000 years. Can we really plan 10,000 years into the future?

參考第 16 堂透過敘述資料支持科學論證的訣竅。

Of course we can't. We have no idea what the world will be like then. There is no way we can claim that we will be able to store nuclear waste for 10,000 years. Any plan to do that is clearly unacceptable.

Of course, calling storage unacceptable is itself an unacceptable answer. We have the waste, and we have to do something with it. But the problem isn't really as hard as I just portrayed it. We don't need absolute security for 10,000 years. A more reasonable goal is to reduce the risk of leakage to 0.1%—that is, to one chance in a thousand. Because the radioactivity is only 1000 times worse than that of the uranium we removed from the ground, the net risk (probability multiplied by danger) is 1000 x 0.001 = 1—that is, basically the same as the risk if we hadn't mined the uranium in the first place. (I am assuming the linear hypothesis—that total cancer risk is independent of individual doses or dose rate—but my argument won't depend strongly on its validity.)

Moreover, we don't need this 0.1% level of security for the full 10,000 years. After 300 years, the fission fragment radioactivity will have decreased by a factor of 10; it will be only 100 times as great as the mined uranium. So by then, we no longer need the risk to be at the 0.1% level, but could allow a 1% chance that all of the waste leaks out. That's a lot easier than guaranteeing absolute containment for 10,000 years. Moreover, this calculation assumes that 100% of the waste escapes. For leakage of 1% of the waste, we can accept a 100% probability after 300 years. When you think about it this way, the storage problem begins to seem tractable.

However, the public discussion doesn't take into account these numbers, or the fact that the initial mining actually removed radioactivity from the ground. Instead, the public insists on absolute security. The Department of Energy continues to search Yucca Mountain for unknown earthquake faults, and many people assume that the acceptability of the facility depends on the absence of any such faults. They believe that the discovery of a new fault will rule Yucca Mountain out. The issue, though, should not be whether there will be any earthquakes in the next 10,000 years, but whether after 300 years there will be a 1% chance of a sufficiently large earthquake that 100% of the waste will escape its glass capsules and reach groundwater. Or, we could accept a 100% chance that 1% of the waste will leak, or a 10% chance that 10% will leak. Any of these options leads to a lower risk than if the original uranium had been left in the ground, mixing its natural radioactivity with groundwater. Absolute security is an unnecessarily extreme goal, since even the original uranium in the ground didn't provide it.

The problem is even easier to solve when we ask why we are comparing the danger of waste storage only to the danger of the uranium originally mined. Why not compare it to the larger danger of the natural uranium left in the soil? Colorado, where much of the uranium is obtained, is a geologically active region, full of faults and fissures and mountains rising out of the prairie, and its surface rock contains about a billion tons of uranium. The radioactivity in this uranium is 20 times greater than the legal limit for Yucca Mountain, and it will take more than 13 billion years—not just a few hundred—for the radioactivity to drop by a factor of 10. Yet water that runs through, around, and over this radioactive rock is the source of the Colorado River, which is used for drinking water in much of the West, including Los Angeles and San Diego. And unlike the glass pellets that store the waste in Yucca

Mountain, most of the uranium in the Colorado ground is water-soluble. Here is the absurd-sounding conclusion: if the Yucca Mountain facility were at full capacity and all the waste leaked out of its glass containment immediately and managed to reach groundwater, the danger would still be 20 times less than that currently posed by natural uranium leaching into the Colorado River. The situation brings to mind the resident near Three Mile Island who feared the tiny leakage from the reactor but not the much greater radioactivity of natural radon gas seeping up from the ground.

I don't mean to imply that waste from Yucca Mountain is not dangerous. Nor am I suggesting that we should panic about radioactivity in the Los Angeles water supply. The Colorado River example illustrates only that when we worry about mysterious and unfamiliar dangers, we sometimes lose perspective. Every way I do the calculation, I reach the same conclusion: waste leakage from Yucca Mountain is not a great danger. Put the waste in glass pellets in a reasonably stable geologic formation, and start worrying about real threats—such as the dangers of the continued burning of fossil fuels.

A related issue is the risk of mishaps and attacks during the transportation of nuclear waste to the Yucca Mountain site. The present plans call for the waste to be carried in thick, reinforced concrete cylinders that can survive high-speed crashes without leaking. In fact, it would be very hard for a terrorist to open the containers, or to use the waste in radiological weapons. The smart terrorist is more likely to hijack a tanker truck full of gasoline, chlorine, or another common toxic material and then blow it up in a city. Recall from the chapter on terrorist nukes that al-Qaeda told José Padilla to abandon his effort to make a dirty bomb and instead focus his efforts on natural-gas explosions in apartment buildings.

Why are we worrying about transporting nuclear waste? Ironically, we have gone to such lengths to ensure the safety of the transport that the public thinks the danger is greater than it really is. Images on evening newscasts of concrete containers being dropped from five-story buildings, smashing into the ground and bouncing undamaged, do not reassure the public. This is a consequence of the "where there's smoke there's fire" paradox of public safety. Raise the standards, increase the safety, do more research, study the problem in greater depth, and in the process you will improve safety and frighten the public. After all, would scientists work so hard if the threat weren't real? Scientists who propose rocketing the waste to the sun, or burying it in a subduction zone in the ocean, also seem to be suggesting that the problem is truly intractable, and that premise exacerbates the public fear.

見第 7 堂說明論點為何重要的方法。

04 社科

The (Futile) Pursuit of the American Dream
（徒然）追尋美國夢

Barbara Ehrenreich

Because I've written a lot about poverty, I'm used to hearing from people in scary circumstances. An eviction notice has arrived. A child has been diagnosed with a serious illness and the health insurance has run out. The car has broken down and there's no way to get to work. These are the routine emergencies that plague the chronically poor. But it struck me, starting in about 2002, that many such tales

5

> ### Barbara Ehrenreich 芭芭拉・埃倫里奇
>
> 　　調查記者兼作家，文章見於《哈潑》（*Harper's*）、《國家》（*The Nation*）、《紐約時報》與其他眾多期刊，亦著有多本涵蓋各式主題的書籍，其中包含 2005 年所出版的《M 型社會白領的新試煉》（*Bait and Switch: The (Futile) Pursuit of the American Dream*，原書名意為「引誘轉移：（徒然）追尋美國夢」），本文即出自此書。她的最新著作是 2009 年的《失控的正向思考》（*Bright-Sided: How Positive Thinking Is Undermining America*）。

of hardship were coming from people who were once members in good standing of the middle class—college graduates and former occupants of mid-level white-collar positions. One such writer upbraided me for what she saw as my neglect of hardworking, virtuous people like herself.

> Try investigating people like me who didn't have babies in high school, who made good grades, who work hard and don't kiss a lot of ass and instead of getting promoted or paid fairly must regress to working for $7/hr., having their student loans in perpetual deferment, living at home with their parents, and generally exist in debt which they feel they may never get out of.

Stories of white-collar downward mobility cannot be brushed off as easily as accounts of blue-collar economic woes, which the hard-hearted traditionally blame on "bad choices": failing to get a college degree, for example, failing to postpone child-bearing until acquiring a nest egg, or failing to choose affluent parents in the first place. But distressed white-collar people cannot be accused of fecklessness of any kind; they are the ones who "did everything right." They earned higher degrees, often setting aside their youthful passion for philosophy or music to suffer through dull practical majors like management or finance. In some cases, they were high achievers who ran into trouble precisely because they had risen far enough in the company for their salaries to look like a tempting cost cut. They were the losers, in other words, in a classic game of bait and switch. And while blue-collar poverty has become numbingly routine, white-collar unemployment—and the poverty that often results—remains a rude finger in the face of the American dream.

I realized that I knew very little about the mid- to upper levels of the corporate world, having so far encountered this world almost entirely through its low-wage, entry-level representatives. I was one of them—a server in a national chain restaurant, a cleaning person, and a Wal-Mart "associate"—in the course of researching an earlier book, *Nickel and Dimed: On (Not) Getting By in America*. Like everyone else, I've also en countered the corporate world as a consumer, dealing with people quite far down in the occupational hierarchy—retail clerks, customer service representatives, telemarketers. Of the levels where decisions are made—where the vice presidents, account executives, and regional managers dwell—my experience has been limited to seeing these sorts of people on airplanes, where they study books on "leadership," fiddle with spreadsheets on their laptops, or fall asleep over biographies of the founding fathers.1 I'm better acquainted with the corporate functionaries of the future, many of whom I've met on my visits to college campuses, where "business" remains the most popular major, if only because it is believed to be the safest and most lucrative (National Center for Education Statistics).

But there have been growing signs of trouble—if not outright misery—within the white-collar corporate workforce. First, starting with the economic downturn of 2001, there has been a rise in unemployment among highly credentialed and experienced people. In late 2003, when I started this project, unemployment was running at about 5.9 percent, but in contrast to earlier economic downturns, a sizable portion—almost 20 percent, or about 1.6 million—of the unemployed were white-collar professionals.2 Previous downturns had disproportionately hit blue-collar people; this time it was the relative elite of professional, technical, and managerial employees who were being singled out for media sympathy. In April 2003, for example, the *New York Times Magazine* offered a much-discussed cover story about a former $300,000-a-year computer industry executive reduced, after two years of unemployment, to working as a sales associate at the Gap (Mahler). Throughout the first four years of the 2000s, there were similar stories of the mighty or the mere midlevel brought low, ejected from their office suites and forced to serve behind the counter at Starbucks.

Today, white-collar job insecurity is no longer a function of the business cycle—rising as the stock market falls and declining again when the numbers improve.3 Nor is it confined to a few volatile sectors like telecommunications or technology, or a few regions of the country like the rust belt or Silicon Valley. The economy may be looking up, the company may be raking in cash, and still the layoffs continue, like a perverse form of natural selection, weeding out the talented and successful as well as the mediocre. Since the midnineties, this perpetual winnowing process has been institutionalized under various euphemisms such as "downsizing," "right-sizing," "smart-sizing," "restructuring," and "de-layering"—to which we can now add the outsourcing of white-collar functions to cheaper labor markets overseas.

In the metaphor of the best-selling business book of the first few years of the twenty-first century, the "cheese"—meaning a stable, rewarding, job—has indeed been moved. A 2004 survey of executives found 95 percent expecting to move on, voluntarily or otherwise, from their current jobs, and 68 percent concerned about unexpected firings and layoffs (Mackay 94). You don't, in other words, have to lose a job to feel the anxiety and despair of the unemployed.

A second sign of trouble could be called "overemployment." I knew, from my reading, that mid- and high-level corporate executives and professionals today often face the same punishing demands on their time as low-paid wage earners who must work two jobs in order to make ends meet. Economist Juliet Schor, who wrote *The Overworked American*, and business journalist Jill Andresky Fraser, author of *White Collar Sweatshop*, describe stressed-out white-collar employees who put in ten- to twelve-hour-long days at the office, continue to work on their laptops in the evening at home, and remain tethered to the office by cell phone even on vacations and holidays. "On Wall Street, for example," Fraser reports, "it is common for a supervisor to instruct new hires to keep a spare set of clothes and toothbrush in the office for all those late night episodes when it just won't make sense to head home for a quick snooze." She quotes an Intel employee:

> If you make the choice to have a home life, you will be ranked and rated at the bottom. I was willing to work the endless hours, come in on weekends, travel to the ends of the earth. I had no hobbies, no outside interests. If I wasn't involved with the company, I wasn't anything (qtd. in Fraser 158).

Something, evidently, is going seriously wrong within a socioeconomic group I had indeed neglected as too comfortable and too powerful to merit my concern. Where I had imagined comfort, there is now growing distress, and I determined to investigate. I chose the same strategy I had employed in *Nickel and Dimed*: to enter this new world myself, as an undercover reporter, and see what I could learn about the problems firsthand. Were people being driven out of their corporate jobs? What did it take to find a new one? And, if things were as bad as some reports suggested, why was there so little protest?

The plan was straightforward enough: to find a job, a "good" job, which I defined minimally as a white-collar position that would provide health insurance and an income of about $50,000 a year, enough to land me solidly in the middle class. The job itself would give me a rare firsthand glimpse into the midlevel corporate world, and the effort to find it would of course place me among the most hard-pressed white-collar corporate workers—the ones who don't have jobs.

Since I wanted to do this as anonymously as possible, certain areas of endeavor had to be excluded, such as higher education, publishing (magazines, newspapers, and books), and nonprofit liberal organizations. In any of these, I would have run the risk of being recognized and perhaps treated differently—more favorably, one hopes—than the average job seeker. But these restrictions did not significantly narrow the field, since of course most white-collar professionals work in other sectors of the for-profit, corporate world—from banking to business services, pharmaceuticals to finance.

The decision to enter corporate life—and an unfamiliar sec tor of it, at that—required that I abandon, or at least set aside, deeply embedded attitudes and views, including my longstanding critique of American corporations and the people who lead them. I had cut my teeth, as a fledgling investigative journalist in the seventies, on the corporations that were coming to dominate the health-care system: pharmaceutical companies, hospital chains, insurance companies. Then, sometime in the eighties, I shifted my attention to the treatment of blue-and pink-collar employees, blaming America's intractable level of poverty—12.5 percent by the federal government's official count, 25 percent by more up-to-date measures—on the chronically low wages offered to nonprofessional workers. In the last few years, I seized on the wave of financial scandals— from Enron through, at the time of this writing, HealthSouth and Hollingers International—as evidence of growing corruption within the corporate world, a pattern of internal looting without regard for employees, consumers, or even, in some cases, stockholders.

But for the purposes of this project, these criticisms and reservations had to be set aside or shoved as far back in my mind as possible. Like it or not, the corporation is the dominant unit of the global economy and the form of enterprise that our lives depend on in a day-to-day sense. I write this on an IBM laptop while sipping Lipton tea and wearing clothes from the Gap—all major firms or elements thereof. It's corporations that make the planes run (though not necessarily on time), bring us (and increasingly grow) our food, and generally "make it happen." I'd been on the outside of the corporate world, often complaining bitterly, and now I wanted in.

This would not, I knew, be an altogether fair test of the job market, if only because I had some built-in disadvantages as a job seeker. For one thing, I am well into middle age, and since age discrimination is a recognized problem in the corporate world even at the tender age of forty, I was certainly vulnerable to it myself. This defect, however, is by no means unique to me. Many people—from displaced homemakers to downsized executives—now find themselves searching for jobs at an age that was once associated with a restful retirement.

Furthermore, I had the disadvantage of never having held a white-collar job with a corporation. My one professional-level office job, which lasted for about seven months, was in the public sector, at the New York City Bureau of the Budget. It had involved such typical white-collar activities as attending meetings, digesting reports, and writing memos; but that was a long time ago, before cell phones, PowerPoint, and e-mail. In the corporate world I now sought to enter, everything would be new to me: the standards of performance, the methods of evaluation, the lines and even the modes of communication. But I'm a quick study, as you have to be in journalism, and counted on this to get me by.

The first step was to acquire a new identity and personal history to go with it, meaning, in this case, a résumé. It is easier to change your identity than you might think. Go to Alavarado and Seventh Street in Los Angeles, for example, and you will be approached by men whispering, "ID, ID." I, however, took the legal route, because I wanted my documents to be entirely in order when the job offers started coming in. My fear, perhaps exaggerated, was that my current name might be recognized, or would at least turn up an embarrassing abundance of Google entries. So in November 2003 I legally changed back to my maiden name, Barbara Alexander, and acquired a Social Security card to go with it.

見第 **8** 堂銜接句子的技巧。

As for the résumé: although it had to be faked, I wanted it as much as possible to represent my actual skills, which, I firmly believed, would enrich whatever company I went to work for. I am a writer—author of thousands of published articles and about twelve nonfiction books, counting the coauthored ones—and I know that "writing" translates, in the corporate world, into public relations or "communications" generally. Many journalism schools teach PR too, which may be fitting, since PR is really journalism's evil twin. Whereas a journalist seeks the truth, a PR person may be called upon to disguise it or even to advance an untruth. If your employer, a pharmaceutical company, claims its new drug cures both cancer and erectile dysfunction, your job is to promote it, not to investigate the grounds for these claims.

I could do this, on a temporary basis anyway, and have even done many of the things PR people routinely do: I've written press releases, pitched stories to editors and reporters, prepared press packets, and helped arrange press conferences. As an author, I have also worked closely with my publisher's PR people and have always found them to be intelligent and in every way congenial.

I have also been an activist in a variety of causes over the years, and this experience too must translate into something valuable to any firm willing to hire me. I have planned meetings and chaired them; I have worked in dozens of diverse groups and often played a leadership role in them; I am at ease as a public speaker, whether giving a lengthy speech or a brief presentation on a panel—all of which amounts to the "leader ship" skills that should be an asset to any company. At the very least, I could claim to be an "event planner," capable of dividing gatherings into plenaries and break-out sessions, arranging the press coverage, and planning the follow-up events.

Even as a rough draft, the résumé took days of preparation. I had to line up people willing to lie for me, should they be called by a potential employer, and attest to the fine work I had done for them. Fortunately, I have friends who were willing to do this, some of them located at recognizable companies. Although I did not dare claim actual employment at these firms, since a call to their Human Resources departments would immediately expose the lie, I felt I could safely pretend to have "consulted" to them over the years. Suffice it to say that I gave Barbara Alexander an exemplary history in public relations, sometimes with a little event planning thrown in, and that the dissimulation involved in crafting my new résumé was further preparation for any morally challenging projects I should be called upon to undertake as a PR person.

I did not, however, embellish my new identity with an affect or mannerisms different from my own. I am not an actor and would not have been able to do this even if I had wanted to. "Barbara Alexander" was only a cover for Barbara Ehrenreich; her behavior would, for better or worse, always be my own. In fact, in a practical sense I was simply changing my occupational status from "self-employed/writer" to "unemployed"—a distinction that might be imperceptible to the casual observer. I would still stay home most days at my computer, only now, instead of researching and writing articles, I would be researching and contacting companies that might employ me. The new name and fake résumé were only my ticket into the ranks of the unemployed white-collar Americans who spend their days searching for a decent-paying job.

The project required some minimal structure; since I was stepping into the unknown, I needed to devise some guidelines for myself. My first rule was that I would do everything possible to land a job, which meant being open to every form of help that presented itself: utilizing whatever books, web sites, and businesses, for example, that I could find offering guidance to job seekers. I would endeavor to behave as I was expected to, insofar as I could decipher the expectations. I did not know exactly what forms of effort would be required of successful job seekers, only that I would, as humbly and diligently as possible, give it my best try.

Second, I would be prepared to go anywhere for a job or even an interview, and would advertise this geographic flexibility in my contacts with potential employers. I was based in Charlottesville, Virginia, throughout this project, but I was prepared to travel anywhere in the United States to get a job and then live there for several months if I found one. Nor would I shun any industry—other than those where I might be recognized—as unglamorous or morally repugnant. My third rule was that I would have to take the first job I was offered that met my requirements as to income and benefits.

I knew that the project would take a considerable investment of time and money, so I set aside ten months4 and the sum of $5,000 for travel and other expenses that might arise in the course of job searching. My expectation was that I would make the money back once I got a job and probably come out far ahead. As for the time, I budgeted roughly four to six months for the search—five months being the average for unemployed people in 2004—and another three to four months of employment (Leland). I would have plenty of time both to sample the life of the white-collar unemployed and to explore the corporate world they sought to reenter.

From the outset, I pictured this abstraction, the *corporate world*, as a castle on a hill—well fortified, surrounded by difficult checkpoints, with its glass walls gleaming invitingly from on high. I knew that it would be a long hard climb just to get to the door. But I've made my way into remote and lofty places before— college and graduate school, for example. I'm patient and crafty; I have stamina and resolve; and I believed that I could do this too.

In fact, the project, as I planned it, seemed less challenging than I might have liked. As an undercover reporter, I would of course be insulated from the real terrors of the white-collar work world, if only because I was independent of it for my in come and self-esteem. Most of my fellow job seekers would probably have come to their status involuntarily, through lay offs or individual firings. For them, to lose a job is to enter a world of pain. Their income collapses to the size of an unemployment insurance check; their self-confidence plummets. Much has been written about the psychological damage incurred by the unemployed—their sudden susceptibility to depression, divorce, substance abuse, and even suicide.5 No such calamities could occur in my life as an undercover job seeker and, later, jobholder. There would be no sudden de scent into poverty, nor any real sting of rejection.

I also started with the expectation that this project would be far less demanding than the work I had undertaken for *Nickel and Dimed*. Physically, it would be a piece of cake—no scrubbing, no heavy lifting, no walking or running for hours on end. As for behavior, I imagined that I would be immune from the constant subservience and obedience demanded of low-wage blue-collar workers, that I would be far freer to be, and express, myself. As it turns out, I was wrong on all counts.

Notes

1 Even fiction—my favorite source of insight into culture and times remote from my own—was no help. While the fifties and sixties had produced absorbing novels about white-collar corporate life, including Richard Yates's *Revolutionary Road* and Sloan Wilson's *The Man in the Gray Flannel Suit*, more recent novels and films tend to ignore the white-collar corporate work world except as a backdrop to sexual intrigue.

2 According to the Bureau of Labor Statistics, women are only slightly more likely than men to be unemployed—6.1 percent compared to 5.7 percent—and white women, like myself, are about half as likely as black women to be unemployed (www.bls.gov).

3 I was particularly enlightened by Jill Andresky Fraser's *White Collar Sweatshop: The Deterioration of Work and Its Rewards in Corporate America* (W. W. Norton, 2001) and Richard Sennett's *The Corrosion of Character: The Personal Consequences of Work in the New Capitalism* (W. W. Norton, 1998).

4 From December 2003 to October 2004, with the exception of most of July, when I had a brief real-life job writing biweekly columns for the *New York Times*.

5 See, for example, Katherine S. Newman's *Falling from Grace: Downward*

Mobility in the Age of Affluence (U of California P, 1999) or, for a highly readable first-person account, G.J. Meyer's *Executive Blues* (Franklin Square Press, 1995).

Works Cited

Fraser, Jill Andresky. *White Collar Sweatshop: The Deterioration of Work and Its Rewards in Corporate America*. W. W. Norton, 2001.

Leland, John. "For Unemployed, Wait for New Work Grows Longer." *New York Times*, 9 Jan. 2005, www.nytimes.com/2005/01/09/us/for-unemployed-wait-for-new-work-grows-longer.html?r=0.

Mackay, Harvey. *We Got Fired! And It's the Best Thing That Ever Happened to Us*. Ballantine, 2004.

Mahler, Jonathan. "Commute to Nowhere." *New York Times Magazine*, 13 Apr. 2003, www.nytimes.com/2003/04/13/magazine/commute-to-nowhere.html?pagewanted=all.

National Center for Education Statistics. Undergraduate Enrollments in Academic, Career, and Vocational Education. *Issue Brief*, Feb. 2004, nces.ed.gov/pubs2004/2004018.pdf.

05 文學

Everything That Rises Must Converge
凡興起之一切必將匯合

Flannery O'Connor

Her doctor had told Julian's mother that she must lose twenty pounds on account of her blood pressure, so on Wednesday nights Julian had to take her downtown on the bus for a reducing class at the Y. The reducing class was designed for working girls over fifty, who weighed from 165 to 200 pounds. His mother was one of the slimmer ones, but she said ladies did not tell their age or weight. She would not ride the buses by herself at night since they had been integrated, and

Flannery O'Connor 富蘭納瑞・歐康納（1925-1964）

　　美國作家暨散文家，出生於喬治亞州薩凡納城（Savannah, Georgia）。著有兩本長篇小說與超過三十篇短篇小說，〈凡興起之一切必將匯合〉出自她的第二本短篇小說集，是 1965 年在她身後才發表的作品集。她的寫作風格經常被歸為南方歌德式（Southern Gothic），這種故事類型以美國南方為背景，故事角色經常面臨恐怖的處境。

because the reducing class was one of her few pleasures, necessary for her health, and free, she said Julian could at least put himself out to take her, considering all she did for him. Julian did not like to consider all she did for him, but every Wednesday night he braced himself and took her.

She was almost ready to go, standing before the hall mirror, putting on her hat, while he, his hands behind him, appeared pinned to the door frame, waiting like Saint Sebastian for the arrows to begin piercing him. The hat was new and had cost her seven dollars and a half. She kept saying, "Maybe I shouldn't have paid that for it. No, I shouldn't have. I'll take it off and return it tomorrow. I shouldn't have bought it."

Julian raised his eyes to heaven. "Yes, you should have bought it," he said. "Put it on and let's go." It was a hideous hat. A purple velvet flap came down on one side of it and stood up on the other; the rest of it was green and looked like a cushion with the stuffing out. He decided it was less comical than jaunty and pathetic. Everything that gave her pleasure was small and depressed him.

She lifted the hat one more time and set it down slowly on top of her head. Two wings of gray hair protruded on either side of her florid face, but her eyes, sky-blue, were as innocent and untouched by experience as they must have been when she was ten. Were it not that she was a widow who had struggled fiercely to feed and clothe and put him through school and who was supporting him still, "until he got on his feet," she might have been a little girl that he had to take to town.

"It's all right, it's all right," he said. "Let's go." He opened the door himself and started down the walk to get her going. The sky was a dying violet and the houses stood out darkly against it, bulbous liver-colored monstrosities of a uniform ugliness though no two were alike. Since this had been a fashionable neighborhood forty years ago, his mother persisted in thinking they did well to have an apartment in it. Each house had a narrow collar of dirt around it in which sat, usually, a grubby child. Julian walked with his hands in his pockets, his head down and thrust forward and his eyes glazed with the determination to make himself completely numb during the time he would be sacrificed to her pleasure.

The door closed and he turned to find the dumpy figure, surmounted by the atrocious hat, coming toward him. "Well," she said, "you only live once and paying a little more for it, I at least won't meet myself coming and going."

"Some day I'll start making money," Julian said gloomily—he knew he never would—"and you can have one of those jokes whenever you take the fit." But first they would move. He visualized a place where the nearest neighbors would be three miles away on either side.

"I think you're doing fine," she said, drawing on her gloves. "You've only been out of school a year. Rome wasn't built in a day."

She was one of the few members of the Y reducing class who arrived in hat and gloves and who had a son who had been to college. "It takes time," she said, "and the world is in such a mess. This hat looked better on me than any of the others, though when she brought it out I said, 'Take that thing back. I wouldn't have it on my head,' and she said, 'Now wait till you see it on,' and when she put it on me, I said, 'We-ull,' and she said, 'If you ask me, that hat does something for you and you do something for the hat, and besides,' she said, 'with that hat, you won't meet yourself coming and going.'"

Julian thought he could have stood his lot better if she had been selfish, if she had been an old hag who drank and screamed at him. He walked along, saturated in depression, as if in the midst of his martyrdom he had lost his faith. Catching sight of his long, hopeless, irritated face, she stopped suddenly with a grief-stricken look, and pulled back on his arm. "Wait on me," she said. "I'm going back to the house and take this thing off and tomorrow I'm going to return it. I was out of my head. I can pay the gas bill with that seven-fifty."

He caught her arm in a vicious grip. "You are not going to take it back," he said. "I like it."

"Well," she said, "I don't think I ought..."

"Shut up and enjoy it," he muttered, more depressed than ever.

"With the world in the mess it's in," she said, "it's a wonder we can enjoy anything. I tell you, the bottom rail is on the top."

Julian sighed.

"Of course," she said, "if you know who you are, you can go anywhere." She said this every time he took her to the reducing class. "Most of them in it are not our kind of people," she said, "but I can be gracious to anybody. I know who I am."

"They don't give a damn for your graciousness," Julian said savagely. "Knowing who you are is good for one generation only. You haven't the foggiest idea where you stand now or who you are."

She stopped and allowed her eyes to flash at him. "I most certainly do know who I am," she said, "and if you don't know who you are, I'm ashamed of you."

"Oh hell," Julian said.

"Your great-grandfather was a former governor of this state," she said. "Your grandfather was a prosperous landowner. Your grandmother was a Godhigh."

"Will you look around you," he said tensely, "and see where you are now?" and he swept his arm jerkily out to indicate the neighborhood, which the growing darkness at least made less dingy.

"You remain what you are," she said. "Your great-grandfather had a plantation and two hundred slaves."

"There are no more slaves," he said irritably.

"They were better off when they were," she said. He groaned to see that she was off on that topic. She rolled onto it every few days like a train on an open track. He knew every stop, every junction, every swamp along the way, and knew the exact point at which her conclusion would roll majestically into the station: "It's ridiculous. It's simply not realistic. They should rise, yes, but on their own side of the fence."

"Let's skip it," Julian said.

"The ones I feel sorry for," she said, "are the ones that are half white. They're tragic."

"Will you skip it?"

"Suppose we were half white. We would certainly have mixed feelings."

"I have mixed feelings now," he groaned.

"Well let's talk about something pleasant," she said. "I remember going to Grandpa's when I was a little girl. Then the house had double stairways that went up to what was really the second floor—all the cooking was done on the first. I used to like to stay down in the kitchen on account of the way the walls smelled. I would sit with my nose pressed against the plaster and take deep breaths. Actually the place belonged to the Godhighs but your grandfather Chestny paid the mortgage and saved it for them. They were in reduced circumstances," she said, "but reduced or not, they never forgot who they were."

"Doubtless that decayed mansion reminded them," Julian muttered. He never spoke of it without contempt or thought of it without longing. He had seen it once when he was a child before it had been sold. The double stairways had rotted and been torn down. Negroes were living in it. But it remained in his mind as his mother had known it. It appeared in his dreams regularly. He would stand on the wide porch, listening to the rustle of oak leaves, then wander through the high-ceilinged hall into the parlor that opened onto it and gaze at the worn rugs and faded draperies. It occurred to him that it was he, not she, who could have appreciated it. He preferred its threadbare elegance to anything he could name and it was because of it that all the neighborhoods they had lived in had been a torment to him—whereas she had hardly known the difference. She called her insensitivity "being adjustable."

"And I remember the old darky who was my nurse, Caroline. There was no better person in the world. I've always had a great respect for my colored friends," she said. "I'd do anything in the world for them and they'd..."

"Will you for God's sake get off that subject?" Julian said. When he got on a bus by himself, he made it a point to sit down beside a Negro, in reparation as it were for his mother's sins.

"You're mighty touchy tonight," she said. "Do you feel all right?"

"Yes I feel all right," he said. "Now lay off."

She pursed her lips. "Well, you certainly are in a vile humor," she observed. "I just won't speak to you at all."

They had reached the bus stop. There was no bus in sight and Julian, his hands still jammed in his pockets and his head thrust forward, scowled down the empty street. The frustration of having to wait on the bus as well as ride on it began to creep up his neck like a hot hand. The presence of his mother was borne in upon him as she gave a pained sigh. He looked at her bleakly. She was holding herself very erect under the preposterous hat, wearing it like a banner of her imaginary dignity. There was in him an evil urge to break her spirit. He suddenly unloosened his tie and pulled it off and put it in his pocket.

She stiffened. "Why must you look like *that* when you take me to town?" she said. "Why must you deliberately embarrass me?"

"If you'll never learn where you are," he said, "you can at least learn where I am."

"You look like a—thug," she said.

"Then I must be one," he murmured.

"I'll just go home," she said. "I will not bother you. If you can't do a little thing like that for me..."

Rolling his eyes upward, he put his tie back on. "Restored to my class," he muttered. He thrust his face toward her and hissed, "True culture is in the mind, the mind ," he said, and tapped his head, "the mind."

"It's in the heart," she said, "and in how you do things and how you do things is because of who you *are*."

"Nobody in the damn bus cares who you are."

"I care who I am," she said icily.   5

The lighted bus appeared on top of the next hill and as it approached, they moved out into the street to meet it. He put his hand under her elbow and hoisted her up on the creaking step. She entered with a little smile, as if she were going into a drawing room where everyone had been waiting for her. While he put in the tokens, she sat down on one of the broad front seats for three which faced the aisle.   10 A thin woman with protruding teeth and long yellow hair was sitting on the end of it. His mother moved up beside her and left room for Julian beside herself. He sat down and looked at the floor across the aisle where a pair of thin feet in red and white canvas sandals were planted.

His mother immediately began a general conversation meant to attract anyone   15 who felt like talking. "Can it get any hotter?" she said and removed from her purse a folding fan, black with a Japanese scene on it, which she began to flutter before her.

"I reckon it might could," the woman with the protruding teeth said, "but I know for a fact my apartment couldn't get no hotter."

"It must get the afternoon sun," his mother said. She sat forward and looked up   20 and down the bus. It was half filled. Everybody was white. "I see we have the bus to ourselves," she said. Julian cringed.

"For a change," said the woman across the aisle, the owner of the red and white canvas sandals. "I come on one the other day and they were thick as fleas—up front and all through."

"The world is in a mess everywhere," his mother said. "I don't know how we've let it get in this fix."

"What gets my goat is all those boys from good families stealing automobile tires," the woman with the protruding teeth said. "I told my boy, I said you may not be rich but you been raised right and if I ever catch you in any such mess, they can send you on to the reformatory. Be exactly where you belong."

"Training tells," his mother said. "Is your boy in high school?"

"Ninth grade," the woman said.

"My son just finished college last year. He wants to write but he's selling typewriters until he gets started," his mother said.

The woman leaned forward and peered at Julian. He threw her such a malevolent look that she subsided against the seat. On the floor across the aisle there was an abandoned newspaper. He got up and got it and opened it out in front of him. His mother discreetly continued the conversation in a lower tone but the woman across the aisle said in a loud voice, "Well that's nice. Selling typewriters is close to writing. He can go right from one to the other."

"I tell him," his mother said, "that Rome wasn't built in a day."

Behind the newspaper Julian was withdrawing into the inner compartment of his mind where he spent most of his time. This was a kind of mental bubble in which he established himself when he could not bear to be a part of what was going on around him. From it he could see out and judge but in it he was safe from any kind of penetration from without. It was the only place where he felt free of the general idiocy of his fellows. His mother had never entered it but from it he could see her with absolute clarity.

The old lady was clever enough and he thought that if she had started from any of the right premises, more might have been expected of her. She lived according to the laws of her own fantasy world outside of which he had never seen her set foot. The law of it was to sacrifice herself for him after she had first created the necessity to do so by making a mess of things. If he had permitted her sacrifices, it was only because her lack of foresight had made them necessary. All of her life had been a struggle to act like a Chestny without the Chestny goods, and to give him everything she thought a Chestny ought to have; but since, said she, it was fun to struggle, why complain? And when you had won, as she had won, what fun to look back on the hard times! He could not forgive her that she had enjoyed the struggle and that she thought she had won.

What she meant when she said she had won was that she had brought him up successfully and had sent him to college and that he had turned out so well—good looking (her teeth had gone unfilled so that his could be straightened), intelligent (he realized he was too intelligent to be a success), and with a future ahead of him (there was of course no future ahead of him). She excused his gloominess on the grounds that he was still growing up and his radical ideas on his lack of practical experience. She said he didn't yet know a thing about "life," that he hadn't even entered the real world—when already he was as disenchanted with it as a man of fifty.

The further irony of all this was that in spite of her, he had turned out so well.

In spite of going to only a third-rate college, he had, on his own initiative, come out with a first-rate education; in spite of growing up dominated by a small mind, he had ended up with a large one; in spite of all her foolish views, he was free of prejudice and unafraid to face facts. Most miraculous of all, instead of being blinded by love for her as she was for him, he had cut himself emotionally free of her and could see her with complete objectivity. He was not dominated by his mother.

The bus stopped with a sudden jerk and shook him from his meditation. A woman from the back lurched forward with little steps and barely escaped falling in his newspaper as she righted herself. She got off and a large Negro got on. Julian kept his paper lowered to watch. It gave him a certain satisfaction to see injustice in daily operation. It confirmed his view that with a few exceptions there was no one worth knowing within a radius of three hundred miles. The Negro was well dressed and carried a briefcase. He looked around and then sat down on the other end of the seat where the woman with the red and white canvas sandals was sitting. He immediately unfolded a newspaper and obscured himself behind it. Julian's mother's elbow at once prodded insistently into his ribs. "Now you see why I won't ride on these buses by myself," she whispered.

The woman with the red and white canvas sandals had risen at the same time the Negro sat down and had gone further back in the bus and taken the seat of the woman who had got off. His mother leaned forward and cast her an approving look.

Julian rose, crossed the aisle, and sat down in the place of the woman with the canvas sandals. From this position, he looked serenely across at his mother. Her face had turned an angry red. He stared at her, making his eyes the eyes of a stranger. He felt his tension suddenly lift as if he had openly declared war on her.

He would have liked to get in conversation with the Negro and to talk with him about art or politics or any subject that would be above the comprehension of those around them, but the man remained entrenched behind his paper. He was either ignoring the change of seating or had never noticed it. There was no way for Julian to convey his sympathy.

His mother kept her eyes fixed reproachfully on his face. The woman with the protruding teeth was looking at him avidly as if he were a type of monster new to her.

"Do you have a light?" he asked the Negro.

Without looking away from his paper, the man reached in his pocket and handed him a packet of matches.

"Thanks," Julian said. For a moment he held the matches foolishly. A NO SMOKING sign looked down upon him from over the door. This alone would not have deterred him; he had no cigarettes. He had quit smoking some months before because he could not afford it. "Sorry," he muttered and handed back the matches. The Negro lowered the paper and gave him an annoyed look. He took the matches and raised the paper again.

His mother continued to gaze at him but she did not take advantage of his momentary discomfort. Her eyes retained their battered look. Her face seemed to be unnaturally red, as if her blood pressure had risen. Julian allowed no glimmer of sympathy to show on his face. Having got the advantage, he wanted desperately to keep it and carry it through. He would have liked to teach her a lesson that would last her a while, but there seemed no way to continue the point. The Negro refused to come out from behind his paper.

Julian folded his arms and looked stolidly before him, facing her but as if he did not see her, as if he had ceased to recognize her existence. He visualized a scene in which, the bus having reached their stop, he would remain in his seat and when she said, "Aren't you going to get off?" he would look at her as at a stranger who had rashly addressed him. The corner they got off on was usually deserted, but it was well lighted and it would not hurt her to walk by herself the four blocks to the Y. He decided to wait until the time came and then decide whether or not he would let her get off by herself. He would have to be at the Y at ten to bring her back, but he could leave her wondering if he was going to show up. There was no reason for her to think she could always depend on him.

He retired again into the high-ceilinged room sparsely settled with large pieces of antique furniture. His soul expanded momentarily but then he became aware of his mother across from him and the vision shriveled. He studied her coldly. Her feet in little pumps dangled like a child's and did not quite reach the floor. She was training on him an exaggerated look of reproach. He felt completely detached from her. At that moment he could with pleasure have slapped her as he would have slapped a particularly obnoxious child in his charge.

He began to imagine various unlikely ways by which he could teach her a lesson. He might make friends with some distinguished Negro professor or lawyer and bring him home to spend the evening. He would be entirely justified but her blood pressure would rise to 300. He could not push her to the extent of making her have a stroke, and moreover, he had never been successful at making any Negro friends. He had tried to strike up an acquaintance on the bus with some of the better types, with ones that looked like professors or ministers or lawyers. One morning he had sat down next to a distinguished-looking dark brown man who had answered his questions with a sonorous solemnity but who had turned out to be an undertaker. Another day he had sat down beside a cigar-smoking Negro with a diamond ring on his finger, but after a few stilted pleasantries, the Negro had rung the buzzer and risen, slipping two lottery tickets into Julian's hand as he climbed over him to leave.

He imagined his mother lying desperately ill and his being able to secure only a Negro doctor for her. He toyed with that idea for a few minutes and then dropped it for a momentary vision of himself participating as a sympathizer in a sit-in demonstration. This was possible but he did not linger with it. Instead, he approached the ultimate horror. He brought home a beautiful suspiciously Negroid woman. Prepare yourself, he said. There is nothing you can do about it. This is the woman I've chosen. She's intelligent, dignified, even good, and she's suffered and she hasn't thought it *fun*. Now persecute us, go ahead and persecute us. Drive her out of here, but remember, you're driving me too. His eyes were narrowed and through the indignation he had generated, he saw his mother across the aisle, purple-faced, shrunken to the dwarf-like proportions of her moral nature, sitting like a mummy beneath the ridiculous banner of her hat.

He was tilted out of his fantasy again as the bus stopped. The door opened with a sucking hiss and out of the dark a large, gaily dressed, sullen-looking colored woman got on with a little boy. The child, who might have been four, had on a short plaid suit and a Tyrolean hat with a blue feather in it. Julian hoped that he would sit down beside him and that the woman would push in beside his mother. He could think of no better arrangement.

As she waited for her tokens, the woman was surveying the seating possibilities—he hoped with the idea of sitting where she was least wanted. There was something familiar-looking about her but Julian could not place what it was. She was a giant of a woman. Her face was set not only to meet opposition but to seek it out. The downward tilt of her large lower lip was like a warning sign: don't tamper with me. Her bulging figure was encased in a green crepe dress and her feet overflowed in red shoes. She had on a hideous hat. A purple velvet flap came down on one side of it and stood up on the other; the rest of it was green and looked like a cushion with the stuffing out. She carried a mammoth red pocketbook that bulged throughout as if it were stuffed with rocks.

To Julian's disappointment, the little boy climbed up on the empty seat beside his mother. His mother lumped all children, black and white, into the common category, "cute," and she thought little Negroes were on the whole cuter than little white children. She smiled at the little boy as he climbed on the seat.

Meanwhile the woman was bearing down upon the empty seat beside Julian. To his annoyance, she squeezed herself into it. He saw his mother's face change as the woman settled herself next to him and he realized with satisfaction that this was more objectionable to her than it was to him. Her face seemed almost gray and there was a look of dull recognition in her eyes, as if suddenly she had sickened at some awful confrontation. Julian saw that it was because she and the woman had, in a sense, swapped sons. Though his mother would not realize the symbolic significance of this, she would feel it. His amusement showed plainly on his face.

The woman next to him muttered something unintelligible to herself. He was conscious of a kind of bristling next to him, muted growling like that of an angry cat. He could not see anything but the red pocketbook upright on the bulging green thighs. He visualized the woman as she had stood waiting for her tokens— the ponderous figure, rising from the red shoes upward over the solid hips, the mammoth bosom, the haughty face, to the green and purple hat.

His eyes widened.

The vision of the two hats, identical, broke upon him with the radiance of a brilliant sunrise. His face was suddenly lit with joy. He could not believe that Fate had thrust upon his mother such a lesson. He gave a loud chuckle so that she would look at him and see that he saw. She turned her eyes on him slowly. The blue in them seemed to have turned a bruised purple. For a moment he had an uncomfortable sense of her innocence, but it lasted only a second before principle rescued him. Justice entitled him to laugh. His grin hardened until it said to her as plainly as if he were saying aloud: Your punishment exactly fits your pettiness. This should teach you a permanent lesson.

Her eyes shifted to the woman. She seemed unable to bear looking at him and to find the woman preferable. He became conscious again of the bristling presence at his side. The woman was rumbling like a volcano about to become active. His mother's mouth began to twitch slightly at one corner. With a sinking heart, he saw incipient signs of recovery on her face and realized that this was going to strike her suddenly as funny and was going to be no lesson at all. She kept her eyes on the woman and an amused smile came over her face as if the woman were a monkey that had stolen her hat. The little Negro was looking up at her with large fascinated eyes. He had been trying to attract her attention for some time.

"Carver!" the woman said suddenly. "Come heah!"

When he saw that the spotlight was on him at last, Carver drew his feet up and turned himself toward Julian's mother and giggled.

"Carver!" the woman said. "You heah me? Come heah!"

Carver slid down from the seat but remained squatting with his back against the base of it, his head turned slyly around toward Julian's mother, who was smiling at him. The woman reached a hand across the aisle and snatched him to her. He righted himself and hung backwards on her knees, grinning at Julian's mother. "Isn't he cute?" Julian's mother said to the woman with the protruding teeth.

"I reckon he is," the woman said without conviction.

The Negress yanked him upright but he eased out of her grip and shot across the aisle and scrambled, giggling wildly, onto the seat beside his love.

"I think he likes me," Julian's mother said, and smiled at the woman. It was the smile she used when she was being particularly gracious to an inferior. Julian saw everything lost. The lesson had rolled off her like rain on a roof.

The woman stood up and yanked the little boy off the seat as if she were snatching him from contagion. Julian could feel the rage in her at having no weapon like his mother's smile. She gave the child a sharp slap across his leg. He howled once and then thrust his head into her stomach and kicked his fret against her shins.

"Behave," she said vehemently.

The bus stopped and the Negro who had been reading the newspaper got off. The woman moved over and set the little boy down with a thump between herself and Julian. She held him firmly by the knee. In a moment he put his hands in front of his face and peeped at Julian's mother through his fingers.

"I see yoooooooo!" she said and put her hand in front of her face and peeped at him.

The woman slapped his hand down. "Quit yo' foolishness," she said, "before I knock the living Jesus out of you!"

Julian was thankful that the next stop was theirs. He reached up and pulled the cord. The woman reached up and pulled it at the same time. Oh my God, he thought. He had the terrible intuition that when they got off the bus together, his mother would open her purse and give the little boy a nickel. The gesture would be as natural to her as breathing. The bus stopped and the woman got up and lunged to the front, dragging the child, who wished to stay on, after her. Julian and his mother got up and followed. As they neared the door, Julian tried to relieve her of her pocketbook.

"No," she murmured, "I want to give the little boy a nickel."

"No!" Julian hissed. "No!"

She smiled down at the child and opened her bag. The bus door opened and the woman picked him up by the arm and descended with him, hanging at her hip. Once in the street she set him down and shook him.

Julian's mother had to close her purse while she got down the bus step but as soon as her feet were on the ground, she opened it again and began to rummage inside. "I can't find but a penny," she whispered, "but it looks like a new one."

"Don't do it!" Julian said fiercely between his teeth. There was a streetlight on the corner and she hurried to get under it so that she could better see into her pocketbook. The woman was heading off rapidly down the street with the child still hanging backward on her hand.

"Oh little boy!" Julian's mother called and took a few quick steps and caught up with them just beyond the lamppost. "Here's a bright new penny for you," and she held out the coin, which shone bronze in the dim light.

The huge woman turned and for a moment stood, her shoulders lifted and her face frozen with frustrated rage, and stared at Julian's mother. Then all at once she seemed to explode like a piece of machinery that had been given one ounce of pressure too much. Julian saw the black fist swing out with the red pocketbook. He shut his eyes and cringed as he heard the woman shout, "He don't take nobody's pennies!" When he opened his eyes, the woman was disappearing down the street with the little boy staring wide-eyed over her shoulder. Julian's mother was sitting on the sidewalk.

"I told you not to do that," Julian said angrily. "I told you not to do that!"

He stood over her for a minute, gritting his teeth. Her legs were stretched out in front of her and her hat was on her lap. He squatted down and looked her in the face. It was totally expressionless. "You got exactly what you deserved," he said. "Now get up."

He picked up her pocketbook and put what had fallen out back in it. He picked the hat up off her lap. The penny caught his eye on the sidewalk and he picked that up and let it drop before her eyes into the purse. Then he stood up and leaned over and held his hands out to pull her up. She remained immobile. He sighed. Rising above them on either side were black apartment buildings, marked with irregular rectangles of light. At the end of the block a man came out of a door and walked off in the opposite direction. "All right," he said, "suppose somebody happens by and wants to know why you're sitting on the sidewalk?"

She took the hand and, breathing hard, pulled heavily up on it and then stood for a moment, swaying slightly as if the spots of light in the darkness were circling around her. Her eyes, shadowed and confused, finally settled on his face. He did not try to conceal his irritation. "I hope this teaches you a lesson," he said. She leaned forward and her eyes raked his face. She seemed trying to determine his identity. Then, as if she found nothing familiar about him, she started off with a headlong movement in the wrong direction.

"Aren't you going on to the Y?" he asked.

"Home," she muttered.

"Well, are we walking?"

For answer she kept going. Julian followed along, his hands behind him. He saw no reason to let the lesson she had had go without backing it up with an explanation of its meaning. She might as well be made to understand what had happened to her. "Don't think that was just an uppity Negro woman," he said. "That was the whole colored race which will no longer take your condescending pennies. That was your black double. She can wear the same hat as you, and to be sure," he added gratuitously (because he thought it was funny), "it looked better on her than it did on you. What all this means," he said, "is that the old world is gone. The old manners are obsolete and your graciousness is not worth a damn." He thought bitterly of the house that had been lost for him. "You aren't who you think you are," he said.

She continued to plow ahead, paying no attention to him. Her hair had come undone on one side. She dropped her pocketbook and took no notice. He stooped and picked it up and handed it to her but she did not take it.

"You needn't act as if the world had come to an end," he said, "because it hasn't. From now on you've got to live in a new world and face a few realities for a change. Buck up," he said, "it won't kill you."

She was breathing fast.

"Let's wait on the bus," he said.

"Home," she said thickly.

"I hate to see you behave like this," he said. "Just like a child. I should be able to expect more of you." He decided to stop where he was and make her stop and wait for a bus. "I'm not going any farther," he said, stopping. "We're going on the bus."

She continued to go on as if she had not heard him. He took a few steps and caught her arm and stopped her. He looked into her face and caught his breath. He was looking into a face he had never seen before. "Tell Grandpa to come get me," she said.

He stared, stricken.

"Tell Caroline to come get me," she said.

Stunned, he let her go and she lurched forward again, walking as if one leg were shorter than the other. A tide of darkness seemed to be sweeping her from him. "Mother!" he cried. "Darling, sweetheart, wait!" Crumpling, she fell to the pavement. He dashed forward and fell at her side, crying, "Mamma, Mamma!" He turned her over. Her face was fiercely distorted. One eye, large and staring, moved slightly to the left as if it had become unmoored. The other remained fixed on him, raked his face again, found nothing and closed. 5

"Wait here, wait here!" he cried and jumped up and began to run for help toward a cluster of lights he saw in the distance ahead of him. "Help, help!" he shouted, but his voice was thin, scarcely a thread of sound. The lights drifted farther away the faster he ran and his feet moved numbly as if they carried him nowhere. The tide of darkness seemed to sweep him back to her, postponing from moment to moment his entry into the world of guilt and sorrow. 10

15

20

Index of Templates

索引 # 學術寫作句型

範本 1：提出「他人論點」（p. 34）

▶ A number of _____ have recently suggested that _____.

最近有些_____提出，_____。

▶ It has become common today to dismiss _____.

今日，我們普遍不去考慮_____。

▶ In their recent work, Y and Z have offered harsh critiques of _____ for _____.

Y 和 Z 在最近的研究中，對_____提出了嚴厲的批評，說他_____。

範本 2：提出「一般論點」（pp. 34-35）

▶ Americans today tend to believe that _____.

美國人向來相信_____。

▶ Conventional wisdom has it that _____.

一般看法是_____。

▶ Common sense seems to dictate that _____.

基本常識似乎認定_____。

▶ The standard way of thinking about topic X has it that _____.

關於 X 這個主題，標準的思維模式是_____。

▶ It is often said that _____.

大家常說_____。

▶ My whole life I have heard it said that _____.

我一生中總不斷聽到別人說_____。

▶ You would think that _____.

或許你會認為_____。

▶ Many people assume that _____.

許多人假設_____。

範本 3：將他人論點轉換成自己的論點（pp. 35-36）

▶ I've always believed that _____.

我一直認為_____。

▶ When I was a child, I used to think that _____.

小時候，我常覺得_____。

▶ Although I should know better by now, I cannot help thinking that _____.

雖然我現在想法更周延了，但不禁還是認為_____。

▶ At the same time that I believe _____, I also believe _____.
我既認為_____，又認為_____。

範本 4：提出暗示或假設的想法（pp. 36-37）

▶ Although none of them have ever said so directly, my teachers have often given me the impression that _____.
儘管我的老師們未曾直言，他們卻常給我這個印象，_____。

▶ One implication of X's treatment of _____ is that _____.
X 對_____的論述蘊含了_____之意。

▶ Although X does not say so directly, she apparently assumes that _____.
雖然 X 沒有明講，但她顯然假設_____。

▶ While they rarely admit as much, _____ often take for granted that _____.
雖然他們不會承認，但是_____經常把_____視為理所當然。

範本 5：提出一個尚未定論的爭議點（pp. 37-39）

▶ In discussions of X, one controversial issue has been _____.
On the one hand, _____ argues _____. On the other hand, _____ contends _____. Others even maintain _____.
My own view is _____.
在對於 X 的討論中，一個爭議點一直是_____。一方面，_____指稱_____。另一方面，_____聲稱_____。有些人甚至堅持_____。我自己的看法是_____。

▶ When it comes to the topic of _____, most of us will readily agree that _____. Where this agreement usually ends, however, is on the question of _____. Whereas some are convinced that _____, others maintain that _____.

談到_____這個主題，我們多半會異口同稱認為_____。然而，到了最後，卻往往在_____的問題上產生歧異。儘管有些人相信_____，有些人仍主張_____。

範本 6：持續關注他人論點 (p. 39)

▶ In conclusion, then, as I suggested earlier, defenders of _____ can't have it both ways. Their assertion that _____ is contradicted by their claim that _____.

那麼最後，如同我先前提到，主張_____的論點有無法克服的矛盾。他們說_____，這和他們_____的主張是相悖的。

範本 7：提出概述和引述 (p. 50)

▶ She advocates _____.
她主張_____。

▶ They celebrate the fact that _____.
他們頌揚_____這件事情。

▶ _____, he admits.
他承認_____。

範本 7-1：適合用來概述和引述的動詞（pp. 50-51）

▶ 提出主張

argue 主張、認為

assert 主張、斷言

believe 相信

claim 主張、聲稱

emphasize 強調

insist 堅持、堅決認為

observe 察覺到、注意到

remind us 提醒我們

report 報告；描述

suggest 暗示；意味著

▶ 表示同意、認同

acknowledge 承認、認可

admire 讚賞、誇讚

agree 同意、贊成

endorse 贊同

extol 讚揚、讚頌

praise 稱讚、表揚

▶ 表示質疑或不認同

complain 抱怨

complicate 使複雜化、使更難懂

contend 聲稱、斷言

contradict 駁斥、反駁

deny 否認

deplore the tendency to 強烈譴責⋯⋯

qualify 補充說明；提出但書

question 質疑、懷疑

refute 駁斥、反駁

reject 拒絕、駁回

renounce 宣布放棄

repudiate 否認、駁斥

▶ 提出建議

advocate 提倡、主張

call for 呼籲、要求

demand 強烈要求

encourage 鼓勵

exhort 敦促、規勸

implore 懇求、哀求

plead 懇求、請求

recommend 建議

urge 促請、力勸

warn 警告、告誡

範本 8：介紹引述內容（pp. 55-56）

▶ X states, "＿＿＿＿＿＿"
  X 表示：「＿＿＿＿＿。」

▶ As the prominent philosopher X puts it, "＿＿＿＿＿."
  誠如知名哲學家 X 所言：「＿＿＿＿＿。」

▶ According to X, "＿＿＿＿＿."
  根據 X 的說法：「＿＿＿＿＿。」

▶ X himself writes, "＿＿＿＿＿."
  X 自己說：「＿＿＿＿＿。」

▶ In her book, ＿＿＿＿＿, X maintains that "＿＿＿＿＿."
  X 在她的著作《＿＿＿＿＿》裡，堅持「＿＿＿＿＿。」

▶ Writing in the journal ＿＿＿＿＿, X complains that "＿＿＿＿＿."
  X 在《＿＿＿＿＿》雜誌撰文，埋怨「＿＿＿＿＿。」

▶ In X's view, "＿＿＿＿＿."
  X 的觀點，是認為「＿＿＿＿＿。」

▶ X agrees / disagrees when he writes, "＿＿＿＿＿."
  X 同意／不同意，他說：「＿＿＿＿＿。」

▶ X complicates matters further when he writes, "＿＿＿＿＿."
  X 說：「＿＿＿＿＿」，這使得問題更複雜了。

範本 9：解釋引述內容 （pp. 56-57）

▶ Basically, X is warning _____.
  基本上，X 是在警告_____。

▶ In other words, X believes _____.
  換言之，X 認為_____。

▶ In making this comment, X urges us to _____.
  X 用這個說法，是促使我們要_____。

▶ X is corroborating the age-old adage that _____.
  X 證實了這句亙古名言：_____。

▶ X's point is that _____.
  X 的論點是_____。

▶ The essence of X's argument is that _____.
  X 的論證本質在於_____。

範本 10：表示不同意並說明理由 （pp. 68-69）

▶ X is mistaken because she overlooks _____.
  X 錯了，她忽略了_____。

▶ X's claim that _____ rests upon the questionable assumption that _____.
  X 主張_____，這是立基在_____這個不確定的假設上。

▶ I disagree with X's view that _____ because, as recent research has shown, _____.

我不同意 X_____的觀點，因為最新的研究已經顯示_____。

▶ X contradicts herself/can't have it both ways. On the one hand, she argues _____. On the other hand, she also says _____.

X 是自我矛盾的╱不可能兩面兼顧。一方面，她主張_____；
另一方面，她又說_____。

▶ By focusing on _____, X overlooks the deeper problem of _____.

X 的論點聚焦在_____，卻忽略了_____這個更深的問題。

範本 11：表示贊同，但補充一點不同的看法（pp. 71-72）

▶ I agree that _____ because my experience _____ confirms it.
我同意_____，因為我_____的經驗證實了這一點。

▶ X is surely right about _____ because, as she may not be aware, recent studies have shown that _____.

X 對_____的見解絕對是正確的，因為最新的研究顯示_____，
只是她可能還沒注意到這一點。

▶ X's theory of _____ is extremely useful because it sheds light on the difficult problem of _____.

X 的_____理論極為有用，因為有了它，要解決_____這個難題，
就有了相當樂觀的前景。

▶ Those unfamiliar with this school of thought may be interested to know that it basically boils down to _____.

對這個學派不熟悉的人，可能樂於知道它基本上可歸結為_____。

▶ I agree that _____, a point that needs emphasizing since so many people still believe _____.

我同意_____，這一點是需要強調的，因為太多人仍舊相信_____。

▶ If group X is right that _____, as I think they are, then we need to reassess the popular assumption that _____.

如果 X 團隊提出_____是對的，對此我也同意，那麼對於一般的看法_____，我們就要重新考慮。

範本 12：正反參半，傾向不同意（p. 74）

▶ Although I agree with X up to a point, I cannot accept his overriding assumption that _____.

雖然我某種程度同意 X 的觀點，我無法接受他認為_____的全面觀點。

▶ Though I concede that _____, I still insist that _____.

雖然我承認_____，我仍堅持_____。

▶ X is right that _____, but she seems on more dubious ground when she claims that _____.

X 說_____，這是對的，但她主張_____，好像有點說不通。

範本 13：正反參半，傾向同意（pp. 74-75）

▶ Although I disagree with much that X says, I fully endorse his final conclusion that _____.
雖然 X 所說的我多半不贊同，我倒是完全支持他的最後結論，就是
_____。

▶ While X is probably wrong when she claims that _____, she is right that _____.
X 主張_____，這可能並不正確，但是她說_____，這是沒有錯的。

▶ Whereas X provides ample evidence that _____, Y and Z's research on _____ and _____ convinces me that _____ instead.
儘管 X 對於_____提供充分證據，Y 和 Z 在_____和_____上面的研究卻令我轉而相信_____。

範本 14：正反意見並存（pp. 75-76）

▶ I'm of two minds about X's claim that _____. On the one hand, I agree that _____. On the other hand, I'm not sure if _____.
關於 X 所主張的_____，我覺得各有道理。一方面，我同意
_____，另一方面，我不確定是否_____。

▶ My feelings on the issue are mixed. I do support X's position that _____, but I find Y's argument about _____ and Z's research on _____ to be equally persuasive.
我對於這個議題有點猶豫。我的確是支持 X_____的立場，但是我發現
Y 關於_____的論點和 Z 對於_____的研究也都同樣有說服力。

範本 15：標示出誰在說什麼（pp. 81-82）

▶ Although X makes the best possible case for _____, I am not persuaded.

雖然 X 的_____立論甚佳，但我仍無法苟同。

▶ My view, however, contrary to what X has argued, is that _____.

然而，我的觀點和 X 所主張的相反，我認為_____。

▶ Adding to X's argument, I would point out that _____.

為了補充說明 X 的論點，我想指出_____。

▶ According to both X and Y, _____.

根據 X 和 Y 雙方的看法，_____。

▶ Politicians, X argues, should _____.

X 認為政治人物應該_____。

▶ Most athletes will tell you that _____.

大部分的運動員會跟你說_____。

▶ X argues _____.

X 認為_____。

▶ I agree, as X may not realize, that _____.

我同意_____，而 X 可能不明白。

範本 16：取代第一人稱「我」（pp. 83-84）

▶ X is right that _____.

X 認為_____，他說得沒錯。

▶ The evidence shows that _____.

證據顯示_____。

▶ X's assertion that _____ does not fit the facts.

X 主張_____，這與事實不符。

▶ Anyone familiar with _____ should agree that _____.

熟悉_____的人應該都會同意_____。

▶ But _____ are real, and are arguably the most significant factor

in _____.

然而_____是真的，而且可能是_____的最大因素。

▶ X is wrong that _____.

X 認為_____，這是不對的。

▶ X is both right and wrong that _____.

X 認為_____，這可以說對，也可以說不對。

▶ Yet a sober analysis of the matter reveals _____.

然而這個問題的一項慎重分析顯示出_____。

▶ However, it is simply not true that _____.

然而，_____完全不是事實。

▶ Indeed, it is highly likely that _____.

甚至於，非常有可能_____。

▶ Nevertheless, new research shows _____.

然而，新的研究顯示_____。

範本 17：嵌入發言標記（pp. 85-86）

▶ X overlooks what I consider an important point about _____.
關於_____，X 忽略了我認為的一個重點。

▶ My own view is that what X insists is a _____ is in fact a _____.
我自己的觀點是，X 堅持是_____的問題，事實上是_____。

▶ I wholeheartedly endorse what X calls _____.
我完全支持 X 所稱的_____。

▶ These conclusions, which X discusses in _____, add weight to the argument that _____.
X 在_____所探討的這些結論，進一步證明了_____的論點。

範本 18：納入反對意見（p. 93）

▶ At this point I would like to raise some objections that have been inspired by the skeptic in me. She feels that I have been ignoring _____.
現在，我想提出一些反對的意見，是我內心的懷疑者告訴我的。她覺得我忽略了_____。

▶ Yet some readers may challenge my view by insisting that _____.
然而，有些讀者可能會質疑我的觀點，堅持說_____。

▶ Of course, many will probably disagree on the grounds that _____.
當然，很多人或許會不同意，理由是_____。

範本 19：指出反對者的身分 (pp. 93-95)

▶ Here many _____ would probably object that _____.

　許_____可能會反對_____這件事。

▶ But _____ would certainly take issue with the argument that _____.

　但是_____一定會對_____的論點提出異議。

▶ _____, of course, may want to question whether _____.

　當然了，_____可能會質疑是否_____。

▶ Nevertheless, both followers and critics of _____ will probably argue that _____.

　不過，_____的支持者和批評者都可能有不同看法，主張說

　_____。

▶ Although not all _____ think alike, some of them will probably dispute my claim that _____.

　雖然並非所有的_____想法都一致，其中一部分人可能會質疑我的主張，說_____。

▶ _____ are so diverse in their views that it's hard to generalize about them, but some are likely to object on the grounds that _____.

　_____之間的想法差異太大，很難一概而論，但是其中一些人可能會反對，理由是_____。

範本 20：以非正式方法帶出反面意見 (pp. 95-96)

▶ But is my proposal realistic? What are the chances of its actually being adopted?

但是我的提議可行嗎？它被真正採納的機會有多少？

▶ Yet is it necessarily true that _____? Is it always the case, as I have been suggesting, that _____?

然而_____必定是正確的嗎？真的一直像我所認為的那樣，_____嗎？

▶ However, does the evidence I've cited prove conclusively that _____?

然而，我所援引的證據可以確實證明_____嗎？

▶ "Impossible," some will say. "You must be reading the research selectively."

有人會說：「不可能，你的解讀以偏概全。」

範本 21：讓步之餘仍堅持立場 (p. 101)

▶ Although I grant that _____, I still maintain that _____.

雖然我承認_____，我仍然堅信_____。

▶ Proponents of X are right to argue that _____. But they exaggerate when they claim that _____.

X 的擁護者說得沒錯：_____，但是他們主張_____是有點言過其實了。

▶ While it is true that _____, it does not necessarily follow that _____.

_____是事實沒錯，但未必能由此推斷_____。

▶ On the one hand, I agree with X that _____. But on the other hand, I still insist that _____.
一方面，我同意 X 說的_____，但是另一方面，我仍然堅持_____。

範本 22：點出在乎這個論點的人 (pp. 107-109)

▶ _____ used to think _____. But recently [or within the past few decades] _____ suggests that _____.
_____過去認為_____，但是最近（或者在過去數十年間）_____指出_____。

▶ This interpretation challenges the work of those critics who have long assumed that _____.
這個解釋挑戰了某些批評者的論點，他們長久以來認定_____。

▶ These findings challenge the work of earlier researchers, who tended to assume that _____.
這些發現挑戰了早期研究人員的研究成果，他們多傾向於認定_____。

▶ Recent studies like these shed new light on _____, which previous studies had not addressed.
諸如此類的新近研究重新釐清了_____，而先前的研究未能處理到這部分。

▶ But who really cares? Who besides me and a handful of recent researchers has a stake in these claims? At the very least, the researchers who formerly believed _____ should care.
但是有誰真的關心？除了我和近來的少數相關研究人員之外，還會有誰？起碼過去相信_____的那些研究者應該關心吧。

▶ Researchers have long assumed that _____. For instance, one eminent scholar of _____, X, assumed in _____, her seminal work on _____, that _____. As X herself put it, "_____" (_____). Another leading scientist, Y, argued that "_____" (_____). Ultimately, when it came to _____, the basic assumption was that _____.

But a new body of research shows that_____.

研究人員長期以來一直認定_____。舉例來說，一名聲譽卓著的 X 學者在_____領域的開創性研究_____當中，就認為_____。如 X 本人所言：「_____」（_____年）。另一位頂尖的科學家 Y 則主張「_____」（_____年）。最後，說到_____，過去的基本看法是_____。

然而，多項新的研究顯示_____。

▶ If _____ stopped to think about it, many of them might simply assume that _____. However, new research shows _____.

如果_____思考這個問題，其中許多人或許會單純認為_____。然而新的研究顯示，_____。

▶ These findings challenge _____' common assumption that _____.

這些發現挑戰了_____的普遍假設，那就是_____。

▶ At first glance, _____ might say _____. But on closer inspection _____.

乍看之下，_____可能會說_____，但更仔細一看，其實是_____。

範本 23：表明你的主張何以重要（pp. 112-113）

▶ _____ matters/is important because _____ .

_____ 之所以很重要，是因為 _____ 。

▶ Although X may seem trivial, it is in fact crucial in terms of today's concern over _____ .

雖然 X 可能看似微不足道，事實上，以今日人們對於 _____ 的關心來看，它極其重要。

▶ Ultimately, what is at stake here is _____ .

最後，真正事關重大的是 _____ 。

▶ If we are right about _____ , then major consequences follow for _____ .

如果我們對於 _____ 的看法是正確的，那麼在 _____ 方面將產生重大的後果。

▶ These conclusions/This discovery will have significant applications in _____ as well as in _____ .

這些結論／發現不僅在 _____ 方面有著重大的影響，在 _____ 方面也是。

▶ Although X may seem of concern to only a small group of _____ , it should in fact concern anyone who cares about _____ .

即便可能只有一小群 _____ 人士關心 X 這件事，實際上任何在意 _____ 的人，都該對此關心。

▶ These findings have important implications for the broader domain of _____.

這些發現對於更廣泛的_____領域有著重大的意義。

▶ My discussion of X is in fact addressing the larger matter of _____.

我對主題 X 的討論，事實上是在探討_____這個更大議題。

▶ My point here (that _____) should interest those who _____. Beyond this limited audience, however, my point should speak to anyone who cares about the larger issue of _____.

我的論點（_____）應該會讓那些_____的人產生興趣。不過除了這些有限的讀者之外，任何關心_____這個更大議題的人，希望都能聽聽我的論點。

範本 24：常用轉接語（pp. 121-123）

▶ 補充

also 再者；此外	indeed 甚至；而且
and 而且；然後	in fact 事實上
besides 此外	moreover 此外
furthermore 此外；再者	so too 也是如此
in addition 除此之外	

▶ 詳述

actually 實際上	to put it another way 換而言之
by extension 進而；乃至於	to put it bluntly 恕我直言
in other words 換而言之	to put it succinctly 簡而言之
in short 簡而言之	ultimately 歸根究柢
that is 也就是說	

▶ 舉例

after all 畢竟；終究
as an illustration 作為例子
consider 考慮
for example 例如

for instance 例如
specifically 具體來說
to take a case in point 舉一個實例

▶ 因果

accordingly 因此
as a result 結果
consequently 結果
hence 因此
since 既然；因為

so 所以
then 那麼；於是
therefore 因此
thus 因此

▶ 比較

along the same lines 以相同的方式
in the same way 以相同的方式

likewise 同樣地
similarly 類似地

▶ 對比

although 雖然；儘管
but 但是
by contrast 相較之下
conversely 反過來說
despite 儘管
even though 即使；縱然
however 然而
in contrast 相比之下

nevertheless 儘管如此；然而
nonetheless 儘管如此；然而
on the contrary 相反地
on the other hand 在另一方面
regardless 不管怎樣地
whereas 然而
while yet 然而

▶ 退讓

admittedly 不可否認地；誠然　　　naturally 自然；當然
although it is true 雖然沒錯　　　of course 當然
granted 誠然；的確　　　　　　　to be sure 不可否認地

▶ 結論

as a result 結果　　　　　　　　in sum 總而言之
consequently 結果　　　　　　　therefore 因此
hence 因此　　　　　　　　　　thus 因此
in conclusion 最後；總之　　　　to sum up 總而言之
in short 總而言之　　　　　　　to summarize 總而言之

範本 25：後設評論的用法（pp. 149-152）

避免誤解

▶ Essentially, I am arguing not _____, but that we should _____.
　基本上，我所主張的並非_____，而是我們應該_____。

▶ This is not to say _____, but rather _____.
　這並不代表_____，而是_____。

▶ X is concerned less with _____ than with _____.
　X 對於_____關注得較少，對於_____則較多。

詳細說明先前的論點

▶ In other words, _____.
　換言之，_____。

► To put it another way, _____.
換句話說，_____。

► What X is saying here is that _____.
X 在這裡所說的意思是_____。

提供文章指引

► Chapter 2 explores _____, while Chapter 3 examines _____.
第二章探討的是_____，而第三章則檢視_____。

► Having just argued that _____, I want now to complicate the point by _____.
方才我們已經提出了_____的論點，現在我想要透過_____的方式，把這個論點說得更複雜一點。

從泛論到實例

► For example, _____.
舉例來說，_____。

► _____, for instance, demonstrates _____.
比方說，_____就顯示出_____。

► Consider _____, for example.
舉例來說，試想_____的情況。

► To take a case in point, _____.
舉一個典型的例子，_____。

指出某主張的重要性

▶ Even more important, _____.
更重要的是，_____。

▶ But above all, _____.
然而最重要的是，_____。

▶ Incidentally, we will briefly note, _____.
附帶一提，我們將略為談到_____

▶ Just as important, _____.
同樣重要的是，_____。

▶ Equally, _____.
同樣地，_____。

▶ Finally, _____.
最後，_____。

預期可能的反對，並據理回應

▶ Although some readers may object that _____, I would answer that _____.
雖然有些讀者可能會反對說_____，我的回答是_____。

總結論點

▶ In sum, then, _____.
因此，總而言之，_____。

▶ My conclusion, then, is that _____.
因此，我的結論是_____。

▶ In short, _____.
簡言之，_____。

文學寫作：先聽聽別人怎麼說（pp. 204-206）

▶ Critic X complains that Author Y's story is compromised by his _____ perspective. While there's some truth to this critique, I argue that Critic X overlooks _____.
評論家 X 抱怨作者 Y 從_____的角度敘事，顯得故事沒那麼精采。
雖然這篇評論說得不無道理，但我認為評論家 X 忽略了_____。

▶ According to Critic A, novel X suggests _____. I agree, but would add that _____.
根據評論家 A 的說法，X 小說暗示了_____。我同意這個看法，但要補充的是_____。

▶ Several members of our class have suggested that the final message of play X is _____. I agree up to a point, but I still think that _____.
班上的幾位同學提出，X 戲劇最終所要傳遞的訊息是_____。我大致上是同意的，但仍然認為_____。

▶ On first reading play Z, I thought it was an uncritical celebration of _____. After rereading the play and discussing it in class, however, I see that it is more critical of _____ than I originally thought.
初次讀到戲劇 Z 時，我以為它只是不經深思一味頌揚_____。然而，經過重新閱讀並在班上討論之後，我發現它對_____的分析比我原本想得要深刻得多。

▶ It might be said that poem Y is chiefly about _____ . But the problem with this reading, in my view, is _____ .

可能有人會說 Y 這首詩主要是關於 _____ ，但我認為這樣解讀的問題在於 _____ 。

▶ Though religious readers might be tempted to analyze poem X as a parable about _____ , a closer examination suggests that the poem is in fact _____ .

儘管宗教讀者可能想把 X 這首詩解讀成一個關於 _____ 的寓言 ；仔細閱讀之後會發現這首詩其實是 _____ 。

文學寫作：回應他人論點（p. 206）

▶ Ultimately, as I read it, _____ seems to say _____ . I have trouble accepting this proposition, however, on the grounds that _____ .

最後，以我的解讀，《 _____ 》似乎是要說 _____ 。然而我不大同意這個立場，理由是 _____ 。

▶ At the beginning of the poem, we encounter the generalization, seemingly introducing the poem's message, that " _____ ." But this statement is then contradicted by the suggestion made later in the poem that " _____ ." This opens up a significant inconsistency in the text: is it suggesting _____ or, on the contrary, _____ ?

這首詩的一開始，我們讀到一個大致的概念，似乎是在傳達這首詩的訊息，這個概念是「 _____ 」。然而這個說法又與詩中後來暗示的「 _____ 」產生矛盾。這顯示出此文本有個重大的前後矛盾之處 ：到底它是在暗示 _____ ，或者恰好相反，是在暗示 _____ ？

▶ At several places in novel X, Author Y leads us to understand that the story's central point is that _____. Yet elsewhere the text suggests _____, indicating that Y may be ambivalent on this issue.

在 X 這部小說中有多處，作者 Y 讓我們以為_____是故事的核心，然而文本在其他地方又暗示了_____，這說明 Y 對此議題態度可能是模稜兩可的。

文學寫作：找出作品裡的矛盾（pp. 210-213）

▶ It might be argued that in the clash between character X and Y in play Z, the author wants us to favor character Y, since she is presented as the play's heroine. I contend, however, that _____.

也許有人認為在 Z 這部戲劇裡，X 和 Y 這兩個角色矛盾，作者是要我們支持 Y，因而將她塑造成劇中英雄。然而我確認信_____。

▶ Several critics seem to assume that poem X endorses the values of discipline and rationality represented by the image of _____ over those of play and emotion represented by the image of _____. I agree, but with the following caveat: that the poem ultimately sees both values as equally important and even suggests that ideally they should complement one another.

幾位評論家似乎都假設 X 這首詩認同_____形象所代表的紀律和理性的價值觀，超過認同_____形象所代表的玩樂和情感的價值觀。這點我同意，但是我要附帶一提：這首詩終歸還是將兩種價值觀等同視之，甚至暗示了最理想應該要互補才是。

▶ Some might argue that when it comes to the conflict over _____, our sympathies should lie with _____. My own view is that _____.

也許有人會認為，就_____這件事的矛盾上，我們應該要支持

_____。我個人的看法卻是_____。

文學寫作：提出證據支持自身論點 (p. 214)

▶ Although some might read the metaphor of _____ in this poem as evidence that, for Author X, _____, I see it as _____.

雖然有人可能將此詩中_____的比喻當作證據，認為對作者 X 來說，

_____，我卻將之視為_____。

▶ Some might claim that evidence X suggests _____, but I argue that, on the contrary, it suggests _____.

有些人也許主張 X 這個證據暗示了_____，但是我認為正好相反，

它暗示著_____。

▶ I agree with my classmate _____ that the image of _____ in novel Y is evidence of _____. Unlike _____, however, I think _____.

我同意同學_____的看法，在 Y 這部小說中的_____圖像代

表的是_____。然而我和_____看法不同的地方在於，我認

為_____。

科學寫作：提出普遍理論（p. 225）

▶ Experiments showing _____ and _____ have led scientists to propose _____.

有些實驗顯示_____以及_____，這使得科學家提出了_____。

▶ Although most scientists attribute _____ to _____, X's result _____ leads to the possibility that _____.

雖然多數科學家把_____歸因於_____，但 X 的研究結果_____顯示有_____的可能性。

科學寫作：指出研究目的（pp. 226-227）

▶ Smith and colleagues evaluated _____ to determine whether _____.

史密斯與同僚評估了_____，以決定是否_____。

▶ Because _____ does not account for _____, we instead used _____.

由於_____無法說明_____，我們改採_____。

科學寫作：提出研究數據（pp. 228-229）

▶ （平均值）± （變異量）（單位）, n =（樣本數）.

▶ We measured _____ (sample size) subjects, and the average response was _____ (mean with units) with a range of _____ (lower value) to _____ (upper value).

我們測試了 _____ （樣本數）受試者，平均反應為 _____ （平均值附單位），介於 _____ （較低值）到 _____ （較高值）之間。

▶ Before training, average running speed was _____ ± _____ kilometers per hour, _____ kilometers per hour slower than running speed after training.

訓練前之平均跑步速度為每小時 _____ ± _____ 公里，比訓練後慢了 _____ 公里。

▶ We found athletes' heart rates to be _____ ± _____ % lower than nonathletes'.

我們發現運動員的心率比非運動員低了 _____ ± _____ %。

▶ The subjects in X's study completed the maze in _____ ± _____ seconds, _____ seconds slower than those in Y's study.

X 研究中的受試者在 _____ ± _____ 秒之內走完迷宮，比 Y 研究中的受試者慢了 _____ 秒。

科學寫作：解釋實驗結果（pp. 231-232）

▶ The data suggest / hint / imply _____.
這份資料大致顯示／似可顯示 _____。（中等信賴水準）

▶ Our results show / demonstrate _____.
我們的結果顯示 _____。（高等信賴水準）

▶ Our data support / confirm / verify the work of X by showing that

_____.

我們的資料證實 X 的研究，因為它顯示_____。

▶ By demonstrating _____, X's work extends the findings of Y.
藉由證明_____，X 的研究延伸了 Y 的研究結果。

▶ The results of X contradict / refute Y's conclusion that _____.
X 得到的結果與 Y 的_____結論相反。

▶ X's findings call into question the widely accepted theory that _____.
X 的研究結果造成人們開始懷疑_____這個廣為接受的理論。

▶ Our data are consistent with X's hypothesis that _____.
我們的資料與 X 的_____假說是一致的。

▶ One explanation for X's finding of _____ is that _____.
An alternative explanation is _____.
針對 X_____的研究結果，有一個解釋是_____，另一個可能的解釋則是_____。

▶ The difference between _____ and _____ is probably due to _____.
_____和_____之間的差別很有可能是_____所造成。

科學寫作：提出不同看法 (pp. 234-238)

▶ Now that _____ has been established, scientists will likely turn their attention toward _____.
既然_____已經確立，科學家很有可能將注意力轉朝_____。

▶ X's work leads to the question of _____. Therefore, we investigated

_____.

X 的研究導致產生_____的疑問，因此我們對_____進行了調查。

▶ To see whether these findings apply to _____, we propose to

_____.

為了了解這些研究結果是否適用於_____，我們打算_____。

▶ The work of Y and Z appears to show that _____, but their

experimental design does not control for _____.

Y 和 Z 的研究表面上顯示出_____，但是他們的實驗設計並沒有控

制_____。

▶ While X and Y claim that _____, their finding of _____ actually

shows that _____.

X 和 Y 雖主張_____，他們的研究結果_____事實上顯示

_____。

▶ While X's work clearly demonstrates _____, _____ will be

required before we can determine whether _____.

雖然 X 的研究清楚顯示出_____，還是需要_____才能決定是否

_____。

▶ Although Y and Z present firm evidence for _____, their data can not

be used to argue that _____.

雖然 Y 和 Z 提出有力證據證明_____，他們的資料卻不足以主張

_____。

▶ In summary, our studies show that _____, but the issue of _____ remains unresolved.

簡而言之，我們的研究顯示_____，但是_____的議題仍懸而未決。

科學寫作：預測反對的聲音（p. 241）

▶ Scientists who take a _____ (reductionist / integrative / biochemical / computational / statistical) approach might view our results differently.

採用_____（還原／整合／生化／計算／統計）方法的科學家，對我們的結果可能會有不同的看法。

▶ This interpretation of the data might be criticized by X, who has argued that _____.

X 可能會批評這項資料的解讀，他曾主張_____。

▶ Some may argue that this experimental design fails to account for _____.

也許有人會認為這個實驗設計無法說明_____。

科學寫作：說明論點的重要性（p. 242）

▶ These results open the door to studies that _____.

這些結果為_____的研究開啟了大門。

▶ The methodologies developed by X will be useful for _____.

X 所發展出來的研究方法將對_____有所助益。

▶ Our findings are the first step toward _____ .
我們的研究結果是邁向_____的第一步。

▶ Further work in this area may lead to the development of _____ .
這個領域的深入研究可能導致_____的發展。

社會科學寫作：發展論點（pp. 249-252）

▶ Economics research in the last fifteen years suggested Friedman's 1957 treatise was _____ because _____ . In other words, they say that Friedman's work is not accurate because of _____, _____, and _____ . Recent research convinces me, however, that Friedman's work makes sense.
過去 15 年內的經濟研究大致顯示，傅利曼於 1957 年所發表的專著_____，原因在於_____。換言之，他們認為傅利曼的研究不正確，理由是_____、_____、_____。然而近來的研究則令我相信，傅利曼的研究是有意義的。

▶ In recent discussions of _____, a controversial aspect has been _____ . On the one hand, some argue that _____ . On the other hand, others argue that _____ . Neither of these arguments, however, considers the alternative view that _____."
近來關於_____的討論中，一直有個爭議之處在於_____。一方面，有人認為_____。另一方面，又有人主張_____。然而這兩種論點都未考慮到另一個觀點，也就是_____。

▶ Although I agree with X up to a point, I cannot accept his overall conclusion that _____ .
儘管我某種程度同意 X 的說法，我不能接受他的整體結論_____。

▶ Although I disagree with X on _____ and _____, I agree with her conclusion that _____.

雖然我在_____和_____方面並不認同 X 的看法，但我認同她的結論_____。

▶ Political scientists studying _____ have argued that it is caused by _____. While _____ contributes to the problem, _____ is also an important factor.

研究_____的政治科學家主張這是由_____所造成，雖然_____確實是問題的起因之一，_____亦是一個重要因素。

社會科學寫作：指出現有研究的缺口（pp. 253-254）

▶ Studies of X have indicated _____. It is not clear, however, that this conclusion applies to _____.

X 的研究已經指出_____，然而，這項結論是否可應用於_____並不清楚。

▶ _____ often take for granted that _____. Few have investigated this assumption, however.

_____經常把_____視為理所當然，然而很少有人對這個假設進行調查。

▶ X's work tells us a great deal about _____. Can this work be generalized to _____?

X 的研究對於_____做了很多說明。這份研究是否能推論到_____上面呢？

社會科學寫作：指出他人觀點（p. 256）

▶ In addressing the question of _____, political scientists have considered several explanations for _____. X argues that _____. According to Y and Z, another plausible explanation is _____.

在處理_____的問題上，政治學家已經考慮過_____的幾種解釋。X 認為_____，而根據 Y 和 Z 的看法，另一可信的解釋則為_____。

▶ What is the effect of _____ on _____? Previous work on _____ by X and by Y and Z supports _____.

_____對於_____的效應為何？過去針對_____，由 X 以及 Y 和 Z 的研究皆主張_____。

社會科學寫作：資料討論（p. 262）

▶ In order to test the hypothesis that _____, we assessed _____. Our calculations suggest _____.

為了驗證_____這一假說，我們估算了_____。計算結果顯示_____。

▶ I used to investigate _____. The results of this investigation indicate _____.

我曾經調查過_____。這項調查的結果顯示_____。

社會科學寫作：預測可能反對的聲音（pp. 263-264）

▶ _____ might object that _____.

_____可能會反對_____。

▶ Is my claim realistic? I have argued _____, but readers may question _____.

我的主張是否務實？我主張了_____，但讀者也許會懷疑_____。

▶ My explanation accounts for _____ but does not explain _____. This is because _____.

我的解釋說明了_____但並未說明_____，這是因為_____。

社會科學寫作：說明論點的重要性（p. 265）

▶ X is important because _____.

X 很重要，因為_____。

▶ Ultimately, what is at stake here is _____.

歸根究柢，重要的是_____。

▶ The finding that _____ should be of interest to _____ because _____.

研究結果發現_____，_____應該會感興趣，因為_____。

Translation

範文中譯

---

01 別怪吃的人 Don't Blame the Eater（pp. 268-271）

假如真有報紙標題是為了登上傑・雷諾脫口秀的開場獨白而量身訂做，那就是這個了。本週兒童迎戰麥當勞，控告該企業害他們發胖。這不就像是中年男子控告保時捷害他們被開超速罰單？到底還有沒有個人責任存在？

不過呢，我傾向於同情這些肥胖的速食常客，或許是因為我曾經也是這種人吧。

小時候，我是標準的八〇年代中期鑰匙兒童，父母離異，爸爸離家建立新生活，媽媽把很長的時間投注在工作上，才能支付每月的帳單。我呢，每天的午餐和晚餐不外乎是麥當勞、塔可鐘、肯德基跟必勝客。當時和現在一樣，美國的小朋友只吃得起這些東西，沒得選。不到十五歲的年紀，我那曾經瘦瘦高高的五呎十吋身材，就塞滿了 212 磅無力的少年肥油。

後來我還滿幸運的，念了大學、參加海軍後備隊，也參與了一本健康雜誌製作。我學會管理自己的飲食。但是大多數像我過去一樣、靠著速食度日的青少年，並不願意改善他們的生活方式：他們從那座金色拱門下方走過，踏上可能一生肥胖的命運。這不完全是他們的錯 —— 我們所有人都有責任。

1994 年以前，兒童罹患糖尿病多半是因為遺傳的關係 —— 只有 5% 的案例是由肥胖引起，後者也就是第二型糖尿病。現在根據國家衛生研究院的統計，美國兒童罹患糖尿病的新案例當中，有 30% 以上屬於第二型糖尿病。

花在治療糖尿病的費用也暴增了，這一點也不意外。美國疾病管制與預防中心估計，在 1969 年的健保成本當中，糖尿病就佔去了 26 億美元，現在更已來到驚人的一千億。

我們不是應該知道一天不能吃兩餐速食嗎？這是一個論點沒錯。但是消費者——尤其是青少年——到底還能上哪兒找吃的？全美有超過一萬三千家麥當勞，我向你保證，隨便開車經過哪條大街都會看到一家。不然你把車開回街上，看有哪裡可以買到葡萄柚。

選擇性已經夠少了，再加上我們對吃進去的東西缺乏足夠的資訊，使得問題更為複雜。速食不像食品雜貨，包裝上並沒有提供熱量表。速食廣告也不像菸草廣告那樣有標示警語。調理食品也不在美國食品藥品管理局標籤法的規範之內。少數食品供應商會應要求提供熱量資訊，但是民眾也未必看得懂。

舉例來說，我們公司網站上列出雞肉沙拉的熱量為 150 卡，副餐的杏仁和麵條的熱量（另加 190 卡）則分開列舉。再加上一份 280 卡的沙拉醬，就是總熱量 620 卡的健康午餐。但不只是這樣，閱讀沙拉醬包背面的小字，你會發現其實一包內含 2.5 份，要是整包倒下去，熱量瞬間飆到 1040 卡左右，達到政府建議之每日熱量攝取量的一半，這還不包括那杯 450 卡的超級杯可樂。

想笑這些孩子控告速食業者的話，儘管笑吧，搞不好下一個告速食業者的就是你。這跟菸草業者的案例一樣，州政府可能遲早會發現，麥當勞和漢堡王每年所花的十億廣告費用，和他們與日俱增的健保費用之間有直接關聯。

我要說，速食業真的是岌岌可危。業者正在向兒童推銷一種確定危害健康的產品，並且沒有標示警語。他們最好能提供營養資訊作為人們選擇產品的參考，這麼做既是保護消費者，也是自保之道。沒有這種警告標示，我們只會看到越來越多肥胖的病童和怒而提告的家長。我說，無論如何，該面對的就面對吧。

02 隱藏的唯智主義 Hidden Intellectualism（pp. 272-279）

每個人多少都認識一個深諳「街頭智慧」、但是學校表現卻不怎麼優秀的年輕人。我們總是會想，好可惜啊，這麼聰明，生活大小事樣樣精通，如果把聰明才智用在學術研究上面就好了。我們卻沒想過，其實可能是大學院校錯失機會，沒有好好利用這種街頭智慧，並把它們導向學術研究一途。

同時我們也沒有考慮到，大學院校之所以忽視街頭智慧在智識上的潛能，其中的一個主要因素在於：我們把街頭智慧和反智識聯想在一起。我們把教育生活，也就是心智生活，想得太狹隘也太偏限，限制在那些我們認定本身就很重要、屬於學術性質的主題。我們認定智識可以用來談論柏拉圖、莎士比亞、法國大革命與核分裂，卻不能用來談論汽車、約會、時尚、運動、電視或電玩。

這種假設的問題在於，任何主題及其引發的討論之教育深度和重要性，這兩者之間並沒有必然的關聯性。再怎麼看似微不足道的主題，真正的知識分子都可以對其提出周延的問題，把它變成自己的工具；即便是最豐富的主題，換做傻子也有辦法讓它變得枯燥無味。這也是比起許多教授對莎士比亞或全球化的深思，喬治·歐威爾探討便士明信片的文化意涵之論文要來得重要許多（頁104-116）。

假如學生想躋身知識分子之列，確實需要閱讀一些具智力挑戰性的寫作範文——歐威爾便是一個很棒的典範。但是，假如我們鼓勵學生先讀一些他們有興趣的主題，而不是我們有興趣的主題，他們反而容易表現得像個知識分子。

　　我自己青少年時期的經驗就是個很好的例子。在我尚未進入大學之前，我真的很討厭看書，只對體育感興趣。我唯一想讀或能讀的只有運動雜誌，我為之著迷，不管是四〇年代後期發行的《運動》雜誌、1954 年創刊的《運動畫報》，乃至於一年發行一次的職業棒球、足球、籃球指南，我都是忠實讀者。我也喜愛約翰・圖尼斯和克萊爾・畢為男孩子寫的運動小說，愛看運動明星的自傳如喬・迪馬喬的《有幸成為洋基人》與鮑伯・斐勒的《三振的故事》。簡單來說，我就是你們口中典型的反智青少年 —— 或者說，很長一段時間以來，我認為自己是這樣。然而最近我開始覺得，我對運動勝於學校作業的偏愛，與其說是反智主義，倒不如說是唯智主義來得恰當。

　　我兒時成長的芝加哥住宅區，在二次大戰後成了一個種族大熔爐，當時我住的地方是不折不扣的中產階級街區，但是僅一街之隔 —— 絕對是被不動產公司集中在那兒的 —— 住的都是些才從南方和阿帕拉契山區的戰後失業潮當中出走的非裔美國人、原住民和「鄉下」白人。要界定出這種分界實為棘手之事。一方面，像我這樣「整潔體面」的小男生，和那些我們喚做勞動階級「小混混」的人之間，還是得維持一個界線，意思就是說，應該還是要表現出一點書卷味兒的聰明氣息。另一方面，我每天都要在運動場和街坊鄰里碰到這些小混混，我渴望得到他們的認同，如果以這個目的來看的話，表現得一臉書卷氣就一點兒用也沒有。那些小混混要是察覺到你對他們擺架子，便要衝著你說：「看什麼看？你這自以為了不起的笨蛋。」有個皮衣少年就是一邊扒走我口袋裡的零錢，一邊這樣罵我，連我的自尊也一併扒走。

　　於是，我在成長過程中一直處於左右為難的境地，一方面要表現得很聰明，一方面又怕表現得太聰明會被揍；一方面不能破壞我的大好未來，一方面又得給那幫小混混留下好印象。以我當時所過的生活，這種衝突歸結起來就是身強體壯和能言善道二選一。以我居住的鄰里和就讀的小學來看，一個小男生是別無選擇的，只能選擇「強壯」才能生存。我到現在都還記得，當時我和死黨們對於誰是「全校最強壯的傢伙」爭執個不休，爭論起來也挺複雜的。如果你和我一樣，完全不是打架的料，那就只好退而求其次，講話得要笨口拙舌的，把會透露讀寫能力的蛛絲馬跡都給藏得好好的，什麼文法正確和發音正確的都不行。

於是就某方面而言，大概沒有誰的青少年時期能比我的還要反智得更徹底。然而現在回想起來，我發覺事情並沒有這麼簡單，我和五〇年代本身並不是純粹對唯智主義懷有敵意，我們的內心是有所掙扎矛盾的。瑪麗蓮‧夢露與退休棒球球星喬‧迪馬喬仳離後，於 1956 年與劇作家亞瑟‧米勒結婚，此舉象徵著文藝怪咖對決運動咖的勝利，暗示當時社會風向正在改變。根據幫貓王寫傳記的彼德‧古拉尼克的說法，在 1956 年的總統大選中最後，連貓王都放棄了艾克（譯註：艾森豪），轉而投給阿德萊。他告訴記者說：「我是不懂知識分子那一套，不過我跟你說啊，老兄，他懂的最多了。」（頁 327）

雖然我當初也覺得自己「不懂知識分子那一套」，但現在我反而明白，我當時不知不覺正接受著成為知識分子的訓練。其實就是從那個看似俗不可耐的爭論開始的：哪個男生最強壯。我現在明白了，在我和朋友們對球隊、電影、強壯分析個沒完沒了的時候 —— 不用說，真正的暴徒對這種分析是不屑一顧的 —— 我早已背離書呆世界，我正在練習成為一名知識分子，那時我並不知道，原來自己是想要成為知識分子的。

我認為，就在我和朋友們討論強壯和運動當中，就在我閱讀運動書籍雜誌之時，我開始學習智識生活的基本元素：如何提出論證、權衡不同種類的證據、遊走於特論與通則之間、概述別人的觀點、參與對話一起討論。正因為當時閱讀以及爭論運動和強壯的問題，我才從中體驗到什麼叫做提出一個通則，什麼叫做重申並回應一個反論，還有從事其他理性探討活動是怎麼一回事，包括寫出我現在正在寫的這種句子。

只不過一直到很久以後，我才逐漸明白，運動的世界比學校更引人入勝，因為它比學校還需要動腦筋。畢竟在運動這個領域裡，充斥著各種挑戰的論點、爭辯、可分析的問題與錯綜複雜的統計資料，你可以關心的事有這麼多，學校顯然是無法提供的。我相信街頭智慧能在我們的文化中擊敗讀書智慧，而非如我們以為的它非關智識，實是因為它比學校文化還能夠徹底滿足對知識的渴求，學校文化則相形見絀，也不真實。

街頭文化也能滿足人們對社群的渴求。當你參與運動方面的討論時，你就成為一個社群的一分子，這個社群不限於你的家人朋友，是全球性、公開性的。學校作業只會讓你遠離人群，而職棒冠軍賽或泰德·威廉斯的四成打擊率卻可以產生話題，讓你和素未謀面的人們互相討論。運動不僅帶你進入一個充滿辯論的文化，而且是一個超越個人的大眾辯論文化。我不會怪我念過的學校沒把智力文化搞得像是一場超級盃，不過，運動界和演藝界深諳如何組織和表現智力文化，他們懂得利用本身類似遊戲般的元素，轉換成引人注目的公共奇觀，這就更有可能成功吸引到像我這種年輕人的注意力，我的學校沒能從他們身上學到一絲一毫，我認為這點難辭其咎。

另外有一點我過去不曾明白，而現在學生也沒發現，因而造成了悲劇的結果：真實的智力世界──不是在學校裡，而是存在於外面浩瀚世界裡的那種智力世界──其組織非常類似團隊運動的世界，有著相互競爭的文本、詮釋和評估，而一些說明為何該讀或該教某些文本的理論，也都在相互競爭。而且團隊競爭關係也很複雜；不管是作家的「粉絲」、智力系統、研究方法，或是各種主義之間，都在相互鬥爭。

學校的確是個充滿著競爭的地方，你越是往上爬，這種情況越叫人反感

（尤其今日開始採用高風險測驗更是如此）。在這種競爭型態之下，計分的標準不看你提出論證，而是看你能否展現知識和廣泛閱讀，也看你有沒有辦法拜託老師幫你加分，或者用盡各種本事證明你高人一等。簡而言之，學校競爭只學到運動文化裡較無魅力的特色，卻排除那些可以創造人與人之間緊密結合和社群的特色。

我念過的學校非但無法像運動到那樣令人愉快又投入，亦沒有好好把握機會利用智力世界和運動的共通元素，即戲劇和衝突。這導致我當時並沒有看出運動和學術界之間的相似之處，假使當初我有看出來，我從一種論述文化跨越到另一種論述文化將更為容易。

教育者嚴重低估了包括運動在內的許多領域對讀寫訓練的潛在幫助（也不只對男性有幫助），對他們來說，運動彷彿是學術發展之大敵，無法當作學術發展的一個途徑。然而，假如這個論點暗示著為什麼應該指定學生閱讀其有興趣的讀物和主題，當然也暗示著這種策略有其條件限制。一聽到有機會撰寫自己對汽車的熱愛，學生總是感到興奮無比，然而這些學生往往對該主題還是寫得很差、沒有深度，跟叫他們寫莎士比亞或柏拉圖是沒什麼兩樣的。以下和我先前提出的論點實屬一體之兩面：學生對一個主題感興趣的程度，和他們表現在寫作或言談中的思維或語言品質，並沒有必然關聯。誠如大學教授奈德・拉夫所言，我們的挑戰「並不在於開發學生的非學術興趣，而是要讓他們透過學術的眼光來看待那些興趣。」

學生須「透過學術的眼光」來看待他們的興趣，意即光是靠著街頭智慧是不夠的。把學生的非學術興趣當作學術研究的對象是有用的，這能引起他們的注意，克服他們的無聊和疏離感。但是這種策略不見得能讓他們更進一步用學術方法嚴謹探討他們的興趣。另一方面，教學時無須避諱讓學生去寫汽車、運動或服裝時尚，唯須要求他們「透過學術的眼光」來探討這些興趣，這個意思是說，要用思辨分析的方式，去思考和撰寫汽車、運動與服裝時尚，用這種方式把它們看作大文化裡正在發生的各個小層面。

假如我的看法無誤，那麼大學院校若未能鼓勵學生以學術之外的興趣作為學術研究的材料，實是失去了一個機會。有些學生不用這種方法便可能完全排斥學術活動，一旦謝絕任何可鼓勵這類學生參與學術活動的主題，對大學院校來說是一個不利因素。假如學生對彌爾的《論自由》提不起興趣，卻願意全心投入閱讀《運動畫刊》、《時尚》或者探討嘻哈音樂的《源頭》雜誌，這就是應指定他們閱讀這些雜誌的強烈動機，而非經典名著。假若撰寫關於《源頭》雜誌的學期報告，能讓學生迷上閱讀和寫作，終有一天他們可以探討《論自由》的可能性就非常大。即便走不到這一步，閱讀雜誌也能夠增進他們的讀寫力和思考力，聊勝於無。因此，就教育學上來說，將運動、汽車、時尚、饒舌音樂等其他類似主題，納入課堂教學單元之規畫是有意義的。我要的學生是能針對《源頭》中的議題寫出論據精闢且切中社會問題的分析，而不是那種只會死氣沉沉地解釋《哈姆雷特》或蘇格拉底《申辯》篇的學生。

03 核廢料 Nuclear Waste（pp. 280-287）

隨著人們體認到化石燃料發電廠的危險，尤其是產生二氧化碳導致全球暖化的危險，使得核能開始顯得更具吸引力。但核廢料 —— 那些壽命長達數千年之久的高放射性廢料 —— 又該何去何從？我們有權力把這種東西留給後代子孫嗎？

未來上任的每位總統，都將可能面對各種重大科技議題，核廢料便是其一。這似乎是個無解的問題。鈽的半衰期為兩萬四千年，這還僅是眾多高放射性廢料的其中一種而已。即便經過如此漫長的歲月，鈽的強烈放射性也只能減少一半。經過了四萬八千年之後，其所放射出的致命輻射仍然有原本的四分之一。就算是經過了十萬年，輻射量還是在其剛離開反應爐時的百分之十以上。萬一外洩到地面，接觸到人類的供水該怎麼辦？我們如何能保證這種原料能夠安全的存放十萬年？

儘管如此，美國政府堅持尋求「安全的」核廢料處置，他們設計了一座原型的核廢料貯存場，設置在內華達州的雅卡山地底深處。為了確保核廢料的安全，貯存室距離地表有 1000 英尺之深。僅是貯存現有核廢料的一部分，也需要將近 2 平方英里的龐大面積，預估成本將高達一千億美元，營運費用更需要額外花上數千億。雅卡山區地震頻仍也讓計畫雪上加霜。僅是過去十年間，方圓 50 英里內已發生過不下 600 次規模超過 2.5 級的地震。更嚴重的是，這個地區最早就是由火山活動所形成，儘管那已是數百萬年前的事，我們又如何確定這座設施不會因火山再度爆發而被摧毀？

人們為了解決核廢料存放問題，提出過不少替代方案。何不乾脆把廢料送進太陽裡？這恐怕不是個好方法，因為有些火箭一發射就墜毀了。有科學家提出以容器裝盛後沉入海底，找個可以利用地殼板塊活動將這些原料隱沒的地區，最終就可埋入數百英里深的地底。只不過，從科學家們提出的這些建議看來，似乎更顯出問題的嚴重性。

最糟糕的是，目前所產生的核廢料早已超過雅卡山的負荷量，那些廢料不會消失，而未來的總統您還在考慮製造更多核能，您瘋了嗎？

容我坦言

反核狂潮已經強烈到了一個地步，我覺得一定要在本章開頭先把反核觀點說明一下，至少也會略提他們的激憤之處。這些都是您當了總統之後，一定會聽到的論點。無論您是反核或挺核都無所謂，核廢料就是在那裡，而您就是得處理。這是您無法可以逃避的議題，如果要把事情做對（同時要讓民眾相信您正在做對的事），您就必須懂物理學。

當我計算數字時發現，比起不這麼做，將核廢料貯存在雅卡山所產生的危險已經算小，況且跟其他我們沒考慮到的危險比起來，這種危險更是小得多。儘管如此，這個爭議糾紛依舊持續。有更多的研究需要進行，然而每多做一點研究，似乎就會發現新的問題，加深民眾的恐懼和懷疑。我把這一節的標題訂為「容我坦言」，乃因我發現我無法袖手旁觀，我無法只提出物理說明，而不表示個人評估。我在這本書裡多半試著說出事實，而且就只提出事實，讓各位去下結論。在這個小節當中，我坦言我要倒戈。要我公平我做不到，因為事實似乎強烈指向一個特定結論。

我和科學家、政治家，以及許多關心的市民都討論過雅卡山的事情。政治家多半認為這是科學問題，科學家又多半認為這是政治問題。雙方一致贊成進行更多調查——科學家贊成乃因這本就是他們的工作，政治家贊成是因為他們認為研究便可得到關鍵問題的答案。我並不這麼認為。

我在這裡列舉一些相關事實。雅卡山的地下隧道設計可容納七萬七千噸高放射性廢料。起初，這種廢料當中最危險的並不是鈽，而是鍶 -90 這類的核分裂碎片，鍶 -90 是一種不穩定的原子核，是鈾的核分裂產物。由於這種核分裂碎片的半衰期比鈾來得短，因此其放射性大約是原礦的一千倍。這種廢料（不含鈽，鈽也是反應爐內的產物，我稍後再解釋）須耗費一萬年才能衰變回鈾礦採出時的放射性強度。主要也是根據這個數字，目前找的存放地點都是一萬年內安全無虞的地點。過了那個時候，我們所面臨的情況會比把鈾礦留在地底不開採要好。這麼說來，也許一萬年的保障已經夠好了，不用到我在本章緒論所說的十萬年。

一萬年的歲月依然漫長得令人難以置信。一萬年之後，世界會變成什麼樣子？我們回顧歷史，體會一下一萬年到底有多久。一萬年前，人類才剛接觸農業，又過了五千年才發明書寫。我們真能計畫一萬年後的未來嗎？當然不能。我們完全無從得知到時世界會變成什麼樣子。我們不可能聲稱有能力把核廢料貯存一萬年之久，任何打算貯存的計畫，顯然都是無法接受的。

當然，拒絕核廢料存放計畫也是不被接受的答案。我們有核廢料要處理，這是不爭的事實。但是問題倒也沒像我剛才講得那麼困難，我們也不需要一萬年那麼久的安全保障。比較合理的目標是將外洩風險降低至 0.1%，也就是千分之一的機率。因為核廢料的放射性只比我們從地底採出的鈾礦高一千倍，淨風險（危險乘以機率）便是 $1000 \times 0.001 = 1$，這和我們一開始就不把鈾礦開採出來，所要承擔的風險是一樣的。（我預設的是線性假說——總癌症風險與個別劑量或劑量率無關——但是，我的論點並不強烈倚賴線性假說的正確性。）

再者，也不需要整整一萬年都維持在 0.1% 的安全性。三百年後，核分裂碎片的放射性將減弱為十分之一，僅是剛採出鈾礦的一百倍。因此，屆時我們已不需要把風險控制在 0.1%，可容許核廢料完全外洩的機率提高到 1%，比起保證一萬年不外洩，這就容易得多。另外，這個計算的前提是核廢料 100% 全數外洩。如果核廢料只有 1% 外洩，那麼三百年後我們可以接受的外洩率就是 100%。用這種方式思考，核廢料貯存的問題似乎就有解。

然而輿論並未將這些數字考慮進去，也沒有考慮到當初一採礦，實際上就已將放射性從地底釋出。輿論反而堅持要絕對安全。能源部繼續對雅卡山展開搜查，希望找出尚未發現的地震斷層。許多人假設，只要找不到地震斷層，該座貯存設施就可以被接受。他們認為一旦在雅卡山發現新的地震斷層，就不必考慮其為貯存地點。然而，問題不在於未來一萬年間會不會發生地震，而是三百年後是否有 1% 的機率會發生足以讓 100% 的核廢料（或是 100% 的機率洩漏 1% 的核廢料，或 10% 的機率洩漏 10% 的核廢料）外洩的大地震，致使核廢料溢出玻璃膠囊，接觸到地下水。上述這些選項所帶來的風險，都比把原鈾礦留在地底或任其天然放射性混入地下水都要來得低。沒必要那麼極端以絕對安全為目標，因為即便把原鈾礦留在地底都無法絕對安全。

倘若我們問，為什麼要拿原始開採出的鈾礦來跟貯存核廢料的危險相比，為什麼不拿留在土壤中的天然鈾礦所造成的更大危險相比？這麼一問，問題便更好解決了。絕大多數的鈾礦來源是科羅拉多，這個地區地質活動頻繁，斷層與裂隙遍布，大草原上群山聳立，地表岩石的鈾含量約有十億噸。這種鈾的放射性是雅卡山法定上限的二十倍，至少需要一百三十億年，而不是區區幾百年，放射性才能降低到十分之一。然而那些穿過、環繞、覆蓋這種放射性岩石的水，最終流入科羅拉多河，成為它的水源，美國西區許多地方都仰賴科羅拉多河提供飲用水，包括洛杉磯和聖地牙哥。貯存在雅卡山的核廢料至少還有玻璃囊包覆，科羅拉多地底的鈾幾乎都是水溶性的。我們可以做個帶點荒唐的結論：萬一雅卡山的貯存設施全部裝滿核廢料，並且全部的核廢料即刻就從玻璃容器中外洩，也成功接觸到地下水，當前天然鈾溶入科羅拉多河所造成的危險，仍然是其二十倍。這讓我們聯想到，三哩島附近居民對反應爐的微量洩漏憂心忡忡，卻沒那麼擔心地底溢出放射性更強的天然氡氣，是一樣的情況。

我並不是要暗示雅卡山的核廢料沒有危險性，也不是要暗示我們應該對洛杉磯的供水感到恐慌。我舉科羅拉多的例子，只是想說明，去恐懼那些神祕陌生的危險，有時會失去洞察力。無論我用什麼方法計算，得到的結論如出一轍：雅卡山的核廢料外洩不會造成重大危險。把核廢料放入玻璃膠囊，存放在具有地質穩定性相當高的結構中，然後去擔心真正的威脅吧──例如繼續燃燒化石燃料所造成的危險。

還有一個相關的風險問題，就是在核廢料運往雅卡山的途中，有可能發生事故或遭到攻擊。當前的計畫要求核廢料須以厚實的強化混凝土圓罐裝載，須可承受高速撞擊而無洩漏之虞。事實上，恐怖分子要打開這種容器沒那麼容易，要利用核廢料製造放射武器也非輕而易舉。恐怖分子要是聰明，倒不如去劫持裝載汽油、氯或其他常見有毒物質的油罐車，開到城市中引爆，這種機率還比較大。記得談論恐怖分子核武的那一章裡提到，蓋達組織要荷塞‧帕迪拉別把力氣耗費在製造髒彈（譯註：一種放射性炸彈）上面，專心策畫著用天然氣炸掉公寓大樓。

　　為什麼我們在擔心核廢料的運送問題？諷刺的是，我們為了確保運輸安全而做到這種程度，反倒讓民眾以為危險性比實際要來得高。你們可以想像一下，晚間新聞傳出有人將混凝土圓罐自五樓高的建築拋下，砸毀地面後彈起而且毫髮無傷，民眾竟然還不放心。這都是公共安全「無風不起浪」的悖論所造成的後果。提高標準，提升安全性，進行更多研究，更加深入探討問題，在這個過程中，你一邊改善安全也一邊嚇壞民眾。畢竟那些威脅要不是真真切切，科學家們需要如此煞費苦心嗎？那些提出要把核廢料用火箭送上太陽，或者埋進海底隱沒帶的科學家，就好像在告訴大家，這個問題真的沒得解，這樣的前提只會讓民眾產生更深的恐懼。

04（徒然）追尋美國夢
The (Futile) Pursuit of the American Dream（pp. 288-301）

　　我撰寫過許多有關貧窮的題材，因此常從人們那裡聽到一些駭人聽聞的處境。房東寄來了逐客通知，孩子被診斷出罹患重疾但保險卻已到期，但汽車故障無法上班。這些緊急事故不斷上演，折磨著那些長期貧窮之人。不過，大概是從 2002 年開始，我才突然發現，很多這種艱苦的故事，竟是發生在那些曾經頗負名望的中產階級身上——都是些大學畢業、曾經擔任白領階級中層職位的人。有位作家便屬於這種情況，她曾指責我忽視了像她這樣認真工作又善良的人。

你去調查一些像我這樣的人吧，沒有在高中未婚生子，功課好又認真工作，不會阿諛奉承，可不但得不到升遷，領的薪水也不合理，淪落到只能賺七美元的鐘點費，助學貸款一延再延，在家當啃老族，債務纏身，再怎麼還也還不清。

白領階級向下沉淪的故事，不能像寫藍領經濟悲歌的報導一樣輕描淡寫帶過。無情的人習慣把藍領經濟悲歌歸咎給「錯誤的選擇」，譬如沒取得大學文憑、沒攢夠錢就生小孩，或者沒能含著金湯匙出生。但是對於那些經濟困頓的白領階級，我們卻不能責怪他們無所作為，畢竟他們「什麼都做對了」。他們憑著本事取得高學歷，犧牲自己對哲學或音樂的年少癡狂，耐著性子修完金融或管理這種枯燥乏味的務實科目。某些案例的淪落人還是高成就人士，正因為他們在公司的職位夠高，裁去他們可省下一筆可觀的成本。換言之，在一場經典的「先引誘再轉移」的遊戲中，他們成了輸家。正當藍領階級的貧困已叫人麻木、見怪不怪，白領階級失業問題 —— 且通常連帶造成貧窮問題 —— 仍然朝著美國夢發出怒吼。

我知道自己對企業界的中上層階級所知甚少，直到目前為止，我對企業界的認識也是透過低薪的底層人物。我曾經也是其中一員，為了替上一本書《我在底層的生活》進行調查，我在連鎖餐廳當過服務生，也做過清潔的工作，還曾經是沃爾瑪的「夥伴」。和所有人一樣，我也曾經以消費者的身分接觸企業界，和職位很低的人打交道，像是零售店員、客服人員或電話推銷員。至於決策階層 —— 副總裁、業務執行、地區經理 —— 我倒是很少接觸。我只有在飛機上看過這類人士，他們讀著關於「領導力」的書籍、翻翻筆電裡的試算表，或者讀著開國元勛的傳記，讀著讀著就睡著了 [1]。我和未來的企業人士比較熟，大部分都是在我訪問大學校園時認識的。在大學裡，「商科」依然是最熱門的主修科目，不說別的，光是最保險也最賺錢就足夠令它成為大熱門了（資料來源：National Center for Education Statistics 國家教育統計中心）。

但是在企業的白領員工當中，有越來越多麻煩 —— 即使還不到悲慘 —— 的徵兆出現。首先，從 2001 年的經濟不景氣開始，高資歷與資深人員的失業率便持續攀升。到了 2003 年末，也正是我展開這次計畫的時候，失業率達到 5.9% 左右。然而，與過去幾次經濟衰退的情況相比，這波失業潮裡面有相當大的一部分是白領的專業人士，將近百分之二十的比例，約一百六十萬人[2]。過去的不景氣主要衝擊的是藍領階級，這一次，媒體選擇同情那些相對菁英的人士，包含專業、技術和管理階層的員工。舉例來說，2003 年 4 月，《紐約時報雜誌》刊載了一則封面故事，引發熱烈討論，故事是關於一位年薪三十萬美元的電腦業主管，在失業兩年後只好到 Gap 當店員（出處：Mahler）。自 2000 年開始的整整四年之中，類似的故事時有所聞，不僅強人垮台，連中層階級也逃不過淪落的命運，他們被逐出辦公室，不得不到星巴克站櫃臺。

今天，白領的工作不安全感已不再取決於景氣循環 —— 股市一跌便惴惴不安，股市好轉就鬆一口氣[3]，也不只發生在如電信或科技這種少數不穩定的部門，亦不侷限於如銹帶或矽谷的少數地區。經濟也許開始好轉，公司也許開始賺錢，然而裁員的危機卻沒有解除，彷彿是一種反常的天擇，淘汰庸才也就算了，連有才幹的成功人士也一併淘汰。自九〇年代中葉起，這種無限期的篩選過程儼然成為一種制度，只不過換上各種好聽說詞，像是要「縮編」、「合理精簡」、「智慧精簡」、「重組」、「縮減層級」—— 現在還可以加上一條：白領職務外包給廉價的海外勞力市場。

二十一世紀前幾年最暢銷的一本商業書，裡頭用了一種比喻：「乳酪」（代表著穩定又有報酬的工作）的確被搬走了。2005 年針對主管人員所進行的一份調查發現，有 95% 的人預料將離開現職，轉換新跑道，不管是自願或非自願；有百分之 65% 的人擔心無預警遭到解雇或裁員（出處：Mackay，頁94）。換言之，不需要等到沒了工作，就能感受失業的焦慮和絕望。

第二個麻煩的徵兆姑且可稱做「過度僱用」。就我的理解，當今企業的中高層主管和專業人員，就跟那些賺取微薄薪水、要兼兩份差才能餬口的人一樣，經常面臨超長工時的問題。撰寫《工作過度的美國人》一書的經濟學家茱莉葉・舒爾，以及撰寫《白領階級血汗工廠》的商業記者吉兒・安德烈斯基・弗雷瑟，描述倍感壓力的白領員工，白天在辦公室裡工作十到十二個小時，晚上回到家還得繼續用筆電工作，就連假日也有接不完的電話，生活跟公司綁在一起。弗雷瑟提到：「以華爾街的公司為例，主管經常會吩咐新進員工在辦公室裡放一套備用衣物和牙刷，遇到必須熬夜趕工、不可能讓你回家打個盹兒的時候，就可以派上用場。」她引述了一名英特爾員工的話：

> 如果你選擇兼顧家庭生活，你的排名和評鑑就會墊底。我願意工作到天長地久，要我週末進公司也肯，出差到天涯海角都無怨尤。我既沒有嗜好也沒有休閒活動。如果我不忙公司的事，我就什麼也不是了（引述自Fraser，頁 158）。

顯然，在我過去忽略的一個社經團體當中，正發生著嚴重的問題，我以為他們過得安逸自在，用不著我操心。我向來以為安逸的地方，現在卻苦痛頻增，於是我決定介入調查。我選擇採用撰寫《我在底層的生活》一書時的調查策略：不讓自己記者身分曝光，親自探訪這個新世界，看看是否能直接體驗並了解這些問題。人們是否不斷被革職？要怎麼樣才能找到新工作？假如事情真如部分報導所言，已經病入膏肓，何以沒人出來抗議？

這次的計畫非常明確：找一份工作，而且是一份「好」工作。白領職位，有健保、五萬美元上下的年收入，足以讓我穩穩當當躋身中產階級之列。這份工作將令我得以一窺企業中層員工的生活，而且是難得的親身體驗。費盡心力找這種工作的過程，自然會讓我成為一名最窘迫不安的白領企業員工──失業的白領階級。

由於我盡可能不想讓自己的身分曝光，因此我必須先排除一些領域，如高等教育機構、出版業（報章雜誌、書籍）與非營利自由組織。我在這些領域都有可能被認出來，比起其他求職者，也許就會獲得差別待遇──比較容易被錄取吧，希望是這樣。不過上述限制也沒有縮小多少範圍，因為白領專業人士的工作場所本來就以其他營利事業的行業為主，包含銀行業、工商服務業、製藥工業與金融業。

一旦我決定踏入企業界──而且是我不熟悉的行業──我就必須把根深蒂固的態度和觀念拋開，或至少暫時放下，包括我長久以來對美國企業和企業領導人的批評。七○年代我初出茅廬、剛擔任調查記者時，就批評過當時即將主導健保系統的一些企業，包括製藥公司、連鎖醫院與保險公司。後來到了八○年代，我轉而調查藍領及粉領員工所遭受的待遇，將美國無可救藥的貧窮水準──根據聯邦政府官方統計為 12.5%，更新的統計則為 25%──歸咎於非專業工作者長年低薪的結果。過去幾年當中，我抓住這波金融醜聞──從安隆風波到現在的南方保健與霍林格國際事件──證實企業內部日盛的腐敗風氣，是一種罔顧員工、消費者甚至股東權益的內部掠奪模式。

但是為了達成這次的計畫，我必須盡量把這些批判和懷疑暫時擱下或拋諸腦後。喜歡也好，不喜歡也罷，大公司是全球經濟的主導體，也是我們日常賴以生活的企業形式。我一邊用 IBM 筆電寫這篇文章，一邊啜飲著立頓紅茶，身上穿著 Gap 的衣服──全部都是大公司的產物。大公司才能讓飛機啟動（雖然未必會準時）、讓我們有得吃（還越吃越多），總的來說，就是「讓夢想實現」。我向來是企業界的門外漢，動輒狠批怒斥，現在我竟然想踏入其中。

我知道這種試驗對就業市場來說並不全然公平，單講一個原因好了，以一個求職者來說，我本身的條件相當不利。其一，我已步入中年，年齡歧視是企業界公認的一個問題，就算也不過才四十郎當，我肯定會被刁難。不過，這個弱點絕不是只有我才有，很多人——從失去依靠的家庭主婦主夫，到被裁員的公司主管——發現自己到了該退休安心養老的年齡，卻還在找工作。

再者，我從未在大公司裡做過白領工作，這也是我的不利因素。我有一次在政府單位工作，是在紐約市預算局，大約做了七個月，算是一次專業的辦公室工作經驗。工作內容就是白領在做的那些，不外乎開開會、消化報表、寫備忘錄。不過那是好久以前的事了，那時還沒有手機、PowerPoint 或電子郵件。我現在設法要進入的企業界，裡面的一切對我來說都很陌生，包括績效標準、評鑑方法、溝通用語甚至溝通模式。但是我學得很快，你在新聞業非得這樣，希望靠著這點還可以應付得來。

第一步，要先取得一個新身分和相關個人經歷，這麼說，也就是一份履歷表。換身分比想像中來得容易。譬如說，你只要走到洛杉磯的阿爾瓦拉多街和第七街口，就會有人湊過來小小聲說：「身分證，要不要弄身分證。」不過我走的是合法途徑，因為我希望有工作上門的時候，證件已經全部備妥。或許是誇張了點，我擔心的是我現在用的名字可能太好認，要是一搜谷歌就會跑出一堆資料，那就糗了。所以 2003 年 11 月的時候，我在法律上改回了娘家姓：芭芭拉·亞歷山大，還用這個名字申請了一張社會安全卡。

履歷表儘管得偽造，我還是希望盡可能反映我的真實技能，我深深相信，不管我到哪一家公司上班，這些技能還是可以創造價值。我是一位作家，發表過的文章不計其數，含合著在內，共寫過十二本非小說類書籍，我知道「寫作」在企業界裡通常可以解釋成公關或「傳播」。很多新聞學院也會教授公關，可能理當要如此，因為公關完全就是新聞業的邪惡分身。記者追尋的是真相，公關卻被要求要隱瞞真相，甚至得造假。假如你的雇主，譬如說是製藥公司好了，聲稱一款新藥可以治癒癌症和勃起功能障礙，你的工作就是推銷，而不是去調查公司根據什麼做出這些聲明。

這我還做得到，反正也只是暫時的。甚至，很多公關平常在做的事我都做過：我寫過新聞稿、遊說編輯或記者用我寫的故事、準備過新聞資料袋，也曾協助安排記者會。身為一位作者，我也一直和出版社的公關密切合作，我發現他們很有聰明才智，各方面都和我非常契合。

多年來，我亦活躍於各種志業活動，對願意僱用我的公司來說，這個經驗也必能化為某種重要資產。我策畫也主持過會議；我在許多形形色色的團隊裡做過事，經常是擔任領導的角色；在大眾面前講話對我也能泰然自若，發表長篇大論或是小組討論時做個簡報都不成問題，這些都相當於「領導」技能，應該對任何公司來說都是資產。至少我可以自稱是「活動策畫」，有能力把集會區分為全體大會和分組會議、安排新聞報導、規畫後續活動。

即便只是約略打個草稿，這份履歷表也花了我好幾天準備。我得安排一些願意為我說謊的人，作證我曾經在他們那裡有過出色的表現，萬一哪個潛在雇主致電給他們才不會露出馬腳。我很幸運有朋友願意幫我，他們有些人工作的公司也小有名氣。雖然我不敢聲稱自己曾在這些企業裡上班，畢竟打通電話給人事部就穿幫了，我在想可以佯裝曾為他們「提供諮詢」多年，應該可以順利過關。簡單講，我給芭芭拉・亞歷山大弄了一份漂亮的公關經歷，偶爾穿插了點活動策畫的部分。我在精心打造新履歷的過程中下了不少掩飾功夫，屆時擔任公關萬一需要進行一些挑戰道德尺度的專案，這也算是先做好準備了。

不過，我可沒有瞎掰自己沒有的情感或習氣，來美化我的新身分。我不是演員，況且就算我想裝也裝不來。「芭芭拉・亞歷山大」只是芭芭拉・埃倫里奇的掩護，她的行為不管是好是壞都是我的。事實上，以實際的角度來看，我也不過是把職業從「自僱人士／作家」改成「待業人士」——不細看還察覺不出差別。大部分的日子我還是在家打電腦，只不過現在不做調查和寫文章，而是研究哪些公司可能僱用我，然後聯繫他們。這個新名字和假履歷只是我的門票，讓我躋身於失業的白領美國人之列，終日尋覓著薪水不錯的工作。

這個計畫起碼得有個基本架構；由於我正踏上一個未知的旅程，我得為自己設計幾個方針。第一條規則就是無所不用其極找到工作，任何形式的幫助我都來者不拒。舉例來說，不管是什麼樣的書籍、網站或公司，只要有提供求職指南，我都會好好利用。我會努力讓表現符合上面的要求，直到不負所望。我不知道到底需要什麼樣的努力才能成功找到工作，唯將盡可能以謙卑勤勉之心，盡我最大的努力。

第二條規則是，我已經做好準備，為了工作，甚至只是面試，我哪兒都去。我在聯繫潛在雇主的時候，也會告知工作地點不拘。本次計畫期間我住在維吉尼亞州的夏洛茨維爾，但是我已經準備好到美國任何地方找工作，假如找到工作，我會在當地住上幾個月。我也不挑產業 —— 除非是可能會被認出的產業 —— 不會嫌它乏味或違反道德。第三條規則是，只要收入和福利有達我的要求，第一份工作我就要接受。

我知道這次計畫需要投注可觀的時間和金錢，所以我空出十個月的時間，並預留五千美元應付交通和求職過程可能需要的其他開支。我預計找到工作就賺得回來，說不定還多賺很多。至於時間，我預計找工作大約得耗上四到六個月 —— 2004 年的失業人士平均花五個月找到工作 —— 另外加上三到四個月實際工作（出處：Leland）。我會有充分的時間體驗白領失業人士的生活，並且探索他們試圖重返的企業界。

打從一開始，我對「企業界」這個抽象概念的想像就像是一座山上的城堡，戒備森嚴，環繞著層層關卡，玻璃牆在藍天下閃爍著誘人的微光。我知道需要一番漫長而艱辛的努力，才到得了大門口。不過，我曾經成功踏上遙遠而崇高的學術殿堂，我耐得住性子又詭計多端，我耐力十足且意志堅定，所以我相信，這次我也做得到。

事實上，我籌備的這個計畫可能達不到我要的挑戰。我是祕密記者，當然不可能體會白領職場的真實恐怖，因為我不靠這個生存和獲得自尊。和我一同找工作的人，可能都不是自願落得如此下場，他們不是因為公司裁員，就是個人被解雇。對他們而言，失業就等於落入痛苦的深淵。他們的收入慘跌到只剩失業保險給付；他們的自信心跌入谷底；關於失業人士心理創傷的文章不計其數，憂鬱症、離婚、嗑藥甚至自殺，一下子都找上門來。我做臥底求職不可能發生這種災難，之後的上班人生也不會這樣。我不會一夕之間淪入貧窮，也不會感受到被拒絕的痛苦。

我從一開始也預期，這次的計畫的艱鉅程度，會遠比我寫《我在底層的生活》時來得低。體能上算是很輕鬆，不用刷刷洗洗，不用扛重物，不用連續走或跑上好幾個小時。至於行為表現上，低薪藍領工人向來得卑躬屈膝、言聽計從，我想，這次這種事不會發生在我身上，我應該可以更自由做自己和表達意見。事實證明，我的想法沒一樣是對的。

註解

(1) 如果要深入了解與我相隔遙遠的文化和年代，我最喜歡參考的是小說，這回連小說也派不上用場。五〇年代和六〇年代是有些小說描述白領企業生活，也寫得十分精采，理查‧葉慈的《革命之路》和史龍‧威爾森的《身穿灰色法蘭絨西裝的男人》便是其中兩部。更近代的小說和電影則對白領職場少有著墨，有也只是作為桃色事件的背景。

(2) 根據美國勞工統計局的資料，女性的失業率只比男性稍高，為 6.1% 對上 5.7%。而白人女性（譬如我）的失業率約是黑人女性的一半（www.bls.

gov）。

(3) 我尤其受到兩本書的啟發：吉兒・弗雷瑟的《白領階級血汗工廠：美國企業界工作與報酬之惡化》（2001 年，W・W・諾頓出版），與理查・桑內特的《職場啟示錄：走出新資本主義的迷惘》（1998 年，W・W・諾頓出版）。

(4) 從 2003 年 12 月到 2004 年 10 月期間，除了 7 月多數日子外，我為《紐約時報》撰寫雙週專欄，是我短暫做過的真實工作。

(5) 可參考凱薩琳・紐曼的《失去恩寵：在富裕之年向下流動》（1999 年，加州大學出版社），或可參考梅爾以第一人稱撰寫、可讀性相當高的《主管憂傷》（1995 年，富蘭克林廣場出版社）。

05 凡興起之一切必將匯合
Everything That Rises Must Converge（pp. 302-323）

醫生要朱立安的母親減掉二十磅的體重，這對她的血壓比較好。於是星期三的晚上，朱立安只好帶著她搭公車，前往市區參加基督教女青年會的減肥班。這個減肥班是為年過五十的女性勞工所開設的，她們的體重落在一百六十五到兩百磅之間。他的母親算是其中比較苗條的，不過她說，年齡和體重是女人的祕密，她們是不會透露的。自從取消種族隔離之後，她就不願意晚上獨自搭公車，而且上減肥班是她少數的樂趣之一，為了健康著想也非去不可，加上又是免費的，所以她跟朱利安說，希望他能看在她為他做過的事情份上，勉為其難抽出一天帶她去上課。朱立安不喜歡一一去回想她為自己做的一切，不過每到星期三晚上，他還是會打起精神帶她去上課。

她站在玄關的鏡子前，戴上帽子，差不多準備好要出發了。而朱立安呢，他一邊等著，兩隻手擱在背後，彷彿被釘在門框上，如聖塞巴斯蒂安等待萬箭穿身一般。帽子是新買的，可花了她七塊半美金。她不停說道：「也許我不該花七塊半買這帽子，對，不該買的。我這就別戴了，明兒個拿去退了，早知道就別買。」

朱立安抬起眼睛望著上蒼。「不，你該買的，」他說道，「快戴上，該走了。」這頂帽子有夠難看，帽緣是紫色絨面的，一邊垂下、另一邊翹起，其他地方是綠色的，活像個棉絮爆出來的坐墊。他覺得這頂帽子是沒那麼滑稽，勉強可以說活潑俏皮又可憐兮兮。能為她帶來快樂的都是些小東西，而這些小東西弄得他好鬱悶。

她又一次舉起帽子，慢慢地放在頭上。兩撮灰髮落在她那紅潤的雙頰上，但是那雙天藍色的眼睛，既純真又未因人生閱歷而改變，她十歲時的眼睛肯定就是這樣。若非她是個寡婦，含辛茹苦供他吃穿上學，至今仍供他生活，「直到他能自立自強」，那麼她也許就是個得要他帶進城的小女孩呢。

「行了，行了，」他說，「走了吧。」為了催她出發，他逕自開了門，往小路上走去。天空泛著死氣沉沉的紫羅蘭色，在它的映襯之下，房子顯得黑漆漆的，這一棟棟圓鼓鼓的豬肝色大怪物，儘管每棟都長得不一樣，倒是醜得如出一轍。四十年前這裡曾是個上流社區，因此他母親執意認為，他們在這裡買了棟房子真是聰明之舉。每棟房子都圍著一圈窄窄的灰塵項圈，裡面通常坐著一個髒小孩。朱立安手插著口袋走著，頭低低的往前伸，兩眼呆滯無神，他已下定決心，在他為了滿足母親的快樂而犧牲自己的這段期間，要讓自己徹底麻木。

門關上了，他回過身，看到一個矮矮胖胖的身影朝他走來，頭上正戴著那頂糟糕的帽子。「哎呀，」她說，「人生只有一回，多付點代價也是值得的，至少不會跟別人撞衫。」

「總有一天等我開始賺錢，」朱立安語帶沮喪地說著 —— 他知道這是遙不可及的事 ——「那可笑的玩意兒你想要就要。」但是首先他們得搬家才行。他想像著有這麼一個地方，離他們最近的左右鄰居也有三英里之遠。

「你做得挺好的，」他母親一邊戴上手套，一邊說著，「你畢業也才一年，羅馬不是一天造成的。」

基督教女青年會減肥班裡頭，她是少數幾個會戴帽子手套來上課的人，也是少數有個念過大學兒子的人。「這需要時間，」她說，「況且世道這麼混亂。這頂帽子戴在我頭上比其他人都來得好看。不過，老闆娘拿出來的當兒，我說：『把那玩意兒拿走，我才不會把它戴在我頭上。』然後她說：『你試了再說也不遲。』她幫我戴上的時候，我說：『噯喲！』然後她說：『要我說的話，你和這頂帽子真是相得益彰，而且，走在路上絕不會有人跟你戴一樣的帽子。』」

朱立安心想，她為什麼不自私自利一點，她為什麼不是個酗了酒便衝著他大吼大叫的醜老太婆，這樣他倒還會認命點。他向前走著，沉浸在沮喪裡，彷彿在殉難的過程中信心全失。她見他愁眉苦臉、絕望又惱怒的表情，便驟然停下腳步，露出悲傷的神情，她拉住他的手，「等我一下，」她說，「我回家去把這玩意兒給摘了，明天拿去退。我簡直是昏了頭，七塊五都夠我付煤氣費了。」

他粗暴地抓住她的手說：「不要拿去退，我喜歡。」

「唉，」她說，「我不該……」

「你就別說了，好好享受吧。」他口中嘟囔著，心裡又更加沮喪了。

「世道那麼亂，」她說，「我們有福可享真是奇蹟。我告訴你，現在簡直是反了。」

朱立安嘆了一口氣。

「當然，」她說，「你哪裡都可以去，只要別忘記自己是什麼人。」每次朱立安帶她去上減肥課的時候，都要聽她說一遍。「班上多半不是我們這種人，」她說，「不過我對誰都可以很親切，我知道自己是誰。」

「他們才不管你親不親切，」朱立安嚴厲地說，「知道自己是誰只對一個世代有好處。你壓根兒不知道你現在的處境，你也不知道自己是誰。」

她停下來看著他，眼中閃著怒火。「我當然最清楚自己是誰，」她說，「假如你不知道自己是誰的話，我真替你感到羞愧。」

「噢，該死的！」朱立安說。

「你曾祖父以前是這裡的州長，」她說，「你祖父是個地主，可發達呢。你的祖母是高德海家族的人。」

「你看一看四周，」他緊張兮兮地說，「現在知道你在哪裡了嗎？」他忽地把手一揮，指著四周的這片街坊，隨著夜幕低垂，看起來好像也沒那麼骯髒破舊了。

「你猶然是你，」她說，「你曾祖父擁有一大片農場和兩百名奴隸。」

「現在已經沒有奴隸了。」他怒沖沖地說。

「他們以前當奴隸，過得還比現在寬裕。」她說。朱立安發現她又開始講這個話題，便發出了痛苦的呻吟。她就像一列行駛在通行線上的火車，每隔幾天就會開到這裡來。沿途的每個停靠站、轉乘站、沼澤地他都知道，在什麼時間點，她的結論會堂皇進站，他也一清二楚，她會說：「這太荒謬了，簡直不切實際。他們是該站起來，沒錯，但是只能在他們的範圍內。」

「我們跳過這個話題吧。」朱立安說。

「我覺得可憐的，」她說，「是那些黑白混血兒，他們真可悲。」

「不要再說了好嗎？」

「假如我們是黑白混血兒，那種心情肯定是五味雜陳。」

「我現在就五味雜陳了。」他呻吟道。

「那不然我們聊點愉快的事，」她說，「我記得小時候到祖父家裡去，房子裡有兩座階梯通往真正的二樓——一樓是煮飯的地方。那時我喜歡待在樓下的廚房裡，因為牆壁的味道好聞。我會坐著把鼻子湊在灰泥上，然後深深吸氣。事實上，那個地方是屬於高德海家族的，但是你祖父切斯特尼支付了貸款，才給他們保住了那棟房子。當時他們家道中落，」她說，「然而無論是否家道中落，他們從未忘記自己是什麼人。」

「想必是那棟破爛不堪的大宅提醒了他們。」朱立安咕噥著。他一提起這房子總是語帶不屑，然而一想起卻又心生嚮往。他在孩提時期曾經見過一回，那時房子還未被賣掉。兩座樓梯早已腐爛、被拆除了。現在是黑人在住。但是那房子依然在他腦海裡，的確就如他母親所見過的模樣。那房子經常在他夢裡出現，夢裡他會站在寬敞的門廊上，聽著橡樹葉沙沙作響，再漫步穿過挑高的門廳，進入相通的客廳，然後凝望著磨破的地毯和褪色的窗簾。他想，有能力欣賞那房子的不是母親，而是自己。他愛它那破爛的優雅更勝一切，也因為那房子之故，他們住過的所有社區對他而言全是折磨——他母親卻完全分不出有什麼差別，她稱自己的遲鈍是「適應力強」。

「我還記得我的奶媽，那位黑人老婦卡洛琳，世上沒有人比她還要好，我向來很尊敬我的黑人朋友們，」她說，「我願意為他們做一切事，而他們會……」

「看在老天的分上，能不能停止這個話題？」朱立安說。每當他獨自坐公車時，會特意坐在黑人旁邊，好似為了彌補母親的罪。

「你今晚動不動就生氣，」她說，「你沒事吧？」

「我沒事，」他說，「別煩我了。」

她撇起了嘴。「哎呀，看來你心情真的不好，」她說道，「我就不跟你說話了。」

他們到達公車站。放眼望去一班車也沒有，朱立安雙手仍然塞在口袋裡，他伸出頭，一臉不悅望著空蕩蕩的街道。這會兒不但得搭公車，還得等公車，那股沮喪之情猶如一隻灼熱的手，悄然地襲上他的脖子。聽到母親痛苦地嘆了一口氣，他才意識到母親的存在。他冷冷地看著她。她把身子挺得直直的，頭上那頂帽子愚蠢至極，戴著它彷彿戴著一面旗幟，象徵著她幻想出來的尊嚴。他的內心有一股邪惡的欲望，想要摧毀她的意志。他突然鬆開領帶，將它抽下、放進口袋裡。

她身體僵硬了起來。「為什麼每次你帶我進城，都得**這**副德行？」她說，「為什麼你非要存心讓我難堪？」

「如果你永遠不知道自己的處境，」他說，「好歹能知道我的處境。」

「你看起來就像是個 —— 惡棍。」她說。

「那我肯定就是個惡棍。」他嘀咕著。

「我乾脆回家好了，」她說，「我不會打擾你。如果你連幫我這點小事都做不到……」

他翻了個白眼，把領帶重新戴上。「恢復我的階級。」朱立安嘀咕有詞。他把臉湊到母親身邊，小聲地生氣說：「真正的文化是在腦袋裡，**腦袋**，」他敲著自己的頭說，「是腦袋。」

「是在心裡，」她說，「且是在你的行為舉止上，而你的行為舉止則來自於你**是**什麼人。」

「在那該死的公車上，沒有人在乎你是什麼人。」

「我在乎。」她冷冷地說。

亮著燈的公車出現在前一座山頭，朝他們駛來，他們走到馬路上，好迎上前去。他扶著她的手肘，把她抬上嘎吱作響的階梯。她面帶微笑上了公車，彷彿正走進一座客廳，眾人早已在裡面等候著。朱立安去投代幣，而她則在公車前面向著走道的寬敞三人座當中，挑了一張坐了下來。座椅的另一端，坐了一位有著暴牙、金黃色長髮的瘦弱女子。朱立安的母親朝她挪了過去，好在身邊留個位子給朱立安。他坐了下來，目光望向走道對面的地板，那兒擺著一雙穿著紅白色帆布涼鞋的削瘦的腳。

朱立安的母親立刻找件普通事攀談起來，看看有沒有誰想聊一下。「這天氣還會不會更熱啊？」她一邊說著，一邊從皮包裡拿出一把摺扇，那是一把畫有日本風景的黑色扇子，朝著自己搧了起來。

「我覺得可能會，」暴牙女人說，「但是我住的公寓已經熱到不能再熱了。」

「它一定有曝曬在午後的陽光。」他母親一邊說著，一邊往前坐一點，朝著車內四處打量。有一半的位子都坐了人，清一色是白人。「看來這班車都是自己人。」她說。朱立安感覺有點侷促不安。

「偶爾也要改變一下，」走道對面的女人說話了，就是那雙紅白帆布涼鞋的主人。「前幾天我上了一班公車，他們人多得跟跳蚤似的，前前後後都是。」

「這個世界四處紛擾，」他母親說，「真不知道我們是怎麼讓它走到這步田地。」

「我氣的是那些好人家的男孩子，竟然偷起汽車輪胎，」暴牙女人說，「我告訴我兒子，我說你也許不富裕，但你是有家教的，要是被我發現你去湊上一腳，我會讓他們送你進少年感化院，到你該待的地方去好好待著。」

「有訓練會有效的，」她母親說，「你的孩子念高中嗎？」

「九年級。」那女人說。

「我兒子去年剛大學畢業，他想當作家，不過還沒開始，目前在賣打字機。」他母親說。

那女人把身體往前一傾，朝著朱立安端詳了一下。他惡狠狠地看了她一眼，於是她靠回了椅背上。走道對面的地板上有一份被丟棄的報紙，他起身去撿了過來，在面前張開報紙。他的母親壓低了音量，小心翼翼地要繼續交談，不料走道對面的女人卻大聲地說：「哎呀挺不錯的，賣打字機跟當作家也差不了多少，直接轉行很容易。」

「我告訴他，」他母親說，「羅馬不是一天造成的。」

報紙後面的朱立安正退回自己內心深處的腔室，大部分時間他都在這裡消磨度過。這是一種精神泡泡，每當他無力參與周遭正發生的一切時，就會把自己安頓在這裡。待在泡泡裡面很安全，外面任何事物都無法穿透進來，但又可以同時看到外面並做出判斷。唯有在這個地方，他才能不與同胞們的普遍愚行一般見識。他的母親未曾進入這個天地，但是從這裡，他又能將她給看個透徹。

這位老女士相當聰明，而他認為，若是她能夠從正確的前提出發，她還會變得更好。她照著自己幻想世界的規則過生活，而她從未踏出那個世界一步。那個世界的規則便是：她先把事情弄得一團糟，藉此創造出一個必須為他犧牲自己的必要。假如他允許了她的犧牲，也只是因為她缺乏先見之明，才把犧牲當成必要。她終其一生，在沒有得到切斯特尼財產的情況下，努力表現地像個切斯特尼家族的人，也把她認為一個切斯特尼家族之人該擁有的一切，都給了他；但是，她說，既然努力能帶來樂趣，又有什麼好抱怨的呢？況且你一旦成功，就像她一樣，回首過去坎坷路是多麼有意思！他無法原諒她竟然享受這種努力，還有她竟然認為她成功了。

她說自己成功了，意思是說她成功地把他撫養長大、供他念大學，而他也的確成長得很好 —— 一表人才（她放著自己的牙沒補，好讓他矯正了牙齒）又聰明（他明白自己就是太聰明才無法成功），而且有著大好前程（哪有什麼大好前程）。她替他的憂鬱找藉口，說是還在成長的關係，他的偏激想法也是缺乏實際經驗之故。她說他還不懂什麼叫「生活」，他甚至尚未進入現實世界 —— 而他卻已經像個五十歲的男人一般，對這個世界不抱任何幻想。

這一切更諷刺的是，儘管有她在，他還是成長得很好。儘管念的僅是三流大學，他也憑著自己的積極進取得到了一流教育。儘管在一顆小小心智的主宰下長大，他卻發展出一顆大大的心智。儘管她每個想法都愚昧至極，他卻沒有偏見，也不怕面對現實。最不可思議的是，他對母親的愛沒有蒙蔽他的眼，這就和他母親不同，情感上他早已不受母親束縛，可以完全客觀地看待她。他並沒有受到母親的支配。

公車晃了一下，停了下來，也把他從冥想中搖醒。一名女子從後面跟跟蹌蹌地碎步往前，差點沒跌在他的報紙上，好在她把自己扶正了。她下了車，一位魁梧的黑人上了車。朱立安壓低了報紙，好瞧上一眼。看著每天上演的不公平正義，給他帶來某種滿足。這證明了他的觀點，方圓三百英里之內，沒幾個人值得認識。這位黑人衣著體面，拎了一個公事包。他四下張望之後，選擇坐在紅白帆布涼鞋女人那排座位的另一端。他坐下後旋即攤開報紙掩住自己。朱立安的母親立刻用手肘不斷地戳他的肋骨，「現在你知道為什麼我不願意自己搭公車了吧。」她小小聲說。

那位黑人才一坐下，穿著紅白帆布涼鞋的女人馬上起身，往公車後面走去，坐了剛才下車的那個女人的位子。朱立安的母親俯身向前，對她投以一個讚許的眼神。

朱立安起身走到對面，在那位穿著帆布涼鞋女人剛才的位子上坐了下來。他從這個位置平靜地望著他母親。她的臉已經因憤怒而漲紅。他用一種陌生人的眼神注視著她。他突然緊張了起來，彷彿已公然向母親宣戰。

朱立安想跟黑人攀談，聊聊藝術、政治或任何超出周圍的人理解範圍的主題，但是那個人仍然埋首看報紙。他要不就是無視旁人換位子的舉動，要不就是根本沒發現。朱立安想要表達同情之心，也無從下手。

朱立安的母親用指責的眼神盯著他的臉，暴牙女人也興味十足地看著他，好似他是一種她沒見過的怪物。

「能借個火嗎？」朱立安問那黑人。

那黑人把手伸進口袋，掏出一盒火柴給他，目光卻絲毫未離開過報紙。

「謝了。」朱立安說。他傻楞地握著那火柴一會兒，門上「禁止吸菸」的標誌睥睨著他。光這樣是嚇唬不了他的；他沒有菸。幾個月前，他就因為買不起菸而給戒了。「對不起。」他嘀咕著把火柴還了回去。黑人拉下報紙，怒目看了他一眼，然後收下火柴，拉上報紙繼續閱讀。

朱立安的母親一直凝視著他，不過並沒有趁勢佔他便宜。她的雙眼依然神傷，臉色也紅得不自然，彷彿是血壓升高之故。朱立安不讓臉上流露出絲毫的同情，他佔了上風，極力想要保住優勢、堅持到底。他想要給她一個能讓她收斂一段時間的教訓，可是好像使不上力，沒辦法持續下去。那位黑人再也不肯從報紙後面探出頭來。

朱立安交疊雙臂，淡漠地看著前方，面對著母親卻又好像沒看見她，彷彿拒絕承認她的存在。他想像著一幅畫面，畫面中公車抵達了他們的站，他仍坐在位子上不動，當她說：「你不下車嗎？」他會看著她，好像看著一個冒冒失失跟自己說話的陌生人一樣。他們下車的地方是個街角，經常空無一人，不過卻燈火通明，就算她獨自一人走四個街區到基督教女青年會，也沒什麼大礙。他決定等到那一刻來臨，再決定是否讓她自己下車。他得在十點的時候去接她，但是他可以讓她懷疑著他會不會出現。她沒理由認為自己可以老是依賴他。

他再度回到那個零星擺設了幾座大型古董家具的挑高房間，他的靈魂剎時間放鬆了一會兒，旋而又意識到母親就坐在自己對面，剛才的幻想便萎縮了起來。他冷冷地打量著她，她那穿著小巧便鞋的雙腳，像個孩子似的懸盪著，搆不大著地板。她對著他做出一個誇大的責備表情，他感覺自己完全與她無關。在那個當下，他非常樂意賞她一記耳光，如同給自己管教之下特別惹人厭的那個孩子一記耳光一樣。

他開始想像可以教訓她的各種行不通的方法。他可以跟某個卓越的黑人教授或律師交朋友，並且還帶他回家作客。他這麼做是完全正當的，但是她的血壓會飆升到三百。他可不能把她逼到中風，而且他也從未成功結交到黑人朋友。他曾試著在公車上結識幾個條件較好的類型，也就是那些看起來像教授、牧師或律師的黑人。有天早上，他坐在一個看起來頗為優秀的深棕色男人旁邊，那人用渾厚嚴肅的聲音回答了他的問題，結果他卻是從事殯葬業的。又有一天，他坐在一個抽雪茄的黑人旁邊，那人手指上還戴著一只鑽戒，就在生硬的寒暄了幾句之後，那人就按了下車鈴，然後起身，爬過朱立安的身體準備離開時，還順手塞了兩張彩券在他手裡。

他想像母親臥病在床、已病入膏肓，他只能給她找個黑人大夫。他玩味著這個主意好幾分鐘，接著便拋掉這個點子，因為一瞬間他又看到自己以支持者的身分參加靜坐示威抗議。這是有可能發生的，不過他並未在這個點子上徘徊。他反而往最恐怖的想像靠近，他帶著一位疑似黑人的美麗女子回家，做好心理準備吧，他說，你拿這事兒一點辦法也沒有，這是我所選擇的女子，她既聰明又尊貴，還很善良，她吃了不少苦，而她一點兒也不覺得是種樂趣。就迫害我們吧，快點迫害我們吧。把她趕出去吧，但別忘了，這麼做也等於是把我趕出去。憤慨中他看到走道對面的母親，面色發紫，朱立安瞇起眼睛，將母親縮小到如她道德本性的侏儒般大小，她就像具木乃伊般坐著，頭上那頂帽子就像一面可笑的旗幟。

公車停下時，他的身體一傾，再度把他從幻想中甩出。車門在惱人的嘶一聲後打開，一名黑人女子從黑暗中上了車，她的身材高大、衣著豔麗，一臉悶悶不樂，一同上車的還有一個小男孩。這位小孩大概四歲，穿著格紋短套裝，戴著提洛爾帽，上面插著一支藍色羽毛。朱立安希望小男孩能坐在自己旁邊，然後那女人擠進母親旁邊的位子。他覺得這樣安排再好不過了。

那個女人一邊等代幣，一邊環視車內尋找座位 —— 他一心盼望她能選上那個最不想讓她坐的位子。她身上有個什麼東西，讓朱立安覺得很眼熟，但他說不上來是什麼。以女人來說她算是高大，她的表情堅定，不只準備好遭遇抵制，也打算挺身抵制。她厚實的下唇下垂著，彷彿是個警告標誌：「別惹**我**」。她那臃腫的體態外面包著一件綠色的皺紗洋裝，雙腳都溢出紅鞋之外了。她頭戴一頂醜陋不堪的帽子，紫色絨面的帽緣一邊垂下、一邊翹起，其他部分是綠色的，活像個棉絮爆出來的坐墊。她拎著一只巨大的紅色手提包，彷彿塞滿石頭似的，鼓得不得了。

朱立安大失所望，因為小男孩爬上了母親身旁的空位。所有的小孩子，不分黑白，在他母親眼裡全都屬於同一類：「可愛」。而且她認為，整體而言，黑人小孩又比白人小孩更可愛。當小男孩爬上座椅的時候，她給了他一個微笑。

同一時間，那女人朝著朱立安旁邊的空位逼近，用擠的坐了上去，這讓朱立安十分惱火。當這女人在他身旁坐下時，他看到母親的臉色為之一變，這才令他心滿意足，因為他發現母親對這件事比他還要反感。她的臉色幾乎蒼白，眼中流露出隱約認出了什麼的神色，好似因看到了什麼可怕的衝突，霎時一陣厭惡一般。朱立安明白，那是因為就某種意義上來說，她和這女人交換了兒子。雖然他母親不會明白這件事的象徵意義，但她感覺得到。而朱立安顯然喜形於色。

他身旁的女人喃喃自語，說著一些別人聽不懂的話。他察覺到身旁有某種毛髮豎立的感覺，像隻生氣的貓咪那樣發出無聲的怒吼。除了那筆直地立在臃腫綠色大腿上的紅色手提包，其他的他什麼也看不見。他腦中顯現這女人剛才站著等代幣時的模樣——笨重的體態，從紅鞋一路向上越過結實的屁股、碩大的乳房、傲慢的臉孔，再到那又綠又紫的帽子。

他瞪大了眼睛。

兩頂一模一樣的帽子，這景象挾著燦爛日出的光輝，在他身上迸濺開來。他臉上突然閃耀著欣喜之色，他不敢相信命運之神竟給她母親強加了這麼一個教訓。他咯咯大笑了起來，好讓她注意到他，並且看到他所看到的景象。她緩緩地將目光轉向他，眼珠子裡的藍似乎已轉為淤青般的紫。有那麼一會兒，她的無辜讓他有點不自在，但是不消一秒鐘，道義便拯救了他。公平正義賦予他大笑的權利。他咧著嘴的笑容越變越冷酷，直到明顯像是他親口大聲說一般：這就是你的小心眼所應得的懲罰，當會帶給你一次永生難忘的教訓。

母親把目光轉向那個女人，似乎是看著兒子令她受不了，看著那女人還好些。他又再次察覺到身旁一股毛髮豎立。這女人像一座即將爆發的火山般隆隆作響，她母親的嘴角開始微微抽動。朱立安心裡一沉，他從她臉上看到復原的初兆，他明白，這件事只會讓她一時覺得有趣，不會是什麼教訓。他母親的目光持續在那女人身上打轉，臉上泛起一抹被逗樂的笑容，好似那名女子是隻偷她帽子的猴子。黑人小孩抬起頭，用一雙興致昂昂的大眼看著朱立安的母親，他已經試著吸引她的注意力好一會兒了。

「卡佛！」那女人突然說，「過來！」

卡佛發現大家終於注意到他了，便把腳抬起來，轉身朝向朱立安母親，咯咯地笑了起來。

「卡佛！」那女人說，「你聽到我說了沒？快過來！」

卡佛從座椅上滑了下來，卻仍背靠著椅子底座，蹲在地上。他調皮地把頭轉向朱立安的母親，而她正對著他微笑。那女人伸出一隻手，從走道的另一邊把將小男孩抓到自己這裡。小男孩把自己站直，旋而又仰掛在母親膝上，對著朱立安的母親咯咯地笑。「他是不是好可愛啊？」朱立安的母親對著暴牙女人說。

「我想是吧。」暴牙女人說得不太肯定。

黑女人使勁地把小男孩扶正，但是他小心翼翼地掙脫，一溜煙又跑到對面，爬上他心愛的人身旁，放聲地咯咯大笑。

「我想他是喜歡我。」朱立安的母親一邊說著，一邊對著黑女人微笑。每當她要對下等人表現得特別親切時，就會露出這種微笑。朱立安發覺一切全完了，那場教訓就像落在屋頂上的雨，從她身上滾落了。

那女人站了起來，使勁把小男孩從座位上拽走，彷彿要把他從傳染病源旁邊救走。朱立安可以感受到她的憤怒，因為她沒有像他母親的微笑一般的武器。她狠狠地拍了他兒子的腿，他哀嚎了一聲，接著用頭頂她的肚子，還哭鬧著踢她的小腿。「你乖一點。」她嚴厲地說。

公車停了下來，一直在看報紙的那個黑人下了車。那女人挪了過去，砰地一聲重重把小男孩放在她和朱立安之間，緊緊抓住小男孩的膝蓋。而小男孩旋即用手遮住自己的臉，透過指縫偷看朱立安的母親。

「我看到你囉！」朱立安的母親說，並且也用手遮住自己的臉，偷看小男孩。

那女人拍掉小男孩的手。「不要丟人現眼，」她說，「再這樣我就把你揍扁！」

好在下一站他們就要下車了，朱立安真是感到慶幸。他伸手拉了下車鈴，與此同時，那女人也伸手拉鈴。噢，我的老天啊，朱立安心想。他有一種可怕的直覺，當他們一起下車時，她母親會打開錢包，賞那小男孩一枚五分錢。這個舉動對她母親來說，就好像呼吸一樣自然。公車停住了，那女人起身衝到前面，並把不情願下車的小男孩一把拖在身後。朱立安和母親也起身尾隨在後。

當他們靠近車門的時候，朱立安試圖要幫母親拿包包。

「不用，」他母親嘀咕道，「我要給那小男孩一枚五分錢。」

「不行！」朱立安怒沖沖地小聲說著，「不行！」

她低頭對著小男孩微笑，並且打開了包包。公車門一開，那女人拎起小男孩的手臂，小男孩懸在她臀邊，一起下了車。一到了街上，她便把他放下，還搖晃了他。

朱立安的母親走下公車臺階時，不得不把錢包闔上。但是一落地馬上又把錢包打開，在裡面翻找。「我只找到一枚一分硬幣，」她低聲說道，「但是看起來像是新的。」

「不要這麼做！」朱立安咬牙切齒地說。轉角那兒有一盞街燈，他母親趕緊跑到燈下，好往手提包裡瞧個仔細。那女人正迅速地沿著街道走遠，小男孩還拎在她手上，向後懸著。

「喂，小男孩兒！」朱立安的母親一邊喊著，一邊加快腳步，就在街燈柱那兒追上了他們。「這裡有一枚閃亮的一分錢幣，送給你。」她拿出了錢幣，在微弱的光線下閃耀著青銅的色澤。

那高大的女人轉身佇立了一會兒，因為強忍著怒氣，肩膀高高聳起，表情也變得僵硬，瞪著朱立安的母親。然後就在一瞬間，她好像一座機器，只要再加一點壓力，就整個爆發了。朱立安看見拿著紅色手提包的黑色拳頭揮了出去。他閉上眼睛、瑟縮在一旁，聽見那女人吼著：「他誰的錢也不要！」當他睜開眼睛的時候，那女人正逐漸消失在街頭，小男孩掛在她肩上，眼睛瞪得大大的。朱立安的母親跌坐在人行道上。

「我叫你不要那麼做了，」朱立安怒斥著，「我叫你不要那麼做了！」

他在她前面站了一會兒，咬牙切齒地低頭看著她。她伸直了雙腿，帽子落在大腿上。朱立安蹲下來凝望她的臉，那張臉面無表情。「你真是罪有應得，」他說，「快起來吧。」

他撿起她的手提包，把掉落的物品放回去，然後拾起她大腿上的那頂帽子。他瞥見掉落在人行道上的那枚一分錢幣，也撿了起來，當著她的面放進錢包裡。接著他站了起來，俯身向前，伸出手要拉她起來，她卻一動也不動。朱立安嘆了口氣。他們兩旁聳立著黑色公寓大樓，零星點綴著燈亮的小方塊。在這個街區的盡頭，有個男人從一扇門中走出，往反方向走去。「行了吧，」朱立安說，「假如有人碰巧經過，看你坐在人行道上，好奇想知道為什麼怎麼辦？」

她握住了他的手，用力喘了口氣，便使勁一拉讓自己站起來，然後佇立了一會兒，身體微微搖晃，彷彿黑暗中的燈光全打在她身上。她那黯然而困惑的目光終於定焦在他的臉上。他並沒有試圖掩飾自己的怒氣。「希望這次你能學到教訓。」他說。她把身子往前傾，用眼睛掃視他的臉，似乎想搞清楚他是誰。接著，彷彿在他身上找不到熟悉之處，她便動身，逕往反方向走去。

「你不是要去基督教女青年會嗎？」他問。

「我要回家。」她嘀咕著。

「好吧，要用走的嗎？」

她的回答就是繼續往前走。朱立安兩手背在身後，尾隨母親。他覺得不能讓這次教訓就這樣煙消雲散，有必要解釋一下它的意義，倒不妨讓她明白到底發生了什麼事。「別以為她只是個盛氣凌人的黑女人，」他說，「她代表的是全體有色人種，他們不再收取你那帶有優越感的一分錢。她就是你的黑人翻版，她可以和你戴一樣的帽子，而且無可否認的，」好端端的他非補上這句

（因為他覺得有趣），「她戴起來比你好看。這一切的意義就是，」他說，「舊世界已然消失，舊禮儀也已過時，你的好意一文不值。」他想起自己失去的那棟房子，一陣心酸。「你不是你所以為的那種人了。」他說。

她繼續埋頭往前走，絲毫沒理他。她的頭髮一邊已經散掉，手提包落在地上了也不理會。朱立安彎腰將它撿起，然後遞給她，但是她並未接下。

「你不用表現得一副世界末日似的，」他說，「又不是世界末日。從現在起，你得活在一個嶄新的世界，你得改變自己，面對一些現實。振作起來，」他說，「這要不了你的命。」

她的呼吸急促了起來。

「我們還是等公車吧。」他說。

「回家。」她聲音沙啞地說。

「我很討厭看你這個樣子，」他說，「跟個孩子似的。我還指望你表現好一點。」他打算就地止步，逼她停下來等公車。「我不走了，」他說著便停了下來，「我們要搭公車。」

她彷彿沒聽見他說話，逕自往前走。他向前邁了幾步，抓住她的手臂，讓她停下來。他一看她的臉，不禁無法呼吸。那是一張他未曾見過的臉龐。「叫爺爺來接我。」她說。

他看著她，受到了打擊。

「叫卡洛琳來接我。」她說。

朱立安非常震驚，他鬆手放開了她，而她再次東倒西歪地往前走，好像長短腿一般。彷彿有一股漆黑的浪潮將她從他身邊捲走。「媽媽！」他喊著，

「親愛的，我心愛的，你等等！」她身體一垮，便摔在人行道上。他衝向前去，跌坐在她身邊，哭喊著：「媽媽！媽媽！」他將她翻過身，她的顏面已經嚴重扭曲，其中一隻眼睛瞪得大大的，微微向左移動，彷彿一艘斷了錨的船。另一隻眼睛則依然凝視著他，再一次掃視了他的臉，感覺一無所獲，便闔上了。

　　「你在這等著！在這等著！」朱立安一邊哭喊，一邊跳起身，朝遠方燈火聚集處奔跑求救。「救命！救命啊！」他大喊道，但他的聲音微弱，連一絲聲音都發不出來。他越是加快腳步，燈火越是往遠處漂移，他的雙腿跑到已然麻木，彷彿怎麼跑也到不了目的地。漆黑的浪潮將他沖回母親的身邊，時時刻刻不讓他進入愧疚和悲痛的世界。

EZ TALK

全美最強教授的 17 堂論文寫作必修課

150 句學術英文寫作句型，從表達、討論、寫作到論述，建立批判思考力與邏輯力
"They Say / I Say": The Moves That Matter in Academic Writing

---

作　　　者：Gerald Graff 杰拉德・葛拉夫
　　　　　　Cathy Birkenstein 凱西・柏肯斯坦
譯　　　者：丁宥榆
審　　　訂：周中天
主　　　編：潘亭軒
責任編輯：鄭莉璇
封面設計：賴佳韋工作室
內頁設計：陳語萱
內頁排版：張靜怡

發 行 人：洪祺祥
副總經理：洪偉傑
副總編輯：曹仲堯
法律顧問：建大法律事務所
財務顧問：高威會計事務所

出　　　版：日月文化出版股份有限公司
製　　　作：EZ 叢書館
地　　　址：臺北市信義路三段 151 號 8 樓
電　　　話：(02) 2708-5509
傳　　　真：(02) 2708-6157
網　　　址：www.heliopolis.com.tw
郵撥帳號：19716071 日月文化出版股份有限公司

總 經 銷：聯合發行股份有限公司
電　　　話：(02) 2917-8022
傳　　　真：(02) 2915-7212
印　　　刷：中原造像股份有限公司
初　　　版：2018 年 10 月
初版 7 刷：2022 年 2 月
定　　　價：450 元
Ｉ Ｓ Ｂ Ｎ：978-986-248-758-7

全美最強教授的 17 堂論文寫作必修課：150
句學術英文寫作句型，從表達、討論、寫作
到論述，建立批判思考力與邏輯力 / 杰拉
德・葛拉夫 (Gerald Graff)，凱西・柏肯斯坦
(Cathy Birkenstein) 著；丁宥榆譯 . -- 初版 . --
臺北市：日月文化，2018.10
400 面；16.7×23 公分（EZ Talk）
譯自：They say / I say : the moves that matter
　　　in academic writing
ISBN 978-986-248-758-7（平裝）

1. 英語　2. 論文寫作法
805.175　　　　　　　　　　　　　　107015068

"They Say / I Say": The Moves That Matter in Academic Writing, 3rd ed.
This edition published by arrangement with W. W. Norton & Company, Inc.
through Bardon-Chinese Media Agency
Complex Chinese translation copyright © 2018 Heliopolis Culture Group Co., Ltd
ALL RIGHTS RESERVED